Watch Me Fall Apart

Scars Run Deep 2

Lola Rooney

For Him

1

"Ohhhhh, Jeremy."

"What did you just call me?"

I froze in place and held my breath, a habit of mine when I know I've screwed up. Like, hugely, monumentally, I-can't-believe-this-is-actually-happening screwed up. Looking down at the face of the guy whose lap I was straddling—a guy whose name was definitely *not* Jeremy—I tried to read his level of outrage, which isn't an easy thing to do in the semi-dark when you're semi-drunk and your body still thinks it's possible you're going to have sex at any moment.

"Nothing, baby," I said, caressing his face and pressing my chest against his seductively, hoping he'd reached that level of intoxication where a nice, warm distraction will make you forget anything, even something like—

"Did you just call me by my brother's name?"

Well, something like *that*.

Pushing me off his lap and lurching to his feet, Alex (my soon-to-be ex-boyfriend) swayed in place for a second before turning to me and roaring, "What the fuck, Sally? Did you cheat on me with my own brother? With Jeremy? Did you?"

"Oh, come on, Alex. You told me you guys share

everything," I replied.

Another habit of mine, especially when I'm not exactly sure where my pants are, is to try to diffuse a sticky situation by making light of it. Has this tactic every actually worked for me? I can't really recall. Though, I can say that on this particular occasion, as Alex stared at me, eyes blazing, then yanked me out of his room and down the hall and shoved me out of his apartment, locking the door with an echoing click, it occurred to me that it might be time to re-think my habits. Especially my habit of wearing my ugliest underwear on the nights I planned on having sex with my boyfriend—because what was the point in wearing pretty lingerie when he was just going to rip it off in five seconds anyway?

Bad choice, Sally, I admonished myself. *Next time remember, you never know when you might end up on full-display of the entire neighbourhood without your clothes on.*

Though, considering how quickly things had been progressing in that bedroom, it was pretty lucky I was wearing anything at all.

As I hopped from one foot to the other, shivering on the porch, I glanced quickly up and down the dark street and considered my options.

A: Run the five blocks to my own apartment, hoping nobody sees me (unlikely).

B: Stay right where I am and pray one of Alex's roommates comes home before I freeze to death.

C: Bang on the door and scream bloody-murder.

I opted for C. If I was going down, I saw no reason not to take Alex down with me.

"Open the goddamn door, Alex!" I pounded on the door with my fists, shouting loud enough for all the neighbours to hear, and probably their neighbours too. My mother had always told me I had the finest set of lungs she'd ever laid ears on. Might as well put them to use.

"Let me back in the house. Let me in, Alex. Alex Compton. Alexander Compton the Third!" We wouldn't want anybody wondering who to hold accountable tomorrow, would we? "Please open the door! I'm freezing out here. I didn't mean what I said. I'm so sorry!"

Nothing. Not a sound. Not even the creak of a floorboard to let me know he was on the other side of the door listening. Was he even listening? Maybe if I cranked it up a notch.

"It doesn't matter to me, anyway. Erectile dysfunction is actually very common!" *There. Bet he heard that.* "Come on, Alex. I'm begging you. At least give me my clothes!"

Nope. Nada. Not even a well-timed "shut up." I was beginning to admire his self-control.

It started to dawn on me that I might really be stuck outside, in five degree weather, after midnight, in my underwear. Not that anyone would be much surprised. If my friends heard about this they probably wouldn't even blink, and I couldn't exactly blame them. Things like this just tended to happen to me, weekly, almost like clockwork. Humiliation was sort of my specialty, my calling, my destiny. There were times when I almost welcomed it. It's reassuring to know that you're getting exactly what you deserve, there's a symmetry to it, a comforting balance.

Even if karma can be a real bitch sometimes.

I heard laughter coming from the street behind me, the audience I'd been screaming so hard for, though suddenly nothing about my situation seemed particularly funny. Who did Alex think he was anyway? Sure, I was easy and I was a cheater and I deserved whatever I got, but what about him? Was he so much better? Hadn't I caught him coming on to Melissa just the week before? Who knew how much farther he'd taken it with other girls when I wasn't looking. It wasn't like he was a saint. Why was I the one being leered at on the porch? Was this justice?

Squaring my shoulders, I launched myself at the door one last time, shrieking and pounding at it with both my hands and feet, even body-checking it a few times for good measure—a move that left a pretty sizeable bruise on my hip, but was still worth it to see the windows rattle. (*Let's see him sleep through that!*) And all the while I yelled every curse word I could think of, a not-for-children's-ears string of obscenities so dirty I heard my fan club behind me exclaim, "Oh shit!" and "Damn!" in response.

I was really ramping up for my big finale, winding myself into a towering fury the likes of which sleazy Alex had probably never seen, when the door suddenly swung open in front of me.

I staggered forward and almost fell, caught just in time by a pair of strong hands gripping me at the waist. Straightening up quickly—and realizing as I did just how drunk I still was—I looked into the surprised face of a guy who was definitely not Alex. His searing blue eyes stared into mine, his expression changing from shock to something indecipherable, before glancing at the street behind me.

"Mind if I come in?" I asked with my most winning smile as I heard the catcalls being launched our way.

"No, don't go, baby!" someone called. "I can keep you warm better than that guy."

With a last grim look over my shoulder, My Rescuer pulled me inside and shoved the door closed behind him, leaving us alone in the dimly-lit hallway.

Without missing a beat, I spun around and sprinted sloppily down the hall toward Alex's bedroom door.

"Don't bother," My Rescuer said. "He's not there. He locked it and went out the back door."

"Bastard!" I swore, jiggling the door handle to Alex's room uselessly. "My clothes are in there."

My chest still heaving from all the screaming, I turned around unsteadily. Now that the alcohol which had been kept at bay by my burst of adrenaline was again circulating freely through my system, I noticed how tilty the walls had become. My blurry vision wouldn't allow me to make out much more of my mysterious saviour than his short, dark hair and the fact that he was leaning against the wall, as far away from me as possible.

Well, that could be remedied pretty easily.

I walked toward him wearing my most sultry expression and placed a hand on his chest.

"Well, now that we're alone," I said.

He was my best bet at a warm bed for the night, after all. I knew all of Alex's other roommates were out, too. And they all locked their doors at night, the untrusting bastards. I had to sleep somewhere.

As I sidled up to him, I felt him place his hands lightly on my hips, his fingers warm against my cool skin. I wondered what his name was. There were half-a-dozen guys living in the house and I'd met a few of them, but it was hard to keep track of them all. Had we ever met before? I didn't really think it mattered. If he was anything like Alex he'd be an enthusiastic (if quick) participant in what I had in mind and then pass out so I could get some sleep. I leaned into him, sure to press my arms in at my sides so my boobs popped the way I wanted them to, and I felt his hands tighten on me.

Sally," he said.

I smiled easily and flipped my blonde hair over my shoulder. He knew my name. This was going to be a cinch.

"You know, I was thinking…" I began, running my index finger down the front of his grey t-shirt.

"Sally…don't," he said.

My eyes snapped to his face. Only then did I notice he wasn't looking at my face or my breasts but down at the floor, and his hands were actually holding my hips away from his body instead of pulling them closer.

I snorted in disbelief and his blue eyes met mine. "Real charmer," I said, and smacked him once on the shoulder before passing out right then and there.

I woke up with a splitting headache and the smell of oranges in my nose. The room was bright with sunshine and I pressed my arm over my eyes to block it out, wondering why Alex had opened the blinds so early when he usually slept until noon on the weekends. Then, in a sour rush, all the events of the night before spooled out like memory vomit and I groaned and rubbed my face with both hands.

Peeking through my fingers, I scanned the room around me: empty. The door was open a crack. Maybe my bed buddy had slipped out to go to work or something, though I tried not to be too hopeful. I might still have to face him.

Feeling under the covers, I discovered I was still wearing my underwear, which was a little puzzling, but not entirely unheard of. Maybe he'd put them back on me after he was done. Stranger things had happened. I also had on a men's t-shirt with a cartoon on the front—I couldn't tell exactly what it was, a rock with feet?—and my bra underneath that. Which was strangest of all. I'd known guys who could take off my bra with the flick of a finger, but putting it back on was always far beyond their abilities, or interest. Either this guy worked at a lingerie store, or he hadn't managed to get it off to begin with.

It was nice of him to give me a shirt to wear, though. Alex usually insisted I sleep naked so he could touch whatever he wanted whenever he chose, and I always woke up shivering. He was a covers hog.

Sitting up in bed I looked around the room. It was different than any guy's bedroom I'd ever seen. First of all, there was no sports equipment anywhere. No baseball bats, no hockey sticks, no tennis rackets. Instead, there were two full bookcases and piles of books on the dressers and the bedside table. I spied a stack of thick textbooks on the desk by the window, beside a laptop which was on, lines of indecipherable numbers and letters covering the screen.

My stomach plummeted.

What'd you do last night, Sally? Oh nothing. Alex dumped me so I decided to hook up with a super dork.

There was only one way to salvage this situation: Get out of here before the dork came back. I was on my feet and halfway to the door before I realized the one flaw in my plan. No clothes. My dress from last night was still in Alex's room, and even if he had come back and unlocked it, did I really want to face him this soon after the throw-you-out-of-my-apartment-half-naked debacle? I still wanted to give him a piece of my mind, but preferably fully clothed, and after he'd cooled down a little. If I saw him this morning he was likely to throw me outside again and I'd be right back to square one.

I sat back down on the mattress and pressed one foot on top of the other. There was nothing I could really do except wait for the dork to come back and beg him to retrieve my dress for me. And my purse, which had my car keys in it. There was nothing to do but wait.

I was about ready to start going through his dresser looking for a pair of jeans that might fit me—my memory of him from the night before was sketchy, but I thought it was possible he was hipster-nerdy enough to own skinny jeans—when my eyes fell on a pile of magazines on the floor. I picked up the one on top of the stack. On the glossy cover was a drawing of a blonde girl falling through a maze of evergreen branches, her face filled with fear, her fingers reaching. Her hair was very yellow and the rest of the cover was overwhelmed with the hues of blue and green of the overlapping branches and leaves. The title, *The Forever Place*, was printed across the top in white.

"That's one's great," a voice said. "Are you a *Forever* fan?"

Dropping the magazine on the bed I swung around to find My Rescuer, the dork himself, leaning on the desk, watching me. I had no idea how long he'd been standing there, which was fine. I had no problem with being looked at, though I wished he hadn't caught me touching his things. Now we had to have a conversation.

Sigh.

"Is it an art magazine or something?" I said.

He had two cups of coffee in his hand and he held one out to me. I took it warily. I couldn't remember the last time a guy had made me a drink that wasn't alcoholic.

He smiled at my question, a quiet smile, really just a twitch at the edges of his mouth, while the rest of his face remained blankly serious.

"No, it's a comic book series," he said. "That's the omnibus, actually. I have some single issues on the floor there."

He nodded at the floor and, if only because it seemed better to talk about comic books than the fact that I didn't know his name, I leaned down and grabbed the pile, spreading them out on the bed.

The other covers were just as colourful, the blonde girl always prominent. In one she was holding a bloody dagger, and in another she was standing at the edge of a cliff, the wide sky behind her.

"I didn't know they made comics big like this," I said. "I used to read *Betty and Veronica* when I was a kid."

There was that smirk again. "These are a little more violent. Less Jughead, more hollow despair."

"She's cute," I said, pointing at the girl on the cover. "What's her name?"

"Her name's Rainbow," he said. "And yeah, she is."

He picked up one of the issues as he sipped his coffee, and while he examined the cover I looked him over. The boys who lived in the house with Alex were all the same. Trust-fund babies with shiny teeth, all of them tall and broad and handsome, sure of themselves, arrogant as hell, and mean. This guy wasn't like that at all. I remembered from the night before that he was taller than me, but not by much. He looked fit, though definitely not as muscular as Alex, and his clothes were different. They weren't out of style exactly, but they were definitely off-brand and worn. The t-shirt I had on was soft from many washings. I slept in one just like it.

When it came to looks he definitely had a lot more going for him than most of the dorks I saw around campus, milling outside the biosciences complex with their bad haircuts and ill-fitting windbreakers. I couldn't decide if I found him good-looking or not, and then I caught him looking at me, and *oh my*. His eyes were baby blue and unwavering, his gaze so intense it made me uncomfortable, which was strange because normally I liked to be looked at. But when he looked at me, it was different. It was like he was looking for something, something I was sure he wouldn't find. I wanted to look away. I was about to, but he beat me to it.

As I drank the last of my coffee, I realized that was the other thing that made me so uneasy around him. He kept looking away from me, as if I gave him the creeps or something. Hadn't he done the same thing last night? I seemed to remember something like that. What the hell was that about? I could put up with a lot of things—glances down my shirt, hands on my ass, teachers staring at me while they taught. I'd once caught a guy with his camera up my skirt trying to snap a photo of my lady parts—but this? This had never happened to me before.

Still, I got the message. He hadn't even touched me once since he'd come into the room. I was just Alex's trashy girl (or ex-girl, now), a simpleton with a nice rack, an easy lay. He was obviously well-brought up. He'd made small-talk with me, gotten me coffee, but it was clear he wanted me out of there. A repeat of last night was not in the cards for us.

Fine by me.

"Listen, I need to get to work," he said, placing his empty coffee cup on the desk.

Of course he did. Sometimes it seemed like everyone had a job but me, not for lack of trying mind you. Lately I'd been fired from a wide array of illustrious establishments, all of which had names that ended in "place": the copy place, the pizza place, the dry-cleaning place, the coffee place. I was thinking of giving up on all the "places" and just going for a bartending gig—since all my firings had been due to drinking on the job, or coming to work drunk, or hungover, or both, I figured it was my last best chance. At least at a bar they wouldn't be able to smell the liquor coming out of my pores.

Something told me super nerd here had never been fired from anything in his life. He had that clean, honest look about him.

"I really wish I didn't have to, but it's too late to cancel my shift," he went on.

Turning my face away, I rolled my eyes.

I get the picture, buddy.

"I need to go, too," I said swiftly, getting to my feet. "You don't think you could maybe slip into Alex's room…"

Reaching behind him, he handed me my wrinkled dress and purse, which I grabbed gratefully. Flinging off his t-shirt, I pulled the dress over my head and adjusted the cleavage—a necessary step, given how low-cut it was. When I looked back up at him he was staring at the wall. Apparently even a quick strip-tease from me wasn't to his taste. I shook my head as I gathered up his shirt. Some guys were just like this. Once they'd had me they didn't want anything more to do with me. I couldn't exactly blame him. If I had a son I wouldn't want him hanging around me either.

"Thanks," I said, handing him back the shirt. "What show's that from?"

"It's not from a show. It's from Super Mario Bros., the Nintendo game? It's a Goomba." He pointed at the rock on the front of the t-shirt.

I blinked at him. "So, you really are a nerd, huh?"

He gave me a real smile for the first time. His eyes crinkled and his cheeks reddened ever so slightly, which was pretty goddamn adorable. For a second I thought what a shame it was that he couldn't stand to be around me. I'd always had a soft spot for boys who blushed.

"Well, I'm out of here, hot stuff," I said, grabbing my bag and making for the door.

Better not to dwell on the cute dork. Better to get a move on, rip off the Band-Aid, get out the door and on to the next conquest. There was always another guy waiting to grope me, one who wouldn't mind staring at me (or my breasts, anyway) for hours. That was the thing about me and guys. They never said no, and neither did I.

"Wait," he said, "I'll walk you home."

Pausing at the door, I turned to see him shrugging on his backpack and handing me a sweater without explanation.

I watched him, bewildered. "I thought you had to work," I said.

"A little later," he said, "but it's no problem—"

I raised a hand to cut him off. The last thing I needed was a pity escort. "Don't bother. I brought my car."

"Then I'll walk you to your car," he said.

He really wasn't getting the message. Either that, or someone—I was guessing his Mom—had really pounded those manners into him.

"It's okay…" Crap. I still didn't know his name.

"Harrison," he offered. "Leo."

I gave him a tight smile. "Listen thanks for a *fantastic* night, Harrison Leo, but I'll take it from here."

He gave me a strange look as I reached for the door, but I ignored it. All I wanted was to get the hell out of there.

"Sally, wait."

He took my hand and I stopped. His grip was strong, but not insistent. I suddenly remembered the way he'd touched me last night as he'd pulled me through the door. His fingers hot on my waist. His eyes meeting mine, as they were now. He stepped toward me and I wondered, fleetingly, what he would do if I just went ahead and kissed him. Would he blush again, his cheeks warming under my fingers? Would he pull away?

Oh good Lord, Sally. Get a hold of yourself!

Letting me go, he took the door handle. "Let me check first," he said, "make sure he isn't in the hall."

Right. Alex: ex-boyfriend who threw me out of the house. Harrison: dork I slept with last night. Got it.

He left the room for a second, then poked his head back in and gestured for me to follow. I didn't even glance in the direction of Alex's room. At the door, I slipped on my shoes and the cardigan Harrison had given me, at his insistence.

Before I turned to go, he handed me the first issue of *The Forever Place* and said I could keep it for as long as I liked. For some reason, when he handed it to me, I almost wanted to cry. But I didn't, of course. Sally Jarvis didn't cry, not over a guy, not over anything. Sally Jarvis always had fun, no matter what.

"See you around, sweetheart," I said, giving him a wink.

"Stay safe, Sally," Harrison said.

Stay safe? I thought to myself as I walked off the porch.

Where's the fun in that?

2

Alcohol. My confidante, my rainy day friend, my saviour. Most weeks I didn't know how I would make it to the weekend without it—and I hardly ever did—going out drinking on Thursday nights, what I called the "prequel" to the fun I would have on Friday and Saturday. If my friends weren't up for it, if the boys didn't answer my calls, no matter. Alcohol was my perfect companion. When I was buzzed I was my optimal self, the Sally everyone expected, the life of the party. Drinking was like putting on a costume, and being drunk like being a superhero. When I felt the warmth of that beloved brew coursing through me, it was like feeling my super power come alive—the power to hypnotize boys, to laugh everything off, to keep the party going no matter what they did or said to me, no matter what happened.

I'd never loved anything the way I loved alcohol, because alcohol helped me to love myself, or stand myself anyway, for the night at least. The next morning was a whole other story.

"So, he broke up with you?" my friend Emily said as she handed me and the other girls our drinks.

I downed mine in two gulps and smacked my lips. "That's right, and I'm very sad about it." I pouted to emphasize this.

"More drinks!"

"Pace yourself," my roommate Anita said. "We've only been here five minutes."

As she smoothed her thick red hair behind her ear, she narrowed her eyes at me, a frown marring her sweet, freckled face. I didn't like that look, like I was a dog she thought might be about to break off its leash and run rampant through town. I didn't want anyone or anything to get in the way of my buzz and my fun and my goal to get over Alex as quickly as possible. Tonight was my night to really let loose and put last weekend behind me by doing naughty things with a brand new naughty boy, or many naughty boys. I really wasn't particular.

"Well, that's not much of a loss, is it?" Melissa said as she picked the olive out of her double martini and popped it in her mouth. "His brother Jeremy is the one you like, right?"

"I believe the word 'love' was tossed around," Anita agreed.

Moving my body to the beat of the music, I looked around the club, making flirty eyes at a few hotties nearby, and avoiding my friends' curious looks. It was true I had imagined I was in love with Alex's younger brother Jeremy for an hour or two last spring, at the height of our week of sneaking around behind Alex's back, when everything had been all about hot texts and secrets and hurried, passionate sex. This "love" had faded somewhat when he'd told me he'd only slept with me to prove to himself that he could bang as many skanks as Alex could. Not that I'd told my friends this.

I had no idea why I'd said his name while making out with Alex, though it might have had something to do with the fact that, as brothers, they looked so much alike, and favoured a lot of the same rough sexual techniques—though I didn't even want to know why that was.

"I'm through with them both," I announced as the bartender set out the line of shots I'd ordered. "They were shit in bed anyway. Couldn't find my G-spot if they had a GPS locator." This was actually accurate. "Bring on the real men of the world, preferably the ones that come with private jets and

Visa Black cards! *L'chaim!*" I did my line of four shots and grinned.

"Yeah, screw them both," Emily agreed, though I was pretty sure I saw her making concerned eyes at Anita.

It was tough finding anyone who could keep up with my endless need for fun distractions. Sometimes, especially when all my friends had given up on me and I found myself on my own at some party, I wondered why none of them seemed to crave the ecstatic oblivion of a new guy's lips and hands and…other things the way I did. Though I never wondered about it for long. I had my good friend alcohol to thank for that.

"Is Lucas bartending tonight?" I asked Emily.

Lucas Matthews, Queen's campus legend and former basketball star—actually, the one guy on the team I'd never scored with, to my dismay—was dating Emily's shy, twin sister Katie. It wasn't often that we saw them out together—they tended to hide away in their cocoon of perfect love—but she sometimes showed up when he was working and we got to witness a hundred women dying of jealousy as he gave her all his attention. Though Katie and I had very little in common, I secretly idolized her for landing Lucas just by being her sweet, artsy self.

Katie was the kind of girl who would never dream of throwing herself at a guy. Katie was everything I would never be.

"He's not working, but they might stop by later," Emily said, her eyes drifting over the bodies on the dance floor. "Oh, what about that one?" She nodded at a guy with longish hair wearing a fitted white shirt. "Is he A material?"

My girls all knew about my choosing process when I was on the prowl. I started by scanning the room, putting out flirty feelers and shaking my ass around to be sure I had their attention. Then I started narrowing the pool down to my top contenders (A, B, and C) before going in for the kill, though sometimes I took all three on test runs before I made my final choice. It was a system I'd honed for years.

"Meh," I said, biting on the straw of my rum and coke. "Let's call him an alternate."

I was far more interested in Mr. Tattoo Arms with the sexy scar above his eyebrow who'd given me a nod on the way into the club. I was itching to give that scar a hot lick.

"Hold the phone," Melissa said, going up on tiptoes to look over my shoulder, her bright blue eyes widening. "I think we've got a contender over here. Not your usual type, but he's definitely got eyes for you."

"Where?" I said, my interest piqued, and we all turned to none-too subtly look. I had no idea what Mel meant by my "usual type"—I was pretty sure I'd tried every single type of guy out there—until my eyes landed on the guy in question. A guy with short dark hair that looked almost black in the dim room, broad shoulders, a slim build, and absolutely mesmerizing blue eyes. I quickly turned away.

Oh, I got it now. She meant the out-of-my-league type, the two-smart-for-Sally type, the has-zero-interest-in-ever-touching-me-again type.

It was Harrison Leo.

"Do you know him?" Anita said. "He's staring at you like…"

"Like what?" I snapped, though over the music I don't think she could really detect my irritation.

Harrison was the last person I wanted to see tonight. I'd had a hard enough time shoving thoughts of his stinging rejection aside all week, and I'd conveniently left him out of my breakup story when I'd recounted it to my friends. The last thing I wanted was his disapproving eyes following me around all night reminding me how little he thought of me.

Somehow his disinterest in me was so much worse than being thrown out of the house by a jerk like Alex Compton. Alex was my equal, a whore just like me. Alex could be replaced in a second. Harrison was the guy who offered to walk you home after your one night stand, and made you coffee, and lent you his comic books. Harrison was the guy I could never have. And we both knew it.

"Like he wants to lick you all over your body," Melissa finished. "Twice."

I rolled my eyes. Melissa was always seeing things wrong. She'd once told me she'd seen Rihanna in the bathroom of a club, and when I'd gone in there it was actually a drag queen, who was white, and needed a shave. Melissa couldn't be trusted.

"Whatever. He's a super dork who lives in the house with Alex. He has Japanese cartoon posters on his walls and is majoring in astrophysics or something. Plus he detests me."

"I'm pretty sure the correct term is 'anime'," Anita corrected me. "And he doesn't look like he detests you." She craned her neck to give him a second look, which given her height of exactly five foot one, wasn't an easy feat. "Actually, he looks kind of familiar. I think I may have met this nerd before. Isn't his name Harrison something?"

"Whew," Mel said, fanning her face with her free hand. "Nerd or not, Harrison's pretty damn hot."

"Oh yeah," Em and Anita said at the same time, both nodding.

"If you say so," I said, using my best nonchalant voice, though of course I knew they were right. The feel of his hand in mine—just his hand, for godsakes—and those blue eyes of his had been on my mind for days, lingering long after I'd pretty much forgotten what Alex looked like. Though I knew it was best forgotten, I wished I could remember what he'd been like in bed, if only to enrich my fantasies.

"*Hawt* with a capital H," Em went on. "He can do math at my place anytime he wants!"

As they all giggled I snuck a quick glance over at Harrison. He was standing with a group of awkward-looking guys who clearly weren't regulars at The Limo. I was actually surprised to see him there, not only because he didn't seem like the clubbing type, but because I'd chosen the club specifically because it was far away from campus and it seemed unlikely I'd run into Jeremy or Alex there. Recently spurned lovers tended to put a kink in my process.

Harrison had his hand on one of his buddy's shoulders, saying something in his ear, and his head was turned away. But just seeing him there, even just the side of his head, did something to me I didn't like. My stomach tightened and my hands started to sweat, almost like it was the end of the night instead of the beginning and I was about to be sick. Then he turned his head and his eyes met mine.

I can't even describe how it made me feel. His look was so direct I could barely stand to look back, though I did. His eyes gripped me, pinned me, impaled me. When I looked away, after five long seconds that felt like an hour, I felt so hot I was surprised my hair wasn't smoking. And I was furious.

"You okay?" Anita said.

The attention of the other two had strayed elsewhere, but Anita was still watching me and I wished she wasn't. The last thing I needed was for her to witness my humiliating crush on a guy who didn't even want me. Somehow her knowing how I felt was worse than feeling it alone. I needed my friends to believe I was happy making out with randoms and dancing 'til I dropped. I needed them to believe it so I could too.

"Screw it," I said.

Thrusting my drink into Anita's hand, I broke away from the pack and stalked right over to Mr. Longish Hair on the dance floor. Alternate or not, he'd been eyeing my ass for the last ten minutes, and that was good enough for me. I smiled and grasped the front of his shirt and without a single word he slipped his hand under my skirt and shoved my crotch toward his.

Screw Harrison Leo and his eyes and his smouldering looks that made no sense. I was a girl who knew how to get what she needed. If he was going to stare at me all night along, I was going to give him the show of his life.

An hour and two guys later I was beginning to wonder if I'd lost my touch. The guy whose lap I was currently sitting on—let's call him Jim—was a perfectly adequate C choice of the night. Though he wasn't exactly cute—his neck was kind of thick and he had a gap between his front teeth—he definitely hit all the right notes in the hottie department with his well-defined muscles bulging under his t-shirt, his confident swagger and sly grin. And most importantly his body was unmistakably interested in my body, his hands wandering up my legs and under the hem of my top, his lips grazing my ear, all signs pointing to yes, yes, yes. So why did I feel about as turned on as I did at the dentist?

It really wasn't so much that I'd lost my touch, but that A, B, C, and all the rest of the alphabet had. This moment right now, when I had my hooks in a guy real good and he was raring to go, this was usually the pinnacle of my night. I'd yearned for this all week, this feeling of being perfectly desired, almost worshipped. I lived for this. I loved this. It was one of the reasons I'd stayed with Alex as long as I had—he'd always come through for me in the appreciation department. He'd practically built a shrine to my breasts. Night after night I could count on him to want me just as much as he had the first night we met when we'd done it in his car, and on his porch, and on the kitchen table. But at this point even if Alex had materialized under me and made all the rights moves I didn't think it would have done it for me. What the hell was wrong with me tonight?

It might have been the booze, which they must have been watering down because the more I drank—and I had drunk a lot, much more than usual for a Friday night—the less buzzed I felt. And being good and liquored up was the main ingredient of all my most slutty endeavours. I needed to be aware of what was going on, but not entirely cognizant of the details—like the cheesy things he was whispering in my ear, or the way he was pulling my hair a little too hard, or how many people were watching.

Or maybe it was just one pair of eyes I wanted to obliterate, one blue pair, which had been following me all night long, and which for some reason I couldn't seem to block out or ignore, my own eyes searching his out as other guys put their arms around my shoulders, and fed me shots, and pulled me up onto a speaker to dance. They were always, *always*, trained on me, watching with unwavering focus, unrelentingly observing, judging, disapproving. He was the one ruining my night, stealing my most sacred ritual—the Friday night hookup—right out of my hands. How could I concentrate with him staring at me like that? Of course I was feeling off. Of course I wasn't on top of my game with him standing there, reminding me of how little he thought of me. This was all his fault!

"Well, whadya say?" Mr. Muscle Man murmured into my hair, the tips of his fingers grazing the underside of my bra. "Your place or mine?"

"Neither," I replied, yanking his hands out of my top and gripping the edge of the bar as I attempted to hop off his lap. I had a bone to pick, and it wasn't his. Unfortunately the shift in my weight on his crotch was giving him entirely the wrong impression.

His hands tightened around my waist. "That's not the tune you were singing a minute ago, sweetie," he said, pressing his groin into my thigh.

I sighed hard and kicked him in the shin with my heel, causing him to curse loudly and catapult me out of his lap, which was a little messier than I'd wanted but entirely effective. I kept going without a backward glance as Mr. Muscle Man and his buddies called me a slew of filthy names that barely made an impression. It wasn't like I hadn't been called worse a hundred times before.

Harrison and his ragtag gang of wallflowers were stationed around the same table they'd been all night, and as I stalked up to them with my fight face on I saw that for the first time Harrison wasn't looking at me but past me at the bar stool I'd just vacated so spectacularly.

"Hi *Harrison*," I said, sneering his name as best I could.

"Sally," he said distractedly. He was having trouble coaxing his eyes to look at me, though when he finally did they roamed all over my head from crown to chin, as though searching for some secret flaw. "Are you all right?"

All right?" I snapped. "Of course, why wouldn't I be?" I hated the way he was examining me, like he thought I might have lice. I folded my arms around my belly and scowled.

The taunts from the direction of the bar got louder as a couple of thugs moved through the crowd and I held out my arm to give them the finger without even turning around. They called me a whore for good measure and I cringed inwardly, grinding my teeth, knowing Harrison had heard them.

Just perfect.

Without warning, Harrison's hand was on my shoulder, his side pressing into mine as he tried to step past me. I noticed the determined set of his jaw as I looped my arm through his to stop him—and just in time, too. There was a startling tension in his muscles, as though he planned to punch through a wall.

"Whoa, where do you think you're going?" I said, pulling him back toward me.

The crowd surged around us, forcing us closer together, and for a second my chin was pressed into his shoulder and one of his arms was draped over my back in an approximation of a hug. We struggled apart pretty quickly but that didn't stop my skin from tingling in all the spots where our bodies had been touching, this sudden surge of the feeling I'd been chasing all night taking me so much by surprise that I almost forgot to be pissed off.

"They can't get away with talking to you like that," Harrison said, his words aimed into my hair just as my stool buddy's had been only minutes before, but *oh my* how differently my lady parts felt. They were practically singing.

Don't you dare fall for this one, I scolded myself. *Don't for a second think you're good enough for him.*

"Sure they can," I said. "They're just saying what everybody's thinking, aren't they? At least they're honest about it, unlike some people."

Taking a step back, he levelled me with another one of his looks. "What people?" he said with real confusion in his eyes. "What do you mean?"

"You know exactly what I mean," I said meanly, and then, more because of how mad I was at myself for still wanting him to touch me, I shoved him in the chest with both hands. "Stop staring at me like that. Stop watching me all the time. Who the hell do you think you are, anyway?"

The song transitioned to a faster one with a demanding bass line, but nothing could drown out the tone of disappointment in his voice. Even when I stood up for myself I wasn't up to his standards, apparently. "Sally, I didn't—"

"Whatever," I said, cutting him off.

Turning away from him I placed my hands on the table and found all of his friends openly staring at the two of us. Only one of them had his mouth hanging open, though.

"Hey," I barked. I think I saw the face of the one sitting closest to me practically shatter with fright. "So, is someone going to get me a drink, or what?"

Two guys wrestled each other to the bar in their eagerness to get me a cocktail and when they returned I felt the gentle pressure of Harrison's hand on my lower back as he introduced me to his friends, and goddammit if I didn't lean into it.

"Sally, meet Roger and Johnny and Winston and Mo."

I gave them my most civil hello and they waved and clinked their glasses with mine like we were toasting at a wedding. Winston giggled for absolutely no reason, and asked me if I liked my drink. I took a sip and made enthusiastic sounds of appreciation and they smiled like it was the most amazing thing they'd ever heard. It was funny, they were all odd-looking—Mo's hair was blonde and because he was chubby he sort of looked like an overlarge cherub—and not at all the type of guys I would ever have considered A material, but I'd never been treated so politely at a bar before. It was surreal, almost like a bland but comforting dream.

A commotion at the other end of the club caught our attention and we all turned to see a tall, chiseled, dreamboat coming through the door, a small but stunning, dark-haired girl at his side—Lucas and Katie. A small smile graced my lips as I saw the embarrassed look on Katie's face as their entrance earned the rapt attention of everyone around. Katie hated to be stared at, but I couldn't really blame the crowd. Lucas was gorgeous all by himself, but together the two of them were dazzling. They were like a double rainbow. You just couldn't look away.

Lucas quickly herded Katie toward her sister, Em, and the other girls, I heard someone over my shoulder mention the words "Kindergarten Killer" and shook my head.

"Do you know those two?" Roger asked, his eyes still shinning with awe at being in the presence of campus royalty.

"Katie's a friend of mine," I said as I glanced over at Anita, holding her drink out to Katie for a sip.

"Did she really kill that guy?" Mo asked.

It was inevitable. No matter how much time passed, the legend of the girl who stopped the Kindergarten Killer was one poor Katie just couldn't shake. Luckily, the paparazzi weren't still following her around as they had been the first few weeks after she'd ended Brandon Tomko, the guy who'd murdered her babysitting charge when they were children and stalked her for months. Over a year had passed since the news vans had moved on, but people just never got tired of hearing the story. I guess that's just how it goes when you're a national hero.

"She defended herself," I replied. "She was very brave."

"She's amazing," Roger said, craning to keep Katie in sight through the crowd.

Yep, amazing. That was Katie. Amazing and tough and kind and lovely and adored like a queen by all.

Me? Not so much.

"Well, boys," I said, "it's been a pleasure, but I should get back to my friends."

I deposited my empty glass on the table and tried not to notice their crestfallen looks. I might have taken one of them home with me if I didn't think the real me, the me who wasn't on her best behaviour, wouldn't give them all a stroke and destroy their faith in women forever. Besides, virgins weren't really my thing.

Steadily avoiding Harrison's gaze, I turned toward the back of the club, looking for my A choice from earlier in the night. He'd seemed like he had the ability to wipe all thought from my mind for a good ten minutes at least.

I hadn't made it far before I felt a warm hand on my arm, a hand that sent a thrill right through my skin and into my bones.

"I think your friends are that way," Harrison said into my ear. He gestured toward the dance floor where all four girls were dancing, Emily pulling Katie along, her drink held over her head, Melissa's long straight hair fanning out around her, and tiny Anita sandwiched somewhere in the middle.

"Those weren't the friends I was talking about," I replied, pulling my arm free.

Enough was enough. Who was he, my Dad?

I turned to face him and his face was as stoic and unreadable as ever.

"You think you know something about me, don't you?" I said, yelling a little so he could hear me over the noise. "You think you know what I'm like? Well, guess what? You're exactly right. That's exactly what I'm like."

His eyes, those blue eyes so breathtaking I wanted to wade right in and get lost in them forever, looked at me sadly. He started to shake his head.

"This is who I am, Harrison," I said, backing away. "I'm the girl everyone's gone home with. Slutty Sally's the name and I'm not worth your time, so why don't you just leave me be? I don't need you to save me. I'm perfectly happy down here in the dirt."

He looked like he was about to respond when I turned and walked away, and this time he didn't follow. I felt an odd sensation come over me, like being plunged into a tank of water, my own screams in my ears, and all I wanted was for someone to make it stop. I could have chosen A, B, or someone else altogether, but I wasn't quite sure any of them would do the trick anymore. Which was why, five tequila shots later, I found myself pressed against the brick wall behind the club by none other than Mr. Muscle Man himself, who was more than happy to scrape and grind and tear at me with all of his bubbling resentment. And I was perfectly happy to let him.

"You know," he panted, "I would have taken you to my place, treated you real nice, even let you sleep over." He ripped my underwear off with a single jerk of his hand. It felt like scratching a particularly elusive itch. I almost smiled. "But that isn't how you like it, is it? This is what you wanted all along."

My ass scraped against the brick as he ground his crotch into me. That was going to leave a mark, and not the first of its kind, either. I gripped his shoulders as he struggled with his belt and I heard the sound of his zipper. His fingers were cold as they yanked down on the neck of my shirt, exposing my breasts.

"You're a dirty girl, aren't you? And dirty girls deserve to get it just like this."

A wave of nausea washed over me and my head rolled back, smacking against the wall. This was taking way too long, and we'd only been outside for about five minutes.

Threading my fingers through his hair, I pulled his head out of my cleavage so I could look him in the face. "Stop talking and just do it already," I said.

His eyes narrowed and he didn't take his eyes off mine as he forced himself into me, hard. My tail bone slammed into the wall with the force of his thrusts and I cried out in pain.

"You think you can tell me what to do?" he said as he continued to pound my body with his and I dug my fingers into his shoulders.

At the moment when my pain peaked, even the litres of alcohol in my veins not enough to dull this feeling, Billy's face rolled through my mind—as it always did, his cruel smile and his tiny, glinting eyes—and my utter disgust with myself was complete.

This is what I am. This is what I deserve. This is all I'll ever have.

I moaned in misery and Muscle Man sneered at me. "Don't act like you didn't ask for this," he said hoarsely, "you stupid, little wh—"

My feet hit the ground hard and my arms swung backward, grasping the wall behind me. Blearily I looked around, unable to understand what had happened or what I was hearing. Had he dropped me?

Then my eyes focused downward and I just stared in disbelief.

Harrison was crouching over the body of the guy who up until a second ago had been pressed against me. Neither of them were moving, but it was clear that Harrison had just punched him, probably more than a few times, because his knuckles were bloody and his face screwed up in a look of such utter loathing I almost didn't recognize him.

In my surprise I slid down the wall, landing on my bottom on the filthy cement and Harrison looked up at me, releasing his fist and sitting back.

"Harrison, stop," I said uselessly, because of course he'd already stopped.

He started to get up, reaching toward me. "Are you—"

"Don't!" I cried, covering my eyes with one hand and pressing my knees together. I had no idea where my skirt was exactly, but I was pretty sure it wasn't covering much. "I don't want you to see me like this," I whispered.

I just wanted him to go away, couldn't he understand that? Couldn't he just leave me to ruin myself alone?

"Please just go away."

I shut my eyes tighter as I heard him approaching my side. Then I felt something being pressed into my hand and the soft graze of his fingers smoothing my cheek. I pressed my forehead into my kneecaps.

"You're better than this," he said into my ear, and then I heard him walk away.

3

The knock on my door pulled me out of a strange dream in which a girl I'd lived next to in the third grade and I were running away from a masked man through a forest. We kept almost getting away, but then I would circle back and leave one of my hair ribbons on the path so he would know which way we'd gone. When I ran out of ribbons I started pulling out my own hair.

My hands flew to my head, reassuringly patting my long blonde (if a little matted) locks as Anita tentatively poked her head into the room. I let my head fall back on the pillow as I breathed a sigh of relief. By the end of the dream I'd had only a single lock of hair left hanging over my forehead, the trail littered with my tresses.

Sure, I was hot, but even I couldn't rock the cancer patient look.

Unfortunately, my relief was fleeting because right on its heels came the excruciating memory of everything that had happened the night before. And I mean everything. Every hideously ugly, humiliating and upsetting moment.

"Oh, you're alone," Anita said, the surprise obvious in her voice, "I didn't think…"

She didn't think I would have left the club by myself is what she wanted to say, which made sense. On any other Saturday morning she would have been exchanging awkward pleasantries at the kitchen table with Alex or whatever random I'd brought home from the club, while trying to forget all the sex noises she'd heard through the wall the night before—at least until I'd bought her that pack of ear plugs.

As my friend perched on the side of my bed I realized she was going to expect some kind of explanation for why I'd returned home *before* she had last night, and alone—an explanation I was in no mood to give, since thinking about last night even for a single second was making my insides contract with extreme rejection.

I rubbed my eyes, my fingers coming away black with leftover mascara. God, I didn't even want to know what I looked like. As I grimaced, Anita held out the orange mixing bowl she'd brought in with her.

"Are you going to hurl?" she said, aiming the bowl at my face.

Yep, she knew me.

Except by the time I'd used the money Harrison had put in my hand last night to grab a cab and dragged myself into the apartment, my buzz had long since worn off. I'd spent the next two hours vomiting my guts out, all long before Anita had even arrived home. Instead of feeling queasy as I usually did after a night of partying, I felt like a tin can that had been emptied, my insides scraped raw. There was nothing left to hurl.

"I'm good," I said, sitting up in bed with a shiver. It was starting to get draughty in the apartment and it wasn't even October yet.

As I gathered the covers around me, I tried to shake off the humongous thundercloud I was sitting under, full of lightning bolts shaped like shame. Unless I wanted to face the Spanish Inquisition, I was going to have to fake my usual sunny disposition, and fast, like really fast, like right now.

"How'd your night end up?" I said. "Did Melissa throw

up bellinis into your hair again?"

This had actually happened once last semester when Anita had leaned down to tie her shoe just as Mel's drinks came out in a disgusting peach-coloured stream. We were never going to let her live that one down, though it was really Anita who was the most traumatized by the episode.

Anita cringed and punched me on the arm. "No!" she said. "Emily was the problem last night, actually. She kept dancing with this guy, getting him to buy us all drinks, almost letting him kiss her, then turning away. He got our coats, hailed us a cab, and then she wouldn't even give him her name. I hate to say it, but she's such a tease. I think you've been rubbing off on her."

"Thanks a lot!" I said, giving her a playful shove, pretending to be offended, when really the comparison had cheered me up a little bit. I liked my friends thinking of me as the girl who could wrap men around her little finger, a girl who was rash and impulsive and didn't care what anyone thought. I had been that girl just a few days ago, hadn't I? Where exactly had she gone? "And what about you? See anyone you like?"

"Nah," Anita said, wrinkling her nose.

Anita never saw anyone she liked anywhere, and as far as I knew she'd never had a boyfriend. Nobody was ever good enough. It was the kind of thing that I usually puzzled over without really thinking about it, but this morning, when everything seemed somehow more real and less funny than usual, I wondered who she was waiting for. At some point I was going to have to get her to talk about it. Just not today.

"So," my friend said, giving me a curious look, "are you going to tell me where you disappeared to last night? I saw you talking to that guy Harrison…"

She left the sentence hanging in the air, and I picked at my cuticles, ignoring it.

"Or do you want me to wait until you get drunk again and trick you into telling me?"

"That totally doesn't work," I scoffed, folding my arms.

As my forearms dug into my belly, I almost gasped with

pain (cleverly turning it into a cough at the last second) because my stomach was so sore. Did I have bruises? It had happened before, though they'd never hurt this bad. As I gingerly explored my side with the tips of my fingers, I began to mentally search the apartment for my flask of liquor. I could stand anything, even a couple of broken ribs, with some hair of the dog.

"I've seen it work on more than one occasion," Anita replied. "That's how we found out you skinny-dipped with that girl the summer before first semester, and she gave you the best orgasm you'd ever had."

"At the time," I added as I tried to slip into my robe without displaying any of my body. I was still wearing my skimpy skirt and glittery tank top from last night, which showed an astonishing amount of skin. Normally I would have happily pranced around the room naked, but today I didn't want anyone seeing my body before I had a chance to examine it myself. "Best orgasm at the time. That was before I met Kevin Lagaros."

"What ever happened to Kevin?" Anita mused, lying down in the warm spot I'd just vacated on the bed.

"Gay," I replied, typing the belt of my robe. "I think I was his 'college experiment.' But oh man, the things he could do with his tongue."

I winked at her and she giggled.

There was something so awful about the way I was lying to her, and how easily she believed me. Sure, I lied all the time, pretending I was happy, happy, happy. Pretending I never had a care in the world. The difference was that usually I believed it myself. When I had to force it, and still nobody could tell the difference, that was just sad.

I'd reached the door and was almost out in the hall, heaving a sigh of relief, when I heard her say, "What's this?" and I turned around. My breath caught in my throat as I saw that she'd picked up *The Forever Place* from my nightstand and was turning it over in my hands.

In a sudden burst of speed I was sure I hadn't displayed

since I'd tried out for the track team in grade seven, I sprinted across the room and grabbed the comic out of her hands.

"That's nothing," I said, hastily rolling it up and shoving it in the pocket of my robe. Anita stared at me like she'd only just noticed that I actually was bald. "It's just…something Alex gave me once. And…it makes me sick just looking at it," I lied, rolling my eyes for emphasis. "It's porn."

Anita frowned at me. "Alex reads pornographic comic books?" she said skeptically. "Alex knows how to read?"

I chuckled and pushed my hair behind my ear, and as I did the sleeve of my robe fell down, exposing my elbow. Even before her eyes zeroed in, I knew. I slapped my hand over my elbow and turned for the door.

"Did you hurt yourself?" Anita said. "There's a scrape or…"

"I'm fine!" I said, practically scurrying for the bathroom. "You know how I am when I'm drunk. I probably fell."

"Fell? Where did you fall? Let me see." She was right on my heels like some kind of haunting conscience, looking for answers, and I didn't have any to give.

As I made it to the bathroom door she reached for my arm and I jerked it out of her hands, causing her to stumble back a step. She gave me a wide-eyed look. "Sally, what—"

"Can't you just leave me alone?" I cried, slamming the door behind me, like I was a hormonal teenager and she was my mom.

Way to fake it, Sally, I thought. *That wasn't weird at all.*

I leaned my head on the back of the door and sighed.

It wasn't long before I had the apartment to myself. As usual on Saturdays, Anita was out of the house early to meet a group for a class project and then she had a shift at the kids play centre where she worked. She was such a busy bee with her study sessions and tutoring and trips home to visit her parents. Sometimes I wondered if I could have found a best friend who was more completely my polar opposite if I'd actually tried. But I hadn't tried. One day Anita had just gone from being one of a group of girls I was friends with to the one who made sure I knew my class schedule, and offered to share an apartment with me, and made sure I ate enough veggies. She was amazing—my saviour—and I wasn't even sure why she bothered with me, though a part of me felt that maybe I was just another attractive project for her, another thing she needed to clean up, to worry over, to perfect. Not that I was complaining.

I usually teased Anita about her unrelenting pace, even on the weekends, telling her if she didn't relax she'd do everything there was to do in the world before she turned thirty and then she would simply die a sad, exhausted prude. Today, I was just glad to have the place to myself.

Alone in front of the bathroom mirror, I stared myself in the face. For some reason I felt as though I hadn't seen myself in a very long time, and look at me now with black mascara circling my eyes and smudged over my cheeks, my lips bare and raw as if they'd been bitten, the whites of my eyes red from all the vomiting. God, I looked like death, and Anita hadn't even blinked an eye, which was somehow worse. It meant this was how I looked most Saturday mornings. It meant this was the norm.

My body was another story. I'd taken a couple of pulls on my flask before undressing and balancing on the edge of the bathtub to look at myself in the mirror over the sink, twisting this way and that to get the whole picture. It really wasn't that bad on the whole—a few scrapes on my ass, bruises in the shape of fingerprints across my ribs, a couple of scratches (from the brick wall) on my elbows, a stinging tenderness between my legs. To be honest I found my body far more resilient than my face, my breasts still full and my stomach flat no matter what I did to it, or let someone else do. I hadn't lost anything permanently last night. My scrapes would heal, my face could be washed clean. I was still desirable, still the tight hottie who could bring a roomful of guys to their knees with the flick of her hair.

So, why did I feel like such a piece of shit?

As I rubbed off my makeup with a cotton ball, I thought about *him*—I hadn't even gotten his name—Mr. Muscle Man who'd treated my body like a lump of raw meat to be pounded. It wasn't always like that. Alex had been demanding in bed, but never as rough as that. Still, it wasn't the first time a guy had been overly aggressive with me. I didn't even fault him for it. Sure, he was a dirtbag, and I would never have let any of my friends go near him, but I'd chosen him for a reason. That was the way I wanted it sometimes, hard and rough. Pain was stronger than ecstasy, it obliterated everything in a way I craved on certain nights. Passion could fade halfway through but pain couldn't be ignored.

He wasn't the problem. What he'd done to me wasn't the problem.

I eyed the comic book in my robe pocket as I hung it up behind the door.

I knew exactly who the real problem was, and he was about to get a piece of my mind.

I waited across the street, crouched behind a parked car sort of like a stalker. Actually, exactly like a stalker. I'd had one myself first semester—a homely boy named Jim who I'd slept with out of pity and had latched on like a crab. This was before I'd instated my "no virgins" rule—and whenever he'd popped up out of nowhere it was always from behind a parked car or a mailbox or a tree. At least I didn't plan on saying, "Fancy meeting you here," and wiggling my eyebrows like a psycho.

After an interminable fifteen minutes of staring at the front door until everywhere I looked all I could see was door handles, Harrison finally made an appearance. The sight of him was like being hit in the face. He glanced down the street to the left and then started right, facing me head on for only a second, but just that moment, the sweep of those blue eyes, was enough to bring everything crashing back: my legs bare and trembling, the vicious look on his face, the sickening sound of his knuckles hitting their mark mixed in with my own self-loathing.

This was exactly the problem. This right here! It was only because he'd seen me that I felt so awful, so completely destroyed. This is what it was to have a witness. I couldn't just brush off the night, wring it out like beer soaked into a shirt, and move on. It was recorded now, in precise, exacting detail. I couldn't get the way he'd looked at me out of my head, or what he'd said—*You're better than this.*

But I wasn't better. I didn't *feel* better. All he'd done was make me feel so much worse.

Standing up so fast I got a head rush, I ran down the street after Harrison.

To hell with keeping out of sight. To hell with everything!

"Hey!" I yelled, and as he turned around, surprise dawning on his face, I threw the rolled-up comic book right into it. "Here's your goddamn comic back. Stay the hell out of my life!"

I spun on my heel and started walking away, though that was nowhere near everything I'd planned to say. I was so worked up I didn't even know what I was doing anymore.

Wait," he said, jogging to catch up with me. "Don't walk away. I was just on the way to your place."

"What?" I said, incredulous. I swung around again, my hair flying. "Why the hell would you do that? How do you even know where I live? You're not my boyfriend, Harrison."

His face was unreadable as ever and he had his hands held up as if he was worried I might hit him, which wasn't outside the realm of possibility.

"I got your address off Alex's phone. And I know I'm not your boyfriend, but I was concerned. You were in bad shape last night. I should never have let you make your way home alone. I shouldn't have pummelled that guy either." A flicker of the anger I'd seen in him the night before passed over his face. "Even though he definitely deserved it. But I shouldn't have just left you there."

"I'm fine!" I snarled, folding my arms and once again wincing as my hands hit that tender spot.

Instantly Harrison was by my side, his hand running

down the back of my jacket, his body so close to mine and that smell of oranges making me dizzy. "You're not fine," he said, his voice low and laced with concern.

"You have *got* to be kidding me!" I roared, pulling out of his grasp. "You don't get to decide if I'm fine or not. You don't get to decide if I need help. That's up to me and only me. I don't need you beating the crap out of every guy who touches me in a way you don't like. Stop fussing over me like I'm a child!"

So there I was ranting and punching the air with my finger and basically acting like a lunatic. To his credit, Harrison stood his ground and didn't show a trace of embarrassment, though people were definitely looking.

"This isn't me," I went on. "This mess, it's not who I am. I don't lie to my friends. I don't nurse my bruises and hide away and cringe every time I remember the things I've done. I have nothing to hide. You're the one who's making me feel this way. You're the one who's screwing with my head!" I poked myself in the temple so hard I almost saw stars.

"Sally," he said in his calm, measured way, in that voice like velvet. "That was never my intention. You have to know —"

"No!" I was really on a roll now and nothing was going to stop me. I felt like I was on a stage, like this was the speech of my life. I paced up and down the sidewalk, unable to slow down. "You think just because you saved me from freezing to death you know me or something? Is that what you think? Well, here's something I bet you didn't know. I used to be numb. I used to feel nothing except a vague sense of satisfaction after a good lay and the calm thrill of my buzz. I used to be perfectly fine. I had a process that was working for me, a perfect formula. And then you came in with your goddamn t-shirt and your goddamn comic book and now all I do is feel things, and everything I'm feeling is bad!"

He was watching me go back and forth, his posture tense, his head turning left and right like he was watching a game of tennis. But he didn't say a word. He didn't even care enough to do that.

I said, "You think just because you screwed me—"

With a sudden jerk he took me by the elbow, gently but firmly, and led me straight into the driveway of the house two doors down from his, not stopping until we were away from the street, standing between the brick walls of the houses on either side.

I flung his arm away. "What? Afraid your neighbours are going to hear that you did the town skank?"

As he walked up to me, uncomfortably close, I could see he was breathing hard, though when he spoke his voice was hardly above a whisper.

"Don't call yourself things like that," he said. "And you might not want to admit it, but I don't think either of us wants Alex to overhear that I slept with his ex-girlfriend of exactly one week. Especially since no such thing ever happened."

"What?" I had been scowling at the ground, but my eyes snapped to his face when he said that. "We didn't—"

"Of course we didn't!" he said, shaking his head at me, his facade cracking just a little as he frowned at me. "My God, Sally, you literally passed out in my arms. What kind of guy do you think I am?"

Well, that silenced me. I couldn't think of anything to say. What kind of a guy did I think he was? Exactly like every single guy I'd ever been with, every guy who'd had absolutely no problem doing me, drop-down drunk or sober, conscious or not. I looked down, chastened.

"I guess I thought…" I stepped away and leaned against the house.

"I carried you to the bed, got you dressed, and tucked you in," he said. "I slept on the couch."

"You didn't even sleep in the bed with me?" For some reason, I found this even more impressive. It seemed to show some kind of super-human restraint. I was impressed, or at least I was for a couple of seconds, until I saw the look of disbelief on his face.

He leaned his shoulder into the wall beside me, training

those breathtaking eyes on my face. "No, I didn't," he said, and there was a hint of sadness in his voice. "I don't get into bed with a girl unless I'm invited."

My head was buzzing with confusion, or maybe it was just because of how close to me he was standing. I tried to remind myself that he'd essentially rejected me, naked. If there were levels of not wanting a girl, that had to be the highest. And yet, he'd rescued me—even though I hadn't needed him to. He'd been on his way to check on me. For some reason he seemed to care and that, more than anything else, had me staring into his eyes as if I was mesmerized.

Like a lovestruck school girl! Like some sappy teenager with hearts on her binder!

His hand was resting, ever so lightly on my sleeve, and I carefully removed it.

"You know who you are?" I said. "You're the black shadow."

He blinked as though disoriented. "...from *The Forever Place*?"

"Yeah," I nodded. "You're not the assassins who come after Rainbow on the road, or the ghosts who haunt her dreams. You're worse than that. You're the black shadow, the evil she can't ever escape or outrun."

The left corner of his lips turned up in the slightest hint of a smile. "You read it," he said.

"You're not the hero in my story, Harrison. You're the villain." The smile slipped off his face. "So stop being so fucking nice to me."

His phone rang right then, at the exact moment I stopped speaking, and I felt a little let down. Because let's face it, that was a pretty good line I'd just thrown at him and I hadn't even had the chance to turn and walk away.

It seemed to be a serious phone call, because Harrison stood up straight as soon as he saw who was calling, and his face was suddenly alert. The call was short. He said yes and no and that he'd be there in five minutes.

"You're going?" I said, flabbergasted. I'd just compared

him to an evil, lurking presence set to destroy me and he was just going to walk away? Really?

"I have to go right now," he said distractedly, looking out toward the street and pulling at the hair on the back of his head.

Then, without warning, he leaned in and kissed me on the cheek, his lips cool, though I felt heat flare up in my belly as he lingered, for just a split-second. And before I could blink the desire from my eyes he was gone.

I don't know where the day went. I wandered stupidly, blindly, trying to sort through my conflicting and riotous feelings. I even made my way to campus, thinking I might sit in on a class—something I'd only done consistently for one week in the four since school had begun—only to realize as I wandered the empty halls that it was *Saturday*.

As I made my way back home, which took far longer than it should have because I kept losing track of where I was going and getting lost, I decided that whatever that kiss on the cheek had meant, it changed nothing. I'd said everything I ever wanted to say to Harrison. I'd said it all. He was the black shadow and I didn't want him destroying me. That was that, end of story.

Done and done.

By the time I got back to the apartment it was dark and my feet were aching. All I wanted to do was collapse on the couch with my flask (which badly needed a refill) and doze while watching some stupid comedy show until it was time to go out. Because of course I was still going out. It was Saturday night, after all.

As I put my key in the lock the door fell open and Anita stared at me with slightly wild eyes.

"I'm *so* sorry," she said right away, and I remembered the spat we'd had that morning and how rude I'd been.

"What are you apologizing for?" I said. "I'm the one who's sorry." I pulled her into a hug and she patted me on the back, almost absentmindedly, which wasn't unusual. Anita wasn't much of a hugger.

As I pulled off my cream-coloured trench coat and hung it on the hook by the door, I noticed there were a few coats I didn't recognize mixed in with ours.

"I mean, I'm really sorry," Anita repeated, a note of pleading in her voice. "Remember when I said he looked familiar…"

Frowning at her, I rounded the corner and saw four unfamiliar faces turn toward me.

No, scratch that. Three unfamiliar faces.

The fourth face belonged to Harrison Leo.

4

"What the hell, Anita?" I whisper-yelled at my roommate as we stood in the kitchen pouring diet coke into glasses. Because the kitchen was essentially a part of the living room I couldn't freak out at her in the way I would have liked, which would have included big hand gestures and swearing, and possibly some strangulation. "What. Is. He. Doing. Here?"

A girl with long curly hair leaned over the couch to ask if she could have water instead and Anita said "Sure!" more enthusiastically than she needed to, and smiled. Then she turned her regretful face to me.

"He's in our class. That's where I know him from," she explained as she loaded glasses onto a tray. "We're studying and Alana asked if she could bring her friend along. I had no idea it would be Alex's roommate. How could I know?"

I leaned against the counter, absolutely refusing to look in Harrison's direction. I knew it wasn't Anita's fault he was here. It wasn't anybody's fault, which was so very disappointing. It was nice to have someone to yell at.

"On a Saturday night?" I said. Didn't these people have priorities?

"It was the only night everyone was free," Anita replied,

"and we have that test on Monday."

"What test?" I said confusedly. "What class is this for?"

Anita rolled her eyes and gave me a look that reminded me of my last year of high school. I'd gotten that look a lot, from my Math teacher, my French teacher, even my Gym teacher. One good thing about being in university was that nobody cared if I didn't know the name of my classes, or when they were, or when the mid-term was. Nobody cared at all, which suited me just fine.

Or at least, nobody except Anita.

"Twentieth-century British lit?" Anita said. "The only class we have together?"

"I know," I retorted, though we both knew I'd really had no idea what she was talking about. Picking at my sweater churlishly, I muttered, "At least you could have reminded me about the study group."

Anita motioned toward the fridge with her chin. "I did!" she said. Under a magnet shaped like a peace sign was a piece of paper with the words *SALLY: Study Group Tonight!* written in big red letters. I scowled at it.

Picking up a bowl of chips and the tray of glasses, Anita whispered, "What does it matter anyway? You said you're not interested in him, right?"

"I said he couldn't stand me," I said sullenly.

Oh yeah, and also I screamed at him in the middle of the street earlier today, and slept mostly naked in his bed, and just being near him makes me feel like crap, but I can't get him out of my head, or my life, apparently.

"You'll win him over! That's your specialty," Anita said brightly as she walked back into the other room.

Peering into the living room through the gap below the cabinets I saw Harrison nod thank you to Anita as he took a drink, and then his eyes met mine and he raised his eyebrows at me in some combination of apology and bewilderment.

Winning people over, my specialty? Nope, my specialty seemed to be pure, unadulterated torture.

Pouring myself my own glass of water—there was no

beer in the fridge, sadly—I thought over my options.

A: Hide in my room for the rest of the night. (A little ungrateful, since I was pretty sure Anita had arranged for the study group to be here instead of at the library to force me to participate.)

B: Pretend to get a call from a friend in an emergency and run out the door. (Still ungrateful. See A.)

C: Cry. (Pathetic.)

D: Grin and bear it.

Though C was in the running for a good ten seconds, I knew D was the only choice I could make. So, plastering my face with that grin, I careened into the living room and announced—still avoiding Harrison's eyes—that I would be joining them as soon as I changed my clothes. A guy with horn-rimmed glasses glanced up and nodded, but the rest of them, already deep into *Sense and Sensibility*, didn't even bother looking up, Anita included.

Okay, so I was still running to my room, which was cheating a little, but I really did have to change. Not because my clothes were inappropriate—though if study group had been scheduled an hour later I easily could have been in my clubbing attire already—but because even though I hadn't looked at Harrison for more than a second, my body seemed to be keenly aware of him. I was all sweaty!

Was I nervous because of the way I'd overreacted earlier (I had reluctantly come to this conclusion during my long day of walking), because I felt like he was judging me (I still did, didn't I?), because his rejection put me so off-balance, or because of…something else?

I pulled my sweater over my head and stared down at it, contemplating this "something else" for way longer than I should have.

Something else was a bad idea, a curse, a guaranteed letdown. Something else would only lead to tears, and I'd already done enough crying to last me a lifetime. Besides, even if *I* was getting all nervous because of "something else" it didn't mean—

There was a short knock on my bedroom door, which startled me so much I dropped my sweater, and then the door swung open and Harrison was looking at me. And unlike our late-night dance in the hallway, this time I was wearing my sexy black underwear and no bra at all.

We both froze, his mouth half-open, whatever words he'd been about to say stalled on his lips, and though it was only for a moment I saw his eyes dip below my chin and felt the hot trail of his gaze. And all at once I knew "something else" wasn't just an idea in my head alone.

Then his eyes slammed to the ground. "I am *so* sorry," he began, and before he could close the door with himself on the other side of it, I ran forward and shut it for him. Yeah, I still wasn't wearing a top, but I had nice boobs anyway, and they seemed to want to be seen in this moment by this boy. These boobs had done a lot for me. Who was I to overrule them?

Now that I was standing so close to him, Harrison was resolutely staring at the floor as though the secret to world happiness was carved into the floorboards.

"Relax, sweetie," I said, placing a hand on his arm just to make him jump. "It's not like you haven't seen most of it before."

I crossed the room to my closet and was just reaching for a top when I felt a slight breeze and realized I hadn't crossed the room alone.

Harrison had followed me.

Harrison who was now standing right behind my mostly naked body, warming the skin of my back with his proximity and making other parts of me perk up involuntarily. A thrill ran down my spine and all the way to my toes. He was standing less than a foot away from me, in my bedroom, with the door closed, and my clothes off. I wasn't sure exactly how, but something else had very suddenly become something very real.

I could feel his breath against my shoulder. I could feel him wanting to say something, but hesitating, holding back.

I half-turned my head toward him, my temperature rising, and said his name, at which point his eyes met mine—oh God, those *eyes*—and he blinked as though he was startled to see me there, still without a top on, almost within his reach. Flustered, his cheeks pinking, he reached past me and grabbed a chambray shirt from my closet, placing it in my hands.

Mystified, and coming down fast from my sudden arousal—could I really call it arousal? Maybe I was just overheated from all that exercise—I quickly snapped on my bra and pulled the shirt on over it. I'd just begun to button it up when I felt the barely-there touch of Harrison's fingertips as he pulled up my sleeve and ran his thumb over the scab at my elbow.

"Hey!" I said, twisting all the way around this time, and pulling my arm from his grasp. I wasn't sure exactly why, but this was so much worse than when Anita had seen my scrapes. This was humiliating. "Mind if I put some pants on before we get all up close and personal, sweetheart?"

Which was the first time those words had ever passed my lips, that's for sure.

As I yanked on a pair of jeans, I glanced up at his face again and saw a startling fervour in his blue eyes, a violent stirring like a wild wind, barely contained. I was sure I'd seen it, but a second later it was gone and Harrison had retreated to his original spot by the door.

"Thanks," I said, raising my eyebrows at him pointedly as if to say, *Now's when you explain what the hell that was about.*

"You're hurt," he said, his voice low.

So that was it. It wasn't my luscious curves that had drawn him toward me. It wasn't my body, it was the marks that covered it, the bruises and the scrapes I'd been so eager to hide that morning. And now he'd seen them all, every alluring bruise and cut.

Just wonderful.

"It's not that bad," I said dismissively, shrugging my shoulders. "It's nothing. It doesn't even hurt."

He was having trouble looking me in the eye again. I got that. I was tainted now, ruined. I was damaged goods. Or at least that's what I imagined he was thinking until I saw his deeply furrowed brow and the way he was holding his hands in front of his stomach, squeezing them into fists.

"I should have hit him harder," he said. I noticed he had bandages on four of his knuckles.

Man was he the king of mixed messages, or what? I didn't even know what was going on now. Was he into me? Repelled by me? Did he have rage issues? Was he secretly The Hulk? In true Sally fashion I decided to dismiss these questions as an unsolvable puzzle—similar to Anita's cleaning schedule—and ignore them altogether.

Stepping toward Harrison, I placed my fingers on top of his and they loosened.

"Harrison," I said, and this time I waited until I really had his attention, his gorgeous eyes drifting up to mine. "I'm really fine. It's nothing at all, just a few scratches. Look, I can even do this." I danced a little jig in front of him and he didn't exactly smile, but he shook his head as if he wanted to chuckle, but couldn't manage it.

God he was a serious guy. Didn't he ever relax?

"What happened to that guy, anyway?" I said. I'd left my partner in destruction lying on his face in the alley without a backwards glance.

"I waited until you got in the cab—I was just standing a few doors down—and then I came back," Harrison said. "I wasn't sure I was done teaching him a lesson. But his buddies were already taking him back inside. He was still there when I left. I guess a bloodied nose and a few minutes of unconsciousness shouldn't get in the way of a night out. They didn't even ask him why he was beat up."

"A guy like that?" I said wryly. "I'm guessing these kind of things happen to him all the time."

"And you?" Harrison said. "Do these kind of things happen to you all the time?"

I frowned and looked over at the window, at the leaves fluttering in the wind, their shadows dancing on the blind. What was it about Harrison that always left me with a twinge in my gut and nothing to say?

Harrison sighed and rubbed his head. "Sally, I'm sorry. That was incredibly rude and it's obviously none of my business. I'm sorry about…" his eyes searched the room "…everything that happened in the last five minutes." He gave me a pained look. "All I came in here to say is that I heard what you said earlier about wanting me to stay away from you. If that's what you want, then I will. I had no idea this study group was going to be at your apartment. My friend Alana drove me or I would have noticed the address."

He was agreeing with me. He was saying he'd do exactly what I'd asked.

Funny how when you get what you want it's never what you want anymore.

"One thing you should know about me, Harrison," I said with an embarrassed smile, "I don't really mean half the things I say. Especially things I yell at people on crowded sidewalks."

He raised an eyebrow. "Oh, really?" he said.

"Yeah, so just, you know," I made a chopping motion at my neck, "forget everything I said this morning. You're not the black shadow. You're not ruining me. I tend to have a talent for doing that all on my own."

He seemed to want to say something, but I stuck out my hand before he could speak.

"What do you say, friends?" I said.

He took my hand but didn't shake it. "What about Alex?" he said, and I was surprised at how many hours it had been since I'd even thought about my ex-boyfriend at all.

"Alex used to eat my fries because he said he didn't want me to lose my figure," I replied with a wicked twinkle in my eye. "Fuck Alex."

"Fuck Alex," Harrison agreed, the corners of his lips turning up at last, and we shook on it.

5

I spent most of the next hour trying to convince myself I didn't have a crush on Harrison Leo. It was a nice distraction, since the study group was boring as hell and the absolute last way I wanted to be spending my evening. If it had been literally any other kind of social gathering I wouldn't have had the time to be thoughtful. I would have been too busy mingling and laughing and flirting and using every one of my feminine wiles on every guy in the room. Being the life of the party was sort of my natural state. Lucky for me, this study group was at no risk of becoming a party any time soon.

Wresting my elbow on my brand new spiral notebook—Anita had given it to me on the first day of class and I had yet to take a single note in it—I put my chin in my hand and watched Harrison. He was the type of guy who liked to participate in group discussions but didn't dominate the conversation or try to force through his opinion by bulldozing everyone around him—I'd seen Alex do this on more than one occasion. When Frank started talking at the same time as him, which Frank tended to do, he always stopped and graciously insisted that Frank speak first. And yet, I got the impression everyone was waiting to hear what Harrison had to say, because he really seemed to know his stuff. I was clued in enough to realize that it was a rare person who was good at both English and science—what was his major again, Microbiology? It was a little intimidating, and also kind of hot. I'd assumed he was a nerd, but I hadn't had any concrete proof. Now I could see he wasn't just a medium smart guy who liked to read, he was multifaceted smart. And guys as smart as that didn't go for girls like me. They just didn't.

Not that I wanted him to anyway. Hadn't we just made a pact to be friends? If I did have a crush on him—I was still holding out some hope that the condition could be reversed—it wasn't something I was ever going to act on. My God, I wasn't Marianne, falling for Mr. Willoughby who was way out of her league and then letting herself get totally crushed when he left her for that snotty rich chick. I was no idiot. I knew where I belonged and what I should hope for. Harrison Leo was a dream I had no right to have.

The whole thing was kind of a huge bummer, and it didn't help that the only distraction available was Jane Austen. School was something I put up with because it gave me an excuse to live away from home in a place where there was a huge number of single, hot, and horny guys. My attitude toward my education was simple. I would do what I needed to stay enrolled and pass at least most of my classes, but nothing more. I tried to attend each class at least once every two weeks and to be there for most tests, and I usually bought the textbooks, or "befriended" a guy in the class who had bought the textbook.

My inability to take my schoolwork seriously was something Anita and I often argued about, arguments she usually won because I refused to admit the truth. I couldn't explain how the very sight of campus made my stomach turn, how sitting in class made me twitch, how out of place I felt there, how panicked, how wrong. I couldn't explain to her that it brought me back to another school, another time, when the answers that had once come so easily had abandoned me, and everyone had always seemed to be looking and laughing, how awful I had felt then, how ashamed, how stupid.

I couldn't explain any of this to Anita because I didn't understand it myself. It was just easier to say that an academic setting wasn't for me—easier, because whatever the reason it *was* true. I would never excel at school. I was never going to be a lawyer or a professor or an engineer, or anyone who made their living by using their brain. Everybody had their strengths and I knew what mine were. I was a good-time girl, not an intellectual, and I didn't want to pretend to be something I wasn't. That was just too pathetic.

Study groups like this were my nightmare. It was just like being in class; I felt so completely out of place. All the talk-talk-talking made me fidgety and irritable and not even having Harrison's handsome face so close by was any help, at least not as we were nearing the one-hour mark. It was almost worse having him there to watch me flailing helplessly in the ocean of literature, biting at my hangnails and sneaking off to my room to refill my flask from the bottles lined on top of my bureau.

God, I loved my handy, little flask. When I felt its familiar weight in my pocket I knew all my anxieties, all the unwanted memories would soon be fading away, and I wouldn't have to remember the girl I'd once been, a girl who'd loved to learn, or the reason I'd left her behind. I wouldn't hear Billy's voice in my head—*Stick to what you're good at, Sal*—or remember what they'd all called me, and why. My flask could make even a study session bearable by giving me the gift of forgetfulness.

On my way back from my third visit to my room for a refill—third and last I'd decided when I'd had to give up on refreshing my lipstick because I couldn't figure out which set of lips in the mirror was mine—I tripped on the corner of the rug and nearly fell. Harrison was up in a flash, grasping me by the waist with his impressively strong hands.

"You okay?" he said to me as I steadied myself against him.

Hmm, his chest seemed to be pretty well-defined, I noticed with appreciation. And though his eyes seemed a little dismayed, I liked the way he kept watching me as I took my seat on the couch. Was this what it was like to be friends with guys? All the sizzle of see but don't touch? Because if so, I was going to try it more often.

"Okay, so that leaves the essay questions," said the curly-headed girl named Alana, "which are a total nightmare. I thought since he was giving them to us ahead of time they would be a cinch, but, like this one: Which character in *Sense and Sensibility* is Austen's favourite? How the hell are we supposed to know that? Oh wait, I'll just go dig up her grave and ask her."

"Yeah," I agreed. I was really digging this Alana chick. I liked her ire, and her highlights. "What the hell's that about, right?"

Alana was nodding at me, like she really appreciated my support, and suddenly I felt like she really got me and I got her. I got all of them. Even if Anita was eyeing me in a strange way, and that guy with the glasses whose name I didn't know kept trying to look down my shirt. For the first time all night I really felt at ease with them.

What a pal my flask was. I knew he wouldn't let me down.

"It has to be Marianne," Glasses said. "I mean, she's the only reason I kept reading. That Edward guy? If I ever met him in real life I'd punch him in the face, and not because of what he did to Elinor. Because he's so freaking boring!"

"Punch him in the face," I repeated. "I dig it, man. I really do."

Harrison, who was sitting in the armchair to my left, sat up as I said this, and Anita got up and went into the kitchen.

"We shouldn't discount the less appealing characters," Harrison said. "Fanny Dashwood is deliciously awful. You could make the case that she is that way because Austen had such a good time writing her."

See what I'm saying? Genius-level smart.

"Here, sweetie," Anita said, handing me a cup of instant coffee. "I made this for you." She stuck the mug under my nose and I took it lazily.

Frank and Alana both started talking at once, and she

waved for him to go ahead. "There's also the mother and the little sister, and Mrs. Jennings. She's funny, right? Austen likes funny."

"Austen likes clever," Anita said. "Mrs. Jennings is *not* clever."

"It's Elinor," I said as I swallowed my first sip of coffee. Anita made the best instant coffee. She always stirred in exactly the right amount of milk and sugar. I had to remember to tell her that. "You have to look at the end, who she matches up with who. Elinor is the one who gets the man she wants, even if Edward is boring as hell. She does the right thing, follows the rules, risks losing him even, because stealing another girl's guy is unseemly. Good girls finish first in Austen's world, and Elinor is always good. Marianne breaks too many rules, so she ends up with Colonel Brandon who's nice and all, but he's no Willoughby, and I can't imagine Austen doing that to her favourite character. I think Elinor is the person Austen wishes she could be. Though I guess an argument could be made for any character in the book. That's probably what the teacher is looking for, an in-depth analysis. I don't think there's any right answer."

They all stared at me as I took another sip of my coffee. Glasses dropped his notebook.

You see? This is why I never spoke up in class. These were exactly the kind of looks I always got: wide-eyed, oh-look-the-stupid-girl-is-talking looks. Luckily, I was too drunk to be bothered about it now.

As Alana and Frank fell back into conversation, I noticed Harrison's eyes were on me again, so warm and blue, and though I couldn't swear to it I thought I saw him wink at me.

Anita leaned toward me and said, "You read the book? I thought you didn't even buy it."

"I read it a long time ago," I said with a shrug. "I just have a good memory. Seriously, you can test me. I can remember every single top of yours that I've borrowed and not given back since the beginning of the year. First there was the blue one with the low-cut back—"

"But—" Anita interrupted, only to be interrupted herself by the doorbell.

As she got up to answer the door I started thinking I should probably retire my flask for the night since I was on to coffee anyway. But then I heard something that changed my mind, and fast.

"Well, if it isn't my gal Sal," a guy's voice said. "If I'd known you were going to be here I wouldn't have taken my time."

I turned around to see Anita giving a sour look to a guy with blonde hair wearing a hoodie and shorts, even though it was almost freezing outside. It wasn't that I didn't recognize him—I sort of did. Or anyway, his muscular shoulders looked familiar—but he fell into the category of guy I'd decided I didn't really need to recall except to know that I'd slept with him at some point and had decided he wasn't boyfriend material. And given the fact that Alex had possessed those boyfriend qualities, and Alex was a huge douchebag, you could say my bar was pretty low and this guy had not reached it. He was the type of guy who, if I'd run into him a few days ago, I would have been pretty glad to come across. He had "easy" written all over him, from his sleazy smile to his low-slung shorts. But it wasn't a few days ago, and I *so* was not in the mood.

But, like the faker I was, I gave it my best shot. After all, I was here to please.

"What're you doing here, anyway?" he said as he planted himself on the couch next to me, wiggling his ass into place in such a way that Alana was forced to move a seat over.

He introduced himself to the others as "Joey With a J," then turned back to me. Behind his head I saw Alana rolling her eyes.

"Did you lose a bet or something" he said. "You didn't seem much like the book learnin' type the last time we hung out."

He nudged me with his elbow and I giggled, as expected. Out of the corner of my eye I noticed Harrison's stomach—

the only part of him I could see—visibly clench.

"Can't a girl broaden her horizons?" I protested and Joey chuckled.

Apparently Joey was in our class and had heard about the study session from Frank, though Frank seemed not to remember this at all. I suspected Joey was the type of guy who listened in on the conversations of hot girls—in this case Alana and Anita—and filed times and addresses away for that night when he had no parties to go to but still hoped to get some action. I knew this type of guy. I was this type of guy.

As Joey put his arm around me, I felt something inside of me tighten, and then loosen. His palm fell over my shoulder, dangling precariously close to my breast and if I had this guy pegged—and I was pretty sure I did—he would be coping a feel in a few minutes. I tried to process how I felt about this, especially since my maybe-crush was sitting a foot away watching us—I didn't even have to look to know this—as Joey's hand swung innocently closer and closer and then lightly grazed the top of my breast.

"Oops," Joey whispered into my ear as I swatted his hand away. "Sorry about that, honey. Sometimes my mitts have a mind of their own, you know?"

Without turning my head, I let my eyes drift over to Harrison's chair to see if he'd seen what had happened, but he wasn't in his seat. That was a relief, but also solidified a realization I'd been slowly coming to since Joey had walked in the door: Harrison didn't want me. He'd made that abundantly clear. Whether I wanted him or not wasn't really relevant. When had my desire every been important to me anyway? It didn't matter who I wanted, it mattered who wanted me. That's what was going to get me what I needed: male desire. The desire of fools like Alex and Joey and whoever came next. The desire I loved to chase.

When Joey leaned in and nuzzled my neck everything seemed suddenly very clear to me, or as clear as anything could be when I'd consumed 30 ounces of whiskey. This was where I belonged; pulled into some guy's lap, enjoying the heat of his wandering hands and not caring who was watching. This was what I knew, and it was such a relief to stop resisting it. This, at last *this*, was what I was good at.

"Actually," Alana said, "Sally just made a pretty insightful comment and we were just about to discuss it further."

Poor Alana. She was still trying to keep the study group going when it had obviously disintegrated. Frank and Glasses were over by the kitchen table chatting up Anita. Everyone's notebooks and copies of the novel were scattered over the coffee table like discarded paper plates. Joey's hand was making its way up the back of my shirt.

"This Sally?" Joey said, moving his knees so I bumped up and down on his lap—a boob-jiggling manoeuvre I was intimately familiar with. "I think you've got that wrong, toots."

Suddenly Harrison was standing behind Alana with a mug in his hand. His stance was tense and when he spoke his words seemed carefully measured.

"Don't you think Sally could have something of value to contribute to the study session?" Harrison said

Uh-oh, I thought to myself. Just that and nothing else: *Uh-oh*.

I tried to ease myself off Joey's lap, but he was holding on too tight.

"Dude," Joey answered, "I once saw Sal here almost hurt herself trying to calculate the tip at a bar. This girl doesn't have two brain cells to rub together, do you, hon?"

I hated it when guys did this, asking me to agree with their insults. Though not quite as much as Harrison seemed to hate it, given the steely look he was giving Joey now and the vein that was throbbing in his neck. As they faced off, Joey still not quite realizing what he'd said wrong—you could tell by the way he was still smiling—I saw my opening.

It was time to take a side.

I put my arm around Joey's neck, pulling him closer, his cheek inches from my cleavage. "Well I might be dumb as a lampost but I sure know how to light up a room, don't I baby?" I said.

Joey nuzzled my chest in appreciation and I tried not to wince at the way his hands were pressing into my bruises.

Harrison's face settled into its emotionless mask, not that it mattered to me. Not that I noticed. I was just trying to figure out how I could get Joey into my bedroom without being too obvious about it when I felt myself tipping sideways as someone hauled me off his lap.

"Sally, stand up," Anita huffed, her hands locked on my arms like shackles.

I stood up, with only a slight wobble, and felt my flask fall out of my pocket and tumble to the ground.

I noticed Anita had that look of finely-tuned fury on her face that she usually reserved for people who abused their pets or spat on the homeless.

"Get out," she said to Joey, pointing imperiously at the door.

The low din of voices in the room suddenly cut out and we were all staring as my tiny roommate took control.

"Wh-What are you—" Joey sputtered, his eyes jumping from me to Anita before she cut him off.

"You think you can come in here, disrupt our night, grope my friend, and call her stupid, and we'll just go along with it?"

She waited a second for an answer, which Joey seemed too shocked to give. He was staring at her like a toddler caught with his hand in the toilet.

"Get out!" she repeated, this time loud enough to get Joey on his feet, though he didn't actually move, as though he still thought this all might be some kind of joke.

"Your friend's a real piece of work, Sally," he said, and it was clear to me he thought I would take his side, as I had earlier. Instead, I stared at my socks.

Anita was still pointing at the door, her arm rigid and motionless as a tree branch. I thought, if she had to, she would have stood waiting forever.

Tearing his eyes from Anita, Harrison stepped forward and grasped Joey by the arm just above the elbow.

"I think it's time for you to go," he said, with (was I imagining it?) real pleasure in his voice. "Now."

As Harrison escorted Joey with a J to the door, Anita turned to me, that furious glare not yet faded from her eyes.

"Why?" she said in a low voice, shaking her head. "Why do you let them? Why do you do it?"

She'd never asked me before. She'd seen me do far worse things, do worse guys. She'd watched me drink myself unconscious, take off my clothes in public, proposition an entire roomful of guys. I didn't know why tonight was the night she was pushed over the edge, but I knew that in the face of her anger, and disbelief, and confusion, and dismay, none of my reasons would make any sense at all. I shook my head, and she sighed and walked away.

6

Harrison closed the door on Joey with a dramatic slam to the delight of the entire study group—there was actual cheering—and the night went on as if my embarrassing display had never happened. Anita turned up the music and got more snacks, and Alana and Frank got tipsy and argued about Virginia Woolf. I sat at the table and laughed when they laughed and watched Glasses continue his determined flirt-carpet-bombing of Anita—who almost seemed to be enjoying it—and tried to avoid both Harrison and Anita's eyes. The look on my friend's face had melted all of my earlier resolve and most of my buzz and I was left with a feeling of generalized disgust and stupidity—which was sort of ironic, since it was Joey's calling me stupid that had caused the whole scene in the first place.

I didn't really see what the big deal was. Everything he'd said was true.

As the night wore on I slipped onto the balcony to escape Frank's deplorable dance moves—it had come to that point of the evening where any suggestion, like a dance-off competition, sounded like a good idea—and I never went back inside. The air was crisp. I pulled the sweater I'd grabbed on the way out around my body and sat in a hot pink plastic deck chair to wait for the study group to disperse. I didn't belong with them. You could see it when they spoke to me, when they looked at me. I didn't belong in there, or with Joey, or with my friends, or with Harrison. Right then I felt like I didn't belong anywhere.

After a while the door to the balcony slid open. I expected Anita's head to peek out, but instead Harrison stepped outside, a cell phone to his ear. He pressed his hip into the iron railing, facing away from me, and I could tell he didn't realize I was out there with him. He thought he was alone.

"No you *don't!*" he said vehemently, hitting the railing with the base of his palm. "Goddammit! Do you hear yourself? Do you hear what you're saying? You—"

He stopped abruptly, interrupted, and listened for a while, then held the phone away from his ear for a few seconds, breathing deeply.

I felt bad watching this private moment, which was obviously very emotional for him. It occurred to me that nobody got that upset unless there was love involved.

He has a girlfriend, I thought. *Of course he does. Great guys like him always do.*

No wonder he'd rejected me so blatantly. He was taken! And Harrison was not the cheating type.

"Fine," he said, his voice cold now, detached. "Just do what you want. Yeah, I know you will."

He ended the call and stared down at the street, and I considered the selfish idea that maybe, if that had been his girlfriend, they'd just broken up.

"Some night, huh?" I said.

Harrison spun around and looked vaguely distressed for about five seconds, probably as long as it took him to recall the ass I'd made of myself earlier. Then he seemed to relax, and took a seat in the other chair, which was fluorescent orange.

"I think 'eventful' is how I'd describe it," he said.

He fished in his pocket and pulled out my flask, holding it out to me. I'd bought it years ago at a novelty store. It was covered in fake white and brown cow fur and looked so ridiculous in his hand I almost started laughing.

"Feels pretty empty," he said as I took it from him.

"Yeah, well, I never study without a buzz on," I replied. "Can't stomach it."

I was being flippant, when really I wanted to sink into the balcony floor. My flask was my secret friend, my therapist, my superhero cape. And like all those things, it wasn't something I wanted to discuss.

"Maybe you should try it sometime," Harrison said.

"What? Studying sober?" I snorted. "Sounds like a blast."

"Maybe not everything has to be a blast," he replied, his voice harder all of a sudden, much more like the voice he'd used while he was on his call. "Who decided that every day has to be a party, that feeling fine, not good, but just fine is such a terrible thing? Maybe you should just…"

He looked at me over the rectangle of light from the door between us, his words trailing off, a perplexed frown wrinkling his forehead. If he thought he'd shaken me with his little outburst, he was wrong. It took a whole lot more than that to scare me off. But I was curious what it was all about. It wasn't just me he'd been ranting at.

"What?" I said, refusing to break eye contact, though he seemed to want to. "Maybe I should just, what? Do this?"

Without thinking twice about it, I tossed the flask over the balcony. Harrison's eyes widened in surprise and we both listened for it to hit the ground five flights below us, but it never did. There was no sound at all.

"There, happy?" I said defiantly, re-crossing my legs and staring him down.

Still blinking in shock, he sat back in his chair and shook his head at me. "You're something else," he said. "Anybody ever tell you that?"

"Honey, you have no idea how many people have told me that."

"I believe it," he said, and there was an appreciation in his voice that warmed me up in a way a guy like Joey never could.

God, he was good-looking. It wasn't only his eyes, which were entrancing all by themselves. It was the way he held himself, the strength in his very posture, and that burning intensity in his every word. Like he was choosing each one carefully, as if every word mattered, as if everything mattered, even what I said and did, even me.

"It's a nice street," he said, nodding at the darkness below us. "Nice and quiet and calm."

"Except for those damn flasks raining from the sky," I added and he gave me one of his almost-laughs, a kind of roll of his stomach and an exhale, which was oddly sexy. "Besides, it doesn't hold a candle to your street. All those lovely neighbourhood block parties, so many young people around. Such a wonderful vibe."

I was being sarcastic, of course. The block he and Alex lived on was known for its ragers. The cops patrolled it nightly.

"How did you ever end up living there?" I asked.

"What do you mean? I'm a party animal," he said with such seriousness I had to laugh.

"Seriously."

"I was in a class with Matt, and I really needed a place to live. When I moved in it was just the two of us. I didn't realize how many of them there was going to be, or how crazy it was going to get. But the rent is so cheap, since there are so many of us. Sometimes I don't even pay at all. They're all so awful at taking care of their money, they write checks for these huge sums and tell me not to worry about it. I make sure the bills get paid on time, the lights stay on. I cook from time to time, clean up. They love me."

"Basically you're their maid."

He shrugged. "It keeps a roof over my head. I'm grateful for that."

Well that confirmed it—he wasn't a rich kid like Alex or Emily. Normally it bothered me when guys didn't have money, though at that moment I couldn't think exactly why.

"So, tell me party animal, what do the kids do these days when they aren't out drinking?"

Now that the high of tossing my flask away had passed, I was beginning to feel a little uneasy about it. That little metal bottle had been with me since my first day in Kingston. It was almost like a security blanket. And though I knew losing it wouldn't actually stop me from drinking—like I'd never chugged out of a bottle before—it would slow me down. And slowing down really wasn't my style.

"Personally, I like to hold up liquor stores," he said, in the dead pan voice I was already beginning to recognize as his joking tone.

"Me too!" I said with an amazed smile. "I knew somebody was trying to move in on my territory. Stay East of Barrie street if you know what's good for you."

"I'll do my best," he said, with a ghost of a smile, his eyes on mine. What was it with those eyes? Every time he looked at me it was as though all the blood rushed straight to my head. "Actually, I have standings plans most nights, nothing quite so interesting, but I could use some company tomorrow. If you'd like to join me, you're welcome, Sally."

I knew I should say no. I knew no good could come of spending more time alone with him. But there was something in the way he said "you're welcome, Sally." It was as though he was really saying, "you're wanted, Sally."

And how could I possibly say no to those eyes?

"Thank you," I said, suddenly formal. "I'd love to."

I wanted this friendship to work. I needed it to work so I could prove to myself that a person like him could want to be my friend, and just my friend. It would be good for me to have a platonic relationship with a guy like him. It made me like myself just a little bit better.

But just friends. That's it. Don't try for more, you stupid girl. Don't ruin it.

"Should I text you, then?" he said shyly, holding out his phone.

My God, if he blushed I didn't think I'd be able to stop myself from ripping off my clothes and throwing myself at him.

Don't Ruin It!

"Like I can afford one of those fancy phones?" I said. "I'm old school. I rock an answering machine, and my phone has a cord."

I took his cell from his hand—it was a flip-phone, which was just too adorable—and typed in my number.

We stood side by side at the railing, the wind blowing my hair onto his shoulder as I tried to ignore the way his elbow and bicep were pressed against mine and how easy it would have been to lean into him, just as I'd leaned into Joey earlier, without caring at all, without feeling even. But Harrison was not Joey. Harrison made me feel too much.

"Brrr," he said, hunching his shoulders. "It's really getting cold, isn't it? If only I had my sweater. But, silly me, I lent it to this girl and she just made off with it. I never saw it again."

I gave him a puzzled look until my eyes snagged on my own sleeve and I realized I was wearing the sweater he'd lent me the other morning, on the way out of his apartment.

"Oh my God!" I said, taking a step back and starting to pull it off. "I'm so sorry! I didn't even realize—"

Leaning toward me, he pressed a finger to my lips and the whole world slowed. My hand fell onto his arm and I had the urge to pull him toward me, but I resisted it. I felt my body practically vibrating at the closeness of his, as if we were magnets, destined to press together, yearning for each other.

"Forget it," he said softly, pulling my arm back into the sleeve. My hair was caught under the wool and he gently lifted it out, his thumb running over my neck in a way that left me short of breath. "You keep it. I like the way it looks on you."

I swallowed hard as he went back inside, my heart pounding, my cheeks hot. I could still feel his finger against my lips long afterwards, as I sat on the edge of my bed in the dark.

Just friends, huh? Man, was I screwed.

I was so distracted that for the longest time I didn't notice the red blinking light of my answering machine. When I pressed it and listened to the automated message, I found myself hoping the one waiting call would be from Harrison, as if my life was a romantic comedy and I would fall back on my pillows, all swoony.

But my life was no romance, never had been, never would be. Billy was the one who'd taught me that, and it was his voice that came out of the machine, gruff, curt, and insistent, that voice that made me cringe whenever I heard it.

"Hello, Sal," he said. "It's that time again, time to pay up. I'll be waiting for your call. And just in case you're thinking of kicking up a fuss like last time, let me remind you that I know where your bodies are buried, figuratively speaking, of course. I know what you've done. I know what you really are, Sally. And don't you forget it."

7

"So, are you going to call him?" Emily said.

"What?" I said a little too sharply. "Of course I am, I mean no. I mean, what?"

Emily pulled the curtain of my changing room open a foot and held up her hands so I could survey the tight red dress she was wearing. "Are you going to call Jeremy," she said. "Who did you think I was talking about?"

I turned toward the wall so she couldn't see the look of panic on my face and pretended to be inspecting the price tag of a pair of skinny jeans.

"Right, of course," I answered. "I think I might have accidentally-on-purpose lost his number."

And I also thought you were talking about Billy. Which would have been pretty crazy, since I've never mentioned him to you. Or anyone.

Emily peered past me at her own reflection in the mirror.

"This makes me look pregnant," she announced before pulling my curtain closed and returning to the cabin next to mine. "Try that stripey top next," she said. "If it doesn't fit you, I want to try it."

"Here, you go first," I said.

I threw the top over the cabin wall and wondered how

long I could stand there hyperventilating and never actually trying anything on before she noticed.

"Excellent," she said. "I look seriously hot in the bra I just bought. Like, if I wasn't myself I would totally make out with me."

I was guessing a pretty long time.

Not that I was really hyperventilating. I didn't have to put my head between my legs or anything. But I was definitely on the wrong side of freaking out, with a little bit of hysteria thrown in for flavour.

Billy had called me. Billy had told me to call him back, and implied pretty heavily that there would be hell to pay if I didn't. Just like he always did, every few months. Just like clockwork.

Only this time I hadn't called him back.

I stopped myself halfway through pulling on a jean skirt with a zipper down the front, the denim pressing my legs together at the knees. I hadn't called him back. It had been more than twelve hours since I'd listened to his message. Actually, to be exact, it had been fifteen hours and forty-two minutes. And who knew when he'd actually left the message. He might have been waiting for more than twenty-four hours by now. A whole day. Just the idea made me feel lightheaded. The next thing I knew I actually was pressing my head between my knees after kicking off the skirt.

A whole day had passed and I hadn't called him. I hadn't even really thought about calling him. It was as if the decision had already been made before I'd even listened to his message. The decision to refuse Billy, to go back on my promise, to stop "paying up," as he called it. The decision to stop.

What the hell was wrong with me?

"What's the matter with you?" Emily said. "You don't seem very excited. Need I remind you that all this stuff is *seventy-five percent* off?"

"Who says I'm not excited?" I said.

After taking a steadying breath, I got to my feet and wiggled into a little black dress that was just like all the little black dresses I already owned. Then I added a sweater to cover up the scabs on my arms and pushed open the curtain to my cabin, presenting myself to Emily who was wearing the stripey top and a skirt so short I could see her red underwear.

As we checked ourselves out in the big mirror, I tried to grin and preen and be the Sally she expected me to be, not just for her, but for me too. I didn't know what had come over me lately, but it was getting to the point that I didn't even recognize myself, and I wasn't sure I liked the change. I'd worked pretty hard on this version of myself, the girl everybody invited to their parties because she was such a blast to be around. The girl who never looked before she leaped. The girl who never worried about her past, or her secrets, or her reputation, because she had none.

I was beginning to yearn for that girl more and more by the minute. I still wanted to be her, but it was getting harder and harder to pull it off.

And if I really pissed off Billy and he came looking to even the score, it would be damn near impossible.

"I kind of look like a playboy bunny in this," Emily said, miming a bunny hop and pursing her lips at the mirror.

"You sure do," I said. When she stuck out her butt I gave it a swat and she laughed. "But I already have that skirt. You can just borrow it."

"Of course you have it," she said, shaking her head at me like I was particularly naughty and not noticing when I gave her a pained look in return.

As the cashier rang up Emily's purchases, she looked down at the items in my arms—a pair of ripped jeans and a sweatshirt—and gave me a quizzical look.

"You're getting hardly anything. Why didn't you take that white dress? It looked awesome on you, and your nipples probably won't even show through that much if you wear it to a club. Or even if they do, who cares?"

I do. I care. All of a sudden, I care. And I don't even know why!

"I have enough dresses," I answered, smiling at the salesgirl as she put my purchases into a bag and wished us a nice day. "What's the point in buying the same thing over and over, anyway? I mean, it's kind of a waste of money, isn't it?"

Emily's phone rang and she pressed it to her ear as we walked out of the store into the chilly autumn wind.

"Hi. Yeah, I'm out with Sally," she said. I figured she was talking to Katie. Ever since they'd made up after all that crap went down two summers ago they were always texting and calling and giggling and sistering. "She's asking me to explain shopping to her. Yeah, I know, she is acting *weird*."

She said the last word louder on purpose so I would hear, but I just looked the other way and let her walk a little ahead of me.

Okay, so I was doing a crappy job of acting like my usual self. Emily certainly didn't seem to be buying it. But how could I shop for myself when I didn't feel like myself?

Emily shoved her phone back into her purse and took my arm. "So, you're not going to call him? Are we crossing him off the list for good?" she said.

I knew she was talking about Jeremy, but I couldn't help but think of somebody else entirely.

"Yeah, I think maybe we are," I agreed. "I don't see any reason why I should ever call him again."

Actually I could think of a lot of reasons. I heap of them. A mountain.

Deciding not to call Billy back was a supremely bad decision, and realizing this was finally the thing that calmed me down. Because if there was one thing that was just like the old me, it was being bad and liking it. Maybe I hadn't changed so much after all.

That wonderful feeling of relief didn't last long.

A few hours later I was sitting in my car with Harrison Leo, feeling so uncomfortable I thought I might roll down my window any minute and howl into the night like some distressed puppy. There was just something about being in an enclosed space with him that made me feel completely alien to myself. I considered that maybe it was because I couldn't

71

remember the last time I'd been in a car with a guy for any reason other than a quickie in the back seat. And that thought got me thinking about having a quickie in the back seat with Harrison, and I felt my whole body flush.

God, even my brain was slutty.

"So, what are we doing here?" I asked.

"We're just waiting," Harrison said.

When I got home from shopping I was greeted by a message on my answering machine from Harrison—not from Billy, as my slamming heart had expected—saying he'd be at my place at around seven. He showed up right on time wearing his black wool coat and backpack, as usual, and I met him at the front of the building rather than letting him come up to the door and have to explain his presence to Anita.

Not that there was anything to hide.

Not that this little excursion meant anything at all, or that I was secretly hoping it was a date or something. Sally Jarvis didn't have dates anyway. She had booty-calls, one night stands, hookups, but no dates. Nope, not a one. And the fact that I didn't think this was a date definitely explained why I was keeping my relationship with Harrison a secret from my friends, and that I'd changed my clothes five times before he arrived, and the way my heart did a flip when his eyes met mine as I came down the walk and he smiled his almost-smile.

Yeah, I was definitely totally on board with this platonic friendship thing. For sure.

He suggested that we walk, but I insisted we take my car on his mysterious errand, and not only because I was wearing my cute burgundy cinch-waist coat that the wind blew right through. There was also the fact that my legs were bare because in my fluster while I was getting ready I'd punched holes through three pairs of nylons. It worked out anyway, since the neighbourhood he'd taken me to wasn't exactly a great one.

Currently we were parked across the street from a dilapidated brown bungalow that looked pretty much abandoned, if not condemned, and had such impressive features as two broken windows, no electricity as far as I could tell, and a front porch that was about to cave in.

Some girls got caviar and roses on their first date; I got parking in the ghetto.

Wait, did I just say date? I meant, casual evening of hanging-out with my new platonic friend. Yeah, that's what I meant.

Harrison was sitting in the passenger seat with his hands on his knees, taping his fingers to the music on the radio. His pose was perfectly relaxed, but I noticed how his eyes never stopped scanning the house, the street, the sidewalk, and how he was almost too still, like a panther poised to spring. But spring on what, or whom?

"It reminds me of the underwater part in *The Forever Place*," I said. "You know when she goes to that abandoned village and meets those creepy people. What are they called, the forgetters?"

"The left-behinders," Harrison said. He'd been looking past me to get a view of the house through my window, but now he looked at me, his expression animated but also suspicious. "But how do you know that? She only meets them in issue three."

I tried to ignore the way my palms started to sweat whenever he looked at me directly like this. "I might have stopped by a bookstore this afternoon and skimmed through a few of them," I said nonchalantly, not revealing that when I said "skimmed" I really meant "read from cover to cover."

He leaned down and riffled through his backpack, eventually pulling out a stack of something. "I guess you won't need these, then," he said.

He handed me issues two through five of the comics, and I grabbed them, flipping through the pages greedily the way I used to do with my fashion magazines in high school. If only I'd known back then that there was an awesome heroine like Rainbow out there, I might have sat with the loner guy with his stack of comics instead.

"Or this," Harrison continued.

On top of the open comic in my lap he placed the rolled

up copy of issue one I'd give back to him the day before. Or, to be more accurate, thrown at his head. As I fingered the pages gingerly, he said, "I'm lending you the other ones, but that one's yours to keep."

"Because I ruined it," I said guiltily, trying in vain to straighten out the cover. Didn't comic book collectors obsess over keeping them in pristine condition? I'd basically mangled his prize possession.

"No," he said softly. "Because I want you to have it."

His words were warm and affectionate, exactly like a caress, and yet we weren't even touching. I'd never known anyone who could make me feel held like this without even putting a finger on me. It made me want to stay in this car with him forever.

"I never thanked you for what you did that night at the club," I said, staring down at my lap. "So, thank you."

"You don't have to thank me," he said.

Reaching forward, he brushed his thumb across my cheek, causing my eyes to nearly drift closed at the sudden unexpected contact. Then, all of a sudden he pulled his hand away and my eyes snapped back open.

"I should have gotten there sooner," he said.

He was frowning now, staring out at the street, and I felt the loss of his touch, his gaze, like a physical ache.

"Hey," I said, tugging on his arm. He looked at me again, but reluctantly. "Nobody's ever fought for me like that before. You have no idea how much it means to me. I'll never forget it."

He shifted in his seat and it seemed for a moment as though he was going to lean toward me. He opened his mouth to say something and I lost myself in those eyes, searching mine, and those lips, which were so sexy, though I hadn't noticed it until that second. I felt myself leaning toward him too, just slightly, and then an odd look passed over his face and his expression closed off again and he sat back in his seat as though none of it had happened. Although it had, I knew it had.

He'd considered me for a minute before rejecting me, again.

Swivelling in my own seat and putting my hands on the steering wheel, I looked over at the house we were staking out and felt the itch to say something outrageous a millisecond before the words were out of my mouth: "So, are we stalking your girlfriend, or what?" I said.

"What?" he said, turning back toward me.

Well, at least I'd gotten his attention.

"Who says I have a girlfriend?" he countered.

"I'm pretty sure I did," I replied sassily. Continual rejection tended to bring out my combative side. "Besides, it's so obvious that you do."

"It is, is it?" he said, the corner of his lip curling.

Stop looking at his lips!

"Well, please, tell me," he said, spreading his hands. "Where's your evidence?"

"Fine," I said, getting my game face on, even though it sort of seemed like a trap. Continual rejection also tended to make me blind to traps, and warning signs, and basically all common sense.

I counted the reasons off on my fingers. "A, you're always getting phone calls and then running off without explanation, like you've been caught cheating or something. B, you could have slept in bed with a half-naked me but opted to sleep on the couch instead. C, the look on your face when you saw my naked boobs." His eyes widened when I said this. "Yeah, that look," I said. "And D, guys like you are always taken. Case closed."

I scowled at him, fully aware that I'd revealed too much but refusing to give a damn. Or anyway, refusing to admit I gave a damn.

Harrison sighed and rubbed his hand through his short dark hair. Then he put his elbow on the dashboard, squaring himself to me.

"First of all," he said, "I've already explained why I didn't sleep with you. If we ever sleep together it will be because you want to, because you specifically request it. I really want to be clear on that."

He seemed to be waiting for some kind of response from me, but my mind had gone blank.

Did he just say "if we ever sleep together"?

"Second, if I got a look on my face when I saw you…without a top on…" I almost smirked at how much trouble he was having getting the words out. "…it was because as much as I wanted to look, it wasn't my right to look. You get that, don't you?"

Did I get that? I wasn't exactly sure. Guys had always just taken whatever they wanted from me, be it a look or a feel or a naked picture. I'd always thought that was how guys showed you they liked you, and so I'd liked it too. Hadn't I?

"Third, I'm not getting calls from a jealous girlfriend, and I'm not cheating on anyone. Because I don't have a girlfriend. And fourth, what exactly do you mean by 'guys like me'?"

He doesn't have a girlfriend. He doesn't have a girlfriend. He doesn't have a girlfriend.

"I just mean, guys like you," I said, feeling a little dizzy from his revelation. "Guys who…worry about you the next day. Guys who listen when you talk. Guys who don't make you feel like…" Like a slut, a whore, a thing they're screwing that can't feel or think or want or need. "Guys who would never choose a girl like me."

I turned away and stared resentfully out the driver's side window. I wanted to blame him for making me feel like a piece of steaming crap, but I knew I couldn't. I'd done it to myself.

"Sally," Harrison said in that low, concerned voice that turned my legs to jelly. I felt his hand on my arm. "I chose you tonight, didn't I?"

But not really. Not the way I wish you would. Not completely.

God, I needed a drink.

I saw movement just outside my field of vision. "Hey, who's that?" I said. I looked up at the door of the house just in time to see it close.

"What? Did you see someone?" Before I had the chance

to answer, Harrison was up and out of the car and all I could do was chase after him. "Did you see someone go in? Was it a guy or a girl?"

"Somebody went into the house," I said, as I joined him on the sidewalk, "but I didn't get a good look." I swallowed, feeling inadequate. "What should we do? Should we go inside?"

I wished I had some idea of what the hell we were doing here, and what the stakes were, though based on the majorly freaked out look on Harrison's face, it seemed they were pretty high.

"No," Harrison said, grabbing me by the hand to stop me, although I hadn't moved. "We can't go in."

Taking out his phone with his free hand, he dialled a number and stared at the house while it rang, but there was no answer. He dialled again and again, but nobody picked up, and the longer it rang the more agitated he became.

"Shit!"

He let go of my hand and turned away from the house, breathing hard and staring at the ground. A gust of wind blew through, stinging my legs and creating a cascade of leaves that tumbled down the street.

I said, "Are you oka—"

"I shouldn't have come here with you," he interrupted, and suddenly it wasn't the wind that was making me feel cold. "I thought...I don't know what I thought. But now... Dammit!"

He threw up his hands in frustration and I tried not to flinch. I knew he wasn't cursing at me, but it still felt like he was.

"I can't believe I let myself get distracted," he said. "I should have thought it through. This was a mistake."

I had no idea what Harrison was talking about, or what had just happened, or why he was so frustrated, but his words echoed in my head just the same.

A mistake. You are a mistake. You are a mistake he made. And now you both know it.

We stood together on the curb, still and separate. "I'll drive you home," I said stiffly and turned toward the car. He followed without another word.

I was going to drive him back to his house, but he said he could just walk from my building and I didn't have the energy to argue the point. We drove in complete silence and by the time we pulled into my parking spot I just wanted him gone. This visit to the land of respectability had been a test which I had clearly failed. It was time to cut my losses. I was already planning to hightail it to the bar down the street just as soon as he was gone. Nothing said pathetic like drinking your sorrows by yourself on a Sunday night. I was almost looking forward to it.

Naturally, because Harrison was Harrison, he walked with me down the path to the front door of my building. Being around a guy as good as him was sometimes a little like torture. I wondered if he knew that.

"You know, I really don't know anything about you," I said. I figured I might as well ask all my questions now, since it seemed like this would be my last chance. "I don't even know your major."

"Computer engineering," he replied. It was the first thing he'd said to me in twenty minutes. "What's yours?"

"Sociology," I said. It was the answer I always gave even though I'd taken so many classes outside my program at this point I wasn't sure I still qualified. "With a minor in stupid," I added, because it was true. I was stupid. My crush on him was stupid. Hoping he had the same crush, also stupid. This whole week had been just one slow avalanche of stupid.

"Don't," he said as I reached for the railing. I just wanted to get up the stairs and through the door to my building, but one word from him and I couldn't do it. "Don't call yourself stupid. You always do that. Don't do that."

I turned to him, tipping my head up to look him in the face, but he was back to his old tricks again, avoiding my eyes, and I had had enough.

"Why won't you look at me?" I blurted angrily. "Am I not even worth a look? Just one last look? Or would that be another mistake?"

I wasn't prepared. I wasn't ready for the sudden flood of feeling that rushed through me as his eyes met mine and I realized that I was kidding myself if I thought this was a crush. This was no crush. I'd gone ahead and fallen for him, stupid girl that I was.

This was what it felt like to really want someone, not just lust after them. This was what my heart felt like when it was all filled up with feelings, real feelings, instead of numbness. This was what it felt like when my heart was about to break.

Then he made an anguished sound in his throat and took my face in his hands. I was so surprised I stumbled back a step or two until I felt the railing pressing into my back, and he followed me.

"You want to know why I won't look at you?" he said, his face so close to mine I could feel the warmth of it burning my cheeks. His eyes bore into mine and I almost couldn't breathe. "When I look at you, I can't think straight. When I look at you, I can't stop. You're not a mistake, you're a distraction. And I don't know what to do about it, Sally. I don't know what to do about you."

Maybe he didn't know what to do, but my body certainly did. My skin tingled with electricity in every place where our bodies were touching, his knee pressing into my leg, his chest heaving against mine. The feel of his fingers against my skin was so thrilling I thought I might black out, and I yearned to lean in and take his mouth with mine.

"I know what to do," I said, running my hands up his back. His body jerked as if I'd electrocuted him.

"Don't touch me," he said, his plea so fierce I dropped my hands immediately. "God, Sally, you make me crazy when you touch me. I can't stand it."

I twisted my arms behind me and took hold of the cold metal of the railing, wondering at the distress on his face.

"Okay," I said. "I won't touch. Not unless you ask me

to."

He still had my cheeks in his hands, and his eyes ran all over my face, just my face, and yet I'd never felt so naked in front of a guy before. Hesitantly, he ran his thumb over my bottom lip and it felt so good I gasped.

"Kiss me," I whispered, and his lips hovered over mine for an excruciating moment before he leaned in, his cheek brushing against mine, his lips against my ear. His hands trailed down my arms and I let go of the railing as his fingers found mine.

"I can't," he said, his breath hot against my hair. I pressed my chin into his shoulder.

"I want you to," I said, trying to express the strength of my desire in these four words. "I want you," I said.

I heard him breathing in my ear and found my own shallow breaths matching his.

"Because I'm such a good guy?" he said. I'd meant it as a compliment, and yet he sounded so deflated when he said it, as though I'd sucker punched him.

Pulling back—though not too far because he was still holding my hands behind my back—I looked up into those devastating blue eyes.

"Because I do," I said and I leaned in to prove it, to take the kiss I wanted to badly, to show him how I really felt.

My lips had just barely touched his when he released my hands and I was left leaning into nothing. My stomach plummeted as I realized he was stepping away from me. I'd tried to kiss him, and he'd actually pulled away to avoid my lips.

"I'm sorry, Sally. I can't," I heard him say, but I didn't see his face because this time it was my turn to stare at the ground, my cheeks flaming with shame. "I'm sorry," he repeated, and then I heard him go.

Was this was it was like? Was this what all those romance movies were about? I thought I knew what a rejection felt like, but I'd never felt anything like this before. I'd never hurt like this before, or at least not in a very long time.

Suddenly I remembered why I'd avoided feeling anything for so long. It was because feelings destroyed me, they crushed me, every single time, and frankly I was sick of it. How had I gone so far off course? I knew who I was and I knew how to handle myself.

I knew what I needed now and it wasn't any tender kiss. It wasn't love.

I needed to tear something apart. I needed destruction. And my life seemed like a perfect place to start.

8

Standing on a table in the middle of the living room, I pulled off my top and flung it into the crowd. As I raised my arms into the air to the sound of their hooting cheers, I realized three things.

1. I didn't know the name of the hotties who were grinding up against me from the front and behind.
2. I didn't think I would be getting my top back, ever.
3. I didn't care.

The bass line booming through the speakers set up on either side of the fireplace thumped through my body, making it impossible to stop moving. With a beer clutched in each hand, I gyrated to the beat, grateful for the ear-splitting music, so loud and constant it was almost like a kind of torture inflicted on prisoners of war—except there was no war, unless you counted the battle I was having with my gut, which kept trying to reject the booze I was funnelling into it, and that really wasn't much of a battle at all since I always won.

Leaning so far back my head was nearly upside-down—I used the arms of one of the hot guys (let's call him Hottie #1) for support—I tipped one of the bottles into my mouth and determinedly gulped the entire thing down. It was a trick I'd learned in high school, and always a real crowd pleaser. Before I had the chance to stand up again someone stuck their tongue down my throat and I shared my last swallow of beer with him. I never even saw his face. The room spun around me as Hottie #2 pulled me upright again and for a second my eyes refused to focus. There was just a blur of bobbing heads and pumping arms, red cups and screaming mouths, and jumping, humping, writhing, groping bodies, and there I was in the middle of it, spinning and laughing and living inside it.

I loved to be inside that noise. There was no room to think in that noise. There was no room to wonder, or to want, or to care in that noise. And that was just fine with me.

As Hottie #1 put his arms around me and dug his hands into the back pockets of my jeans, I looked around for my friends only to realize, a second later, that they weren't at the party with me. This had been happening all night, and tended to put a temporary wrench in my euphoria. At the beginning of the week, actually the very morning after the ill-conceived stakeout with Harrison—which I'd taken to referring to as The Idiotic Incident—I'd tried to convince Anita to drown her sorrows along with me. She'd been quick to inform me that: A, she had no sorrows to drown; B, I didn't have any either, as far as she knew; and C, our British lit test was in thirty minutes and wasn't I coming to class?

I suppose I could have told her everything, beginning with Alex throwing me out on the porch right on down to The Idiotic Incident. I could have made her understand the sheer magnitude of my humiliation—it wasn't like she wasn't already fully versed in my pathetic ways—but for some reason I couldn't get myself to do it. The same stubborn instinct that had led me to keep my nerdy rescuer a secret from the get-go wouldn't let me reveal the grimace-inducing end of the ordeal.

So, naturally, I screamed at her instead as I hugged my bottle of whisky to my chest, calling her a selfish wench—or was it "an unfeeling biatch"?—and telling her not to bother coming back, like some hungover single mother who's just found a bag of joints in her daughter's underwear drawer. I'd assumed she would be back that evening and that we would passive aggressively eat each other's leftovers for a day or two before making up, but she hadn't come home that night, or any other night all week, and Melissa and Emily wouldn't tell me where she was.

Those two were similarly full of excuses when I asked them to be my wing women for the night.

"Tonight?" Melissa protested. "But the housewives show is on."

"I promised Katie I'd have dinner with her," Emily said. "Besides, I went out with you last night."

"Again?" Melissa asked. "Didn't you go out for the last three nights straight? Sally? Are you drunk right now?"

Amateurs, all three of them. I really didn't know why I put up with them. I'd done just fine without them anyway. There were plenty of guys willing to party with me. Sure, I'd had to flip pretty far through my little black book to find them, but desperate times called for desperate measures. And if I'd woken up in a different bed every morning, because I couldn't face the empty apartment alone? Well, so be it. I was doing just fine. I didn't need them, or Harrison, or anyone. All I needed were my adoring faceless boys and my booze and my next thrill.

All I needed was oblivion.

Dimly, I felt Hottie #1's hands wandering up to the clasp of my bra.

"I want to lick vodka off your nipples," he yelled into my ear.

"Yeah!" I yelled back, though truthfully I wasn't all that excited about it. Not that having a guy suck on my breasts wasn't totally hot, but I really liked the bra I was wearing and I knew the second it came off it would go flying across the room.

I knew the type of guys who came to these parties. They couldn't resist a brassiere slingshot.

With clumsy fingers, he fiddled none-too gently with the clasp. I felt a strange sensation in my belly, like an ice cube making its way through my stomach. It was always at moments like this, when some guy I'd been teasing all night did something I didn't like, that I was glad to have my friends nearby. Usually, this was when I lashed out, baring my claws like a crazed honey-badger, and they dragged me away, saving me from myself. It didn't happen every time. It hadn't happened in quite a while, actually. But it was happening now, and for some reason I couldn't find the energy to get mad, not with nobody around to catch me if I fell. This time, I just had to grit my teeth and bear it.

It started with Billy, as my bra fell away. It started with his face, jeering at me, and those squinting eyes of his, looking when I didn't want him to look. Watching as they all laughed. I felt the splash of vodka on my chest, and saw the faces of everyone in the vicinity turn to stare as he leaned over me, but they weren't just anonymous faces anymore. I knew these faces. They were all here, just as they had been that night. That one gaping, this one pointing, all of them wanting something, all of them taking something. Something I didn't want to give. Something I would never get back.

This is what you deserve, said the familiar voice in my head. *This is what you're good for. So, enjoy it, Sal. Drink it in. This is what it is to be loved.*

"Sally?"

It was a girl's voice, a familiar voice. I saw a head of curly dark hair and wide brown eyes, a soft hand on my hair.

"Get off her!" she said.

Hottie #1 stumbled off the coffee table as my eyes focused on a face I knew. Emily! No, that wasn't it. It was the other one.

"Sally, it's Katie," she said. "Come on, step down here. That's it."

She guided me off the table and leaned me against a wall, then started threading my arm into the sleeve of a black jacket.

"Did you just shove that guy off my breast?" I said woozily.

"That's my girl!" said a guy so tall, dark, and handsome I

couldn't help but grin up at him and his honey-coloured eyes and his dimples. It was Lucas Matthews, Katie's partner in perfect love.

Good Lord, either I was so drunk I was hallucinating—fully possible—or when he smiled down at the two of us his shiny, white teeth actually glinted. Then he caught sight of my half-naked body and said, "Oh," and half-turned away in a smooth motion that only a guy of his caliber could pull off without looking foolish.

"You're embarrassing my boyfriend," I admonished Katie. "Stop flaunting your body in that lascivious manner!"

"Help me with her other arm," Katie said to Lucas, ignoring me entirely. I wasn't even bothered. Katie was so classy she probably didn't even hear my dirty words. She probably had a dignified filter in her brain that blocked me out.

Lucas dutifully helped Katie dress me, the two of them making me giggle with their serious faces and continual exchange of concerned glances. Like I couldn't read that code. When I started to slide down the wall, Lucas put his arm around me, pressing me to his side, which was satisfyingly warm and chiseled. I tried to be a good friend and not nuzzle him, or at least not too much.

"Is it just me, or is she more drunk than usual?" Lucas said, hoisting me against him. "Come on, Sally. Try to stand up straight."

"Yes, sir!" I said, waving my arm because I couldn't quite manage a salute.

Katie took out her phone and started texting with impressive speed. "I've never seen her this bad," she said to Lucas. "And that's really saying something."

Her phone buzzed and she looked at the screen, then frowned.

"Sally, how long have you been feeling like this? How many days has it been?"

She looked just like her twin sister Emily, but more worried. Emily never worried about anything. Emily might have taken off her bra with me. Suddenly I wished Emily was there with me instead.

"Who's telling you I've been drunk for days?" I protested. "I won't stand for this kind of slander. I demand a recount!"

Still keeping a tight hold on me as I tried to wiggle out of his grip, Lucas leaned down and said something into Katie's ear. Somehow, even over the music I managed to hear the words "get her outside" and saw Katie nod.

As they started to manoeuvre through the dancing bodies toward the door of the house, I wasn't thinking about the way I was being escorted off the premises like a coke dealer—and how ironic, since we passed a guy named Tilly who actually was a coke dealer on our way out of the room—but about the way Lucas managed to shield Katie, and me by extension, from the press of aggressive bodies by curving a protective arm around and in front of her, the way they seemed connected even when they weren't touching by this complicated series of nods and looks and movements. He never really took his eyes off of her, even when he was looking around. She was always in his line of sight.

It reminded me of someone, but I couldn't remember who.

"You know, this doesn't really seem like your scene, Katie," I slurred as we struggled to get through the door, three abreast. "Wouldn't you rather be at some bohemian art gallery or a poetry slam or an ice cream parlour or something?"

"That's pretty accurate, actually," Lucas said as he sat me down on the porch railing.

Katie made a pretend-scowly face at him and he grinned.

God, they were adorable.

"Lucas, who is going to get the car right now..." she said, giving him a pointed look. He put his jacket around her shoulders, kissed her cheek and descended the stairs to the front walk. "...thought his old roommate Danny's band was going to be playing here tonight. We didn't realize the party would be this crazy."

She sat down next to me on the railing, pressing her hip into mine to anchor me in place.

"Does he kiss you like that every time you separate?" I said.

I leaned my head toward her a little too far—my muscle control wasn't quite what it had been an hour before—and she gently put my head on her shoulder.

"Yeah, he does," she said shyly, and though I couldn't see it, I could hear her sweet smile.

"I want to be just like you when I grow up," I said. "Just like you—talented and smart and beating off murderers with my bare hands—"

"I used a tree branch," she interjected smoothly, though I could tell she didn't want to talk about all the drama from two summers before. "And we're the same age, Sally."

"You're a national hero!" I went on. "You're, like, my idol."

"Uh-huh," Katie said. She looking over my head, watching for the car, and mostly ignoring me.

Perfect people hardly ever acknowledged their perfection. That's what made them perfect.

"You fall for the right kind of guy, too," I said. "And he falls for you back. How do you do that? Can you tell me? Because when it happens to me they just…"

"What?" she said, the timbre of her voice changing suddenly. "When it happens to you they just what?"

What was I even saying? Was I getting myself into trouble? I wished I could keep track of my own words but I knew at this level of Slurry Sally it wasn't even worth trying.

Looking up into her lovely face, the face of a girl who'd been through so much terrible pain and finally found her way to happiness—as I hoped and dreamed I could, and yet knew I certainly never would—I asked the question I couldn't ask anyone else, the question I wouldn't even ask myself: "Why doesn't he love me?"

She stroked my hair, and in typical Katie fashion, she didn't say the easy thing. She didn't lie—lying was something she wasn't playing at anymore. Instead, she said, simply, "I don't know."

I liked her for that. I liked her for her neutrality, her unwillingness to buck me up with false compliments or put me down with truths. She really was a class act.

I heard a car honk from the street and Katie hopped to her feet, holding me steady with one hand. "Time to go," she said.

"Oh, I'm not going," I said. The music was so loud, even outside, that I couldn't make out the song, but it must have been a bad one because the porch was really filling up. A guy holding three cups of beer bumped into Katie and she fell forward into me, almost sending me backward into the bushes. "I'm meeting someone here. I'm just waiting for him to show up."

Katie frowned at me and started to say something but two girls with big hair shoved their way between us and she didn't get the chance. She took a step down the porch stairs and then another as more and more people streamed out of the house.

"Sally, I really don't think—" she began, but the rest of her words were drowned out by the noise.

That's when I saw him walk right past her. I saw Katie do a double take, and then narrow her eyes as he eased through crowd, that slick grin spreading across his face as he took me in.

Here he was, the guy I'd been waiting for, the guy I wanted to spend my drunken hours with, because he wasn't going to tell me he couldn't kiss me, or at least he never had before. And given what I'd told him on the phone, and the way I unbuttoned my jacket as he came toward me, I didn't think he'd be turning me down tonight.

Ex-boyfriends didn't have a lot of uses, but last-minute, grovelling booty calls happened to be one of them.

"Sally!" I heard Katie calling, and between this chest and that pair of legs I saw Lucas come up next to her and the two of them falling into close discussion.

Lucas tried to shoulder his way toward me, but I was already on my way back into the house, an insistent hand pulling me on.

"Bye bye, lovebirds!" I said sunnily, over my shoulder. "I'm fine. Don't worry about me!"

I saw Lucas shake his head and turn back, and Katie pull out her phone again before they were blocked from view.

"Don't worry about you?" Alex said as he reached a hand around my waist and under the jacket, his fingernails scratching my skin. "Cause I'm such a stand-up guy? Cause I'm so forgiving?"

I closed my eyes as the scratch turned to a scrape.

"Because I know what I want," I said, opening my eyes again.

He gave me a dark look and I felt a thrill run through me, the thrill I'd been waiting for, the thrill I knew I deserved.

"Get upstairs and let's do this," he said.

The stairs rose before us and he shoved me forward, his hand hard on the small of my back, and I didn't resist.

I led the way.

I didn't know whose room we were in but I knew they had too many pillows. They scattered across the floor as Alex pressed me against the headboard from behind, reaching around to pull at the button of my jeans. He was breathing hard, his free hand kneading my hip a little more firmly than I would have liked, and when the zipper of my jeans wouldn't cooperate he swore and tried to tear them off by yanking roughly at the material, which cut into my skin.

"Easy cowboy," I said. "It's not a race."

Still struggling with my pants—which were obviously never going to come off all the way if we stayed on our knees like this—he jammed his palm between my shoulder blades, pushing me forward with some force. My cheek slapped against the wall, and suddenly I was wishing I could reach one of those pillows, just so I could have some padding between my face and the wall, not to mention my chest and the headboard. At this rate the rails were going to leave permanent stripes across my breasts, which was so not the kind of look I was going for.

"Don't talk," Alex grunted. "Just shut up, okay?"

It's amazing how you can have sex with someone a hundred times and still manage to get everything wrong. Alex was a willing but middling lover at the best of times. He was strong enough to carry me, which meant we could have sex standing up—a huge plus, in my book—but he wasn't particularly attuned to my needs. More than once I'd wondered if I should draw him a "main attractions" map of my vagina, so he would know which places deserved the most attention. I didn't even know what he thought he was doing right now as he pulled at my hips so I slid down onto the mattress, facedown, my jeans still only half-off, and then flipped me over and lunged at my breast like some crazed vampire, practically biting me.

"Hey!" I said, slapping him upside the head, which didn't even unlatch him.

Was this supposed to be sexy? Did he even know what sexy was anymore?

He was still fully clothed, as he crouched over me, pressing, always pressing me down into the sheets. It was a little suffocating and a lot uncomfortable. Was he even turned on? It was hard to tell in the dark under all that clothing. I certainly wasn't turned on, but I'd learned from past experience that that didn't matter quite so much. As long as my partner in depravity wanted me.

But did he?

The room spun around me slowly, kind of like a leisurely merry-go-around. Alex jammed his knee between my legs, a little too close to my lady parts, then straightened up and looked down at my mostly naked torso.

"Are you going to play nice now?" I said as I struggled to sit up. He grasped me by both shoulders and pushed me back down, which I didn't like. No, I didn't like that at all.

"Who says I'm playing?" he said as he pulled off his shirt.

He smiled humourlessly and that's when I realized something. I'd been with angry men before. Actually, they were kind of my thing. I'd seen how lust made some guys ugly, their words vicious, their thrusts bruising. I'd even been with my share of straight up misogynists, guys who had sex so rough it was like they were trying to punish me. My Muscle Man from the night at The Limo fit into that category. I'd seen it all and I'd put up with it without even breaking a sweat. It was easy to throw your life around when you didn't care much about it. Rough sex was my dirty little secret, my vice, and I knew that one day it would probably get me into trouble. I knew it wasn't any good for me, but I chased after it anyway, because I needed it, because I had to have it.

But just then, looking up at the sneer on Alex's face, I understood that Alex wasn't angry with lust. Alex didn't want me so much he hated me, or hated himself. Alex just straight up hated me. It was written all over his face.

This was revenge sex, plain and simple. Revenge for sleeping with his brother. And there was absolutely nothing that thrilled me about that.

It was tough to know exactly how to proceed. My expertise lay in getting myself into the room with the guy, not in getting myself out. While he was taking off his pants I eased myself backward just enough that I was out of his reach, but that didn't last long. Climbing back onto the bed, he leaned forward, planting an arm on either side of my body.

"Don't tell me you're not in the mood," he said, and I wondered how someone so handsome could manage to make himself so ugly. The features were the same, and yet all the boyish charm was gone. "You're always in the mood."

"Well, not tonight," I said, turning my body to the side and trying to wiggle under his arm. "I think I made a mistake."

Just as my feet hit the floor, he grabbed my arm so tightly I gasped. I struggled against his grip, but it wouldn't give.

"You called *me*, Sally," he said through gritted teeth. "You called me *begging*, and now you're saying no?"

"I think what I'm saying is, *hell no*," I replied, pulling my arm out of his grip with such force his fingernails scratched the scab on my elbow and it started to bleed a little. "I don't know what I was thinking."

But I did know what I was thinking. I knew exactly. I was thinking some quick, hard sex would fix things. I was thinking I could turn back the clock and get the old Alex, a good lay with great hair who never asked questions. I was thinking all my old tricks would still work on this new pain, just as they'd worked so well on the old one. But now I was beginning to think they'd never really worked in the first place. Even if I'd been able to get what I wanted out of Alex—which was clearly not going to happen—where exactly would it have gotten me? Because I'd been drinking this particular cure all week and I sure as hell didn't feel any better.

There was a loud noise out in the hall and both of us looked at the door. I took the opportunity to grab for my jeans, which were balled up on the floor, but Alex kicked them out of the way at the last second.

"Really?" I said. "Don't be a baby about this. There are still plenty of girls at this party for you to screw."

"What if I don't want another girl?" Alex said. Standing up, he towered over me. I'd used to find his bulk sexy, but as he backed me up against the wall I saw it another way. "What if all I want is to screw Sally Jarvis until she screams? Are you really telling me no?"

Outside the door the banging was getting louder and I heard a yell. What were they doing, playing hockey out there?

He reached for the band of my underwear, and I stopped his hand with my own. He grimaced, but didn't try to press further as I stared up at his dark eyes.

"What's the matter, Alex? Never had a girl turn you down before?" I said. "I find that pretty hard to believe."

I shoved my body against his, focusing on the door behind him, but he was like a solid wall, completely immovable. The ice cube was back in my gut, but sliding faster now, filling me with cold. I knew this feeling of wanting to get away but not being able to. Of being made to stand, naked and exposed. Of wanting to cry but not being able to, not while they were watching, not now. I felt Alex's hand circling my ribs and when I blinked the room around us was completely different, much brighter and lined with lockers and there were rows of them, rows of guys, all of them watching, all of them reaching. And I could not get away.

"Get off!" I yelled.

Reaching up with sudden force, I grabbed a hank of Alex's hair and pulled until he screamed, then cut upward with my knee. The banging had finally made it to our door, a hammering and a voice calling someone's name. I ran toward it, grabbing my black jacket and purse as I went, as behind me Alex yelled out one long string of curses interspersed with my name.

Throwing on the jacket, I unlocked the door and breathlessly pulled it open to find Harrison standing on the other side looking sweaty and mildly crazed, his blue eyes darting, and a substantial group of people crowding in behind him.

"Sally!" he exclaimed.

With one hand he reached forward and pulled my jacket closed, but I could already see his other going for the door, and feel the momentum of his body as he tried to get past me to the guy swearing his head off in the dark room.

Dragging the door closed behind me, I pressed both my hands into Harrison's chest and pushed him backward, the two of us stumbling, scattering the gawking people around us. Reaching between our bodies, I buttoned the jacket closed, first one button and then the other.

Then I looked up into those piercing eyes of his and said, "Harrison, I think it's about time you got me the fuck out of here."

9

We burst out of the house like we'd just robbed the joint, only slowing when we reached the corner and Harrison tried to turn one way and I tried to turn another, our bodies connected by our linked hands. I wasn't sure when he'd taken my hand, but there it was in mine, his fingers laced through my own. I stared down at it as we stood on the street corner, the deafening sound of my own pounding heart easing off gradually until there was no sound at all except that of Harrison's breathing and the wind. I wished it would come back, that overwhelming noise, like the music from the party. It was a wonderful hiding place. Without it, I felt terribly unsafe, able to hear anything Harrison might say, anything I might say, able to hear my own thoughts, which were the very last thing I wanted to hear right then.

Dropping Harrison's fingers, I covered my ears with my hands like a little girl who doesn't want to hear her punishment, and closed my eyes.

"Sally," Harrison said.

I heard his voice as if I was listening through a ball of cotton, and squeezed my fingers more tightly together. I didn't want to hear his questions. I didn't want to see the disappointment in his eyes. I didn't want to feel him pulling farther away, to feel that loss again, to feel that pain again, not after what had just happened. Not tonight.

"Sally," he repeated, and this time I felt his hand on my back, just a little lower than the spot where Alex had shoved me hard into the wall, but his touch was so much gentler, and warmer. Even his voice was warmer. I wanted to curl up against the sound of his voice and forget every other word that had ever been said to me, and every word I'd ever said to myself.

I wanted Harrison's voice to be the noise in my head. His voice and nothing else.

"I have to ask you a question," he said.

Why do you insist on being such a slut, Sally? Why are you such an embarrassment, Sally? Why do you keep dragging me back into your life when all I want to do is forget about you, Sally?

I felt him pulling gently at my hands and I let them fall, giving up, knowing whatever he was going to ask it couldn't be worse than what I was thinking. I already knew what he thought of me. If he wanted me to confirm it, then so be it.

He tipped my face upward and I smelled the faint scent of oranges, which had an oddly calming effect on me, almost like a sedative.

"Open your eyes," Harrison said, and I did. My eyelids weren't going to save me anyway. He could already see the disaster that I was. At least with my eyes open I could look at his lovely face, and those beautiful, kind eyes and feel for a moment that he saw something worth seeing. Just for a moment before he asked whatever he was going to ask.

It was a wonderful moment.

"Sally," he said. *Here it comes*, I thought. *Here comes the end.* "Where's your car?"

"What?" I said, shaking my head. "That's what you want to ask me?"

"Well," he replied, looking apologetic, "you're not wearing any pants." We both looked down at my bare legs. Katie's little jacket was barely covering my ass, I was barefoot, and it wasn't exactly warm out. "I figure getting you off the street should be job one."

"Right," I agreed. Safety first, disapproval later. "It's this way, I think."

As we jogged another block to my grey Corolla, I noticed the determined look on Harrison's face, and the way he clenched his jaw. He looked like he was on a mission, like a firefighter or a soldier. Maybe this was his thing—rescuing stupid girls from their own fates, getting them home safe. I was like an assignment for him. It made sense. At least it explained what he was doing here. Maybe he would never ask me anything about what had happened at all. Like a paramedic, he'd bundle me up and stitch up my wounds and take me where I needed to go, and then move one to his next emergency. The idea both comforted and depressed me.

Once we reached the car, he asked for my keys and I handed them over warily. "You know how to drive, right?" I said.

"Sure," he replied as he got into the driver's seat. Though my friends were constantly screaming at me about it, I'd driven myself home completely plastered tons of times, and I'd always felt a lot more confident in my abilities than he looked right now. "Maybe I'm a little out of practise."

He then proceeded to adjust his seat five times—once forward, then too far back, then forward three more times in tiny increments.

"Whatever," I said, leaning my head against the window, which felt nice and cool against my temple and the headache just developing underneath it. On the second try I heard the car start. "Just get me home in one piece."

If you couldn't trust your rescuer to bring you home safe, then who could you trust?

I closed my eyes and felt sleep rushing toward me, like a shade being pulled down when it was still light out. I had two thoughts before I passed out. One was that I hoped I didn't throw up on him. The second was that I hoped he was gone when I woke up.

It would be better to wake up empty than to wake up hopeful and have those hopes dashed when he walked away.

I was done being rescued by Harrison Leo.

When I woke up he was carrying me.

I must have only been asleep for a few minutes, because I was still half-naked and smelling of booze—I could actually smell it coming off my skin. Just great—and it was still dark. The apartment was just as I'd left it, which meant Anita still hadn't come home, and this on top of the fact that I was in Harrison Leo's arms, clasped against his chest, his pulse beating against my cheek, left me feeling infinitely let down and depressed. I wanted this to be real. I wanted him to take me to my bed and take off my jacket and touch me in all the places on my body that were waking up just from being near him. I wanted Harrison to want me, but he didn't, and he never would. So, why couldn't he just leave me alone?

"Put me down," I said suddenly and Harrison paused in his step.

We were crossing the living room, approaching my bedroom. I didn't want him to come into my bedroom. I didn't think I'd be able to take it.

With a sigh, he set me down on the couch, then sat down on the coffee table, facing me.

"I thought you were sleeping," he said in a whisper.

Of course he would whisper, like we were sharing secrets in the dark. Of course he would pull the blanket off the back of the couch and drape it over my bare legs. Of course he'd be a good guy, because that's who he was, but I wasn't a good girl. I was no good at all.

I lay back against the cushions and folded my arms, refusing to look at him. "Thanks for everything. You can go now," I said.

I could feel him staring, but I wasn't going to look. He had to get that this was the end. I needed him to get that. I needed him to finally get that no matter how many times he rescued me, I was never going to change. I would never stop disappointing him. It would be better for him, for both of us, if he just cut his losses and got out now.

"Are you okay?" Harrison said, completely ignoring my words. His gaze dropped to my arm. "Is your elbow—"

"I'm fine," I snapped, cupping the scrape on my arm where the blood had already dried.

Kicking off the blanket, I edged to the far side of the couch and curled into a ball. My legs were still cold from being outside, and my feet were filthy and scratched. My hair was actually wet with sweat from all the dancing earlier, and was looking, I was sure, like some kind of swirling, yellow bird's nest.

I was a putrid mess, and Harrison wouldn't stop looking at me. More than anything I just wanted him to stop looking at me, stop helping me, just stop.

"I want you to get out and leave me alone."

"Sally, what happened?" Harrison said. Not leaving, not even making an attempt to do as I asked, he leaned toward me and put a hand on my arm. I flinched it off. "Just tell me what's wrong."

"What's wrong?" I spat, glaring at him in the semi-dark. "You want to know what's *wrong*?"

Everything, that's what was wrong. Every single thing in my life was wrong, and no matter what I did nothing ever came out right. Every choice I made was wrong. Everything I did and said and was, was all wrong. I might as well have had the word tattooed on my forehead.

A wave of feeling suddenly welled up inside of me, and broken as I was I just wasn't prepared for it. It wasn't just one emotion, but a wadded up, twisted mess of them. It started with the icy panic of being in that room with Alex, and the regret of yelling at Anita, and the disgust of having let all those guys paw me that week, and the anguish of wanting Harrison, and the dread of Billy's phone call, and Billy, and Billy's face, and Billy's voice in my head, that contemptuous, superior voice telling me all the things I already knew, reminding me whenever I could snatch a moment of happiness that it wouldn't last, because I didn't deserve it, because I was nothing, I was dirt, I was only good for one thing, and this degradation, this misery, was all I would ever have.

With an anguished cry I covered my face with my hands and burst into tears.

Melissa was an ugly laugher. We all made fun of her about it. She looked kind of like a maniac when she laughed, her eyes wide and her eyebrows raised, he head flung back. What she didn't know, what nobody knew, was that I was an ugly crier. Not because of the way I looked, but because of its intensity. I never cried in front of anyone, because I knew once I got started I would never stop. I couldn't stop.

That's how I cried that night in front of Harrison.

My wails filled the room, shaky and high-pitched and grating even to my own ears. Before I knew what was happening, Harrison was beside me on the couch, murmuring into my ear, holding me against his chest as I struggled to get loose.

"Don't touch me," I shrieked. "I'm dirty. I'm disgusting."

"You're not disgusting," he said, holding me tightly, even when I kicked and fought to be let go. "You're not dirty, Sally. You're not."

"You don't know what you're saying!" I cried, sobbing, doubled over and clutching my stomach. "I'm no good. I'm human waste. You should just scrape me off your shoe and go!"

"Stop," Harrison said, and there was real feeling in his voice, as if my words were actually hurting him. But how could they? If he didn't care, as I knew he didn't, then how could they?

"You know, you already know the truth. That's why you don't want me. Because you know I let them do whatever they want to me. I should have just let Alex do it to me, too. What does it even matter? They've all had me. They've all had me twice! I'm used up. I'm nothing. I know you know it. Just admit it!" I pushed against him with my hands, but weakly, still weeping so hard I could hardly sit up.

Putting a hand on each of my shoulders, he forced me to look at him. Through my tears, I could only see a blur, even the comfort of his face taken from me. "Stop it, Sally," he said firmly. "I don't know who told you these lies, but that's what they are: Lies. You are not nothing. You are not used up."

I'd never cried this hard before. I'd never gone this far, delved this deep into the well of emotions I kept hidden under layers and layers of forced laughter and fun. I felt a searing pain when I reached the place where those memories hid, those emotions I hadn't let myself feel in, how long was it, four years? Ever since that day. That day when I became Slutty Sally. That day when it all started. That day when the girl I had been was wiped away.

When I spoke next I didn't even know what I was saying. It was as though that girl, the old Sally, was speaking for me.

"You don't know how long ago this started," I said, staring glassy-eyed into the dark. "They took something from me, you know? They removed it. And I was so young when it happened. I've been this way for such a long time now, that I know. There's no getting it back. There's no changing me now. I am what I am. Nobody will ever want me after what I've done. I trick them sometimes, but it isn't real. Nobody will ever love me."

The tears were still coming, like a river, like a waterfall. Harrison tried to wipe them away, but there were always more. That's what I was trying to tell him. There would always be more. He took my face in his hands and my tears ran into his palms.

"It doesn't matter," he said. "None of that matters, do you hear me? You are smart and beautiful and kind. You aren't what anybody says you are. You get to decide what you are, and you are important. You're important to me."

"Don't lie to me," I sobbed. "You don't want me. You don't care about me." Guys always said all kinds of nonsense when they wanted you to stop crying. He would take it all back later. I'd seen it before.

"I do want you," he said. He leaned in and kissed my wet

cheeks, first one and then the other. The shock of feeling his lips against my skin was so strong that I actually stopped crying, right then. "I do care. God, Sally, you have no idea how much."

I stared at his face, so close to mine, and his gorgeous eyes, dark with some overwhelming feeling I didn't understand. I couldn't look away.

"Prove it," I said, a challenge I was sure he wouldn't rise to. I was calling his bluff. This was the part where he would tuck tail and run. "Prove that you want me."

He paused for a moment, and I thought that was an answer. I thought that was it.

And then he kissed me.

I'd been kissed by hundreds of guys. I'd had good kisses and bad, hard and soft and slobbering and half-hearted. I knew every technique, every move. I'd seen it all. But I'd never been kissed like this before.

His lips were soft, coaxing but gentle, warm and sweet. He held my face with delicate fingers, and I grasped his forearms with my hands, holding on. His mouth was unhurried, his lips pressing against mine like a present given instead of taken, though I could sense in the way he was breathing that there was a hunger underneath it, a desire he was suppressing for my sake.

Gently, tentatively, he teased my lips open with his and then stroked his tongue against mine and I felt that touch more keenly than I ever had while doing far naughtier things with far naughtier guys. When he ran his right hand down my back and lightly pressed me toward him something flipped over in my stomach and I moaned against his mouth.

He kissed the edge of my mouth, and my cheek and then continued across my jaw to my ear, where he whispered, "Do you believe me now?"

Did I believe him? I wanted to, that much I knew. I wanted to believe in this heat and this feeling in my belly and this guy, but I'd been fooled before, and I wasn't sure I could stand being wrong tonight. I wasn't sure I was strong enough to believe.

In answer, I wrapped my arms around him and buried my face in his shoulder. "Take me to bed," I said.

Gathering me up again, he carried me the ten feet to my bed and when I wouldn't let him go he gave me what I wanted and got in with me.

This time, as I fell asleep, I didn't hope he would be gone when I woke up. Instead, as I rested my face against his chest, I surprised myself.

I hoped he would stay.

10

At some point in the night I woke up and made it to the bathroom just in time to throw up all the booze from my long night of partying, then wandered back to bed, all without making the tiniest mess, or waking Harrison, or fully waking up myself. This particular talent, which I'd been honing for years, meant that when I finally did wake up the next morning it wasn't to the lurching realization that I was about to explode disgusting everywhere like some kind of party-girl sewage volcano. Instead, I woke up in Harrison's arms.

It was such a foreign sensation to me that before I opened my eyes I couldn't quite figure out why I felt so incredibly comfortable, and warm, and something else that I couldn't quite place but that reminded me of when I used to sleep with our enormous German shepherd as a little girl because I believed he would guard me against the mean little rabbits that lived under my bed. This feeling and this memory left me uncomfortably surprised, like when you discover you've eaten an entire pie when you'd only planned on having one slice. I never thought about my childhood, pleasant as it had been. It was just too easy for my thoughts to wander to other things, things that had happened later, things I wished I could gouge out of my brain with a melon scoop. It was safer to forget. But sometimes all that forced forgetting made me feel like my childhood was lost to me forever, like if there came a time when I wanted to remember I wouldn't be able to.

But I guess I was wrong. Because here I was remembering that five-year-old feeling. I hadn't been able to name it at first, but as I opened my eyes it came to me.

I felt safe.

Then the heavy male arm that was wrapped around me moved just a little bit and I almost lunged for my hair straightener—not exactly a lethal weapon, but the only thing within easy reach of my bed that I could clobber someone with. I'd burned myself on that thing dozens of times and it hurt like a *bitch*!

Turning my head just the tiniest bit to my left, I breathed in the scent of oranges—what was it, his cologne? His shampoo? Did he just eat a lot of oranges?—and the truth finally sunk in.

Harrison Leo was in my bed.

No, scratch that.

Harrison Leo was spooning me in my bed.

I'd learned a long time ago that just launching myself into memories of a night of heavy drinking was often:

A: Traumatizing.

B: Demoralizing—mainly because there would often be long stretches of no memories at all, making me feel like my own brain had been redacted and soon enough the governmental body in charge of depraved activities would close my file for good.

C: Nauseating.

D: Exhausting.

I decided to give it a go anyway, if only so I could parse this whole guy-breathing-softly-in-my-ear situation, which felt so good I was practically purring.

Then my eyes landed on Katie's black jacket lying in the middle of my bedroom floor, and I looked down at my own arms to see them covered in a men's blue button-down shirt.

Which could only mean one thing.

Harrison Leo was spooning me, shirtless.

If there were prizes given out for the quickest time from zero to completely, absolutely, convulsively turned on, I would have won it right then, hands down.

I'd never spooned with a guy before, had never even lingered in bed with anyone the morning after longer than the time it took to remind myself of his name and ask where my underwear had gotten to. I'd always thought of spooning in bed as something married couples did after he got fat and she forgot what her genitals were for, a sad, boring alternative to all the high-energy sexual gymnastics I liked best. I'd never considered that lying next to a guy in bed could be any different than lying next to Anita when we fell asleep on the couch watching a movie; a little comforting, but completely non-sexual.

Man alive had I been wrong.

Harrison's chest was locked tightly against my back, excruciatingly out of my reach, but pleasantly sturdy and warm. One of his arms was belted around my middle and I could just feel the tickle of his chin stubble on my shoulder. Though I wasn't wearing any bottoms, it felt as though he still had pants on—which disappointed me in a profound way—but the way he'd bent his legs, locking my ass against the heat of his crotch, more than made up for it. I had the sudden overwhelming urge to wiggle my ass, just a little, just enough, to see what kind of naughty reactions I could elicit, but I resisted and instead held painfully still.

I didn't want to wake him up. I didn't want the dream to end.

Because of course it would end. That was a given. We'd both found ourselves this morning in some new universe where I loved spooning and the morning sun shone prettily through the window, dappling the bed, and (I was hoping) fairies made us breakfast and morning breath did not exist. It was the only explanation for this lovely boy's presence here, in my apartment, in my bed. Pretty soon the fairy dust would dissipate and everything would go back to normal. Harrison would remember that he didn't belong here, because he didn't want me. He didn't even like me. Unless…

I gasped and half-sat up in bed, Harrison stirring behind me, as the memory of last night's kiss came back to me. That devouring, soul-wrenching, panty-dropping kiss. Pressing my fingers to my lips, which were throbbing at the mere memory, I remembered how he'd carried me to bed and put his shirt on me when I'd ripped off my jacket and held me under the covers—the sound of his heartbeat the soundtrack of my dreams—and then, like a finger held firmly on the rewind button I recalled everything that had come right before those tender moments, the entire catastrophic disaster of the evening, including all the weeping and the yelling and everything I'd told, and everything I could never take back.

I squeezed my eyes shut with mortification for one long second, before leaping out of bed like a jack-in-the-box and scurrying straight for the door.

"Hey," I heard Harrison say, his voice rough with sleep, just as my hand hit the doorknob.

I tried to arrange my face into some version of placidity—or at the very least plain-old hungover sickliness—as I turned around and saw him rising up on his elbow. His cheeks were just a little rosy with sleep, his lips curling into that half-smile that made my toes curl.

"You're wearing my shirt," he said, though from the way he was looking at me, it wasn't the shirt he was interested in.

His eyes didn't linger on my legs or my chest for long, because Harrison wasn't one to leer, but I felt the brief, appreciative look he gave them before his eyes returned to my face. I almost combusted right then and there I was so overcome with conflicting emotions of desire and panic, arousal and hysteria.

"You put it on me," I replied gamely, trying but failing to force a smile.

"Come here," he said, waving me back as I continued to inch toward the door, even as a part of me—and I won't deny it was a forceful part—yearned to do exactly as he asked.

Then I heard the wonderful, heart-leaping sound of the door to the apartment opening and closing and I knew I had the rescue I'd been hoping for.

"I think I hear Anita!" I said a little too loudly and with a little too much enthusiasm, before grabbing for the door handle and swinging myself out of the room, catching just one quick glimpse of Harrison's puzzled expression before I shut the door against him.

I stood there for a moment, staring at the door, as though waiting for it to explode. If this had been a cartoon I would have nailed the door shut, and put on three extra locks, and shoved a couch against it, and a desk, and a TV, and the kitchen sink.

I just needed him to stay in there until I could figure out how to face him, or how to reverse time and redo the entire night.

So, a couple of lifetimes at least.

As I turned my back on the worrying, lockless door, Anita walked into the room carrying two grocery bags, which she set down on the counter.

"Oh!" she said, when she saw me, pressing her hand to her chest. "God, you scared me. I didn't think you'd be up yet. How are you—"

I threw myself into her arms, cutting her off, and kind of suffocating her a little too because she was a foot shorter than me and her face was buried somewhere half in my neck and half in my boobs, but I couldn't help it. I'd never been so happy to see anyone in my life.

When I pulled away she gave me a look that was a combination of relief and worry. Relieved, because our fight seemed to be over—I knew that's what she was feeling, because I was too—and worried because I'd never done anything other than grunt and scowl at her on a hangover morning. Hugging wasn't on the menu. Hugging at nine a.m. meant serious business.

She held up a jug of juice. "I got that tropical punch you

like, but I'm guessing we have other more important things to talk about. Like, whose shirt is that?"

I pulled at the cotton hem of the shirt as I collapsed onto the couch. "Harrison's," I said hopelessly, trying to impart to her all of my explosive alarm in that one word.

It's Harrison's shirt! Harrison's. Shirt. Don't you see?

"Oh good," Anita said, her shoulders slumping with relief, "he found you. Katie called Em, but she was stuck in some three-hour evening class, and I was at my parent's place for my Dad's birthday dinner. I couldn't think who to call, and Mel wasn't answering my texts, but then I thought—"

"Wait, what?" I said, struggling to follow her babbling. "You called Harrison?"

Well, it did make more sense than him just randomly pounding on bedroom doors calling my name for no apparent reason.

Anita nodded. "Katie said you were really out of it and you went off with some sleazy guy she thought was Alex and then she couldn't fine you. I was worried, and I had his number from the study group, so…"

She shrugged apologetically, and I was so wrapped up in my own distress that I almost didn't notice her eyes filling with tears.

"Hey, I'm okay," I said, putting an arm around her shoulder. "You did the right thing. I'm an idiot. I should have someone watching me twenty-four-seven."

"I should never have let you go off partying by yourself all week. I shouldn't have slept at Mel's," Anita said, wiping at her eyes. "I should have been there. I know how you get when…when you're on your own."

You mean near-suicidally careless? You mean so bleakly depressed I might drink myself into oblivion? Is that what you mean?

"I'm sorry I worried you," I said honestly. "I was so stupid. I always take everything way too far."

I hadn't exactly told Anita what I'd been so upset about in the first place, and I could see her wanting to ask, but also not wanting to get into another disagreement. She knew that sharing my deepest hurt wasn't exactly my forte. Little did she know I'd already moved about five hurts passed the one she was dwelling on.

"But nothing happened, right?" she said, looking me over as if trying to find some hidden scar. "I mean, he found you before you got into a bar fight or bit off a guy's testicles or whatever, right? He got there in time?"

The look she gave me was so perfectly serious that I almost started to laugh, even though my gut was swirling with nausea. Bit off a guy's testicles? It's like she thought I turned into a rabid dog when the sun went down.

"Well, yeah, he got there just in time to see me drop-kick Alex in the face," I admitted.

I realized, as Anita's eyes grew wide and she started grilling me for details, that though the whole unsuccessful revenge-sex portion of the evening was hardly the part I was obsessing over, that didn't mean it wasn't the part everyone else would be obsessing over.

"Wait, wait. Back up and start from the beginning," she said, settling into the couch like she really wanted to get into the nitty-gritty of the thing.

I was just trying to figure out how to explain that there was a whole other, much bigger, way more monumental thing going on when a noise came from behind my bedroom door. Like the noise of someone getting out of bed and maybe approaching that bedroom door. Jumping to my feet, I opened my mouth as if to command the door to stay closed, but luckily stopped myself before I actually did so.

Anita looked from me to the door and then down to the shirt I was wearing, a suspicious expression on her face.

"So, after getting there just in time, he also sort of slept over," I explained, staring down at the too-long sleeves of Harrison's shirt, not sure exactly why I was embarrassed.

Anita's mouth opened in surprise. "Oh my God," she whispered, pulling me toward her. "So, you guys, like…" She twirled her fingers in the patented Anita gesture for whoopee.

"No," I said, swatting her hands away. "No, of course

not. Nothing like that."

My friend's expression changed swiftly from scandalized to disbelief, and then finally to impressed, though my emotional roller coaster wasn't quite so optimistic. I wasn't sure why Harrison and I hadn't had sex the night before, but I knew that it couldn't have been my idea to hold off. My memory of everything after that epic kiss was a little hazy, but I knew myself, I knew how I went into autopilot when there was a guy in my bed. I wouldn't have broken off that kiss and then turned over and gone to sleep. Had he turned me down? Had the kiss just been a means to an end, a way to shut me up? Did he really not want me at all?

"If you're wearing his shirt," Anita began, "then he's in there wearing—"

"No shirt," I finished, nodding.

She blinked a few times, digesting this, and I almost wanted to smack her for thinking whatever she was thinking, as if I was the sole proprietor of all sexy thoughts about Harrison Leo.

"And you really didn't…" Seeing my look of infinite distress, Anita changed her tone. "I called him for a reason, you know? He really cares about you."

"I don't know," I said, wrapping my hands around my stomach. "Last night…Oh God, the things I did. The things I said!"

"I'm sure he won't hold it against you," Anita said. "He's a good guy. He's the guy who goes to some party just to make sure you're okay. He's so much better than stupid Alex. Whatever you said, he'll forgive you."

She didn't know, of course. She couldn't know all the secrets I'd told, the humiliating scene I'd made. She thought I was talking about some drunken confession about a sexual exploit. She had no idea what was at stake now. I realized, as she looked up at me, nodding reassuringly, that I couldn't possibly tell her what had really happened. Because there was so much she didn't know, so much I'd always kept from her, so much I couldn't tell peaches-and-cream, straight-laced, get-there-on-time-and-with-a-smile Anita.

I didn't know if I would be able to keep Harrison. I wasn't about to lose my best friend too.

"He's too good for me," I said sadly. "You know he's too good for me."

Anita took a breath before answering, and in that quick second I hung my head. She agreed with me.

"I think he's too good for the girl you pretend to be most of the time," she said, nudging me with her elbow. "But we both know that's not the real you."

Except that was the thing she didn't know, the thing I couldn't tell her. That girl was the real me. Always had been, always would be.

"What exactly does he think you're doing out here?" she asked.

I shrugged. "I don't know," I said. "Talking to you?"

Anita gave me an incredulous look. "You just left him in there with no explanation?" she said.

"Is that not right?" I asked. How was I supposed to know the proper morning-after-non-sex-bed-sharing ritual? This was totally new territory for me.

"Go back in there and talk to him," she said, shoving me toward the door. "And say thank you for helping me, and offer to make him breakfast."

Damn, she was really on the Harrison bandwagon. I kind of wished I'd kept her out of the whole thing. It was going to be so depressing when I had to break it to her that it had all been in her head.

"Like I know how to make breakfast. Burnt toast and runny eggs isn't much of a thank you," I protested. Anything to avoid going into that room. Anything.

"Buy it for him then," she said sternly.

And sit across from him for an hour unable to look him in the eye? No thanks very much. I'd rather slit my wrists.

"Stop pushing me," I whined, trying to wiggle out of her grip.

I was grinding my elbow into her side and she was trying

to readjust her grasp on my arm when the door to my bedroom suddenly opened and Harrison stepped out. He raised an eyebrow at the two of us as we tried our best to look casual and non-violent, releasing each other and plastering on beaming smiles.

He still wasn't wearing a shirt, which made it kind of hard to focus on anything besides controlling my own drool. That chest I'd wanted so much to touch earlier? It really didn't disappoint.

"I was just going to jump in a shower, if that's okay?" Harrison said, looking a little uncomfortable, though I wasn't sure why. Wasn't being stared at by university girls every man's dream?

When I didn't answer him—all the synapses in my brain had stopped firing—Anita directed him to the bathroom and told him where to find a towel and how to make the hot water tap work by jiggling the knob.

I heard the water go on and then she came back, shaking her head. "They didn't make nerds like that when I was a kid," she said, a dazed look on her face. "But don't worry, I know. Hands off." She shook her hands in the air. "I know he's yours."

I smiled at her, but as soon as she turned away that smile vanished just like that feeling of warm safety from the moment before I'd properly woken up.

Harrison Leo, mine? I thought to myself. *Yeah, right.*

And if there was any doubt in my mind on that score, it was finally confirmed when I wandered back into my room and saw the flashing light on my answering machine and listened to the message waiting for me from Billy, his words like a steel collar closing around my neck, sealing my fate, reminding me of who and what I really was.

No matter what Anita thought, no matter what Harrison did or said, I knew the truth.

I had to stop dreaming. The time had come to wake up.

11

I walked into Labour Economics twenty minutes late, avoiding the glaring look from the teacher as I made my way to the back and slumped into a seat. Ten more minutes passed before it even occurred to me to take out a notebook and pen. Needless to say I didn't ingest much information about labour or economics, not that I was much concerned about my marks, since this was the first time I'd been to class in weeks. I didn't even know how I'd been tricked into coming to campus in the first place.

It had all started with Anita asking Harrison all kinds of nosey questions over waffles—which she'd made, of course—the types of questions I suppose I should have asked him the very first time I met him, like which classes he was taking (Digital Systems something something, Fundamentals of blah blah, yada yada Development), and where he worked (he had dual tutoring gigs. One at a local high school, and another in the computer engineering department, mentoring first year students), and where he was from (right here in Kingston). They were pretty chatty as they ate their bacon and sopped up their maple syrup, while I sat listening to a continual loop of Billy's latest message in my head, not eating a bite.

You think you can hide from me? You think that will get you out of it? Because we both know that won't work. There's no getting out of this. Not for you.

I'll admit I zoned out for a few minutes, biting at my cuticles and trying to ignore the headache that even a profoundly good sleep hadn't taken care of. The next thing I knew Anita was announcing brightly that my morning class was right near Walter Light Hall—where Harrison was headed—and wasn't it a coincidence that it started right at the same time as Harrison's first session, and should we be on our way? She practically linked our hands and tucked lunch money in our pockets like a perfect soccer mom. I barely had time to stick out my tongue at her before we were out the door and on our way to school, a sticky note with a classroom number clutched in my hand because Lord knew I would never have found the classroom otherwise. She'd also written the words "Be Nice" and underlined them three times, which I felt was unnecessary.

My not being nice to Harrison wasn't the problem. It was my wanting him to be nice to me, and to keep being nice to me, and to be nice to me forever. That was the problem.

"How are you feeling?" Harrison said carefully as we walked side by side down the sidewalk.

There had been a moment earlier when it had seemed like he was trying to reach for my hand, but I'd stuffed mine in my pockets to avoid that land mine. I didn't need any more sweet gestures to hoard and obsess over once this was over, and it really was going to be completely over soon. I even had a deadline.

I'm coming for you on October 9th, Sal, and you'd better cooperate, or you know exactly what will happen. And who I'll tell. And what you'll lose.

October 9th. Exactly three weeks away. Three weeks until this fantasy life I'd been living would be over. Three weeks until I lost Harrison, one way or another.

"Sally?" Harrison brushed a lock of hair behind my ear, his blue eyes clouded with concern. Without realizing it I'd stopped walking and stood staring at a willow tree across the street. I hadn't even answered his question.

"God, I'm out of it today, huh?" I said, shaking my head and detouring around him to keep walking up the street. "I blame the whiskey…and the beer…and the Tequila shots…"

That's what I sounded like, right? That was a pretty good impression of happy-go-lucky, sloppy, silly Sally, wasn't it? It was so hard to tell from Harrison's stoic expression, though he was frowning just a little. Did that mean he was buying it and he thought I was an idiot, or he wasn't buying it and he was getting ready to call me on it?

And when exactly had I become the type of girl who analyzed a guy's *expression*?

"Listen," he said, "I get that you don't want to talk about what happened last night, and it's not exactly my place to ask…"

Ask what? Ask me what exactly I'd been alluding to when I'd brought up my past? Ask why I'd decided to call up Alex, a guy who'd thrown me outside in the cold half-naked? Ask what had driven me to drink myself into oblivion in the first place?

There were dozens of questions he could have asked that would have made me run for the hills and hundreds of horrendous lies I could have told and then regretted later in my own, personal, self-hating way. But he didn't ask any of them.

Swallowing with some difficulty, Harrison kept his eyes on the ground ahead of us as he said, "I know Alex was in that room with you last night. I heard a few things through the door."

Wonderful. Just absolutely fantastic.

"I need to know," he continued slowly, "did he hurt you?"

"Not as much as I hurt him," I said sassily, mostly just relieved that he didn't want to know anything more. This was his big question? Had Alex forced himself on me? Like that was my most pressing problem.

Taking me gently by the arm, Harrison turned me toward him and gave me a look that wiped the smile from my face. He looked truly pained, as though the very idea of Alex hurting me was twisting a knife inside him.

"It's not a joke," he said. "The things I heard him say to you, no guy should ever say. It's just like the guy that night at The Limo. No one should ever make you feel unsafe like that. Not ever."

I let my eyes drift over to the chain-link fence surrounding the playing fields up ahead, suddenly self-conscious. We were getting into uncomfortable territory now, like why-do-you-do-the-things-you-do territory. This wasn't a place I wanted Harrison to go with me. Not now, and given my three week deadline, probably not ever.

"Nothing happened," I said, looking him straight in the eye, the universal look of truth. "I changed my mind about… what I wanted from him, and he got a little heated. But I took care of it." Or my knee did, anyway. "He wouldn't have forced himself on me, anyway. He wanted me to want him and then to reject me, or something like that. He's always playing these little games."

I was about done with this conversation. The fact that we were talking about a guy I'd nearly had sex with the night before was making me feel ill. I wanted to tell him that I would much rather have been getting naked with him. I wanted to tell him that the whole reason any of it had happened was because I'd wanted to be with him. I wanted to, but what good would it really have done?

"Whatever, he's a child," I said. "I should never have called him anyway. I'm pretty sure he hates me."

"Don't you hate him?" Harrison said, giving me a look of disbelief. The way he gritted his teeth after he said it made me think he was the one who hated him.

"It wasn't a big deal," I replied honestly. "Guys can be assholes sometimes. I'm a big girl. I can take it."

I lifted my chin as I said that, because it was something I prided myself on. I could take it. I could take anything any guy threw at me. I was indestructible that way. I'd had plenty of practise.

"You shouldn't have to take it," Harrison said, his tone gentle but firm, as if he really wanted to get this point across.

This was the problem with good guys. They thought they were a dime a dozen, that they fell from the sky right into our laps. They didn't know how valuable they were, how elusive, how difficult to find. They didn't know how hard it was to let them go.

I tried to avoid looking into those kind eyes. I didn't want to fall into that vortex. I might never find my way out. But it was hard to do when he leaned in close like that, slipping his arms around my waist. I wanted to do the right thing for both of us. I wanted to resist him. But how could I when all I could think about was how incredibly good he'd tasted the night before and how much I wanted to taste him again.

Reaching up, I ran my fingers over the stubble on his chin, my knuckle grazing awfully close to his lips.

"Sally," he said in that low bedroom-voice I craved, "you know that I—"

And then his phone rang.

I actually turned away and gave the grass beside me a devastated glare as he pulled his cell out of his pocket. The conversation was terse and over quickly, but Harrison was obviously preoccupied after he hung up and it was obvious the moment was gone.

As we turned down Union street and approached his building I tried to convince myself it was for the best anyway. How long was I going to let this charade go on? Harrison Leo wasn't for me, goddammit. He was way out of my league and a way better person than me, and just because he hadn't figured that out yet didn't mean it wasn't true. I had to forget everything he'd said to me last night about wanting me, about caring. I had to remember who I really was, the dirty girl who spread her legs for anyone who asked, the type of girl Harrison wouldn't be caught dead with, at least not for long, at least…

"Do me a favour," Harrison said, pulling me toward him by the hand.

When exactly had he taken my hand?

Leaning toward me, he spoke into my ear, his breath tickling my cheek just as it had that morning when I'd been lying in his arms.

"Try not to think terrible things about yourself today," he said, and I froze in surprise. How could he tell what I'd been thinking? Had I been muttering under my breath? I did that sometimes, although usually when I was three sheets to the wind.

"What do you mean?" I said with affected innocence. "Give up my title of Drunken Super-Whore? What would I tell my fans?" I smirked at him, trying my damnedest to shake the serious expression from his face, and failing.

Pinching me playfully on the chin, he said, "Do it for me," and then his lips met mine in a brief, soft kiss before he walked away, leaving me open-mouthed and more confused than ever.

The room was already emptying before I realized class was over and I hadn't taken a single note. A guy with a long face and copper-coloured hair stopped by my chair and smiled at me in a friendly way, and I wondered if maybe we'd been made partners on some project while I'd been daydreaming. I'd once gotten an A in Biology that way.

"It's too late," he said with a grin, "I caught you."

Could he be talking about my topless coffee-table dance of the night before? He didn't seem like the type of guy to show up at a rager like that, but I had run into Katie and Lucas there, after all. Maybe he'd been delivering a pizza or something.

Luckily, given my notoriety around campus, I was used to this kind of attention. I was just about to turn on some no-pictures-please attitude, when he pointed down at my notebook, and the copy of *The Forever Place* I'd strategically opened inside its covers. Because, like I was really going to sit through an hour-long lecture without a distraction.

"Issue number five," he said appreciatively. "It's pretty decent. Things really start to get crazy when you get to seven, though."

"Oh God, I'm dying to read six and seven," I admitted, stuffing the comic into my bag and following him down the stairs to the door. "I've already read this one twice. And the stupid bookstore is always out of stock! I yelled at the manager and sort of let him get a look at my cleavage, but no dice. It's back-ordered or something?"

Long Face Guy laughed and held the classroom door open for me. "They're always back-ordered. Sometimes I go into Toronto just to get my fix. But you can just borrow them from Harrison. He's got them all."

"You know Harrison?" I said in confusion. Looking him over, I realized he did look sort of familiar, except the last time I'd seen him he'd been wearing an unfortunate red shiny shirt that belonged in 1997.

"I'm Winston, remember?" he said good-naturedly. "We met at that club a couple of weeks back? Harrison mentioned you were getting into *Forever*. He never lends out his comics, so you should feel special. It's cool that you have that in common. My ex-girlfriend always referred to it as my 'immature hobby' but she never got…"

As Winston blathered on about his inability to find a girl who liked comic books, my mind focused on just one thing: Harrison had talked about me to his friends.

I didn't know why it meant so much to me. All of Alex's friends had known we were hooking up of course, but he'd always been hesitant to call me his girlfriend, especially when other girls were around. And I'd always gotten the impression that when he talked about me he talked about my particular "talents" and nothing else. Which was fine. I pretty much did the same where he was concerned. But the idea of Harrison talking about me when I wasn't there, discussing my interests with his pals, it made my stomach flutter and blew away the dark cloud that had been hovering over me since I'd seen that damn blinking light on my answering machine.

He'd kissed me, again. He was telling his friends about me. He'd made small talk with my roommate. He'd told me to be nicer to myself—even if I hadn't quite been able to follow that advice.

Maybe, I thought to myself. *Maybe this means, if he learns the truth about me…Just maybe…*

"Hey," Winston said, as we came out of the building and started down the stairs. "Isn't that him over there?"

He was right. Harrison was talking with someone on one of the campus paths, his head bent toward him. It had only been ninety minutes since I'd last been with him, but that didn't stop my pulse from quickening at the sight of him. Winston waved goodbye as he rushed off to his next class, and I started across the grass, my heart light and a smile on my lips.

Three weeks could be a lifetime if I made the most of them. Three weeks could be forever.

Rushing up behind Harrison, I kissed him on the cheek in a sudden sneak-attack.

"You just missed Winston," I said giddily. Just being in Harrison's radius was like getting a happiness shot straight to my heart. I couldn't stop smiling. "Apparently we're in the same class, which was so boring I wanted to stab myself in the eye. Are you already done with your tutoring gig? Do you want to get coffee because, man I could use a pick me up."

Clearly, talking a mile a minute like a twelve-year-old girl on crack was also a symptom of being close to Harrison, but I didn't even care.

Harrison didn't quite look in my direction as he replied, "I'm just on a break."

His entire demeanour was so different than it had been the last time I'd seen him, very strained and cold, as if he was a police officer getting ready to question a perp arrested for some heinous crime.

Disoriented, I looked over at the guy he was talking to, who smiled at me in a lazy way. He was a strange-looking guy, a little older than us, with enormous eyes, a skinny frame, and long dreaded hair pulled back in a ponytail. By the way he was dressed I wondered if he was homeless. He wasn't wearing a coat, but instead had on several layers of army surplus-type jackets and a threadbare stripped scarf wound a bunch of times around his neck. For a second I wondered if he'd come up to Harrison asking for donations to some charity—although he didn't have a clipboard—but it seemed clear from the way Harrison was looking at him that they knew each other.

"That's just what I was saying to Harry," Ponytail Guy said. "You see? Your girl knows what I'm saying. A pick me up, that's what we need." Then he cupped his hand around his mouth and leaned toward me. I noticed his fingernails were black with dirt. "Harry's not having it. Look, he's giving me his grouchy face."

Actually, I wouldn't have called Harrison's face at that moment "grouchy." I would have called it "seething with rage," though of course his actual expression was mostly blank. It was the vein throbbing in his neck that gave him away. It was odd to see him so angry without understanding why. Did Ponytail Guy owe him money or something?

Harrison didn't reply to the guy's dig, which he'd obviously overheard. He didn't say anything at all, just stared at Ponytail's face, glancing over at me every few seconds as if to make sure I hadn't moved.

"Well," I said, unsure of what I was stepping into, "there's a great coffee house just over here." I pointed across the street. "It's way better than the Starbucks on campus."

"You know sweetheart, I was thinking more along the lines of Benny's up the street. A beer and some fries, that would hit the spot, don't you think?"

I'd barely nibbled at my waffle that morning, but my appetite was coming back now, and there was something very appealing about the idea of having a drink, especially if my next class was as boring as the one I'd just sat through. I figured now that I was on campus I might as well go to all three of the classes I had that day. After all, Anita had gone to the trouble of writing the classroom numbers down on the other side of the sticky note.

"Sounds like a plan," I said happily, looking to Harrison for some sign of agreement.

Ponytail Guy reached for my hand and I was about to give it to him when Harrison suddenly surged forward, putting his shoulder between the two of us and grabbing my hand instead.

"That's enough, Jason," he said gruffly. "I'm not doing this with you today. I told you, no."

"All right, man," Ponytail Guy said, hunching his shoulders and smiling, as if it was all a big joke. "No need to get all riled up. It was nice to meet you, sweetheart."

He held his hand out for me to shake, but Harrison pulled me close to his side, out of his reach.

"Don't touch her," he barked. Before I could quite take in that bizarre exchange, he was pulling me up the path. Ponytail Guy called after us to "Have a great day!" then sauntered off, whistling.

"Okay, what was all that about?" I said as we charged up the path at a brisk pace, weaving around other students as if we were trying to win a race. "Who's Jason? I mean, clearly you're not BFFs. But you were kind of rude to him. And that's coming from me, the girl who once told—"

I'd never been particularly good at sensing when tension had lifted, which had more than once led to my cracking a joke at an inopportune time, and it was clear as Harrison let go of my hand and cut me off that I'd done it again. The tension hadn't died with Jason. The tension was very much still alive.

"This is exactly what I was afraid would happen," Harrison said, raising his voice just enough to shock me, because I'd never heard him do so before.

He looked intensely agitated and he was breathing hard. It dawned on me that he wasn't pissed at this Ponytail Guy/Jason person. He was pissed at me.

"What happened," I said. "What are you talking about?"

I tried to go over the last few minutes in my head, to figure out exactly when I'd made some boneheaded move. But the exchange had been so brief and I'd hardly said anything at all. Did he think I'd been coming on to his friend when I'd agreed to have a beer with him? Is that was this was about?

"You're just like him," Harrison said through gritted teeth. "You don't take anything seriously. You refuse to take care of yourself. You think it's all a game."

I stared at him, a feeling of regret expanding in my stomach. Regret that I'd left myself open for exactly this moment, a moment I'd known would come. Regret that I'd let myself imagine I could avoid it.

He'd figured it out. He'd realized the truth about me.

"I tried to tell you," he said, though he wasn't looking at me but at the tree beside us. He'd already gone back to avoiding my eyes, and it stung like an arrow through the heart. "I can't do this with you." He gestured between us, as if to indicate some invisible cord connecting us, a cord he was about to cut. "I want to, but I can't."

I didn't want to speak. I knew he was right. But the words bubbled out of my mouth anyway. "Tell me what to do," I pleaded, stepping toward him, following his face with mine as he kept trying to look away. "I can be different. I can be better."

It wasn't true. I couldn't be better. I could barely manage to be what I was now. But maybe if he believed I could. Maybe if he would just take my hand again.

"No," he said finally, and I dropped the hand I'd been extending. "This will never work. When I'm with you I'll always feel like… I'm bad for you, and you're bad for me."

He looked me in the eye one last time and I could see right away that he wasn't fooling around. Whatever he'd felt for me, that warmth I'd seen in his eyes just an hour before, it was already gone.

He'd said, "You're bad for me," but I knew what he really meant. I'd known all along.

He meant, "You're bad."

"I have to go," he said, and before I could answer he turned and walked away, leaving me alone.

12

I'd never been miserable without drowning in alcohol at the same time, and it was so much shittier than I thought it would be.

When I'd returned to my apartment after sitting numbly through the rest of my classes, I'd gone straight for the bottles lined on top of my dresser. Jack Daniel, Johnnie Walker, Jose Cuervo, and Jim Beam; all my boys were ready and waiting to help me forget my troubles. I went for Jack first, my hand closing around the square glass bottle. I even went so far as to unscrew it, flinging the cap over my shoulder, but instead of bringing it to my lips I just ended up staring down at the label and watching the brown liquor swirl around the bottom of the bottle. When it came right down to it, I couldn't take that first swig.

I'd been filling myself up with liquor for days like I was refilling a pool, and where precisely had it gotten me? Right here, feeling just as wretched as ever. And if I was being really honest with myself, it had been way longer than a few days. It was probably more like four years that I'd been dealing with any negative emotion I had with a trip to a liquor cabinet, or a visit to a bar, or a swig from my trusty flask. That was four years of running from one disastrous moment to another, four years of vomiting up my troubles, four years of numbing myself against the world.

Though I didn't understand exactly how, I'd definitely gotten the impression that it was my drunken tendencies that had pushed Harrison away, and as much as I wanted to neutralize the awful feelings of rejection and shame that were rising inside me like some unstoppable tide with a barrel-full of whiskey—and maybe a roll in the hay with some random bed buddy—I'd finally come to the conclusion that this bad habit of mine wasn't doing me any favours. In fact, this bad habit was only making everything so much worse.

So, instead of getting dazzlingly trashed and drunk dialling Harrison to prolong both of our suffering, I did the next best thing.

I swung my arm across the bottles and sent them crashing to the floor.

Anita, who had been curling her hair in the bathroom, came running, half her head straight and half curly, and stared at me with wide, fearful eyes. "What's going on?" she cried.

"I'm giving up drinking!" I announced with a dramatic shake of my fist. She nodded weakly, eyeing the glass on the floor and the liquor soaking into the hardwood. "And also sex!" I added impulsively.

"Fuck!" she said, walking right into the room in her bare feet, all thoughts of the glass forgotten. "Are you okay? What happened?"

Yeah, the alcoholic sex-addict suddenly deciding to go dry and celibate really got people's attention.

I shook my head, breathing hard, as she sat me down on the bed.

"Was it Harrison?" she said.

Because she knew. Of course she knew that I loved him. Even though she'd hardly heard any of the story. Even if she didn't know everything he'd done for me. She'd seen enough this morning. She knew this one was different.

"I told you he was too good for me," I said, my eyes filling with tears.

Anita grabbed the Kleenex box from my bedside table and pressed it into my lap, then pulled her phone out of her pocket. "I'm calling in reinforcements," she said.

If you ever want to know if your friends really care about you, just watch what they do when you fall apart. Within a half hour of Anita's call, right around the time my level of self-loathing was reaching a fever pitch, Emily and Melissa and Katie descended on my room like a trio of executive party-planners, determined to cheer me up, or at the very least keep me pleasantly distracted.

I had no idea what Anita had told them was wrong with me, though I imagined there had been some heavy use of the H word—which I had banned about ten minutes after my bottle smashing fiasco. She'd definitely given them the impression that this was nothing like the Alex/Jeremy breakup nonchalance. This was the real deal.

Melissa brought her Golden Girls box set—because, she insisted, "those old broads know how to deal with life's ups and downs"—and her massive makeup kit, so we could do manicures when we got bored out of our minds watching TV. Katie, bless her sweet little heart, brought five gallons of ice cream, a bottle of fudge topping, and gummy bears, though she insisted she would get more if we ran out.

"How are we going to run out?" I said, eyeing the array of junk food covering the kitchen counter. "How depressed do you think I am?"

"It's not about how depressed you are," she said knowingly. "It's about how good you are at being depressed." She held out a bowl heaped with ice cream and poured sprinkles on top. "This is your medicine. Keep eating until you don't need it anymore."

"Yes ma'am," I said, grabbing a spoon.

As if she was trying to prove something about the fact

that being twins didn't mean you were anything alike, Emily, girl after my own heart, brought porn.

"What good is this going to do?" Anita demanded, grabbing the DVD out of Emily's hand. "*Janie's Got Big Guns?* She's giving up sex. This is like waving crack in front of a junkie."

"Nuh-uh," Emily said, shaking her head. "This is about weaning her off sex a little at a time. She can't just give it up cold turkey. Do you know how much sex this girl is used to getting?"

"Hey!" I protested, though nobody else chimed in. "Yeah, okay I've been a total whore," I finally agreed.

"I don't think 'whore' is a constructive word choice," Anita corrected me as she drowned a mountain of gummy bears in fudge. "I think we should go with 'misguided' or 'looking-for-love-in-all-the-wrong-places.'"

I'd never actually been looking for love in all those hot, sexy places, but I decided to let that one go.

"Oh, give me a break," Katie said, pointing at the TV as scenes of choreographed sex flickered across the screen. "Why does porn have to be so ridiculous? It's only giving teenage boys the wrong impression. Like, who exactly is enjoying this position?"

I took a seat on the arm of the couch next to her, a bag of chips in my hand. "Oh yeah, I've done that," I said. "It's only fun for the first ten seconds, then your arms gets pretty tired."

"What do you mean, Katie?" Em said with a smirk. "Are you saying Lucas isn't a wild beast in the sack as formerly reported?"

We all turned to look at Katie, who promptly turned beet red and hit her sister with a couch cushion. Ever since Katie had started dating King Hottie Lucas Matthews we'd all been dying to hear the details of their sex life, which Katie flatly refused to share beyond a few tantalizing hints.

"Can we take the subject of Lucas's prowess off the menu for tonight's entertainment, please?" Katie said. "Tonight is supposed to be about Sally."

"Well, you guys already know all the details of *my* sex life," I said. "So I don't know how entertaining it will be."

"Just tell us one thing," Melissa said to Katie. Grabbing the remote, she fast-forwarded the film. "Have you guys ever done…this?"

Anita giggled and we all turned, once again, to look at Katie, who rolled her eyes. "A lady doesn't kiss and tell," she said. "But since I'm not a lady I'll say that, yes, we did try that a few times, until we got bored of it and moved on to…" she fast-forwarded even further, "that."

"Wow," Melissa said, staring at the screen.

"Hot," Anita agreed, equally mesmerized.

"You're so irritating!" Em cried, throwing that same couch cushion back at her sister, who laughed as she caught it. "You shouldn't be able to have perfect love and perfect sex at the same time. It should be a rule."

"Did I say perfect?" Katie protested. "Lucas is totally not perfect. Sometimes when he makes me breakfast the eggs are undercooked—"

"He makes you *breakfast*?" Melissa moaned.

"And he has trouble getting to places on time. He's always about five minutes late—"

"Five minutes?" Emily said. "I've had guys not show up, like *at all*."

"And sometimes when he kisses me…" Katie trailed off, a shy smile spreading over her face, and it was clear to all of us there was absolutely nothing wrong with Lucas's kisses.

"Ugh, I hate you!" Emily said, grabbing her enormous bowl of ice cream and jamming a huge spoonful into her mouth. "Let's get to the part with the threesome, at least we can guarantee *that's* something Katie and Lucas have never done."

We all turned to stare at Katie one last time and she gave us a look. "You've seen Lucas," she said. "You think I'm going to share him with some other girl? That boy is mine."

The room roared with laughter, and though I couldn't quite join in—I hadn't yet reached the stage where I could pretend I wasn't dying inside—it did make me feel a little better just to be near their lighthearted happiness and to know they were here for me, their affection surrounding me, like a big, five-girl hug.

Hours later, when they'd all passed out in the living room, their nails half-painted and their lips glazed with chocolate, I slipped into my bedroom to grab a pair of socks. The mess of sticky glass and liquor had been mopped up by Anita—she wouldn't even let me help, the sweetheart—but the smell of it still lingered, unbearably strong, even though we'd cracked a window. I felt all the hair on my arms and legs stand on end at the scent, though I tried my best to ignore it. Liquor might have held me, like a lover, for years, but in the end he was like a cheating boyfriend, all those nights passed out in his arms had been nothing more than a lie.

No more, I thought to myself. *No more lying and no more hiding.*

Alcohol, I'm breaking up with you.

As I rooted around in sock drawer, my eyes landed on the chair by the window, covered with discarded clothes, and the grey men's sweater lying on the top. My cold feet forgotten, I pulled the sweater over my shoulders and inhaled that tantalizing scent—faint, but still there—of oranges. And that's when it finally happened, as I crawled onto my bed, the sweater draped over my body like a blanket. That's when the tears I'd been holding in all day finally started to fall. Hugging the sweater like the lover I'd lost, I sobbed into the night.

My weekend of girly wallowing was tons of fun—or, if not exactly fun, at least a welcome comfort—but all good things have to come to an end sometime. Come Monday morning, the girls had all returned to their lives of classes and studying and drop-dead-gorgeous boyfriends, and I had to face the reality of my pathetic life with only Anita by my side.

"Go to class," she encouraged me, sliding a plate of scrambled eggs (with a side of gummy bears) toward me. "The distraction will do you good. Not to mention your grade point average."

"You really think being bored to death is going to help my mood?" I said, picking at my breakfast. "If you really want to cheer me up you could offer to switch lives with me."

I'd always thought Anita's life was so dull, but, dull or not, there was something to say about having nothing to feel ashamed about, because you'd never had the chance to do anything shameful. It certainly seemed way better than being the trashy, used-up, former town whore.

"You know I would, hon," Anita said with a sympathetic twist of her mouth, "if I could."

Sad looks and concerned squeezes and whispered conversations about me just out of earshot; this was what my life looked like now. Anita was right, I had to get out, go to class, get a life. If only to pre-empt the irritation I felt building up inside me at all that concentrated sympathy. Other people's pity was only comforting for so long. Pretty soon I was going to start resenting my friends for being so thoughtful and concerned, which was the last thing I wanted to do.

"You're right," I said, jamming a corner of toast into my mouth. "It's time to get back on the horse." The worried look on Anita's face pushed me to clarify: "I mean the horse of schoolwork, of course."

"I totally knew that's what you meant," she said, as she cleared her plate.

Sure she did. I wondered how long it would be before people stopped assuming I was always talking about sex.

"Oh, you left this in the dryer," Anita said, hoisting a laundry basket full of my underwear onto the stool next to mine. Or, to be more accurate, a basket full of my thongs in various colours.

Yeah, I was guessing it would be a pretty long time.

My course load on Mondays was pretty light, just English in the morning and a Labour Economics seminar in the afternoon. I was looking forward to the seminar because I was planning on badgering Winston into letting me borrow more issues of *The Forever Place*—he hadn't expressly said he had issues six and seven, but I figured he had to know someone who did. I was willing to reach out to any and all comic book nerds on this one. If it came to it, I was even willing to let him just describe the plot to me so I could move on to the next issue the bookstore actually had in stock.

But before I could get to the seminar, I had to make it through British Lit, which had the triple stresses of being the one class I'd never actually attended since the semester had begun, the class for which I'd skipped a test the week before, and the only class I shared with Harrison Leo.

As Anita and I took the stairs up two flights to get to class, I was strongly considering just making a run for it, my eyes scanning my surroundings like I was on a swat team scoping the building for bombs. My escape routes were few and all had their own obstacles.

1. Turn on my heel and sprint back down the stairs.

Obstacle: Anita would surely grab my arm and stop me.

2. Pretend to be following Anita into the classroom, but back away and run down the hall instead.

Obstacle: There was no way Anita wasn't going to foresee this. She was already walking a step behind me in anticipation.

3. Take a seat in class, then got to the bathroom and never come back.

Obstacle: If I tried to leave class with all my things, Anita would definitely get suspicious. Also, being inside the classroom meant Harrison would see me leaving, and avoiding his seeing me, or me him, was the whole point of escape in the first place.

Basically, I was imprisoned in the building, and Anita was my jailer.

As we approached the classroom door, my steps began to slow of their own volition. I knew the moment I saw Harrison everything I'd just spent the weekend trying to forget would come flooding back, everything he'd said to me, both the good and the bad. I wasn't even sure which was worse. But more than that, I knew all the hateful things I thought about myself, and which I'd sort of been able to avoid during my weekend of girly bonding, would come flooding back too. Harrison's very being was all wrapped up in it now. As soon as I saw him it would be like a crowd of bitchy naysayers yelling obscenities in my face. During the short span of my infatuation with Harrison, those naysayers had been not exactly quiet, but at least sort of muted. Now there was nothing to stop them from screaming at the top of their lungs.

Despite all of this, there was still a part of me that badly wanted to see Harrison again, and hoped that as soon as he saw me he'd change his mind about everything and take me in his arms.

It was that hopeful part of me that made me want to kill myself the most.

Noticing my sudden inertia at the classroom door, Anita put her arm around my waist. "I'll be right next to you the whole time," she said supportively. "It's a big class. You don't even have to see him at all."

Except I wouldn't be able to help myself, I knew it. As soon as we walked in, that stupid, hopeful part of me would be searching the rows of seats for his face.

"You'll be okay," Anita said, and I wished I could believe her.

"God, I hate British Lit," I muttered as we walked into class.

We sat in a row close to the middle of the classroom and Anita kept up a steady stream of chit-chat to hold my attention, which, naturally, worked not at all. As luck would have it, there were a bunch of empty seats just three rows ahead of us, so when Harrison walked in and sat down—right next to that girl Alana, who I'd sort of liked right up until that moment—I had a perfect view of the back of his head, his short dark hair I longed to run my fingers through, the back of his neck just begging to be kissed, and those broad shoulders, those arms which had held me so tightly in bed.

Great.

Surprisingly, I didn't feel a sudden swell of self-hatred overcome me, as I'd thought I would. I definitely felt like total crap as I watched him lean over to Alana and write something in the corner of her notebook, and then saw her smack him on the shoulder as they both laughed. (And of course I immediately began to analyze that smack. Was it an affectionate, platonic, I-think-of-you-as-a-brother kind of smack? Or was it a flirty, my-isn't-your-bicep-large, sex-kitten-eyes kind of smack?) But mostly, I felt a sudden constriction of my heart, and a terrible spreading ache of longing to be near him, to have his beautiful eyes looking into mine again, to be the person he was teasing and laughing with, instead of the sad, jealous girl watching from afar.

When Anita grabbed my hand as the professor began his lecture—which basically meant she couldn't take notes all through class—I'd never been more grateful to anyone in my life.

A funny thing happened as class wore on. Desperate to distract myself from the minutiae of Harrison and Alana's interactions, I actually started paying attention. We were studying Virginia Woolfe's *To The Lighthouse*, which I'd read in grade nine, back when I'd been academically precocious, and I found it surprisingly soothing to lose myself in Mrs. Ramsay's motivations and the symbolism of the waves, sort of like flexing a muscle I didn't even know I had. For the first time in the longest time, thinking about schoolwork wasn't making me cramp up with nervousness. By the end of the hour and a half I'd let go of Anita's hand and filled two pages with notes, which was astonishing given the fact that I'd never taken a single note in class my entire university career.

As class came to an end, the professor reminding us to finish the book off with special emphasis on the last chapters—a subtle hint at a possible quiz next class, which I actually wrote down—Anita was drawn into a conversation with Frank about last week's test. My mind was still abuzz with literature as I packed up my things, and though I hadn't forgotten about Harrison's presence in the room, I'd certainly gotten my mind off him, which I was pretty proud about. I was feeling almost optimistic, almost glad I'd come to class in the first place, which was why it was such a punishing blow when I looked up and saw Alana put her arms around Harrison and kiss him.

Most of the students sitting between us had cleared out, so I had a clear view of Harrison's back as he leaned toward her. Watching them, my stomach plummeted so hard it was as though my guts were weighed down with an anvil. I actually gasped and tried to look away, but it was as though my head was being held in place as a film reel of my worst fears played on an enormous screen right in front of me. As Alana was standing directly in front of him, I couldn't see her completely, but I could make out her thick mane of curly hair and see her hands pressing into his back as they kissed and kissed and kissed. Literally the kiss went on for like a full two minutes. I know because I counted. I know because I stood there the whole time and watched.

Pull away, I silently begged him. *Pull away and show me that you didn't want to kiss her. Pull away and shake your head in disgust.*

But he didn't shake his head, or scold her, or push her away from him. None of those things seemed very Harrison anyway—although I'd also never thought Harrison would string me along when he was clearly into another girl, so what did I know? When she finally let him go he laughed and waved goodbye to her as she scampered toward the door, and said something about seeing her tomorrow. I'd had crippling hangovers in class before, but I never came so close to vomiting in a classroom as I did right then, watching Harrison give his half-smile (*my* half-smile) to Alana when she turned at the door and waved.

It finally occurred to me that maybe I should get the hell out of the class myself—especially since my whole body had started to shake like I was some junkie going through withdrawal—when Harrison turned and looked directly at me.

The cinematic feel to their kiss had momentarily made me feel as though I was invisible, like some anonymous moviegoer staring at a screen, so it was somewhat shocking to have Harrison staring back at me all of a sudden. His expression was typically unreadable, but there was something in his eyes that spoke of…what was it? Sorrow? Regret? Pity? I couldn't tell, though I was sure my own feeling of betrayal was written across my face, clear as day.

It seemed as though he wanted to say something, but I sure as hell wasn't sticking around to hear his excuses.

You're better than this, isn't that what he'd said to me? *You shouldn't have to take it*, weren't those his words?

He was the one who'd convinced me to expect more from guys, to expect more from him, and now it looked like he'd been full of shit from the beginning. And I wasn't about to take it lying down.

Just in case he wasn't clear on how much he'd hurt me, I held up the middle finger of both my hands before I turned and followed Anita out of the classroom and out of Harrison Leo's life for good.

13

"So, there are going to be hot guys at this thing, right?" Emily said as I threw the car into park and climbed out.

"Of course," I said, doing my best to sound convincing and not like the epic liar I was. "I promised you hot guys, didn't I? So, hot guys you will get."

It wasn't that there was guaranteed to be no hot guys at the party we were going to. It was possible there might be one or two, just as there might possibly be one or two hot guys at any gathering of twenty-something university students. Of course, the likelihood that any of them would be the type of hot guy Emily was used to—the buff, uber-charming, well-dressed, soon-to-be-sailing-a-yacht-in-some-foreign-sea-with-the-sun-shining-off-his-golden-hair type—well, that was nearly nil. Not that I mentioned this to her.

"Why are you dressed like that, then?" she asked, gesturing at my outfit.

As we stepped into the lobby of the building, I glanced at my reflection in the glass doors. Lately I'd taken to wearing some of Anita's tops because everything I owned was either skin-tight or had a plunging neckline, and I'd noticed that when I wore her clothes instead of mine people were generally nicer to me. It was strange, because it was the exact opposite reaction than I would have expected.

I'd always thought my relentlessly revealing outfits that made all the guys pant like dehydrated Labradors were my ticket to the kind of attention I wanted. But, as it turned out, the only attention I'd gotten had been from the lowest form of male, the handsy type who would invite me to ride him in a bathroom stall. When I wore different clothes, like the jeans, peasant top, and loosely tied scarf I had on under my coat now, I still got some attention—though definitely not as much—but it was of a surprisingly better calibre.

Guys smiled at me now, instead of staring. They started conversations, instead of extending inappropriate invitations for booty calls. And, most interesting of all, girls were talking to me much more too, as if my old clothes were some kind of repellent to them and now that I'd shrugged them off, they were free to approach me for the first time.

The clothes didn't change who I was inside, of course, but they did make it a little easier for me to stand myself.

"Whatever, I look awesome," I replied. I punched in the number I'd written on my hand and the buzzer sounded right away. "Besides, there's no point in giving it all away at first glance. It's better to make them work for it a little."

Emily blinked at me, then rushed to follow me across the hall to the bank of elevators. "Who are you and what have you done with Sally Jarvis?" she said, and I shrugged my shoulders and gave her a patented Sally smile.

As we stepped out of the elevator and walked down the hallway toward the apartment, I felt a few kernels of nervousness begin to pop inside me. When Winston had first invited me to his *Forever* release party—apparently the omnibus had gotten new cover art and this was a super big deal—I'd jumped at the chance to hang out with other people who loved the comic as much as I did. (My excitement had more than doubled when he'd assured me, in a timid mumble, that Harrison would definitely not be there). I'd also thought it would be the perfect opportunity to convince one of

Harrison's friends to give him back the comics he'd lent me—having them sitting in my room was only depressing me—and to get my hands on some later issues. Winston had already lent me issues six, seven, and eight, which ended on an excruciating cliffhanger. I needed to know what happened next, and I was willing to do anything to find out, even hang out with the good friends of the guy who'd pretty much eviscerated my heart.

Reading about Rainbow's adventures was basically the only thing that had gotten me through the last few days, stopping my mind from wandering to the disaster just behind me, and the humiliations waiting ahead. Without the next issue, I felt myself falling into an abyss of staggering depression, which simply would not do. Desperate times called for desperate measures, and some support, which was where Emily came in. Though I'd had to tell a few well-worded fibs to get her on board.

Like the fact that this was predicted to be the party of the year, full of hot guys and booze, and that if she didn't come with me she'd regret it for the rest of her life. You know, not exactly a major lie, just an obscene stretching of the truth until it resembled absolutely nothing like the truth.

I smiled shakily at my friend as we knocked on the door. "Just try to keep an open mind, okay?" I said brightly.

"An open mind?" she scoffed. "I don't plan on using my mind at all tonight."

"Well, that might be kind of a problem," I replied, just as the door opened and Mo and Winston greeted us with big smiles, both of them wearing the green felt hats of the Wittlings (the woodland people who help Rainbow on her journey).

"Welcome to the land of *Forever!*" Winston said, ushering us inside and handing us each a felt Wittling hat with dainty brown horns.

Mo helped a flabbergasted Emily off with her coat. "I made yours myself," he said shyly, gesturing toward the hat in her hands which she'd yet to really acknowledge.

"Super," Em replied, fixing a look of utmost irritation on

me.

Placing my own hat on my head with a wide smile, and subtly gesturing at Em with my chin to do the same—she did not comply—I said to Mo, "Em's new to *The Forever Place*. I real *Forever* virgin. So, you might have to give her some time to get used to all…this."

Just as I finished speaking, Johnny came through the door behind us wearing a black wig with bangs that mostly covered his eyes, a white shift that fell to his knees, and elbow-length, black, kid gloves with very long and pointy fingers.

"Did I hear something about a *Forever* virgin?" he said. "You know we don't allow their kind here."

He grinned encouragingly at Em, possibly to let her know he was only joking. She looked at him as though he'd sprouted a pig snout and was speaking solely in oinks.

"I told you we were all going to be Wittlings this time," Winston huffed at his friend. "No costumes, just *hats*!"

"Oh, come on, guys," Johnny protested. "How could I resist?"

"Yeah, I'm sure this look was a real challenge to put together," Mo said critically, referring to the fact that Johnny, who was Chinese, had opted to dress up as Kas, the only Asian character in *The Forever Place*.

"Hey," Johnny protested, trying unsuccessfully to shake the bangs out of his eyes, "these fingers were really hard to make!"

He pointed accusingly at Mo, knocking the Wittling hat right off his head with the overlong appendage. Mo then proceeded to yank the glove right off and chase Johnny down the hall with it.

Em and I ducked into the living room as Winston tried to mediate, saying, "Guys, *Forever* is a land in search of peace."

"Take me to the beer," Em said through gritted teeth, her hand gripping me at the elbow, and I hurried to oblige.

Maybe, I reasoned, *if I get her just tipsy enough she'll think she's at some kind of themed frat party or something.*

As we were walking to the kitchen, I took in the *Forever*

posters on the walls, the documentary about *Forever* creator Max Heinler playing on the TV, and the guy sitting in the corner wearing a Styrofoam ball covered in cotton balls on his head, this hat apparently meant to represent Lin-Lin, the giant cloud formation that guides Rainbow across the sea.

Or, maybe not.

"What kind of freaky, live-action, dungeons and dragons hell have you dragged me to?" Em demanded as I uncapped a bottle of beer from the fridge and handed it to her. "Is this punishment for that time I let you leave the house with a condom stuck to the back of your leg, because I promise you I didn't *see* it!"

"I just thought it might be nice to spend some time with some different people," I said evasively, grabbing a pile of comics from the counter and leafing through them, looking for issue number nine. "You know, people who share my interests."

"You have interests?" Em said in disbelief, which I tried not to take personally. "And those interests are woodland creatures and…what the hell is that supposed to be?"

She pointed at Mr. Lin-Lin, who waved back.

"Okay, so I didn't exactly realize there were going to be funny hats involved," I said, adjusting my horns. "But I'm a huge fan of *The Forever Place*! These people," I waved around the room a little uncertainly as a guy wearing a full set of deer antlers made of tree branches hit his head on the ceiling, "are my people!"

All right, that was a bit of an exaggeration, but I was trying to make a point.

Em narrowed her eyes at me, but I could already see her softening. "Is this about Harrison?" she said. "Did he get you reading his weird graphic novels and now you're clinging to—"

"Actually, for the sake of accuracy, I feel it's my duty to interject," said Roger, whose name I remembered only because he looked a lot like a Roger I'd slept with first year, except shorter and with patchier facial hair. "Graphic novels are generally a single volume, and the stories longer, spanning the length of what one would expect of a novel. *The Forever Place* is usually referred to as a comic book series, though your confusion is valid, since the term 'graphic novel' is bandied about with such enthusiasm these days."

Em blinked at him and his hat made of leaves for a few seconds, then snatched issue number one out of his hands and said, "Okay, Peter Pan. Give me the gist of the story, and I'm talking the sexy highlights, not the lineages of every family, or whatever. Is there a hot knight to drool over in this thing, or what?"

I smiled to myself as I saw the crowd of boys positioning themselves around my friend, all of them so eager to show off their *Forever* knowledge to a pretty girl, and Em batting her eyelashes and commanding them to get her a seat on the couch and snacks and a better hat because this one was making her hair all flat. She really did have the power to hypnotize men wherever she went, and for once that didn't make me feel competitive. For the first time in a long time I was looking on as other people did the winking, and the arm-touching, and all the other moves of flirtation that I knew so well, and I didn't have the slightest urge to jump into the fray.

I was happy just to sit back with my comic and read.

I was on issue eleven when I looked up from the armchair I was lounging in to see Emily climbing into Tree Antler Guy's lap.

"No keep it on," she said as Tree Antler Guy tried to take off his antlers. "I like it there. It's like I'm sitting in a tree house or something."

From the look on Tree Antler Guy's face, it seemed like he would be doing whatever the hell she said as long as she kept sitting in his lap, including letting her paint the tips of his antlers different colours with the nail polish she had in her purse, as she proceeded to do.

Clearly, my job of getting Em to accept the comic book posse was done.

When Winston sat down on the couch next to me I

decided maybe it was time to stop being anti-social and engage him in conversation. Sure, it was a comic book party, but nobody else had been actually reading the comic books as compulsively as I was. On the other side of the room they were playing a spirited game of charades by acting out scenes from issue two, and there seemed to be some kind of fantasy *Forever* film cast argument going on in the kitchen. I was beginning to look like a hermetic, badly-socialized bookworm, which in this crowd was really saying something.

"How'd you do on that test?" Winston asked, referring to the test in Labour Economics I'd happened to show up for, half-drunk, because I'd followed the guy I'd hooked up with the night before to campus. When I'd walked into class I'd actually thought it was the ladies room.

"Oh, you know, I got a seventy-something," I said evasively.

I hated talking about my marks, especially with a guy like Winston who did things like buy the textbook and sharpen his pencils and care about how he did on tests. Guys like Winston sometimes thought I was out of their league when they saw me at a club, but it quickly became obvious in conversations like this one that those tables could easily be turned.

He stared at me with unexpected intensity. "Seventy-what?" he persisted, adjusting his glasses.

"Like, seventy-seven, I think," I replied, then held up the comic in my hands, eager to change the subject. "But can we talk about Rainbow in issue eleven, please? Because I just don't get what she's thinking when she—"

"Mo!" Winston called to his friend across the room, his hands spread wide. "Sally got a seventy-seven on Paretti's test!"

I slumped down in my seat in horror and tried to hide behind my comic book. I'd thought Winston was my buddy, not the type of vile betrayer who would shout your miserable grade to the entire room. It just went to show you just never knew a guy, even when you were wearing the Wittling hat he'd made you.

Mo turned toward Winston and glared. Winston giggled

like a girl.

"Mo barely passed the class last year," Winston confided in a whisper. "I got a seventy-five, on that test. You should really be proud. Paretti almost never gives out a grade above an eighty. Yours might be the highest in the class."

"That's ridiculous," I said, unable to figure out what game he was playing with me, but knowing I was somehow being duped. "I didn't even study for that test. It must have been a fluke or something. I messed the test up so bad it came back around to good or something."

"Oh please," Em interjected without taking her eyes off the antler she was painting. "Sally got a good mark because she's smart. She just lacks confidence in her own abilities. She's going to be a lawyer."

"Why do you always say that?" I snapped. "I have no intention of becoming a lawyer. That's completely idiotic."

I scowled at her and she shrugged. I hated it when she bragged about me like this, which all my friends did, as if they were reciting from a shared script. Did they think it made me feel better to be insulated by a layer of girls shouting about my cleverness? Did they think that would make it true?

"I knew it," Winston said, nodding his head. "Harrison always goes for the clever girls."

Hearing his name was like a punch in the stomach, and I actually found myself suddenly short of breath, the rest of Winston's words completely lost to me. I felt like I'd been dunked into the ocean, like Rainbow when she gets thrown from the boat and meets the left-behinders, except I couldn't breathe in this underwater world like she could. I could only drown.

Since the subject had already been broached, I decided to take my opportunity and pulled the comics Harrison had lent me from my purse.

"If you could just give these back to him," I said, plunking them in Winston's lap without exactly looking him in the eye. "I'm sure he's been wanting them back."

Winston's face collapsed into a sad grimace as he looked

down at the pile. "I was really sad to hear that you guys didn't..." he trailed off, awkwardly. "I know he blames himself."

"Oh yeah?" I said angrily, flipping through the comic I was still holding with such aggression I almost ripped a page and everyone in the room (except Em) looked at me in horror.

What exactly did Harrison blame himself for? Implying I was a stinking drunk he couldn't stand to be around? Forgetting to tell me he was dating another girl? Tricking me into thinking I could have a better life, and then ripping it away?

Was that what he blamed himself for?

"Things have been really hard for him," Winston went on. "You know, with his brother and all. And that's no excuse, but sometimes he gets so caught up. It's hard for him to focus on anything else. I don't know how he handles it all."

I was so busy cursing Harrison in my mind—or wanting to curse him anyway—that it took a few minutes for me to register what Winston had said.

"His brother..." I said carefully, "the one who's..." I left the sentence open, hoping Winston would fill in the blank.

"Oh, he only has one brother," Winston said. "Jason's just gotten so much worse lately. Harrison's pretty sure he's onto the hard stuff now, you know," he lowered his voice to a whisper, "*heroin.*"

I nodded slowly, trying to put the pieces together. The homeless guy who'd tried to take me for a drink was Harrison's brother? His junkie brother? Was that who was calling him all the time? Was that who we'd sat outside that house waiting for?

You're just like him.

"Jesus," I muttered. No wonder he'd pushed me away. One junkie was enough to deal with.

"And since their parents have passed away," Winston said as I tried not to register my shock at this second revelation, "Harrison just feels responsible. We're always telling him Jason's not his responsibility. You can't help someone like that, someone who refuses to help themselves, someone who's determined to circle the drain no matter what you do. You'll use yourself up trying to help them. But Harrison, he's just that kind of guy. He can't stand by while someone he loves destroys himself. He has to help."

You refuse to take care of yourself. You think it's all a game.

It made a lot more sense now, why he'd been so interested in me. I'd been right about him from the beginning. He'd wanted to save me, to fix me, like he wanted to fix his brother, but in the end I'd been too much of a hassle. He had to focus on what really mattered. He had to focus on the one he thought he could save.

"It's really too bad," Winston said. "We were all so excited about you. I've never seen Harrison happy before. You really made him happy."

I'm bad for you, and you're bad for me.

"Yeah, right," I said under my breath, suddenly overcome with dejection.

I still didn't have the whole story. I didn't know why Harrison was keeping his real girlfriend a secret from his friends. But I knew enough to know that I didn't want to know any more. If Harrison had been a character in *The Forever Place*, he would have been called Harrison the Rescuer. Harrison the Orphan who scoured the land searching for his troubled brother. Harrison the Saviour.

How had I ever thought I was good enough for a guy like him?

I got to my feet and started gathering my things. I shot Emily pointed looks to give her the message I wanted to leave—a message she was ignoring—when there was a knock on the door and a part of me knew.

Alana came through the door first, her hair prettily done up in red ribbons just like Bedly, Rainbow's best friend. She beamed at the room in general as Harrison came through the door after her.

It was hard enough to see his face—his gorgeous eyes searing into mine, a look of surprise changing to something deeper as he stared—but seeing the two of them together was just too much.

What had possessed me to come here, to his friend's house, anyway? Was I some kind of masochist?

I struggled to manoeuvre my way out of the room, which had erupted in applause as soon as they'd walked in—mainly, I had to assume, because of the large, metal, deep-sea diving helmet Harrison was holding in his arms, and not because of the glory of their union as I darkly supposed.

I heard Emily calling my name, but I ignored it as I pulled open one door and then another, desperate to find what I was looking for, so desperate to obey the accusing voices in my head telling me I was stupid to come, stupid to hope, stupid to imagine I could belong anywhere.

Finally I found the bedroom with a window facing the back alley and I yanked it open, hoisting myself onto the ledge so I could climb onto the fire escape and be gone.

I tried to tell you. I can't do this with you. You're bad for me. You're just like him.

Why was it so hard for me to learn this lesson? Why did I have to have it beaten into me again and again?

I wasn't good enough for Harrison. I wasn't good enough for any of these people. No matter what I wore, or what books I read, or what mark I got on a test, I would always be trash with a dirty past I couldn't ever shake.

It wasn't anything to cry over, or to run from, or to drink away. It was just the hard truth.

And it was about time I started facing up to it.

I walked back to my apartment because I'd left my purse and car keys at Winston's and I wasn't about to go back in and get them. Besides, Emily needed the car to drive herself home once she sobered up.

Anita sleepily answered the door when I rang the bell and told me a package had come for me, and she'd left it on my bed.

"A secret admirer?" she said, yawning, and I didn't contradict her. Let her have her little fantasies.

It was a large white box, and there was no note, but I didn't hesitate to open it. I knew who it was from.

Inside was a midnight blue cocktail dress in my exact size, the straps giving the impression, in the moonlight, of iron-blue shackles.

Billy's message was obvious, and it echoed clearly in my head, since I'd come to the same conclusion earlier.

Here's a costume that fits, Sally. Here's a task you can handle.

Here's your destiny, waiting for you, on the bed.

Here's reality.

It didn't even phase me now.

There was a note, pinned to the dress itself, and I brought it over to the window so I could read it.

See you in two weeks, it read. *Love, Billy*.

14

"Would it be totally lame if I said I was proud of you?" Anita said as she zipped up her coat and handed me my coffee in one of the matching travels mugs she'd gotten us both.

"Yes," I said, rolling my eyes. We stepped out of the apartment and I locked the door behind us.

It had been over a week since I'd given up drinking. A week of going to class and taking notes and hitting the books at night. A week of being the roommate Anita had always hoped I would be; picking up groceries, and remembering to hang up my towel, and changing the light bulb in the hall when it went out instead of sitting in the dark waiting for her to come home and do it. A week of being the Sally everyone wanted to see, the Sally who wasn't falling apart or tearing herself apart. The Sally who sort of, mostly, kind of had it together.

Or at least made everyone believe she did.

As we walked toward campus, the first flakes of an early flurry swirling around us, I had to admit that I was a little proud too. Sure, my togetherness was mostly an act. I still craved booze every time I neared a bar—or stepped near that stain on the hardwood in my room that still smelled of

Whiskey laced with Tequila. Whenever I thought of Harrison, my heart still seemed to shrivel inside of me, actually withdrawing from the rest of my organs as if it thought, having messed it up with him, I didn't deserve a living, beating heart. I still had the urge to smother myself in some sweaty, writhing, male body, to melt into passion that would kill all my hurt, for a few minutes at least. It was hard not to pick up the phone and call one of the dozens of numbers I knew would reach a more than willing partner. The phone itself had started to look like a kind of life raft I was letting float further and further away as I drowned.

I wanted to throw myself into my old ways. I yearned to with the ferocious cravings of an addict.

But I didn't.

And that's why I was proud.

Because I didn't.

Instead, I fell back on the one habit I'd let myself keep, and I pretended everything was fine. I stayed home with Anita and watched the new Channing Tatum movie instead of going clubbing. I got into discussions with Winston about *The Forever Place* before class instead of skipping class altogether. I smiled, and flirted, and charmed my new nerdy group of friends, and pretended I was worthy of their attention. I pretended I wasn't depressed and devastated and bleeding internally from a heartbreak that never seemed to heal. I pretended I was a different girl, and everyone around me (even Anita) bought it hook, line, and sinker. I was glad they did because I knew it was my last chance.

An acceptance of my fate had settled in my gut since the party, and solidified as Billy's messages began to come daily, reminding me of what was coming, reminding me of the end. When the day came it would be all over for this Sally. Clean, cheerful, straight Sally. Studious Sally. Acceptable Sally. When he came for me I would be my old self again, Slutty Sally down in the dirt, and I knew in a way that was uncontradictable that I would never be able to find my way back to this pinnacle of myself I'd fabricated.

Even if I didn't have Harrison, this Sally was still pretty good. I was proud of what I'd been able to scrape together, proud of my creation. I would be sad to see her go. I'd liked being her, if only for a week.

She would have made my Mom proud.

After my Consumer Culture course, I sat on a bench on Union street, watching the other students milling around. I might have looked a little crazy, sitting outside in the snow, but truthfully this was my favourite time of day. Campus was crowded because it was between course hours, and I could look around at the other kids chatting and gossiping and moving off in groups of two and three to get lunch or coffee. I couldn't think of Harrison directly—the last thing I wanted to do was start crying in the middle of a crowd—but if I moved my head just right and squinted I could sometimes trick myself into thinking I'd caught a glimpse of him, just his backpack maybe, or his black coat. And for one sweet moment I would feel that thrill of recognition. For one moment I could just be a girl spotting a boy she liked in a crowd and smiling to herself, happy with the secret that she'd seen *him*. That *he* was near.

And then I did see him.

Actually, what I saw first was a small commotion over by the stairs to Goodwin Hall as someone pushed their way through a crowd of students bunched around the doorway, and then threw themselves down the stairs with such force they almost fell.

A girl yelled after him to "relax buddy," though he seemed not to hear, or to notice the snow driving into his face, or the girl he was striding toward, namely me, though I couldn't take my eyes off him.

It was Harrison all right, but looking more harried and wound up than I'd ever seen him. His frame heaved with every breath he took, his entire being giving the impression of a runaway train, hard as steel and just as out of control, about to jump the tracks.

I knew I should let him pass. I knew I shouldn't get involved. But something was wrong, I could see it in his eyes, and seeing him like that was the worst pain I'd ever felt, far worse than losing him to begin with. Watching him hurt was like being dipped in acid. I couldn't just stand by. I had to do something.

"Harrison," I said, lurching to my feet just as he reached me.

He stopped short, practically reeling, staring at me for a moment without really seeing me, his eyes unfocused until they landed on my face.

"Sally?" he said confusedly.

Reaching out, he brushed some snowflakes from the shoulder of my coat, and then just left his hand there, gripping my shoulder, before letting it slide down my back. Then he drew me toward him with a single sweep of his arm and before I knew it I was right up against him, his eyes boring into mine, our lips just inches apart, and every sense in my body screaming yes, yes, yes, as if we'd fast-forwarded to a much hotter, much slicker moment.

I would have let us get there, too. I would have let him take me right there on the pavement if the arm that held me wasn't hard and stiff, and his lips weren't shaking with some barely contained agony I couldn't understand.

I recognized desperate desire when I saw it. Of course I did. I was the goddamn queen of it.

I took his face in my hands as he moved in to kiss me, his lower lip just grazing mine with a tantalizing electricity before I moved my thumb between his mouth and mine.

"What's wrong?" I whispered against his cheek. "Tell me what it is."

Harrison stepped back with a perplexed expression on his face, then suddenly collapsed onto the bench beside us. I sat down next to him, unable to remove my eyes from his face. Squeezing his eyes shut, he mashed the heels of his palms into them, then rubbed at the back of his head, and it was all I could do not to kiss those eyes and those hands and that hair. Anything to make this better. Anything at all.

"It's Jason," he said finally, staring out at the street in

front of us. "I can't find him."

"Your brother?" I said. As he looked over at me with surprise I realized I wasn't actually supposed to know that Ponytail Guy was his brother, since Winston was the one who'd shared that information. "What happened exactly?"

Taking his phone out of his pocket, he shook it as he talked, as if he thought Jason might shake right out of it like a bookmark out of a book.

"He calls me every day at the same time, or if he doesn't call, he comes. He always wants money. And of course I usually say no. I know what he wants it for. Sometimes he calls to warn me that he's about to shoot up, like he wants me to talk him out of it, though I never can. But whatever the reason, he always calls, every day, without fail. That's why I pay for the stupid phone to begin with. Because if he's still calling me at least I can be sure that he's still…"

"Still alive," I finished and he nodded, then started kneading his legs with his hands. The phone slipped from his grasp and I took it and held it. It was burning hot, as if he'd been calling and calling the same number. "How long has it been?" I asked, watching his beautiful, tortured face.

"Two days," Harrison said, shaking his head. "It's too long. Way too long. He always calls me. Something is wrong." A vein bulged in his neck as he swallowed.

"Okay, then let's find him," I said, all efficiency and order all of a sudden, channelling Anita as best I could.

Clicking through to his contacts, I scanned the list which included names like Weird Hair Girl and Freaky Guy and Peter Pills.

"Are these Jason's friends?" I asked, waving the phone in front of Harrison's face until he nodded.

"But I've called everyone twice," he said. "Nobody's seen him."

Clicking on Weird Hair Girl's number and listening to it ring, I said, "If I know junkies and whinos, and I think I do, they have only one answer when someone comes around asking where this guy's at, or whatever happened to that girl, and the answer is, 'I don't know'. They say it automatically. They're all paranoid and expecting the cops to bust down their door any second."

The phone rang and rang without an answer—I could just picture the girl, her hair dyed an unflattering shade of green, her eyes dilated and staring at the wall as the phone rang on and on—so I hung up and moved on to Freaky Guy.

"Lucky for you," I said, "I speak several dialects of drunk, drugged, and high. Let Sally take care of it."

Freaky Guy didn't have any pot to spare because his cupboard was bare—it stuck in my mind because he told me so five times in our five minute conversation, that's how devastated he was about it—but he said he'd seen that bastard Jase the night before, and yeah, maybe he was the one who'd made off with it all.

"Maybe he's at Lillian's. They're always smoking up together without inviting me," he complained.

"I don't know any Lillian," Harrison said, sitting up straighter and watching avidly as I dialled the next number.

I asked for Lillian first, and then Peter, who was talking so fast I knew he was on Coke: "Sure I've got Lillian's number. I keep it here on the inside of my cabinet door because I'm always losing my address book though I should really just memorize it all and keep it in the ultimate vault because our brains are like safes in themselves and no Jason isn't here but I'm always telling him to stop growing that beard and give it all to charity because we're all too heavy with the weight of our souls and all that hair is just another weight around our necks but not the kind that tightens like a noose the kind that just drags us down onto the floor and the tiles catch us and keep us there forever and what was your question?"

Lillian, it turned out, was actually Weird Hair Girl who finally did pick up after about thirty rings. With slow-motion calmness she gave me two more numbers, one for a Bud and another for a Frederico. It was Freddy in the end who made me hand the phone back to Harrison with a triumphant grin and say, "Got him."

Harrison grasped the tiny phone with both hands so hard I thought he might break it and stared at me with such intense focus I could almost imagine it was me he wanted and not the words that were about to come out of my mouth. Why else would he be looking with such mouth-watering eagerness at my lips?

"My best friend Freddy informs me that Jay-Jay is sleeping it off on his couch. It seems he went a little too hard last night and he's been really out of it all day, but he's still 'moving around and all.' Which I guess is how these idiots detect whether their friends are still alive."

My God, was I like these people when I was drunk? Had I ever reached that level of pathetic?

I wanted to say no, but I couldn't.

Speechless, Harrison was still staring, and I realized I hadn't told him the best part. "It's three blocks away," I said, pointing East. "Apartment 4G."

Slumping toward me, Harrison pressed his forehead into my shoulder and, I couldn't help it, I put my arms around him and sucked in that scent of oranges because every girl, even one who's pretending, needs a hit of her drug now and then.

I felt the heat of Harrison's breath against my neck and I flushed. "Thank you," he sighed. "Thank you so much."

His hands found my waist and squeezed and it felt so good I had to wiggle away before I literally moaned in his arms and humiliated myself. The last thing I needed was to confuse gratitude with love.

I got to my feet and it took a moment for Harrison to follow, though when he did he took my hand firmly in his in such a way that would broach no argument.

"Lead the way, Detective," he said.

Jason was, indeed, perfectly alive and sleeping off his high when we found him on Freddy's couch in the most bizarre apartment I'd ever seen, every room devoid of furniture, except for the full dining set in the kitchen—which looked brand new—and the disgusting, rotting, corduroy couch under Jason himself.

It took Harrison quite a while to rouse Jason, who seemed in no mood to get up. When the two of them got into a small argument about it, I had to stall Freddy who, though clearly an idiot and a junkie so far gone he was actually missing teeth, had some very strong ideas about his friends being allowed to sleep off their bad highs in a natural environment of serenity and comfort, like his roach-infested living room was some kind of holistic spa.

In the end, I managed to convince him that brothers like Harrison and Jason had their own code, and they had to work it out between them, in that natural way of brothers, because family took care of family. I went on spouting nonsense like that for a while, walking him deliberately, but subtly, into the next room, and he watched me like he was hypnotized. By the end of my speech he seemed convinced I was on his side, and happily divulged exactly how much drugs were left in the apartment (none), and how much money he and Jason had (none), and what he planned on doing for the rest of the night (confused stoner look that heavily implied, nothing).

Since Jason's apartment wasn't much cleaner or safer than this one, and it didn't seem like he and Freddy could manage to get themselves any higher with no money and dead phones— Freddy had let me check his—we ended up leaving him there with a note pinned to his jacket that he should call Harrison tomorrow, or else! I made it extra threatening by writing it in red lipstick that looked just a little like blood.

Out on the street again, a murky sunlight greeted us, and I saw that this morning's snow had already melted. I assumed Harrison would be on his way home in a jiffy, since the crisis was over and I knew how he felt about being around me, but to my surprise he took my hand with that same firm grip and didn't seem in any way inclined to let it go. I expected him to be delirious with relief, given how upset he'd been earlier, but he still seemed pretty unfocused and said little as I led him up the street toward his apartment.

"Where are we going?" he asked finally, after about ten minutes of silent walking, which was less awkward than you might think. Walking quietly hand in hand with Harrison in the sunshine was actually pretty great—though I sort of wanted to stab myself for thinking so. We'd just passed my apartment. His was another ten minute walk away.

"I figured you'd want to go home," I said, pointing ahead.

Slowing his pace, Harrison shook his head at me. "I don't live with Alex and those guys anymore," he said. "I moved out."

"Oh?" I said. I'd forgotten how long it had been since we'd spoken. A lot could happen in a week. Apparently a guy could leave one apartment and get another in a week. "What for? I thought you said you didn't even pay rent half the time."

He got a funny look on his face. "You think I'd keep living with Alex after what he did to you?" he said. "I wanted to rip his head off every time I saw him." He flexed his hand in mine. "I had to go."

I felt a stirring in my stomach at the idea that Harrison had still been looking out for me, even after he'd said I was no good, but it was hard to get too excited about it when I knew the truth.

He has a girlfriend. Remember Alana? Remember that kiss?

Harrison's eye caught on a guy walking on the other side of the street wearing a hemp poncho and army shorts—shorts! In this weather!—with a duffel bag on his back. I recognized him as one of the guys who hung around outside the shelter on Brock street. Watching Harrison, I noticed the dark circles under his eyes and the fact that he wasn't wearing a scarf or a hat. He looked practically as strung out as Freddy, except without the drugs. He looked about ready to pass out.

"Why don't you come to my place for a few minutes, just to warm up?" I suggested, and Harrison, his eyes still on the homeless man making his slow way up the street, agreed unconsciously and let me tug him inside.

I sat him down on the couch and did my best to make him some strong tea, though tea wasn't exactly my specialty, my warming beverage of choice having been brandy for as long as I could remember. As I pulled the teabags out of the cupboard I wished Anita was home so she could do this for me since she was a big fan of tea, but she was working all afternoon.

"Well, at least it's hot," I said apologetically as I thrust the mug into Harrison's hands. He thanked me and took a sip and then another, and if it tasted like warm socks he didn't let on.

I sat down gingerly on the other end of the couch, facing him. It was strange having him at my place again. It was bringing back all kinds of memories I was supposed to be trying to forget.

Putting the mug down on the coffee table, Harrison looked over at me. "Who told you Jason was my brother?" he asked.

"Winston might have mentioned something," I admitted, hoping I wasn't getting Winston into trouble. "He just wanted to—"

"No, it's okay," Harrison assured me. "I'm glad you already knew. You really saved me today, Sally. I doubt I would have found him without your help. I don't even know how to thank you."

His eyes drifted to the couch cushions and I began to feel uncomfortable. It was obvious he didn't want me to make more of this than it was. He didn't want to thank me and make me think it made everything better. Luckily, I was on the same page.

"Like I said, junkies and drunks are my people," I reassured him. "I'm like their supreme leader. They basically do whatever I say, follow me around like I'm a prophet. You can always count on me to track them down. I've practically got junkie GPS built into my system—"

I would have gone on babbling about my powers of junkie persuasion if he hadn't interrupted me with a vehement, "Sally don't!" and cast a look at me that was more troubled than the one he'd had on his face when we'd been searching for his brother.

I stared at him.

"Don't say things like that about yourself. They aren't

true. None of that is true. You're nothing like them."

I frowned at him. "You said it yourself, and you were exactly right," I said. "I'm no better than them. I'm no good for you. It's really fine."

I got to my feet because having this conversation with him, again, was just too much for me. I didn't want to have to convince him that I was trash just because he'd lost sight of the truth for a few minutes. I didn't think much of myself, but I was at least determined to spare myself that humiliation.

"Sally, stop," Harrison said.

I felt his hand on my arm, and seconds later found myself pivoted around so I was facing him again. His expression was grave and so full of remorse I felt it would be cruel to pull away. So I didn't.

As though pulling out of Harrison's grasp was something I was capable of, anyway.

His voice thick with emotion, Harrison said, "I've felt so guilty about the things I said to you. I need you to know that none of them were true. You're nothing like Jason. You're so much better than him." He peered into my face, trying to catch my eye, but I wouldn't look at him. "I know you must be furious with me for what I said, and I have no excuse. I was just angry with my brother and I took it out on you. It was a deplorable thing to do, and it ended up pushing you away, which was the last thing I wanted."

"It seemed like you wanted it that day," I said, finally looking back at him. "You were pretty sure I wasn't good enough for you. And you were right. Just because you're having a change of heart now…"

I tried half-heartedly to pull away from him, but he only gathered me closer.

"You are absolutely nothing like my brother," Harrison said, pronouncing each word precisely as if that might cement them in my mind. "Do you think Jason would call a half-dozen strangers and chat them up just to help a friend out? Do you think he'd give up his afternoon to scavenge the city with me, or make up a random story to distract a junkie name Frederico, or drop-kick his way out of trouble, for that matter? Jason is both completely self-centered and completely unable to help himself. He puts that burden entirely on the people around him. You are way too awesome and badass to even be mentioned in the same breath as my brother, and I'm sorry I ever did."

I stared at him, uncomprehending and a little resentful. "Harrison," I said hopelessly, "what are you trying to do to me?"

I didn't want to hear this. I didn't want to hope. I'd come to terms with the truth about myself, with what I was and what I would always be. I'd closed the book on me and Harrison and here he was trying to write a new chapter.

Holding me even closer, so my chest pressed against his and our legs intertwined, Harrison gazed at me, his eyes locked on mine.

"I'm trying to tell you the truth," he said. "The only reason I've stayed away is because I was so ashamed of what I said to you. And I'm the only one who deserves to feel ashamed. Do you hear me?"

I tried to turn my head away because it was just too much. Having his eyes one me was just too much. I wanted to dive into their depths. I so wanted everything he said to be true, but...

He took my chin in his palm and gently turned my face back to his. "Do you hear me?" he repeated, his eyes searching mine.

"I'm not the girl for you, Harrison," I said, trying to make my voice confident and strong when really I wanted to quiver with barely contained emotion. "Even if I'm not as bad as your bother, I'm still pretty damn messed up. You might think you want me, but you're wrong."

I wanted to back away, to punctuate my statement with the physical cues it required, but instead I found myself leaning toward him just slightly, and I saw his eyes dip to my lips.

"I beg to differ," he whispered, and then his mouth was on mine.

Harrison Leo kissed like no guy I'd ever kissed before. He kissed with his whole body. Within seconds of our lips touching I was surrendering to his kiss, opening my mouth and letting his tongue find mine and revelling in the heat our bodies were creating as he bent me gently backward, one hand on my lower back and the other positioned squarely on my ass. He literally kissed me dizzy. I might have lost my balance if he hadn't lifted me up, hoisting me onto the back of the couch as he pressed his mouth to my neck, making me sigh involuntarily, the feeling of his tongue against my skin sending thrills all through my body from the tip of my head to my toes. I locked my legs around his, pulling him closer, and he cupped the back of my head with one hand as he ran the other down my thigh.

"Show me where I can touch," he breathed into my ear, making me shiver. "Show me what you want."

Pushing myself back up into a standing position, I boldly took both his hands and placed them on my breasts, exactly over the place where my nipples were straining against my top and bra, and when he rubbed his thumbs gently over those sensitive nubs I arched into him and crushed his lips with mine.

He slipped his tongue back into my mouth, tasting me, and without breaking the kiss I placed his hands on the back pockets of my jeans and quickly unbuttoned my shirt and whipped it off, silently thanking the fashion Gods that by some miracle I had on my sexiest, semi-see-through, black bra. Then I leaned forward and cupped the bulge in his jeans, searching deftly with my fingers for the zipper, until I felt him pull my hand away.

"Wait," he said breathlessly and I smiled at his bashfulness.

"No, I want to," I said, reaching forward again, but instead of letting me touch him, he walked me a few steps backward and sat me down on the back of the couch again.

His hands were on my upper arms. Suddenly I felt like I was being put in a time out, and the reality of what was happening sent a chill down my back.

He didn't want me to touch him.

He was changing his mind. *Again.*

"Okay," I said shakily, trying but failing to smile.

I kind of wished I hadn't thrown my shirt over my shoulder now. It was even more embarrassing to have peeking nipples at this moment.

Flinching out of his hands, I crossed my arms over my chest. "Well, that was fun, anyway. You can just go now."

But he didn't go.

With a heavy sigh, Harrison put his arms around me, trapping me in his embrace, surrounding me with his scent. It was impossible to keep my arms crossed in that position, so I looped them loosely around him, unsure of what was happening now. This road we were on had so many twists and turns I basically had no idea where we were anymore. We could have been halfway to China for all I knew.

Pulling away just slightly, he cupped my cheeks with both hands.

"You think, now that I've got you back, I'm ever going to let you go?" he said. "I'm not going anywhere."

"What are you talking about?" I said, a little angrily, squirming out of his hands. "You clearly don't want me right now, so..."

"Sally," he said patiently, brushing my cheek with his knuckles, "just because I don't want to rush into bed with you doesn't mean I don't want you at all. I think you just felt how much I want you."

I felt my body flush at this suggestion, or maybe it was the way his hand was skimming along the skin of my back.

"There's no reason to rush things," he said, placing a kiss on one side of my mouth and then the other with such gentleness I almost believed him. "I believe in saving my dessert for last, not eating it first."

Trying not to be distracted by his use of the word "eating," I said the first thing that came to my mind.

"Is this because of Alana?"

His hand stilled on my back and he pulled back slowly, giving me a puzzled look. "Alana?" he said. "What? My friend Alana from study group?"

I'd forgotten that she'd been the one to bring him to that study group. The signs had been everywhere.

"I know you're together. I saw you kissing in class, remember?"

The look on Harrison's face was positively baffled. "Alana is Mo's girlfriend," he said, and my gaze, which I'd averted, snapped back to his face. "I don't have any memory of kissing her anywhere for any reason...Although she did hug me in class a few weeks ago...and then you gave me the finger, as I recall." He gave me a pointed look.

"It wasn't a hug," I insisted, though now that I thought about it I realized I hadn't actually seen their faces touch. Harrison's back had been toward me, and I'd seen him lean in, and her arms go around him. "Or if it was, it went on forever."

"She was really grateful," Harrison said, pulling a stray hair out of the side of my mouth. "A kid I tutor at the high school has a father who's a metal worker and I'd just found out he was willing to make the deep-sea diving helmet, you know from *Forever*. It was a gift for Mo."

The two of them arriving together at the party, Harrison carrying the helmet, made a lot more sense now. Though my climbing out the window in horror made less.

"Plus," Harrison went on, "she's one of those over-huggers. Every hug from her goes on for like five full minutes. You just have to wait them out."

The dual embarrassment of having wrongly accused him of going out with Alana, and misunderstanding why he'd pulled away, combined with my intense relief that he wasn't cheating on his girlfriend at this moment, that what was happening between us might actually be real, left me feeling altogether discombobulated.

"I guess I was confused," I admitted lamely, dipping my head.

Harrison replied by leaning in and kissing me on the

cheek, and the jaw, and the neck. My head fell back as my body warmed with amazing speed, and I gripped his torso.

"I thought we were putting this on hold," I said. Not that I was complaining. The work he was doing with his tongue was making my toes curl with pleasure.

"No," Harrison murmured. "I said I didn't want to rush. But there are still plenty of things we can do very, very slowly."

I felt his fingers on the clasp of my bra and looked up at him through my haze of desire.

"May I?" he said, one eyebrow cocked and the beginnings of a grin on his lips.

"Yes," I breathed into his ear, running my fingers through his hair. I felt the clasp open and my bra fall away. "Oh *yes.*"

15

A couple of hours later I was napping on the couch when Anita shook me awake.

Or, to be more precise, I was napping on the couch in Harrison's arms when my eyes snapped open to see Anita's legs in front of me, and when I looked up she nodded in approval and mouthed the word "Hawt!"

Did I mention both Harrison and I were topless?

Wiggling carefully out of Harrison's arms so as not to wake him, I grabbed a shirt and followed Anita into her bedroom, feeling more than a little embarrassed. I'd made out with guys enthusiastically in full view of my friends before without batting an eye, but things with Harrison were different, private. I felt as though Anita had just caught me baring my soul.

There was also the matter of my very recent week of heartbreak over him. As Anita closed the door I assumed I was in for a lecture, but she surprised me.

"So, what have you been up to?" she asked with a massive grin on her face.

"You know, chores, studying, same old, same old," I replied, shrugging my shoulders. We both giggled and then shushed each other, eyeing the door.

"I thought things were over between you two," she said. "This isn't just the death rattle, is it? I mean, are you getting back together?" She pressed her hands together, readying to clap.

"Well, we were never really together in the first place," I said shyly, pulling at the sleeves of his shirt, which I was wearing, again.

"Whatever," Anita said dismissively. "It's been obvious to everyone but you from the beginning that he's totally into you. And don't even try to tell me you're not obsessed with him too." She held up her hand as I began to protest. "No, don't even bother. You're not wearing a bra. That says it all."

I shut my mouth, chastened. I guessed it wasn't so bad if Anita knew I had real feelings for Harrison, since for some reason she didn't seem to think, as I did, that he was too good for me. Still floating on my cloud of happiness laced with desire, I was about to tell her more, starting with what a monumental kisser he was, when she said something that stopped me short and brought reality rushing back, my cloud drifting away without me.

"Oh, a guy named Billy stopped by earlier. I forgot to tell you," she said.

She stepped behind the divider that walled off her closet as I nearly gagged on this news. Billy had been here? In my apartment? With Anita?

Immediately my hands began to shake and I had to take a seat on the bed, painfully aware of Harrison sleeping in the other room. Harrison who I'd naively convinced myself I could have, as if his imaginary girlfriend had been the only impediment. There were plenty of other reasons why I would never be able to keep him, beginning with Billy and what would be happening two days from now. And if Billy had been in this apartment—he'd never come that close before—he was definitely trying to send a message, which I was getting loud and clear.

You are mine, Sally. You do as I say. And don't you forget it.

"You got the note he left on your dresser, right?" Anita said as she appeared around the divider, having changed out of her work t-shirt, combing her hair. "He said he knew you from home? An old friend?"

Her eyes were on herself in the mirror, so she didn't catch the way I cringed in distaste at my sweet friend describing the conversation she'd had with my torturer.

"Yeah, I've known Billy forever," I replied with a dry mouth. "I'm sure I've mentioned him before."

Except not really because I never talk about him voluntarily, ever.

"Cute!" Anita said. "Is he former A material? I mean, not that we want to talk about the past now that you've clearly moved on to better and hotter things."

She was trying to be all sly with the sexual innuendos, but I really just wished she would stop. Like right now.

"No, no," I said, taking the comb out of her hands and turning her toward the mirror so I could brush her hair myself, if only to have something to do with my hands. "Billy was…never that kind of friend. And Harrison and I didn't…He wants to wait."

The words sounded so strange coming out of my mouth that even I felt confused after I'd said them. I hoped Anita wouldn't laugh at me.

She caught my eye in the mirror and raised an eyebrow, the most understated reaction to my pronouncement that I could have hoped for. I knew it had to be taking a lot out of her.

Pursing her lips, she said, "I'm liking that boy more and more by the minute."

Handing the comb back to her, I told her I'd better get back before he woke up, and she nodded cheerfully.

"Sally," she whispered before I made it out the door. "Are you happy?"

It was a heartbreaking question, and not only because she seemed so happy for me, but because I was happy, or had been ever so briefly this afternoon, and I knew my happiness wouldn't last.

"As a clam," I said with wink, and closed the door behind me.

With silent steps I skirted the couch and ran to the dresser in my room, snatching up the note which said about what I'd expected, except much more succinctly: *Two Days*. I crumpled the piece of paper in my palm, trying to crumple the feeling of despair in my heart at the same time. But despair is strong. It doesn't crumple as easily as paper. It can survive anything.

Rousing Harrison turned out to be harder than I imagined it would be, but I finally managed it—it took some kissing in ticklish places—and convinced him to move into my room because Anita had come home. His body was sleepily warm as I led him to the bed. When he pulled me into his arms, feathering kisses across my cheeks and lips, I couldn't help but feel that he was living in a wonderful world from which I'd been ousted. I didn't know how I was going to break it to him that I was just a visitor here. I wouldn't be staying the night.

"I thought we already went over the shirt issue," he said, undoing the two buttons I'd done up and slipping the cotton off my shoulders, his lips quickly following.

I tried to lose myself in the sensation of his mouth on the skin of my neck, my chest, but that note was like a terrible clock ticking down the seconds, the timer suspended over Harrison's head whenever I looked at him. For once I didn't want to abandon myself to lust. These moments with Harrison were too important. I wanted to know him. I wanted to know everything, before it was too late.

I pressed a kiss to his cheek, and then gently pushed him back until his head was on the pillow. I placed my head on his chest, winding my arms around him. He sighed contentedly and ran his fingers through my hair, which might seem like a small thing, but it meant so much to me. I wasn't used to being embraced, held, caressed. It was still a surprise to be touched by a guy without feeling I had to surrender a part of myself in return.

Outside my window, leaves flew wildly on their way down to the ground. I watched them fall to the sound of Harrison's heart beating in my ear.

"Tell me about Jason," I said. "What happened to him?"

Harrison sighed. He was quiet for so long I wondered if I'd made a mistake in asking, pushed too far. I could feel the muscles tensing in his arms just at the mention of his brother. Maybe he wouldn't want to share this part of his life with me. Maybe it was just too painful.

Then, his hand still brushing my hair, he started to speak: "He wasn't always like this. When we were kids he was fantastic, a perfect big brother. He taught me how to play soccer—although I was never very good—how to sneak out of the house, how to tease girls. He was always a little wild, getting into trouble at school, but so charming he could almost always talk his way out of any punishment. He tried to teach that to me too, but I was never as good as him. I wanted to be him when I was little. I idolized him."

I squeezed my eyes shut, trying to hold back thoughts of my own childhood. This wasn't about me.

"He was already drinking too much by the time our parents died," Harrison went on. "I was fifteen, he was seventeen. It was a car accident, just a fluke thing. An old lady who didn't see the light turn red, ice on the road, a telephone pole. Jason was passed out drunk when we got the call. I had to call the cab that took us to the hospital to…identify the bodies."

"My God."

I moved my head up to the pillow and Harrison turned on his side so we were face to face. It seemed right. I didn't want him just to tell this story. I wanted him to tell it to me.

I smoothed my palm over his cheek and imagined the teenage boy he'd been, walking into that hospital, approaching the door that would seal his fate.

"We had no close family. My mother was an only child, and my father's sister died of cancer in her twenties. We convinced them to let us stay together in the house—Jason was nearly eighteen after all—but Jay had to take over the mortgage, which meant he had to drop out of school and get a job right away.

"He was drinking pretty heavily at that point, drowning his grief in booze, and after he lost one job and then another and then stopped looking for a new one, it became painfully clear that he wasn't going to be able to support us. I got a full-time evening job and tried to keep the mortgage payments going, which worked for a month or two, but my grades started suffering. I was falling asleep in class. I just couldn't keep it up.

"Eventually, children's aid came calling. We lost the house, I was put in a group home, and Jason—he'd just turned eighteen—was on his own."

Harrison shook his head, his usually stoic expression cracking with pain, and I kissed his lips lightly, just to let him know I was there, I was with him. I wouldn't let him fall.

"We'd still see each other regularly. He'd come and meet me after school, or he'd come over to my new house. The family I lived with was a little cold, but good to me. They knew it was good for me to see my brother. Or at least, at first."

His blue eyes met mine and I knew we were teetering at the top of the roller coaster. Now was the moment when we went over.

"It happened so quickly. One day he was fine, then he was acting strange, slurring his words, scratching himself like he had lice. He stopped meeting me after school. He was evicted from his apartment. He grew his hair long, started hanging around with a scary crowd. I hoped it was just pot, maybe he was dealing too, but Jason was never one to hold back. He always had to be the most daring, to go the farthest, push the limits.

"The day I found him shooting up in my foster family's garage he told me it was like having them back. When he was high was the only time he forgot they were dead and the awful mess his life had become. He never showed any signs of wanting to stop. He never even bothered to pretend. Who would want to go back to all that pain? Heroin was Jason's new best friend."

I flinched as my own relationship with liquor was reflected back at me in that phrase. I knew a little something about toxic best friends.

"I was a senior in high school when he started coming around asking for money," Harrison said. "He'd always managed on his own until then—though I had no idea how—but all of a sudden he was always broke, always begging. I had a job as a pizza delivery guy, so I had some extra cash. Basically every dime I had started going to support my brother, or rather his habit, though I didn't quite see that at first. He always told me he was hungry, he needed new shoes, new jeans, a haircut. Like I said, he was very charming, very convincing, and I didn't want to believe my brother would lie to me. I wanted to help him."

He clenched his jaw and I could see the anger in him, the pools of betrayal in his eyes, the resentment in his heart.

"After I graduated I chose to stay in town, to go to Queen's, so I wouldn't be too far away from him. So I could keep an eye on him. But I also stopped supporting him, which as you can imagine didn't go over well. He never yells, never threatens me or anything—Jason isn't a violent guy—but he's become even more emotionally manipulative. He's dealing for the most dangerous drug dealer in town, a thug named Lance, and he calls me up whenever he's going over there, telling me it's all my fault that he's been driven to this, blaming me."

I remembered the sagging house we'd parked in front of, the stakeout, and Harrison's insistence that he shouldn't have brought me, that I was a distraction. No wonder. His brother's life had been hanging in the balance and I'd been quizzing him about girlfriends and what he thought of my bare breasts.

"You're a good brother, Harrison," I said, though I wasn't sure he was hearing me. He was closing off again, his face going still and expressionless. "Jason's choices are his own. You can't be responsible for everything he does."

The warmth of his hand left my hip and I realized he was

pulling at the sheets behind me, balling the cotton in his hand as if he wanted to rip them to shreds.

"I want to help him. All I want to do is help him. But all he wants is to make himself worse. And he makes me tell him no over and over." His eyes filled with frustrated tears. He didn't say his next words so much as choke them out. "And every time I say it I know I'm failing him."

"No," I said, wiping the tears from his eyes. "You're not failing him. You're trying so hard for him. He's failing himself."

The look he gave me was agonized, his beautiful eyes swimming with pain. "Then why does it feel this way?" he said.

I'd spent so many years of my life being the mess my friends had to pick up after. It had seemed like the only choice at the time, my only means of escape, and when the hurt inside me was as searing and as all-consuming as it had been, escape wasn't so much a need as a requirement. Destroying myself had seemed like the perfect answer, a victimless crime, nobody hurt except myself. I'd never thought about what it was like for the people watching me destroy myself.

Holding Harrison in my arms, I waited for his limbs to lose their tightness, for his muscles to relax. I thought about the look on Anita's face as she'd said, "Why do you do it?" I thought about the concerned looks my friends gave each other when they thought I couldn't see, and the way they'd showed up at my door with ice cream and porn, and the countless times they'd called to check on me, or pulled guys off of me, or tried to talk me out of having one more drink.

For the first time I tried looking at my mess of a life from their point of view. What was it like being friends with Sally Jarvis? Did it feel like watching your brother kill himself one hit at a time? Did they stay up at night worrying about me? Did they feel like they were failing when I fell down?

I'd never been in the position I was now in with Harrison. I'd never been the comforter. I'd always been the one who needed to be cared for. Nobody had ever tried depending on me, because, let's face it, I wasn't very dependable. Harrison was the first one to ever give me the chance.

Nobody had ever trusted me like this before.

I hoped I wasn't about to screw it all up.

Eventually Harrison fell into a fitful slumber and I snuck out of the room to make us a nutritious dinner of microwave ramen noodle soup and the oatmeal cookies Anita had bought the first week of class when we'd made the vow to stop eating chocolate with every meal. The box was still unopened.

Harrison ate his soup in bed, assuring me he was a very neat eater, and I assured him he could spill as much as he wanted, pointing to my heaping pile of laundry as evidence of my slovenly ways. (He was nice enough to pretend he hadn't noticed.)

I perched on my desk chair as we ate. It felt strange to be out of his reach after everything we'd shared, every place he'd touched, and from the way his eyes kept running over me I knew he felt it too. It was like an ache of longing that grew worse the further we were apart.

God, what had I done?

"I didn't realize you were from Kingston," I said as I bit into a crumbly cookie. "I guess I just thought you were from someplace else, like everyone else."

"Didn't realize you'd landed yourself a townie, huh?" he said good-humouredly. I tried to calm my leaping heart at his use of the word 'landed.' "I know you never thought you'd be so lucky."

I loved the way he slurped his curly noodles. He ate neatly, but noisily. It was pretty adorable.

"You never told me where you're from," he said. "Actually, you've never told me much about yourself at all. Hiding your childhood as a pick-pocket, I'm guessing?"

He was regaining his good mood, joking and teasing, but I couldn't quite join in. It felt terrible keeping the truth from him when he'd just bared his soul, but I couldn't bring myself to tell him everything. Actually, I didn't even consider it. Whatever spell I'd accidentally cast on him to make him like me wouldn't be strong enough to withstand the secrets I had to tell, I knew that. I'd always known that. If he started asking questions about my past, I figured I had three options:

A. Lie outright. (Which wasn't really a choice. I couldn't out and out lie to Harrison.)

B. Avoidance. (A possibility, but it wasn't easy to avoid a direct question, especially one as simple as "What were you like in high school" without being really obvious.)

C. Tell the bare minimum, and no more. (The clear winner. All I had to do was keep myself from babbling and giving myself away. That couldn't be too hard, could it?)

"You got me," I said, playing along with his joke. "Things just weren't going so well for me at that orphanage, but then I met this guy named Dodger and my life of crime really took off."

"All right, Oliver," Harrison said, taking another noisy bite of soup. "What's the real story, then? You grew up in Toronto, right?"

Why was my heart beating like a drum in my chest? All I had to do was pretend. I'd been doing it for years. Why was it that whenever I was with Harrison pretending to be someone I wasn't felt so very wrong?

"Scarborough," I corrected him. "My mother still lives there. She's a librarian."

I picked up my bowl and drank the broth straight from it. I didn't care if it made me look like a child. Anything to not have to look at him while we were talking about my mother.

"Do you get along?" he asked.

I shrugged, like I didn't care. This was how the callous youngsters did it, wasn't it? This was what it looked like to treat your parents like irritating strangers you put up with over the holidays only because you had to, right?

I wished I could not care about my mother, who I hadn't seen in two-and-a-half years. I wished I could go home for the holidays, even just to see her through the window. More than anything, I wished I could face her again.

Harrison was watching me, a curious expression on his face. I realized I'd never answered his question.

"She has Lupus," I said suddenly, regretting the words almost as soon as they were out of my mouth.

Great, because sick parents don't ever get follow-up questions.

Harrison's expression turned serious again and he put his soup bowl aside. "That's awful," he said, his words so genuine I nearly wept.

"She's had it for a long time," I said. "But it means sometimes she can't work. And the medication is expensive." I tried to think of an upside that would turn the conversation away from the uber depressing and back to blandly boring. "That's why I eat a lot of cheap noodles. The education fund she set up when I was born pays for my classes, but not much else. And unfortunately that money can't be used to help her out. It's just for school."

Oh my God, stop babbling!

"It must be nice to have someone to go home to, though," Harrison said, surprising me. He made an effort at a smile. "I'm sure she's so proud of you."

My stomach sank. What had I been thinking, bringing up my mother when his parents were dead?

"I'm so sorry about your parents," I said. "I can't even imagine what it was like for you."

"It was a long time ago," he said thoughtfully. "I'd like to say I don't miss them anymore, but I do. And at the strangest times, like when I see a father lifting up his kid at the park, or when I talk to the parents of the kids I tutor. I guess it never really goes away."

"That just means you really loved them," I said.

I knew about missing a time when things were better, a past just out of reach. He had no idea how much we had in common.

Shaking off the melancholy moment, Harrison said, "So what about siblings?"

I turned around to put my empty soup bowl down on the desk, but something stopped me from turning back to face him. Something that started in my toes and moved up through my body like a current, except slower and colder.

"I have a brother," I said. "He's older. I see him sometimes."

The end. Finito. That's all she wrote, folks.

"You didn't mention your father," Harrison said, his mouth full of cookie.

"Oh yeah," I said. I stared at myself in the mirror leaning on the edge of my desk, behind the rows of hair products and nail polishes. I looked strangely pale, almost like a kid. "He left us when I was four, couldn't take the uncertainty of my mother's illness. I don't remember him."

Please, let that be the end. No more questions. Please.

I heard the bed covers rustling, and then felt his arms come around me from behind, his chin resting on my shoulder, his eyes peeking at me in the mirror. "We don't have to talk about this anymore if you don't want to," he said gently, and I nodded. "But I do have one last thing to ask."

In that moment I had only one desire, and that was for Harrison to ask me anything that didn't have to do with my past or my future. A question that had a time span of one day, that's all I wanted. A question that could fill our time together, the only time we'd ever have. A question that didn't ask too much.

He pressed his lips to my shoulder and then whispered in my ear: "Sally Jarvis, will you go out with me tomorrow night?"

I met his eyes in the mirror and smiled so wide my lips almost didn't fit the glass.

"Absolutely," I said.

16

"So, the lion attacks Pinocchio and, what, mauls him to death?" I said.

We were looking for the address of the low-budget play Harrison's friend Roger was staring in, but I was pretty sure we were on the wrong street. Not that I was particularly worried. I was beginning to get the feeling this play wasn't exactly going to be a masterpiece.

"No, the lion *is* Pinocchio," Harrison corrected me, squinting to see the addresses across the street. "He's a stuffed lion instead of a boy and then he becomes a real lion. It's a reimagining of the fairy tale."

We turned a corner and the little crowd and ticket taker told me we'd found the place. We joined the line on the dark sidewalk and I pressed myself against Harrison's side, slipping my hand inside his coat and running my fingers down the front of his shirt (and down, and down), until I heard him suck in a breath. His hand gripped my hip.

You had to book your opening night on the same day as my very first date with Harrison, huh Roger? You couldn't have waited until, I don't know, next winter or something? Real nice, Roger. Way to go.

I'd been ragging on Roger, who I'd only spoken to once,

pretty hard in my head all day. It was surprisingly comforting.

"You're sure this is what you want to do tonight?" I said, not for the first time that night, though this time I breathed it into Harrison's ear, making his hand slip from my hip to my ass and his eyes dip to my lips, which I licked seductively.

I had to use my promiscuous training for something, didn't I?

Swallowing hard, Harrison shook his head as if to clear it—though I noticed he didn't move his hand.

"You're a vixen, you know that?" he said through gritted teeth. "And I promised him I'd come, or God knows we wouldn't be here right now."

He paid for our tickets, ignoring the cash I tried to force on him, which resulted in a little tug of war as we walked down the narrow hallway to the theatre.

"Oh? Where exactly would we be instead?" I said as I finally succeeded in stashing the bills in his coat pocket. "I thought we were taking it slow."

I blinked at him innocently as other patrons squeezed by us to get into the dark room.

Grinning at me, Harrison whisked me around the corner into the dark theatre with rows of chairs rising away from the stage. He pressed me against the wall in a shadowy corner half in the wings, and then his lips were on my neck and his fingers teasing at the skin just under the hem of my shirt, his hips tight against mine, straining, demanding. He devoured my neck, tonguing, and licking, and kissing his way from one side to the other so that when he finally moved his mouth to mine my eyes nearly rolled back in my head with heightened desire.

"This *is* taking it slow," he said, as I panted against him, desperate to move the hands he's conveniently trapped at my sides so I couldn't quite reach him. "Now let's get us some culture."

"Tease," I muttered, but I was smiling as he released me from my playful cage, tugging me up through the rows to a couple of seats in the middle.

He gestured that I should sit down first and took my coat,

pilling it on his lap with his own. I tried not to be weirded out that a guy was being so nice to me, *me*, or that when he looked at me there was something more than lust in his eyes, or that he'd invited me to see the avant-garde play his buddy was in instead of assuming I wouldn't understand it. I was trying really hard to believe this was my life, and the funny thing was, I almost could.

"If this play ends up sucking, I want you to know that I'm very sorry," Harrison said, his blue eyes settling on my face, "and I'll have to make it up to you."

He was being suggestive and mischievous, as he had all day, stealing kisses and making jokes, almost cheerful. It was so nice to see him in a good mood for once, all the stress of worrying about his brother forgotten, at least for the moment.

Lifting my eyes from the program, my lips already curling into a smirk, I was about to tell him just how he could make it up to me—dirty talk didn't disqualify us from taking it slow, did it?—when I caught a glimpse of a guy sitting a few seats down from us. It was just a flash of the side of his pale face and his floppy blonde hair, and my heart practically leapt into my mouth. Breathing hard, I looked again, but the face staring back at me wasn't the one I expected, and I sat back in my seat as the theatre lights dimmed and then went black, lacing my fingers with Harrison's.

It wasn't Billy, but it might have been. It wasn't him, but it looked like him, it could've been him, it would be him.

In one day. Tomorrow.

Tomorrow I would be his.

It had been happening all day, though I'd tried to ignore it. At the diner as Harrison hemmed and hawed over fries or onion rings. On the street as we walked back to my place. Even in my building. That face in the checkout line, in the park, in the elevator. That resentful face I knew so well, because I'd seen it so many times in my self-hating daydreams. That face. Billy's face.

It was like he was stalking me, which in a way he was. Leaving all those messages, the dress, and the horrifying appearance at my door. I felt as though a net was closing in on me, and I was just watching the ropes squeeze tighter, my opening, my escape route, dwindling to a tiny hole. It had been different the other times. I'd hardly cared where he took me, what he called me. Back then what I did had meant so little to me, and whether he was forcing me or I was doing it of my own volition—I could hardly tell the difference.

But now.

Now everything was different.

The morning felt like a death sentence, and like an inmate on death row, I couldn't even think about it. Hallucinations aside, I wouldn't let tomorrow ruin tonight. I had to concentrate on this moment, this night with Harrison, our last night—though he didn't know it. I had to be blinded to the fact that any pleasure I might find tonight would be my last for a very long time, and will myself to be happy, to enjoy it.

I'd never been one to sulk at goodbyes.

I'd always raised my glass and put on a hell of a show.

As it turned out, the play was even weirder than I'd expected, with all the characters, the lion (played by Roger, a starring role!) and the humans, wearing enormous papier-mâché heads with big round eyes that made everything seem hilarious even when it wasn't. Harrison and I gave the cast a standing ovation—although we were the only ones—and watching him clap I could tell he was truly happy for his friend, that he wasn't just clapping out of obligation. Because that's the kind of guy he was. The guy who rooted for you no matter what. The guy who stood up in a crowd of hecklers and clapped. The guy who had your back.

It only made me want him more.

We waited outside the theatre for Roger for a little while, huddling under my umbrella in the drizzle, but eventually Harrison decided to go in and find him. I told him I'd be fine waiting alone, but as soon as he went back in I regretted it. The cold combined with the wet and the dark only encouraged the melancholy mood I was trying to avoid and I didn't feel comfortable being there without Harrison's enveloping presence next to me. I became suddenly paranoid that any second someone I knew was going to spot me standing outside the theatre and call me out as a faker, an intellectual wannabe, a liar. Even in my more conservative outfit—I'd caved and bought a few new tops when Anita started complaining that her entire wardrobe was on my bedroom floor—I still felt like I stuck out like a sore thumb in this crowd. Like a sniper sitting on a rooftop with me in his sights, I felt as though my real life was readying to strike.

But it was my past that blasted into me instead.

She looked to be about sixteen or seventeen, wearing torn stockings and a too-short skirt—the kind I would have coveted a month before. Her boyfriend was similarly dressed in the kind of dark, angry fashion of kids who want to scare their parents, with greasy-looking hair and slouchy jeans. Even though the rain had trickled to a stop they both looked cold, and the girl in particular was in no mood for the arm he kept trying to put around her shoulder and the phone he kept jamming in her face.

"Leave me alone, Hunter," I heard her say, and instantly, like a TV set changing channels, I wasn't standing on the sidewalk anymore, but in a locker room on that night, with all of them gathered around me, feeling just as cold, and just as young.

Leave me alone! Billy, tell them to stop.

Don't be silly, Sal. This is what you want, isn't it? This is what you're good for. This is what it is too be loved.

The boy held the camera up to her face again and it was clear that he was filming her. She shoved his arm away, but he only laughed and kept at it, circling around her, making her stop in her tracks and glare at him.

"Quit it! Stop filming me!" she said.

"Oh, now she's angry," he replied, standing directly in front of her and slowly moving his phone toward her face.

Stop filming me. Please just go away.

Oh, come on, sweetie. Don't get shy now.

Stop it!

We just came for a show. So, go on. Give us what we came for.

"Hunter! Will you get that thing out of my face?" she exclaimed.

She tried to snatch the phone out of his hand, but he only jerked it out of her reach, laughing and taunting, waving it above her head. As I watched, I didn't see them at all. All I saw were laughing faces and phones aimed at me, from above and below, from all around. Jeering male laughter surrounded me as I cowered in shame, as I tried to hide, and they laughed and laughed and laughed.

"Stop it, Hunter!" the girl cried.

I was standing on the dark sidewalk and I wasn't. I was in the locker room, under the glaring lights, and I wasn't.

"Stop it," I whispered to myself, focusing on the couple still arguing in front of me, the boy's face transforming into Billy's, the phone in his hand turning toward me. "Stop it!"

Without quite realizing what I was doing, I dropped my umbrella and shoved the guy hard with both my hands. Vaguely, I heard his phone clatter to the ground and a girl's voice crying out, but mostly all I heard was Billy's laughter and the six words he'd repeated to me so many times.

This is what you owe me.

"Did you hear her?" I said, pushing harder into his chest, pushing him away from me, pushing them all away. But he was bigger, they were all bigger, and I was just a girl. "She said, stop it!"

My voice was loud and angry, full of all the rage I felt for that innocent girl, the girl I had been, the girl who didn't know how to defend herself against a roomful of boys. The girl who made every wrong decision, and had to live with it after.

The girl who never really lived again.

"All right!" Hunter said, and my eyes focused on the boy I'd knocked to the ground. His coat was bunched in my fists as I loomed over him. He raised his hands in surrender. "I'm stopping."

"What are you, crazy?" the girl said, leaning down to help

up her boyfriend, and handing him his phone. I blinked at them both, trying to reconcile the kids before me with what I'd been seeing just a few moments earlier. "Mind your own business, why don't you."

"I'm...sorry," I said lamely as they started to walk away, the guy still looking a little startled and the girl, who didn't seem the least bit abused, giving me a dirty look over her shoulder. "I didn't mean to."

She was the type of girl I wished I'd been back then. Strong. Cocky. Resilient. Not every girl fell apart over a boy, I reminded myself. Not every girl was as weak as me.

"What was that about?" Harrison said, coming up beside me as I watched the teenagers walking away.

"Oh, nothing," I said. I forced a smile and tried to fight back the myriad of emotions pulsing through my body, none of which I wanted Harrison to know about.

He watched me curiously, his gaze sliding to the backs of those two kids. I could see the rigidity coming back into his body and his face closing off, like a metal gate falling, as he considered whether someone had been trying to hurt me. I knew I had to stop him before it was too late, before the easy, good mood he'd been in all day vanished and I spent the rest of the evening chasing it, desperately trying to get it back.

This wasn't how I wanted to spend our last night together. In fact, I had pretty specific plans for the rest of our night together, and it had to do with desperation of a completely different kind.

"Hey," I said, turning his chin toward me and letting those gorgeous eyes roam over my face.

He never looked away when he saw me anymore. He let every look linger, lighting me up.

"If there's something I want, will you give it to me?" I said boldly.

"You know I will," Harrison said softly. Taking one of my hands in his, he brought it to his lips and kissed it just above the knuckles, as if I was royalty, as if I was a queen. "What do you want?"

Without taking my eyes off his, I stepped forward and slipped my arms inside his open coat, wrapping them around his body. I heard him chuckle quietly as my chest pressed against his. I remembered briefly that we'd stood in this very same position on the night we met. Then, before he could stop me, I slid my hands down and cupped his ass, pulling him toward me, the hardness in his pants connecting with that place between my legs, and I watched his expression change, his eyes going dark with desire.

"You," I whispered into his ear as his hands tightened around me. "I want you."

After the longest ten-minute drive of my life, Harrison and I fell through the doorway into Johnny's apartment, or Harrison's apartment now, I supposed. I heard Harrison tell me Johnny was out for the night, or I'm pretty sure that's what he said. It was a little hard to concentrate when his tongue was on my neck and I was panting raggedly into his ear.

"So this is your new place?" I mumbled as he kicked the door closed behind us without breaking contact with my neck.

"Mmm-hmm," he said.

He sucked my earlobe into his mouth, making me gasp, as I unbuttoned his coat and pushed it off his shoulders, then shrugged out of mine. Both fell to the floor with a thump.

"It's nice," I said.

I ran my hands up his back, inside his shirt, feeling him shiver at my cold fingers, while at the same time billows of heat seemed to be rising between us. Every breath I took made me feel a little dizzy.

"Should I give you a tour?" Harrison said.

I could hear the slight smile in his voice as he worked his way up my jaw toward my mouth and I dug my fingers into this back. Neither of us was in any mood for a tour. In fact, I barely took the apartment in at all as he walked me backwards across the living room toward a door I assumed led to his bedroom, both of us nearly falling flat on our faces when we almost tripped over a pile of computer parts by the door.

"Oops," Harrison said, "that's just—"

"Don't care," I said breathlessly.

Our lips were just millimeters apart now but he'd yet to kiss me, and I didn't think I'd ever wanted any kiss so much in my entire life. To make this abundantly clear, I ran my fingers down my shirt buttons, flicking them open one by one and then flung off my shirt, revelling in the feeling of his eyes on my body and his hands sliding around my torso to rest in the small of my back.

He pulled off his own shirt in that way guys did, by reaching behind their neck and simply pulling, and then his bare chest was under my hands and I heard him suck in a breath as I ran my fingers over his tight abdomen.

Digging the tips of my fingers under the waistband of his jeans, I sat back on the bed, pulling him toward me so that he was standing between my legs looking down at me. He reached forward to touch me, but instead of letting him I pulled up my leg and settled the foot of my high-heeled boot on his chest. His eyebrows rose in surprise.

"Off," I commanded, placing his hand on the zipper, but he shook his head slowly and moved my own hand to the place instead.

"You do it," he said.

I pouted but did as he asked, sitting up straight to pull the zipper down the leather as he ran his hand over my calf, and then up my thigh, distracting me so completely that I almost couldn't get the other boot off at all.

As soon as the second boot hit the ground, Harrison moved toward me, his hands in my hair, his lips against my cheek, the side of my mouth, and even grazing my lips. Then he paused agonizingly and pulled back, stilling my hand which had gone to the button of my jeans.

"You don't have to," he said, brushing a lock of hair away from my face. "I may have gotten a little carried away—" we both grinned, glancing back at the trail of clothes and chaos behind us—"but I still think we should take things slow. There are plenty of things we can do without taking these off."

As if to emphasize this fact, he let his thumb run over my hard nipple through the material of my bra—which really had the opposite effect than he was going for, only making me want to take it right off.

I looked up into his blue eyes filled with concern, with caring—which I had never, ever seen in any guy's eyes after I'd taken my top off before—and then, without breaking eye contact, I shimmied out of my jeans.

"My body, my decision, right?" I said, and he nodded slightly. The sight of all my exposed skin seemed to have robbed him of the power of speech.

It was such an empowering feeling, taking off my own clothes instead of having them ripped off without my say-so, watching him react as I showed him my body rather than reacting as he looked and touched and took for himself.

Feeling bold, I stood up suddenly, causing him to take a startled step back, and unhooked my bra, dropping it onto the substantial pile of clothes we'd created.

Wearing just my black lace underwear, I backed up against the bed and cocked my head. "So?" I said coyly. "Are you coming or what?"

Making a guttural sound in his throat, Harrison closed the space between us in a single step, his mouth descending on mine as we fell back onto the bed. His hands were everywhere, smoothing and touching and teasing, and I wrapped my right leg over his hip to bring us closer still. His lips were insistent, yet gentle too, controlled instead of hard, and I found myself drowning in his scent and the feel of his tongue against mine, his taste and his hands sending jolts of intense pleasure through my body wherever he touched me.

"You're so soft," he whispered into my mouth. I nibbled at his bottom lip, cupping his face in my hands.

I wanted to tell him how much I wanted him, and why I wanted him—*him*—not those other guys who'd been here before, but trying to find the words when so many feelings were tumbling through my body was just too much.

Instead I steered his head down to my chest and he rolled

me onto my back, placing kisses along my collarbone. Snaking my hand between our bodies, I tried to find the top of his jeans—I was determined to get them off this time—but before I could reach I felt my arms being pressed up and my hands folded over my head.

"No, let me," I complained. "I want to."

He wasn't holding my arms in place, but I felt shackled by his rules all the same, rules which seemed to me to be pretty arbitrary. I could be a slip of fabric away from naked, but he couldn't? I wondered suddenly if he had some kind of weird bodily malformation he was trying to hide from me. Then he rolled on top of me, bracing himself so as not to crush me, but I could still feel his body along every inch of mine, his thighs and his chest and his legs and the hard heat of his arousal. Every single part of him felt absolutely perfect.

He looked down at me with that intense gaze of his, and it shocked me as it always did how beautiful he was, and how for all those months he'd been walking around Alex's house, completely unnoticed by me. How had I missed this? How had I missed him?

"You're used to giving when you're in bed with a guy," he said. "You always want to give yourself, give me something, give it away." He was speaking softly, kindly, but they weren't easy words to hear. I wanted so much to look away, but his eyes held me in place. "I don't want it to be like that when you're with me. I don't want you to feel like you have to give me anything. You have to learn to take, to enjoy."

Shifting his weight, he reached up and curled my fingers around a rung of the headboard. Then he was hovering over me again, kissing lightly, ever so lightly down my neck.

"I want you to feel this," he said, his lips grazing my nipples, which were so hard I moaned at even this minute contact. He looked up at me. "Don't let go," he said.

Then his lips were on my breast, nipping and kissing, and I wrapped my legs around him, as waves of pleasure washed over me. Sweat beaded on my skin and my hips bucked involuntarily, heat building between my legs. I strained against the rungs of the headboard, wanting to let go, but loving this feeling of being pleasured, of being tasted, as he continued to ravage my breasts as if they were his only desire.

When I couldn't stand it a second longer, I did let go, but only to run my hands through his hair. He licked my nipple slowly, teasing the tip, and I arched into him, pulling his face back up to mine, searching for his mouth. I couldn't get enough of his taste. I couldn't get enough of him.

Palming my ass, he pressed me against him, his insistent length finding that exact spot, and I gripped his shoulders, wanting so much more.

"How did you get so good at this?" I said deliriously.

Had he been with a lot of girls? I wasn't exactly one to talk, but I suddenly felt self-conscious, imagining him comparing me to other beautiful girls, girls who hadn't spread their legs for every guy in town, girls who didn't shamelessly take off their bras and throw them at him.

He shook his head bashfully and busied himself with kissing the tip of my nose and my temples and my cheekbones, as if every part of me was precious, not just the voluptuous ones.

"You make me good at it," he breathed. "You have no idea what you do to me."

He lips met mine again and I lost whatever I was going to ask next, lost myself entirely in his mouth. I didn't even feel him reaching down between us until his fingers inched under the waistband of my underwear and he paused, expectant.

"Yes," I said, breathing the word. "Yes."

With a hesitant but gentle touch he found the place exactly at my centre and I buried my face in his shoulder, gripping him against me. He took up a rhythm that built into a crescendo of feeling and I rocked against his hand, crying out with pleasure.

"Look at me," he said, as I fell back on the pillow, my body entirely open to him, my legs quivering as my eyes found his and locked.

He pressed his forehead against mine, never easing up on

the relentless rhythm of his hand, and when I reached the peak he held me with his eyes and kissed me over and over until I could kiss no more.

17

I didn't know what time it was. Regular things like time and sleep ceased to have meaning when I was lying in Harrison Leo's arms, our naked limbs tangled under the covers. My cheek pressed to his chest, I stared out the window beside the bed, watching the moon hanging low in the night sky. I felt like that moon, floating in a dark quiet place of peace.

I'd never felt this good after a sexual encounter before. I'd never felt this good in my entire life.

"How many girls have you been with?" I asked, lazily tracing figure eights on his chest.

Harrison was in and out of sleep, snoring quietly in my ear and then waking to kiss me sleepily without opening his eyes. It seemed like the best time to ask this question, which I wasn't quite sure I had the right to ask. Maybe he would just mumble the answer to me in his sleep and forget it.

"You mean…?" he said, his fingers trailing along my back.

Damn. He really was awake.

"Yes, I mean," I said. "I'm just…wondering."

"Does it really matter?"

He didn't seem particularly bothered by the question, just curious. I took this to be a sign that his group of past lovers was more like a few drops in a bucket than a torrential downpour. When I considered my own number I suddenly regretted bringing the subject up at all. Drops or a downpour? Mine was more like a tsunami.

"It doesn't matter," I said, readjusting my position against him. "Forget I even asked."

He shifted around so our heads were both on the pillow facing each other, and my body ached from the loss of contact with his skin.

"I've been with three girls," Harrison said.

He spread his fingers across my middle as he said this— he didn't seem to be able to stop touching me, either—and I tried to form the appropriate reaction.

Three girls? THREE girls?

"Three girls and then me?" I said, trying desperately to keep the shock out of my voice. If his number was three there was absolutely no way I was telling him mine. No way in hell.

He dipped his head, stroking a path between my breasts without actually touching them, making my breath catch. Was he trying to distract me?

"No, three girls including you," he said, and I was glad he couldn't see my face as my eyes bulged with surprise.

Once his eyes returned to my face I'd managed to regain my composure, but he wouldn't hold my gaze. It was like that first day in his room again when I'd thought I disgusted him. But it wasn't disgust at all, I realized now. His expression was always so subdued it was hard to tell, but it was suddenly obvious to me what he'd been feeling then, and now. He was embarrassed.

Placing a hand against his warm cheek, I said, "Did you love them?"

"Yes, I did," he said without hesitation, and in that answer I understood.

Harrison might have been with far fewer partners than me, but he'd still surpassed me in the important ways, that's why he was such a good lover. Harrison had known real love. Harrison knew how to make love. I only knew how to screw.

Now it was my turn to be embarrassed, and a little jealous, if I was honest, of those other girls he'd loved. I moved toward him, planning to hide my face in his neck, but instead he captured my mouth with his and I found myself actually whimpering against his lips as he kissed me thoroughly and completely, pressing me back against the pillow, making my whole body flush. When we broke apart we were both panting.

"I loved them," he explained, "but I never felt with them the way I do when I'm with you. I've never felt this way before."

My eyes locked with his. Had I heard him right? Had he really just, almost, said he loved me? I wanted more than anything to say it back, to tell him I'd never felt anything real for any guy before him, but the moment was too overwhelming. Before I could say a word his lips found mine again and he kissed me over and over, until our lips were raw, until the room spun around us.

Before he drifted back to sleep, I said, "Don't you want to know my number?"

Because as much as I didn't want to tell him, I felt I owed it to him now. I owed him this truth.

He folded me in his arms and kissed me on the top of my head.

"No," he said, and I let out a breath I didn't even realize I'd been holding. "I think that secret is just for you to keep. It really doesn't matter to me who you were with before. As long as you're with me now."

Harrison fell asleep, snoring adorably, but his last words echoed in my ears long after.

As long as you're with me now.

As long as you're with me today and tomorrow and forever.

But I wouldn't be his tomorrow, would I? I wasn't his now and he didn't even know it.

The truth that I'd somehow kept at bay for the last few hours of passion hit me like a ton of bricks. I glanced at the clock, counting the hours. It was already tomorrow, really, though the sun had yet to rise on the day that would take me away from Harrison. It was already the day when I would have to say goodbye to him and leave him behind without any explanation, because of course I couldn't tell him why. I couldn't explain this to him. I couldn't see that look of disgust in his eyes again and realize, this time, it wasn't embarrassment or awkwardness or distraction. This time it was real.

Billy's message on my machine yesterday morning had been very clear. He'd specified the exact time I should meet him and where, as he always did, and I would go, as I always did. Because this was who I was. This was what I did. Harrison was a dream, and this was my real life. Billy was real. His cruelty was real. And Harrison with his sweet words and soft touch and slight smile…Harrison was everything I could never keep.

I watched the sun rise through the window, the dawn of a new day, and placed a last kiss on Harrison's lips before tiptoeing from the room, and the apartment, and his life.

Better not to wake him. Better to let him keep his happy feelings a little longer. Better to be gone when he woke up.

Maybe when he woke he'd think, as I already did, that everything that had happened between us had been nothing but a dream.

Anita was out when I got home—all the better—though she did leave a note on the fridge asking me how my date had gone, hearts and happy faces decorating the scrap of paper. I ripped it from its magnet and crumpled it in my first. She'd also left another note reminding me that she'd gone to her parents' house for Thanksgiving and she hoped I had a good time with my family. In true Anita fashion she'd jotted down the train schedule to Scarborough for me. Because I'd lied, as I always did, and said I was going home for the holiday when I had no intention of doing so. Because she knew nothing real about my family or my mother or my home, just the half-truths and evasive answers I'd provided over the years. Because so much of my life was one gigantic heap of lies.

Like a zombie, I headed to my closet and pulled out the small travel bag I used for only these occasions—how I detested the bright pink material, the optimistic zips and compartments, as if this bag was taking me on an exciting adventure instead of toward my doom—and packed my usual array of items: hairdryer, makeup, shoes, dress. Billy had informed me this would be an overnighter, not a full weekend, so I didn't need to bring much. He would feed me at least, that was part of the deal, part of the illusion. It was such a shame that I'd always eaten the best food on the nights when everything tasted like dirt.

Once I'd packed and showered and dressed myself in one of my old outfits—because this was one occasion when I felt I should look like the slut I really was—there was nothing to do but sit and wait. Right now would have been a brilliant time to relapse and drown myself in alcohol—that was actually how I'd gotten through it all the other times—but the apartment was painfully lacking in booze since I'd foolishly smashed all the bottles a week before. I yearned for that delicious release from reality and found myself licking my lips, dreaming of oblivion.

I briefly considered running to the liquor store, but I somehow felt sure that if I went outside Harrison would materialize on the sidewalk in front of me. Outside was less safe, less hidden than inside, though of course he could just as easily find me here. He knew where I lived. I had to meet Billy at three, but I already knew I would be very early—I felt like a sitting duck. I just wanted to get this over with, to shove myself out the other side where I could pick up the splintered pieces of my life and move on.

Still, there were a lot of hours to wait through, and after I'd unenthusiastically choked down a few bites of breakfast and brushed my teeth and put on my shoes I had no other tasks to tend to.

There were a few things I could have done to pass the

time.

I could have read issue twelve of *The Forever Place*, which Harrison had given me as a present at the beginning of our date, but I didn't feel like I deserved it.

I could have studied for midterms, but school seemed about a million miles away just then, and I had trouble even remembering the names of my classes.

I could have started thinking about Harrison and everything I was losing, about what I was about to do, and what I'd done, and who I was.

It's funny what the mind can do when pressured. Instead of doing any of those things, I sat for those four hours, motionless and silent, and thought of nothing. It was fitting, I thought. My brain was nothing and my body was nothing and my life was nothing. I was nothing.

And nothing I did mattered.

The phone rang a few times while I sat there, but I didn't answer it. I'd turned the volume of my answering machine off so I couldn't hear the messages. As I stood to leave it started ringing again, and I ignored it again, walking swiftly to the door with my suitcase and locking it behind me. It was still ringing as I walked down the hall to the elevator. I heard it right up until the doors closed.

It wasn't a long walk to the street corner where I was to meet Billy, the same street corner he always chose with the depressing coffee shop-pawn shop-barber shop trio of broken-down store fronts, and the punishing wind. I stared up at the cloudy sky as I waited, wishing I could be a cloud, lost in that sea of white, where nobody, even Billy, could ever find me.

He pulled up in his usual sleek, black town car, and I didn't look down from the sky until he rolled down the window.

"Hey, Sal," he said, flashing a smile that made my stomach curdle, "how's my favourite sister doing?"

I pulled open the door and glared at my brother, my jailer, my tormentor.

"Shove over," I said. "I'm not going around to the other

side."

I placed my suitcase in the trunk and then climbed into the car, sinking into the plush leather seat and turning my face to the window. The driver pulled slowly into the mid-afternoon traffic.

"It's good to see you," Billy said, his mock good-humour grating on my nerves. He patted me, a little too hard, on my thigh, and I swatted his hand away.

"Let's just go," I said, jamming my chin into my palm.

All I wanted was for this day to be over, and it had only just begun.

"Whatever you say, sweetheart," Billy said. "Your wish is my command."

As the car sped out of the city I caught a glimpse of the bookstore where I bought my comics. There was a display for *The Forever Place* in the window, piles of comics and a poster of Rainbow staring longingly at the ship that would take her home, tiny on the horizon, gone without her. I felt just like her in that moment, or rather I felt like I was on the boat, but it wasn't going to a home I wanted to visit. It was going to the home I wanted so much to forget.

Thoughts of Rainbow only made me think of Harrison, which only made me feel worse. As the trees closed in around the highway I closed my eyes and wished for another life. But when I opened them again I was still in the car with Billy, rushing toward my unavoidable fate.

I wished I'd never woken up that morning at all.

My brother's condo was the same as the last one he'd lived in, on the twenty-seventh floor of an impossibly tall building in a neighbourhood of tall condo buildings down by the Toronto waterfront. Inside, it was cold and antiseptically clean, the couch dark leather, the kitchen cabinets gleaming black. There was no colour anywhere, and no signs of life—a discarded napkin, a dirty sock. It was museum-like in its hushed stillness.

"If you can afford this, I don't know what you need me

for," I commented as I plunked down on the couch and stared out at the view of the highway and the water beyond. I made remarks like this every time, and every time he had some excuse.

"Oh this place?" Billy said as he poured himself a drink at the counter. "I'm just house-sitting for a friend. You should see my real apartment. It's tiny, the size of a closet. You're living in luxury compared to me, sweetheart, trust me."

But I didn't trust him, for obvious reasons. His excuses had stopped ringing true years ago. A part of me knew I should call him on his lies, that it was possible I was actually doing all this for nothing, that the system he'd blackmailed me into was benefiting only him. But I didn't. I didn't know why the loudmouthed girl I was in the rest of my life collapsed whenever I was near him and I found myself mute, and docile, and easily coerced.

Who was this girl who was letting these things happen to her, who was actually participating in her own demise? Was she really me?

"Here," Billy said, nudging a glass into my hand before taking a seat in the armchair beside me.

I looked down at the heaping drink he'd made me— vodka tonic, his drink of choice, not mine—and saliva filled my mouth in sheer anticipation of the first sip. But I'd made one decision on the long drive over, and that was to face this with my eyes open. I felt somehow that I owed this to Harrison, to myself. I had to be conscious this time, present. I had to face the truth.

"No thanks," I said, placing the beverage on the glass coffee table.

My brother gave me a contemptuous look, then shrugged and turned his face toward the window, his hand hanging over the arm of the chair loosely holding his own glass. He looked so nonplussed, so unfazed by my presence. As if I wasn't even there.

"How's Mom?" I said tightly.

Asking about our mother was opening me up to so much

possible pain—which Billy could inflict so easily, and he knew it—but I couldn't not ask. He was the only one who could give me any news of her.

"She's doing just fine, little sister," he said, smiling a smile that didn't reach his eyes. "Her bills are paid and her pills are delivered and she has nothing to worry about. You should hear her thanking me whenever I come by. Like I'm her saviour. Like I'm God himself."

He chuckled derisively, and I clamped my teeth shut to keep from swearing at him. I hated it when he made fun of Mom. I hated that a turd like him was even allowed to be in the same room as her.

"As long as she's happy," I said. "That's all I care about. That's what I'm doing this for."

"Oh, is that what you're doing this for?" Billy said snidely. "I thought it was out of sheer pleasure. That's certainly the impression you give every weekend when you bang anyone who's willing, maybe even some who aren't, what do I know? Don't try and act like this isn't your dream come true."

"Fuck you," I said quietly, staring down at my knees. "You know I didn't want to come here. That's why you left so many threatening messages, why you came by my apartment to scare me into it." I took a deep breath, gathering my courage for what I was about to say next. "Like a bully having a tantrum when he thinks he's not going to get his way."

"What did you just say?" Billy hissed.

Up until that moment we'd been able to keep a semi-cordial mood to the conversation. Billy liked it that way. Me agreeing with him, or silently taking his jabs. Him acting like the puppet-master while I did what he said, went where he said, withstood anything he could dish out. One thing Billy didn't like was to be contradicted.

"What did you call me?"

He hardly ever raised his voice. It was when it got quieter that you knew you were in danger, and he'd said those last words in a near-whisper.

I looked up at him just in time to see him slam his glass

down on the table, smashing it, sending vodka flying all over me and the couch.

I sat motionless, breathing hard, as Billy leaned over me, pressing his hands into the back of the couch on either side of my shoulders.

"Don't you ever, *ever*, speak to me that way again, do you hear me, whore?" he said, breathing the words right into my face, inches from my nose. "Need I remind you of who got us here, of what you stole from me, from our entire family? Why Mom would be living on the street if I didn't send her money every month, why I have to offer clients this *service* because if I lose even one, we're all fucked? Look at me when I'm talking to you, you stupid, filthy slut!"

Reluctantly, I raised my eyes to meet his. When we were kids people used to remark about how similar we looked, just one year apart, that gorgeous hair, almost like twins. But right now, looking up at him, all I could see in his face was pure evil.

"Am I a bully for asking that you do what you promised and help me support our mother?" he said. "Am I a jerk because I have to hunt you down and keep tabs on you just to make sure you're sober enough to do the only thing you're good for?"

This is what you're good for. This is what you want.

"I'm not even drinking anymore," I said, almost under my breath.

"So, you've been on the wagon for a week and you think you're too good for this now? You think you can get out of your responsibilities? You have a boyfriend and you're in love and you think I'm going to forget?"

I blinked, averting my eyes, his mention of Harrison scaring me in a way his towering over me never could. I didn't want Billy to have anything to do with Harrison. I'd do anything to keep them apart. Anything.

"That's right, sissy, I know about him," my brother said, leaning in to talk directly into my ear. "I know about your precious nerd with the little backpack and the bedroom eyes. Isn't he sweet? Won't he just love to hear all about what you do for me in the city?"

"Don't," I said in a much more panicked tone than I intended. "I won't fight you. Just don't say a word to him. Please, Billy."

As I pleaded, I finally let my eyes meet his.

Straightening up, Billy snorted and stepped carefully away from the glass littering the carpet.

"*Please, Billy*," he mimicked in a sickening falsetto. "That's what I like to hear. I like to hear you begging, Sally. I like it when you show me who you really are."

He walked toward the bedroom, shaking the vodka from his hand. "We leave in an hour," he said. "Fix yourself up. You look like shit."

Curling my legs under me, I laid my head down on the arm of the couch and reminded myself to breathe. In less than twenty-four hours this would be over and I wouldn't have to see him again for months. All I had to do was pretend my way through tonight. I could do that. I'd done it before. It wouldn't be so bad, would it?

But it was.

My decision not to drink myself silly turned out to be a punishing one from the start. I could barely look at myself in the mirror as I put on the dark blue dress Billy had gotten me—so tight I could only take shallow breaths—and doing makeup without actually looking at your own face is quite the challenge, let me tell you. I was hyper aware, as I put my shoes on, and my necklace, and my purse, that each of these things would be taken off me later, by someone's hands other than my own, the hands of someone I'd never even seen before.

You've done this a hundred times, I reminded myself. *You've screwed guys you met five minutes before in the bathroom of some bar. You're a pro at this.*

But it was different when I wasn't the one making the choice, calling the shots. It was different when Billy was forcing me along with a hand at the back of my neck. It was different when they were paying for the privilege and my brother was pocketing the cash.

Being a slut was so different from being a whore.

At least when I was a slut I could look myself in the face.

When Billy saw the product of all my primping, he nodded appreciatively, then snapped his fingers at me to indicate that I should follow him, like I was a dog.

I followed anyway.

In the past he'd always dropped me off at some restaurant on King street, giving me the small advantage of being able to scope out the guy in question over a meal before I had to see his bedroom. But this time was different. Instead of taking me into town he drove along Lakeshore boulevard, eventually turning into another condo similar to his own. He dropped me in front of the lobby doors.

"What about dinner?" I said, gazing up at the building through my tinted window.

"Vince wanted to cook for you," Billy answered with a small grin. He knew meeting the guy at his place was making me uncomfortable, and he was loving every second of it. "Apparently he's a pretty good cook. I'm so jealous."

He puckered his bottom lip before his face cracked into a mocking smile.

Gathering my purse and coat, I opened the door and stepped out. Anything would be better than being along in this car with my brother.

"How much should I expect?" I asked through the open door.

That was another thing. The money was usually exchanged at the table before my brother left me there, a subtle handover, palm to palm. I wondered if I might be able to convince this guy to pay more and then keep some for myself, send a letter to my mother with the cash. I wanted so desperately to have something to give her, something I could say was from me. Something Billy couldn't take credit for.

"Like I'd trust you?" Billy said, slipping on a pair of sunglasses, although the sun had nearly set. "It's all arranged. He'll wire me the money as soon as he's had his fill of you.

And don't try to get anything extra out of him either. I've already told him you're not worth it."

Biting back a curse, I slammed the door on him and watched the car glide into traffic, then turned and took one faltering step and then another into the lobby. I pressed the correct number and waited for the buzzer, then walked into the elevator and down the hall and to the door, all of this done in a kind of fog, imagining I was someone else, somewhere else. Imagining this was not happening, even while I was letting it happen.

I knocked on the door.

A handsome man answered, young enough, through still at least ten years older than me. He had dark eyes and slightly shaggy hair, which clashed somewhat with his immaculate suit, the neck undone, the tie discarded. I might have been attracted to him if I'd seen him from across the room at some club, or sat down next to him at a bar. I might not have cringed inside when he smiled if I hadn't known he was paying for the pleasure of my company.

"You must be Sally," he said.

I noticed a gap between his two front teeth as he spoke. I focused on that flaw.

He's just a person, see? A guy who needs to pay to get laid. He's just as filthy as you are. He's no better than you. He's nothing.

I can do this.

I smiled and let him take my hand in his. "In the flesh," I said with a flirty smile, and stepped inside.

18

"You want me, don't you?"

Vince liked to hear me beg. It might not have been so terrible otherwise. I might have been able to sort of pretend that I wasn't lying naked on the satin sheets of a man I'd only met two hours before, if only he hadn't kept prompting me, like a schoolteacher putting a student through her paces, to confirm my desire.

"Yes," I said in a kind of moan, a kind of whine, though I was pretty sure Vince couldn't tell the difference.

I turned my head to the side so I couldn't see him poised over me in the semi-dark, still wearing his shirt. I hated it when guys insisted I take off all my clothes but then didn't get all the way undressed themselves. At least give me some bare skin to look at while you're pounding into me. At least give me that.

"Do you? Do you want me? Do you want this?"

I felt the pressure of this length, ready to push inside me, but waiting for my confirmation, my say-so.

The irony of this made me want to vomit.

How could I possibly answer him, when every fibre of my being wanted to shove him away and hightail it out of this room, out of this condo, this building, this night, this life? How could I tell him I wanted him when the idea of letting him force himself inside me made my stomach turn? How could I do this with him when all I wanted was to do this very thing with somebody else, and that desire, that real desire, had changed everything for me?

Sex was different now that I'd been in Harrison's bed, lain like this in his arms. Even though we hadn't done it, or maybe because we hadn't, having sex with any guy who looked my way seemed like a betrayal now, a failure of the utmost proportions. I could literally feel my body retreating into the mattress, trying to push itself away from Vince.

Was I really doing this? Was I really going to let this guy screw me when just last night Harrison's hands had touched the same places he now touched, Harrison's mouth had captured mine, as his did now—though Vince's lips were harder, less tender, less caring. Vince's touch was nothing like Harrison's touch and I was pretty sure that when what was about to happen finally happened it would feel nothing like making love to Harrison. I didn't have to experience it to know.

I'd been here before. I knew what I was in for.

I'd just never known there was something better out there for me. Or that there had been. I was pretty sure this moment was about to ruin anything Harrison and I could have had forever.

"I want this," I answered, as required, as demanded. "I want you, please."

I looked up into his face, which was half in shadow, and I tried to see another face there, another pair of eyes, another pair of lips.

But I couldn't.

He thrust into me and I closed my eyes as he moaned with pleasure, trying to keep my body from recoiling. It would only hurt more if I resisted. It was too late to back out now.

"Yeah," Vince said, as our bodies rocked as one. "Say it again."

"Please," I said into his ear, when what I really wanted to

say was *please stop.* "Please don't stop," I said as he pounded into me so hard my body shifted upwards on the mattress, my head shoved up against the metal headboard.

I wondered, if I didn't brace myself against it, could I smack my head hard enough to fall unconscious?

I found myself hoping I would.

Had I really wanted this once? Had I gone out in search of just this experience, this sweaty, forceful, angry experience? Had I yearned for male lust, that most aggressive desire, to be focused on me, thrust into me? Had it really made me feel better?

Or had I always known, deep down, that I was only pretending to want this, because it's all I thought I could get? Slutty Sally, always good for a roll in the hay. Slutty Sally, always down for a screw in your car, or the bathroom, or in the shadows of a building. Slutty Sally who'll do it with anyone, who's always up for it, who doesn't care who you are as long as you give it to her.

Had I been fooling myself all along?

Because as Vince used my body as his personal plaything, I didn't feel anything close to satisfaction, or release, or enjoyment.

I just wanted it to be over.

Placing my hands between the top of my head and the punishing headboard, I stared up at the ceiling and thought about *The Forever Place.* I imagined I was Rainbow in issue one, tripping as she crossed a bridge in her treetop village and falling down, down, down to the forest floor below. I looked around me as I fell through the branches, at the Wittling homes built into the tree trunks and the curious creatures watching me pass. And then the branches closed in over my head and I could no longer see my home above me, or anything of the world, not even the sky. I could see only green everywhere and the ground coming up to meet me, faster and faster.

Until I hit rock bottom.

The next morning was a lot like the one before. I woke up well-rested and took a deep, cleansing breath before turning on my side and seeing whose bed I was sleeping in. Then the cold, creeping tendrils of reality wrapped themselves around me and I felt instantly nauseous and desperate to be gone.

Just like the day before, I tiptoed out of the room without waking my bed buddy, only this time it wasn't a favour I was doing him, it was one I was doing myself.

Once out of the bedroom I ran stark naked down the hall to the perilously bright living room to retrieve my dress from the back of the dining room chair where he'd taken it off me—the remains of our meal looking all the more unappetizing in the daylight—and my underwear from the bathroom doorknob. I looked around for my bra for a while, until I remembered that I hadn't bothered putting one on. Grabbing my purse, coat, and shoes, I left the apartment without so much as a backward glance and did the walk of shame down the hall to the elevator.

Lucky for me, I didn't have to wait long in front of the building in my tight outfit, smudged makeup, and spiked heels—just one step up from wearing a sandwich board that read "I'm a Hooker"—because Billy's town car was sitting there waiting for me.

"Have a nice night?" he said as I got into the car, a smug look on his face.

I glared at him from behind my sunglasses and didn't answer. "You're taking me straight back, right?" I said instead.

"Absolutely, sweetheart," he said cheerily. He was always like this the night after, good-humoured and joking, almost giddy at his luck that he had a sister like me. What a cash cow I was. "Your bag's in the trunk."

I'd enjoyed this ride in the past. It had been nice, then, to sit next to a brother who wasn't putting me down, to know I was the farthest away from another one of these trips as I could possibly be. This time I only felt deadened, as though what had happened the night before had murdered me and I was nothing but an empty capsule of flesh walking around, pretending to be alive.

Only one thing was clear to me, something I dearly wished I'd realized the day before, though I knew there was no use regretting it now. What's done was done. I was done.

"How much did you make?" I said suddenly, pulling the glasses from my face and staring at my loathsome brother.

He shrugged. "It was a business deal," he said smoothly. "There's no exact sum. In exchange for your charming company—" he grinned lasciviously at me—"he agreed to take on my business."

"Last night you said he was wiring you the cash," I pointed out, my suspicion ignited. "What business, anyway? The restaurant?"

I'd always wanted to know as little as possible about how my brother made his money, mainly because everything he did was tinged with sketchiness, his purchases never seeming exactly on the up-and-up. He'd run a boxing club, an Italian restaurant, and a delivery service over the years, each of them eventually folding for unknown reasons, though not for lack of my help.

Now, as he shifted in his seat as though my question had taken him off guard, I wondered why I'd never pressed to know more about how I was helping him, how much money was changing hands, and what precisely he was doing with it.

I knew very well that Billy was self-centred and untrustworthy. I'd learned that lesson the hard way at sixteen. So, why on earth had I trusted him with our mother's care for all these years?

"How much are you sending to Mom?" I demanded. "Look at me, goddammit!"

Billy turned his head toward me with deliberate slowness, his eye finally settling on me with a look of utter disdain.

"Why should I tell you?" he said. "You know you don't have a head for numbers."

"Try me," I said, unwilling to let his insult rattle me.

He smiled then, an almost frightening grin, as though my determination amused him.

"I will send our mother the same sum I send her every month," he answered. "This deal will just keep the cheques coming, as she expects them too. And of course, as you always request, I won't mention your participation in my business so you can keep up the charade that you aren't a whore who fucks the guys I line up for you. I'll leave you out of it, just like you like it."

He reached out to pat my hand but I snatched it away.

"This was the last time," I said, enjoying the sound of the words coming out of my mouth, like music to my ears. "I'm never doing this again."

My statement seemed to have no impact on my brother, who was looking down at his phone.

"You'll do as I say," he said, scrolling up the screen with his thumb.

"No, I won't," I said firmly. I folded my arms over my chest. "It's over, Billy. I don't work for you anymore."

He glanced up at me disinterestedly, before returning his attention to his stupid phone, though only for a second. A moment later I snatched it out of his hand and tossed it under the seat in front of me.

Closing his now empty hand, my brother narrowed his eyes at me.

Are you getting it yet? Are you hearing me?

"This isn't some waitressing job you can just drop because you screwed the manager against the hostess stand," Billy said. I knew by the sharpness of his words that I had his attention now, at least. "I've told you what will happen if you don't provide this service for me. I've told you what I'll do."

"Tell everyone I'm a huge slut?" I said. "Like they don't know that already. Tell all my friends, my boyfriend, my teachers? Go right ahead, Billy. My life is already a huge pile of crap. I'd like to see you try to make it worse. Be my guest."

"Prostitution is illegal, little sister," he said, his lips tight and white with anger. "You'll be expelled. You'll end up in jail."

"So, my pimp is going to turn me in?" I said, raising my

eyebrows at him.

I put on a sweet, high voice. "I wanted to stop, officer, but he threatened to cut off my mother. He picked me up, told me what to wear, where to go. I never saw any money, honest. I thought I was doing the right thing, taking care of my sick parent. It wasn't illegal what I did, was it?" I blinked innocently at him. "He told me it was all right."

"Stop the car!" Billy shrieked, his eyes blazing.

As the car jerked toward the curb he lunged across the seat at me, grabbing me brutally by the forearms. I almost laughed at his sudden, over-the-top rage and the way the spittle collected on his lips when he spoke next.

"No judge would ever believe a slut like you," he threatened, pushing me back against the seat. "If you turn on me I'll turn on you right back. Who do you think they'll believe?"

"A misguided college student, or a sleazy entrepreneur with a string of failed business ventures?" I said, picking at his fingers, though they held fast. "I wonder."

"If you stop helping me I'll stop sending money home," he said. "Do you want to be responsible for cutting off your own mother's medication?"

I considered what he'd said. Was he really that cruel? Would he really abandon his own mother? Then I saw his eyes widen in triumph at my hesitation and I had my answer. I couldn't believe I'd ever doubted it.

Of course he was that heartless, that cruel.

Billy didn't care about anyone but himself.

"I'll get a job," I countered.

He scoffed, as if the idea of me holding down employment was a joke.

"Two jobs! I'll send every dime back to Mom. I bet it'll be more than you're giving her."

"Nobody would hire a dirty slut like you," he said. Shoving me away from him, he leaned over and unlatched the door, pushing it open. "You're nothing but a used up whore and I'm going to make sure everybody knows it. This is the biggest mistake of your life."

"No, my biggest mistake was years ago," I corrected him. "We both know that."

I gave him a meaningful look and he shook his head, turning back toward the window on his side.

"Get out," he said, gesturing toward the open door without even looking at me. "You can walk yourself the rest of the way home."

I wasn't wearing a jacket and there were clouds gathering in the sky, thunder rumbling in the distance. Still, I didn't hesitate for a second before climbing out of that fancy car on the side of the highway.

"You will never own me again," I said, holding the door open.

They were the most liberating six words I'd ever spoken.

"Sweetheart—" Billy began, but I slammed the door in his face before he could finish.

The car took off in a spray of gravel, leaving me by myself, without my bag or an umbrella (or even a bra), but infinitely stronger and safer and happier than if I'd had all those things. No moment had ever felt sweeter than this one, watching Billy speed out of my life for good.

My life might have been a snarled mess, but at least I had this cherry of self-respect to put on top of it.

It wasn't much, but it was something.

By the time I made it back to my apartment three hours later—after walking five kilometres in the cold and rain (in heels!) before I managed to hitch a ride with a young business woman who clearly thought I was a street walker who'd gotten into a bad way—I was shivering, exhausted and feeling the beginnings of the flu coming on.

I sneezed impressively as I slipped off my shoes, looking down at my swollen and blistered feet, then covered my nose and mouth, eyeing Anita's bedroom door. I couldn't let her see me dressed this way, when she probably thought I'd been at Harrison's this whole time. I couldn't let her know about my double life, especially not when I was ready to put it all behind me.

I tried to cross the apartment as quietly as possible—which wasn't easy given how much I was dripping—but then gave up the act when I glanced into her room and saw it was dark and empty. Then I remembered that Anita was out of town. There was nobody here, and nobody coming.

I was alone.

As soon as I realized this, something inside of me ruptured and I sank to my knees on my bedroom rug, unable to make it to the bed. For the first hour or so after Billy had left me by the side of the highway I'd been able to maintain my optimism, which had turned to satisfaction as the rain trickled down my back, then soured to dismay when nobody would give me a ride, and then disgust with myself, and then contempt.

Because no matter what I'd told Billy afterwards, I'd still slept with a man for money the night before. I could still feel Vince's hands on my body, his fingers pulling my hair, his weight on top of me when he'd finally finished, nearly crushing my windpipe. I could still remember how he hadn't moved right away when I'd gasped that he was suffocating me.

Covering my face with trembling fingers, I realized I didn't know who I was anymore. Was I the party-girl who sought out sex to dull her self-hatred, and did it all with a smile? Or was I the new girl I'd been trying to be, the girl who went to class and read comic books and had a sweetly-serious, nerdy boyfriend who was crazy about her? I couldn't be both, that was obvious. Kneeling on the floor, I realized queasily that both of these personas were pretty much lost to me now. I couldn't be my old sex-crazed self because sex wasn't doing for me what it used to. It wasn't really doing anything for me at all. And I couldn't be the new Sally after what I'd done the night before. I'd never be able to keep up the act. Other people might not know what had happened, my girlfriends might not know, my classmates might not know, but I would know. I would know my every action, my every effort to be this person was a lie. I would know what I had done, and who I really was.

You can take the girl out of the whorehouse, but you can't turn the whore back into a girl.

Taking off my sopping clothes, I managed to climb into bed in just my underwear and wrap the blankets around me. The room was spinning and I wasn't sure if it was because I was sick, or because of my reeling emotions. My wet hair clung to my face in strings and my nose wouldn't stop running, but was that because I was crying?

I kept turning over the last twenty-four hours in my head, and then reaching further back to Harrison's face when he'd kissed me, his voice telling me how I made him feel—*you have no idea what you do to me*—his gorgeous eyes. I felt a pain in my gut as though I'd been punched when I realized, again and again, that I couldn't be with him anymore. I'd tainted what we had by running to a stranger's bed mere hours after I'd been in his. How could I ever look him in the eye again after what I'd done? How could I bear for him to look at me, to see me, knowing eventually he would see the truth: That I'd ruined what we had, as I ruined everything.

I could never be with Harrison again. I'd lost him.

And in losing him, I'd lost everything.

My sobs came hard, mixed with bouts of coughing and shivering, until my body was nothing but a quivering, snivelling mess, and I couldn't tell which misery was worse.

At some point in the night I got out of bed, still wrapped in my blankets, and walked unsteadily to the door to turn off the overhead light that had been keeping me awake for hours. It was then that I saw the blinking light of the answering machine and pressed the message button before throwing myself back on the bed.

The first message was from Harrison, and my breath caught at the sound of his voice. He must have left it not long after I'd left his place: "Hi Sally. I just wanted to check that you're all right, since you left without saying goodbye this morning. Or maybe you did say it and I thought it was a dream? I had a wonderful time with you last night. Call me when you get this."

His voice was husky, intimate, still caught in the wonderful warm tendrils of the night before.

I had a wonderful time with you.

I felt so wretched my stomach heaved.

The beep followed, and then there was a message from Melissa asking if I wanted to go shopping, and one from Anita reminding me, on the ride to the airport, that she would be coming back on Tuesday afternoon.

Then another from Harrison, this time a little less confident.

"Hey Sally, are you there? I was thinking of going out for a bite to eat and thought you might like to join me. So...call me back, all right?"

There were two more messages, I could tell by the number of times the machine light flashed. I almost clutched my pillow to my ears so I couldn't hear them. I didn't want to hear the bewildered tone in his voice that I knew was coming, the confusion. I didn't want to hear it dawn on him that I would never be calling back.

Next message: "It's Harrison, Sally. I'm sorry I've left so many messages. I just want to make sure the other night...I hope I didn't upset you. Please give me a call."

I listened to the last message intently, searching his tone for the slightest sound of pain, but all I could hear was resignation. It had been only a day and a half since I'd last seen him, but my silence seemed to have communicated everything I'd been so worried I might have to say in person.

Somehow, he already knew.

"Oh Sally," he said with a sigh. "Is this how it ends?"

No, I thought to myself as I turned onto my stomach, weeping into my pillow. *This isn't how it ends.*

This is how you know it never even began.

19

I really thought that was it. I thought he got it, that he knew it was over between us.

But apparently Harrison wasn't one to give up so easily.

I spent the rest of that day and most of the next in bed, in and out of consciousness, never sure which was worse, the nightmares that invaded my sleep, or the horror of being awake. The flu that had me in its grip was severe and unrelenting, and left me reeling between feverish sweats and chills, aching bones, and exhaustion, all of it riding on a wave of nausea that never seemed to crash. Basically I felt like a pile of crap.

This is what you get for being a whore, I thought to myself. *This is your punishment.*

The apartment was cold and silent, the only sound that of me puking into the waste basket beside my bed, trudging to the bathroom to wash it out, and then barely making it back to bed before I hurled again. Eventually I made camp on the bathroom floor, my cheek resting on the cold tile, which (thanks to Anita) smelled reassuringly of lemon and pine, a nice clean smell. I really didn't know what my life would have been like if Anita had not agreed to be my roommate. I pictured myself eating raw ramen noodles out of the package, pawing through my laundry basket for a top that smelled clean enough, and showing up to class on the wrong day, at the wrong hour, in the wrong building. Anita really was my angel.

"Wish you were here, Anita," I mumbled deliriously as I stared up at the shower curtain. "I could really use an angel right now."

Since I couldn't manage to drag myself into the living room, I couldn't watch TV to pass the time—though I didn't think daytime TV would do much for my gag-reflex, anyway—but luckily I had something even better within easy reach.

I'd barely made a dent in the twelfth issue of *The Forever Place*, which was a double issue, and the comic became my saving grace. On Sunday, once my stomach finally settled, at least a little bit, I managed to get myself back into bed. Snuggled under the covers I poured over that comic, devouring each page with the same intensity I'd once given *Tiger Beat* as a pre-teen. I was glad to have something to lose myself in, something to quiet my rampaging thoughts which, without supervision, tended to stray to places and things I absolutely did not want to think about. Like a certain guy's voice on my answering machine. Or that feeling of yearning as his lips approached mine. Or even the way he said my name, nothing more, just my name.

But nothing good could come of thinking of him now. Nothing but anguish and self-reproach. Nothing but suffering.

And so I read my comic.

Sadly, the comic was kind of a downer, which didn't exactly help my mood. Rainbow was being held prisoner in a tower by Kas and his band of wolf followers. She'd trusted him when she shouldn't have, telling him secrets that he'd used against her, and now she was paying the price. At least half of the issue was filled with fantasy sequences in which Rainbow, sitting forlornly in her cell, imagined how she could escape, until finally coming to the realization that the only way out was to go back and make different choices. She'd been too trusting, too naive. Kas wasn't the problem at all, *she* was the problem.

Lucky for Rainbow, there was a secret trap door in her cell and a helpful Wittling guide who offered to lead her away from the tower and out of Kas's territory so she could get back to her quest and start again, armed with her new wisdom, ready to face the unknown. The issue ended with Rainbow riding an odd creature called a Jubble, sort of a mix between a camel and a lion, setting out over the dunes under a starry sky.

I wondered, if Rainbow could start over, did that mean I could too? Was there some secret passageway in my life that would spit me out in a different place where I could be a different person, all my past mistakes forgotten? Was that even what I wanted? Rainbow had to leave everyone behind, including her best friend Bedly, and her home, even her identity. Is that what it was going to take to remake me? Or could I stay here and keep being this person, whoever she was, and face the future still saddled with all the baggage of my past, my actions, my mistakes?

Was I strong enough to stay?

As afternoon gave way to evening and my head started to pound with a sinus headache—a new delightful symptom to pile on top of nausea, congestion, exhaustion, and a hacking cough—I began to consider the possibility that I might need some medication. Sitting up in bed surrounded by tissues, I thought over my options.

Walk to the pharmacy down the street and get some flu meds. (The sensible choice.)

Drive to a pharmacy two towns over where I could be sure I wouldn't run into anyone I knew because the idea of facing the outside world right now made me feel sicker than the flu. (A mildly deranged choice.)

Become a hermit and never leave the house again because I didn't deserve to be around normal people who didn't sleep with guys for money. (The self-hating, and yet most attractive, choice.)

Though I was leaning heavily toward B, when I stood up and realized how difficult it was going to be just to walk to the front door, I decided driving a car might not be the most intelligent decision right then. So, I pulled my raincoat on over my sweatpants—that's right, it was also still pouring rain—and dragged myself outside where I started the slow, achy, five-block walk to the pharmacy under Anita's umbrella with the panda bears on it.

I was about halfway there when I felt a hand on my arm and turned around to see a soaking wet Harrison standing in front of me.

Right away my knees went weak and I staggered, almost falling into him. His hands shot out and he grasped me by the waist. I felt my pulse quicken and my chilled body begin to warm, just from his touch, even with several layers of clothing between his skin and mine.

Oh God, not good. This is so not good!

Once I was able to catch my breath, I looked up into his eyes—another mistake—and found myself frozen there, unable to move.

"Sally, where have you been?" Harrison said. Water ran down his face but he didn't seem to notice. "I've been calling. Are you all right?"

He seemed so concerned, so caring, and I considered how easy it would be just to make up some excuse and go on as if nothing had happened. He still hadn't let me go and I knew I shouldn't be letting him hold me, or letting my free hand fall on his strong arm, or imagining him pulling me into those arms and holding me forever. But I did it anyway.

What can I say? I'd never been much good at following the rules.

Harrison said, "Anita told me—"

I interrupted him with a sneeze that led to a fit of coughing, finally allowing me to pull my eyes away from his and back away. As soon as I'd lost that contact with his hands I felt my mind clear.

Going back to him is not an option, I reminded myself. *Loving him is not an option. You lost that right, not that you ever had it.*

I had to leave him, cut all ties, and be done with it. I would only be beating him to the punch.

This was for his own good.

"So what, are you stalking me now?" I said, stepping around him on the sidewalk so I could continue on my way. "You're calling Anita about me, waiting for me outside my building?"

I'd done this before, given some poor sap a severe talking to when he'd taken our one-night-stand to be more than it was. I'd rejected guys before, guys who'd wanted more than I could give, who'd thought they'd found love between my thighs when I knew all they'd really found was a mistake. They didn't really love me. How could they? And neither did Harrison.

I just had to remind him why. I had to drive my point home.

Harrison frowned. "I was worried," he corrected me. "I had no idea if what happened between us had hurt you or scared you off. And then Anita told me she was out of town. You weren't answering the phone. I thought it was possible—"

"What? One night in your bed and I'm going to run home and drink myself into a coma?" I said meanly. "I'm not your junkie brother, Harrison. And you're not that good in bed." I waited a beat for those words to sink in. "Trust me. I have a lot to compare it to."

I knew those words had to be a double blow, reminding him of his inexperience and re-enforcing my claim that he was a bad lover—which couldn't have been farther from the truth—but I couldn't tell if my digs were hitting home. His face was expressionless once again, though he did seem mildly confused. If he'd been Alex he would have been raging at me already. He would have been walking away already. But Harrison wasn't Alex. I was going to have to up my game.

Another coughing fit came over me and I turned away, covering my mouth.

"What are you doing out on the street?" Harrison said, trying to take my arm, but I pulled it away. "You're sick. You should be in bed."

"Don't tell me what to do!" I cried.

Now I was walking quickly, walking away, hoping he'd

just let me go, but he kept pace with me easily. How was it that the rain didn't seem to bother him at all, when each gust of wind almost bowled me over? When I could tell I wasn't going to outrun him I slowed down, feeling spent.

"Just leave me alone," I said. "The other night was a mistake. I don't want to see you anymore."

I could tell this time my words really reached him, because he stepped in front of me, blocking my way. "A mistake?" he said, and as he spoke I heard the echo of those same words when he'd said them to me the night we staked-out the crack house.

I shouldn't have brought you here. This was a mistake.

I knew how it felt to hear those words. I knew how much they hurt.

He stepped under the umbrella and I tried to keep my face neutral, hostile even, but it was so hard when he was so *close*. Even under all that wet I could just smell that orange scent of his and all I wanted was to let him take me home to bed, strip off my clothes—sickness be damned—and make love to me. Because I knew I'd never get the chance again. I would never feel like this about anyone again.

And no one would ever feel like this about me, ever.

"What happened?" Harrison said, getting right to the heart of things, knowing there had to be more to it than what I was saying.

Which of course there was, not that I could explain it to him.

"I was wrong, that's all," I said, raising my chin, trying to sound confident, resolved, but my voice faltered when my eyes dipped to his lips.

"What were you wrong about?" he said.

His eyes never left my face as he stepped closer still, brushing a stray drop of rain from my cheek and then leaving his hand there. His thumb rubbed my skin lightly and my hand shook as I clutched the umbrella handle between us, not that I was paying much attention to the rain anymore, or my aching body, or anything or anyone else.

Focus, Sally. Finish this now. Don't open yourself up to even more pain. Don't let him suck you back in.

"Sally," Harrison said in that low, tender voice that made me melt, and I knew in a second his lips would be on mine and I wouldn't be able to say no. I had one second to decide. One second until I broke my own heart and his. One second to feel this, for the last time.

He came so close. His lips grazed mine, just the slightest of touches, before I pushed him back with an anguished cry, the umbrella skittering to the ground between us.

For once Harrison looked truly astonished.

My mind went back to the moment on campus when he'd pulled away from me and accused me of being just like Jason, and I found his words forming on my tongue.

"I can't do this with you," I said. "This will never work."

He stood very still, his eyes finally slipping from my face, coming to rest on my right shoulder. He recognized these words. He knew what the end sounded like.

"I'm bad for you and your bad for me," I choked out, wiping the water from my face uselessly, because there was always more.

Harrison shook his head at me. For once he didn't look tense, like he was waiting for some fight that might come at any moment. Instead, his shoulders we slightly slumped, his head bowed. He looked defeated. And yet still he shook his head, as if he didn't believe me, as if he knew that every word I was saying was bullshit. He knew, but he also knew there wasn't a thing he could do about it.

And that was the closest to an agreement as I was going to get.

"Goodbye, Harrison," I said in my hardest tone, hard enough to hold back the tears gathering behind my eyes. Hard enough to get me past him and up the block, to get away. Hard enough to carry me through this, or so I hoped.

I was going to need all the help I could get.

I slammed the bottle in its paper bag down on the coffee

table and stared at it through watery eyes. It wasn't my fault the pharmacy was right next to a liquor store, was it? I couldn't take the blame for that lucky urban planning decision, nor could I really be made to explain why, after rushing down the aisles to grab the three first packages of cold and flu medication I could find, I'd rushed just as breathlessly into that liquor store. I'd snatched up the first whiskey bottle I saw and brandished it to the clerk at the cash like a weapon, throwing the bills at him and whisking out the door into the rain before he could give me my change.

None of this was my fault, not really. The mistake that had started this crazy, out-of-control roller coaster that was my life had been made so long ago. I couldn't still be held accountable for it, could I? I couldn't be expected to answer for these crimes, not when I had started out as the victim.

Could I?

Wiping the tears from my cheeks, I broke open the first box of pills and swallowed two with a glass of water. Then I went back to staring at the bottle as I waited for the drugs to take effect and carry me to sleep.

I didn't know why this final, miserable moment, the moment of the end of Harrison and I, was making me think so much about that day when I was sixteen, but it did. Because that's when all of this had started, when my life had been wrested out of my hands and jerked in a completely different direction. By Billy. And by him, Connor Buckley. Just thinking his name made me wince.

Don't you want to kiss me, Sally? Isn't that how all good dates end?

Reaching blindly for the bottle, I unscrewed the top and upended it, taking one gulp, two, three.

Connor Buckley, captain of the football team, star forward, charming devil. Connor Buckley who said he'd had his eye on me ever since he'd become friends with my brother, although I had my doubts. Why on earth would he look at me, when he could have any girl he wanted? Why would he want to kiss me, who'd never kissed a boy before, me who'd never even been on a date?

Come on, Sally. Just let me. It doesn't have to mean anything. I treated you nice, didn't I? Just let me touch.

More swigs from the bottle, until it was practically half empty and my vision swam and I had trouble sitting up straight.

He had beautiful eyes, Connor did. They were a lot like Harrison's eyes, now that I thought about it. Although Connor's were steely and hard when he'd shoved his hand up my skirt. Harrison would never have looked at me that way. Harrison was ten times the man Connor Buckley could ever be. And Billy too. Billy and Connor, like two pythons with snapping tongues, circling me, taunting me.

And now, Billy's voice filled my head and I couldn't let go of the bottle.

Dimly I heard the phone ringing.

What did you do to him, Sal? What the hell happened? Run get help! Run! Oh God, Sal, what did you do?

You're going to fix this for me. You're going to make it up to him. Whatever I say, that's what you're going to do. Don't you dare cry!

This is what you wanted, isn't it, Sally? You wanted all the boys to like you, didn't you? This is what you asked for. This is what you deserve. This is what it is to be loved.

Dirty whore. Stupid slut.

Slutty Sally. Slutty Sally. Slutty Sally.

I didn't know when I picked up the box. I didn't remember making the decision, only opening my mouth and swallowing. Only ripping open the next box, snapping out the pills, filling my palms and swallowing, swallowing. Washing them down with whiskey. Gagging on the sheer number of them clogging my throat. And swallowing, swallowing, swallowing.

Nobody will ever love you now.

The phone rang again, the shrill note insistent, and I picked it up and barked, "What?" into the receiver. There was a voice on the other end of the line, but I couldn't hear what it was saying. I couldn't hear anything over the singing, or was it screaming? Was I screaming?

You're nothing. You're used up. You're ruined.

One last box, one last handful of pills. It was harder to get these ones down. My lips wouldn't work. My arms were heavy. I could barely lift the bottle. I could barely see the pills, which were so small and rolling everywhere. I could barely see anything at all.

Nobody will ever love you ever again.

I fell back against the couch cushions and thought about that word, "ever." How it was so permanent. How it went on forever. How the choices we made never really left us, they lasted, they followed. They could never be escaped.

I didn't know how much time passed. I heard a loud noise to my right and wondered if it was the storm trying to crash into the apartment. I imagined it busting through the door, dead, wet leaves sweeping in, splattering the lamps and the rug and the couch, the ceiling ripped away, all my things soaked or swept away.

And me along with it.

There was a loud bang and I thought, *It's happening now,* and then someone was calling my name and holding my head and gathering me in their arms.

How nice of the storm to cradle me, I thought. *What a lovely way to go.*

I smelled the sweet smell of oranges before I closed my eyes and didn't open them again for a long time.

20

And then I did open my eyes and everything was different.

I was in a room with white vertical blinds over the window. They were the ugliest vertical blinds I'd ever seen, which was saying something since vertical blinds were, in general, pretty hideous. I tried to turn my head away so I wouldn't be staring at the window with its monstrous vertical blinds, and that's when I noticed how weak I felt, my head wobbling on my neck, my throat painful and raw. The room I was in was small and painted light blue. There was a painting of the seashore across from my bed, beside the door, and everything smelled like industrial floor cleaner.

Oh, I get it. I'm in hell.

I was tucked so tightly into bed that I couldn't move my arms—a sensation I hadn't felt since I was very small—my mother had always been an overly aggressive tucker—and as I wiggled weakly, trying to free at least one shoulder, I realized it wasn't the sheets that were holding me down, it was the person who's head was pressing the sheets down. The sleeping person with his head on my arm. The lightly snoring person whose short dark hair I ran my fingers through, startling him awake.

"You're awake!" Harrison exclaimed, his eyes snapping to my face. It was a pretty funny thing to say, considering he was the one who'd been sleeping.

But Harrison didn't look like he was in a laughing mood. His face was pale, almost sickly, under the stubble covering his jaw. He had bags under his eyes as though he hadn't slept a wink, though he'd been asleep just a second before, and the look he was giving me was slightly wild, as though he couldn't believe what he was seeing. I pulled one arm out from under the covers and he grasped my hand like a drowning man clinging to a life raft.

He looked such a mess I suddenly had the maternal urge to wrap him in a blanket and cuddle him.

"Your hair's sticking up," I said instead, and he nodded, but didn't move a muscle to brush it back down.

There was something strange about the way he was looking at me with his bloodshot eyes, as though he was afraid to look away. A troubling thought fluttered at the edge of my mind—or was it a memory?—but I swatted it away.

"Why'd you do this, Sally?" Harrison said hoarsely, as if he was in pain.

The memory fluttered closer.

"What did I do now?" I said flippantly, because there were so many things I might have done wrong. I was always messing things up and making bad decisions. I was the girl who got shoved onto the porch in her underwear for saying her boyfriend's brother's name in bed. If he was going to make me guess, this could take all day.

Harrison rubbed roughly at his face with his hands, leaving it looking red and irritated. He seemed truly not to want to say what he was about to say, which made me feel incredibly uneasy.

"Try to remember what happened last night," he finally said, his grip on my hand becoming more gentle, his thumb tracing soft circles on mine.

He nodded encouragingly, but his eyes told a different story. His eyes, full of concern, seemed to want me *not* to remember. Or was it just that *he* didn't want to remember?

"I was sick all day," I said, as if it was obvious. "I had the flu." Though, I noticed, all my flu symptoms were gone now, as though they'd been sucked right out of me.

An image flashed through my mind of bright lights in my eyes and a tube approaching my face, the feeling of being emptied.

"And then what happened?" Harrison said softly.

"I saw you outside in the rain," I said, more slowly, more uncertain. "You tried...you tried to kiss me."

But I'd pulled away from his kiss. There'd been a good reason for it, an important reason. Why couldn't I remember what it was?

Another image, this time of a woman with a clipboard standing beside the bed in this room, Harrison arguing with her. I felt my own hands covering my ears as I turned on my side, turned away.

"And then what happened?" Harrison repeated, his words not much above a whisper.

"And then..."

It all came back to me then, not in a smooth flood of memories, but in jagged and painful flashes, like hammer blows. I remembered what I'd done with Vince, and the ride in the car with Billy, and coming back, my walk in the rain. I remembered being sick, and vomiting, and knowing I'd lost Harrison forever, and seeing him on the street, and the liquor store, and the pills and the liquor, and the pills and the pills and the pills.

And vaguely, very dimly, I remembered making the snap decision to take my own life.

Because it wasn't worth very much anyway. Because I wasn't worth very much to anyone.

"Get away from me," I said shakily.

Every single terrible feeling I'd felt over the past two days washed over me and I found myself riddled with self-loathing. Clamping my eyes shut, I struggled to pull away from Harrison's grip, to scramble to the other side of the mattress, but he put his arm around me to keep me close.

"Get away from me," I cried, kicking out with my feet, shoving the covers off the bed. "I'm no good! I'm disgusting."

"No, Sally," Harrison said. His grip on me wasn't tight, just firm. His voice was even, sure, as if I wasn't having a tantrum right in front of him. "I'm not going anywhere. I'm staying here, with you."

But I didn't want him to stay. I didn't want him to see me like this, at my absolute lowest, my most pathetic. I didn't want him here as I remembered getting my stomach pumped while he watched, as I remembered the counsellor asking me if I wanted to die.

What type of person tried to kill themselves? The ruined type, that's who. The lost causes. The dregs of society. I wanted to run away from him, let him remember me how I was—fun and sexy and mischievous. I didn't want him to see this. I'd worked so hard to never let anyone see this.

There was nothing fun about hospitals.

There was nothing sexy about bed pans.

There was nothing mischievous about the girl who didn't want to live.

"Please just go," I said painfully, turning my head away. "I don't want you to see me like this."

"Sally," Harrison murmured, his voice a low rumble, "just look at me."

When I didn't turn my head, he reached over and cupped my cheek, and I leaned into his palm, which was so soft and comforting. I just couldn't help myself. Before I knew it, I'd turned around and I was in his arms. He climbed onto the bed and gathered me toward him, lining my body up with his, his strong arms encircling me, holding me, securing me, his face inches from mine on the pillow. That heartbreakingly beautiful face with its blue, blue eyes that always seemed, like none before, to be looking directly into my soul.

It was so hard to look at him and know he was looking back at me, seeing me as I was. Seeing the real me.

We lay that way for a while, until the tightness in my chest began to ease. Only then did I realize that Harrison was shaking in my arms and my hair was wet from the tears running silently down his cheeks.

"This is my fault," Harrison began, and right away I shook my head. I would not let him blame himself for what a good-for-nothing, slutty, screw-up I was. Not a chance.

"No," I said. "No."

I held his face in my hands, wiping his tears away with my thumbs.

"I can't believe I could have lost you," he choked out, and he seemed so full of anguish, his entire body twisted with it, that all I could do was silence his words with a kiss.

When our lips met, the world stilled. I felt Harrison's mouth against mine, opening, responding, and both our heart beats calming, until there were no more tears, and the pain of it all began to fade just a little, just enough.

He still seemed to want to speak, to explain—when really I was the one who needed to explain—and I decided to let him. Because if Harrison was still kissing me, still holding me, maybe I didn't understand anything. Maybe it was time I listened.

Gliding his hand up and down my back in a reassuring motion, Harrison began to speak.

"I'm not good at saying what I feel," he said. "I'm not like you. You're so free, so open with your opinions, your feelings. I've never been that way." He shook his head, his eyes trailing down to my arms. "I should have told you as soon as I felt it, as soon as I knew it. Maybe if I had you wouldn't have done this. You must have felt so alone."

His expression hardened as he shook his head, reproaching himself. This time it was my turn to take his chin and make him look at me.

"You didn't leave me alone," I told him. "I pushed you away. Because you're too good for me. I shut you out. It's not your fault."

"Of course it's my fault," Harrison said, tightening his arms around me, his voice tortured. "I should never have let you shut me out. I should have told you."

"Should have told me what?" I demanded in exasperation. I had no patience, that morning, for beating around the bush.

Harrison drew his hands up to my cheeks, his eyes unwavering as he said, "I should have told you how *much* I'm in love with you."

For a moment I could hear nothing but the beating of my own heart. Or was it his? It was hard to tell the difference.

"In love with *me*?" I croaked, my throat suddenly dry.

He was mad, delirious from lack of sleep. He felt guilty because of what I'd done and he wanted to make me feel better. That's why he was telling me this lie. It was the only explanation.

"That's a terrible lie to tell," I said. I pulled my face out of his hands, retreated from his touch, lowering my eyes. "And I should know," I said. "I know a thing or two about lies."

As I folded my arms around myself, Harrison's looked like he was about to contradict me—not that it would have worked. I knew a whopper when I heard one—but then he seemed to reconsider. He laid down on his back so I was staring at the side of his head, and looked up at the ceiling.

"I'm not lying," he began, and held up a hand to stop me before I could interrupt, "but I can tell you're going to need some convincing. So here goes."

Huddling on my side of the bed—which was really more like one-third of the total area of the mattress. He took up an awful lot of space—I gave him a surly look, but didn't try to stop him. If he wanted to keep the charade going a little while longer then let him. I knew he wouldn't be able to convince me. Guys like Harrison Leo didn't fall for girls like me. I'd spent enough time in the last few weeks learning that lesson. Nothing he said now would make me unlearn it.

"I've fallen in love with you three times," Harrison said, which was a pretty impressive opener. He certainly had my attention. "The first time was last spring. I'd seen you a few times around the house with Alex already, but this was the first time he introduced us."

My eyes widened and Harrison smiled at the ceiling.

"Don't worry," he said. "I know you don't remember. There was a party going on at the house and Alex was pretty drunk, you less so. He'd collapsed on the couch and a song you liked was playing. You were trying to get him to get up and dance with you. I came into the room and Alex introduced us. He told me to dance with you. He said, 'Do a guy a favour and dance with her so she'll shut up.' Something like that. I remember being so offended that he'd spoken that way about you, but you didn't seem particularly bothered. You beamed at me and draped your arms around me and we danced. Not very well, mind you. I sort of tripped around for about a quarter of the song. Then someone dragged you away. But before you went you kissed me on the cheek and thanked me for the dance. And I was done for."

"I sort of remember that," I said, thinking back. "I mean, I remember dancing with a sweet guy who had warm hands. You held me really close."

"Yeah well, I thought it would be my only chance to hold a girl as beautiful as you. I figured I'd better make the most of it," he said, with his signature grin.

"Was that really you?" I said with some amazement.

I focused on the fact that I'd actually been in Harrison's arms all those months before to stop myself from focusing on the fact that he'd called me beautiful. Because that wasn't something I could focus on. Not if I didn't believe him.

"That was me," Harrison said with a nod at the ceiling tiles. "That was us. That was the first time I fell in love with you."

I folded my hands under my cheek and let myself be drawn into the story. It was a nice story anyway. It was romantic. Even if it wasn't true. Even if he was making it up. I couldn't hurt just to listen, could it?

"The second time was…more complicated," he said.

He turned his head to glance at me and I felt caught in his gaze. He didn't turn completely toward me, but he kept his head turned my way, telling this part of the story to the wall behind me, his eyes coming and going from my face.

"I'd pretty much managed to forget about you. You were with Alex, after all. Well, Alex and also Jeremy…"

"You knew about that?" I said, startled, and he gave me a rueful look.

"You can hear an awful lot through the walls in that house. And the laundry room shared a wall with my room."

My heart sank as I remembered the quickie I'd had with Jeremy in that room late one night, my back up against the wall—Harrison's wall.

Harrison reached out and touched my knee and I didn't pull away. "I didn't think less of you for it," he said.

"Please," I said cynically. "If there's anyone who's absolutely in the wrong it's the girl cheating with her boyfriend's brother. How could you not think I was a terrible person?" I felt my cheeks heat up with shame.

"Well, Alex wasn't exactly being faithful, either," Harrison said and I nodded. No surprise there. "And to be honest you didn't really seem to be having much fun. It sort of seemed, from the little I saw anyway, that you were trying to punish yourself."

God, he really had me pegged, didn't he?

Getting back to the story, he said, "Then there you were, all of a sudden, standing at my front door in your underwear in the dead of night. I could say I fell for you again right then, when you fell into my arms half-naked and tried to seduce your way into my bed." He smiled again, as if the memory was so adorable, while I wanted to climb under the covers and die. "But my feelings were confused by the fact that you were always drunk or drinking when I saw you. I found myself feeling overwhelmingly protective of you, and also a little afraid."

"Afraid?" I said in disbelief. His eyes jumped from the window down to me. "You didn't seem scared to me. You were always staring at me. I thought I disgusted you, or maybe you just found it embarrassing to be around me."

Harrison's hand, which he'd somehow left on my knee

without my noticing, moved to my waist, which he pinched playfully. "I couldn't take my eyes off you because of how gorgeous you are." He paused for a moment, so those words could sink in. Which they sort of did, without my permission. "And also because I was concerned you were going to get yourself hurt. At The Limo right after you and Alex split? You seemed out to taunt every sketchy guy there. I couldn't bear to think of them hurting you. I wanted to crush each one that manhandled you."

"And then you had your chance," I said with fake brightness.

While I was screwing him like the whore I am.

"I went a little out of my head that night," Harrison admitted, his fingers tightening on me just slightly as he remembered. "I've never hit another guy like that before. But when I heard him say those words to you, I just sort of lost control."

"Don't apologize," I said, taking his fingers before they curled into a fist and holding them in mine. "I guess he deserved what he got."

"You guess?" he said. "There's no guessing about it. He deserved it." His eyes searched mine before slipping back to the window again.

"I guess you could say I was hypnotized by you, mesmerized. Here you were, this wildly beautiful girl, smart without knowing it—" he moved a finger to my lips to quiet me before I could call myself stupid, and I let him—"who was so different from me. I wanted you so badly, that day in the car waiting for Jason. I was falling for you again, but you were like a dangerous beast, like a tiger. I wasn't sure I could tame you. I wasn't sure I could keep up with you."

"I thought you didn't want to be with me because I was a dirty slut," I said, hanging my head.

Drawing his arm around me, Harrison pulled me in toward him, then slipped his hand around the back of my head. I looked up at him hesitantly.

"It kills me to hear you use that brutal, ugly word about

yourself, Sally," he said. "It only puts you down and paints a picture of you that's far from true. Can you promise that you won't use it again, that you'll stop calling yourself Slutty Sally? Can you do that for me?"

His blue eyes swam with sorrow as he spoke. I think I would have agreed to anything he asked me in that moment, even to bring him the moon or to build him a kingdom of gold. Anything to stop him from feeling this pain. Anything.

"I promise," I said honestly, and he drew me in closer and kissed the top of my head.

"Now, where was I?" he said. He seemed to have perked up some all of a sudden. I wondered if it had to do with the fact that I'd essentially let him pull me back into his arms little by little. The damn sneak.

"So there I was trying my damnedest not to fall for you again, and pretty much failing, and then there was that kiss…"

Oh God, that kiss. That first kiss.

"And then I spent the night in your bed…"

Shirtless! Let's not forget shirtless!

"And I was pretty much head over heels for you again," he said.

"Didn't last very long, did it?" I said, slapping him on the chest. "If I remember correctly, it was that same day that you accused me of being just like your brother and pushed me away again."

He brushed a thumb over my cheek. "You can be in love with someone even when you're pushing them away, can't you?"

Could you? I guess you could. Wasn't that what I was trying to do to Harrison at that moment?

"Those few days away from you were torture," Harrison admitted. "And at the same time Jason was being erratic. Then I ran into you sitting on that bench, and you helped me find him—something I'd really lost hope of doing at that point—and I fell in love with you a third time right then."

He pressed his forehead against mine and I felt the soft tickle of his words. "You: the clever, charming, amazing girl in front of me. The girl who isn't afraid to yell at a guy on a crowded sidewalk, or walk into a drug den. The girl who isn't embarrassed to dance on a table, or read a nerdy comic book series, or be seen with a guy who wears t-shirts with silly cartoons on them. The girl who breezes through her classes and thinks nothing of it. The girl who always under-estimates herself, and yet always surprises me. The girl who makes my heart leap in my chest every time I see her. I'm in love with you, Sally. Only you. Always and forever, you."

Let it be true. Let it be true. Let it be true.

I felt his mouth moving toward mine. I heard the voice in my head telling me he was lying. Telling me I didn't deserve him. Calling me every name in the book. But this time, for the first time, there was a louder voice in there, drowning him out. It was Harrison's voice, Harrison's words still coursing through me, shooting around in my head and my heart, taking me over.

Harrison saying he wanted me. Harrison saying he loved me three times over.

Harrison Leo saying he was mine.

"You love me?" I said, into his lips. Because I was never going to tire of hearing it. And if I was going to truly believe it, I was going to have to hear it again and again.

"I do," Harrison said, "and I always will, just as long as you don't try to leave me again." He fingered the hospital bracelet on my wrist and I nodded weakly.

"I promise," I said as his lips found mine and I filled with the deliciousness of him, the intensity of him, the incredible feeling of him in my arms where, I almost believed, he'd come to stay.

Almost.

21

For a day that had such an optimistic start, it certainly got pretty weepy. In between more visits from the counsellor and nurses and the doctor, I had a steady stream of my own visitors, starting with Anita, who rushed into the room looking wild-eyed and unkept—a very strange look for her. She was usually so immaculate.

As Harrison considerately excused himself to go get a cup of coffee, she plunked down on the edge of the bed, handed me a piece of pumpkin pie wrapped in cellophane, and burst into tears.

"Don't cry," I said, smoothing her short hair. "That counsellor with the clipboard who keeps threatening to put me on a psychiatric hold might walk in here any second. We don't want her locking you up, too."

"Can they really keep you here?" Anita said, wiping her wet cheeks with the back of her hand. "What about school?"

Count on Anita to think school would be my biggest concern.

"Don't worry," I said, leaning in to whisper in her ear.

"Harrison's casing the joint right now. He'll bust me out if it comes to it."

I thought at the very least that would get a smile out of her, but instead she only nodded slowly, looking thoughtful.

"He's a great guy," she said. "Thank God he was there. I mean, if he hadn't broken the door down…If he hadn't found you…"

The tears were threatening to fall again, and I pulled her into a hug just so I wouldn't have to see them.

"But he did find me," I said. "He did."

"I left you alone," Anita whispered. "I'm so sorry."

"Don't," I rushed in. "It's Thanksgiving. Of course you went to be with your family. That was exactly right. I feel bad enough that you had to cut your weekend short because of me. Because I'm such a mess. But I'm so—"

"You're so nothing," she interrupted. "You're awesome. And I can't believe I could have lost you."

I shook my head at her. "Why are you so good to me?" I said. "All I do is mess up and all you do is worry about me, and clean up after me, and wait for my next disaster. You deserve so much more from a best friend. I'm always dragging you down."

"Don't you say that!" Anita said. She was so adamant I couldn't help but shut my mouth. "I don't know what I would do without you! I'd probably schedule my life into oblivion and never live at all. You bring in the laughter, Sally (well, usually). You bring in the spontaneity, and the fun, and the silliness that's always been missing from my life. Sure, you mess up. But you're not afraid to mess up, not like me. And you always look at me like I'm the most awesome thing ever, even though I know you must think my life is boring as hell. You make me feel like I am awesome, sometimes anyway. My God, losing you would be like…like losing the best part of myself. I don't know what…I can't imagine…"

Then she was crying too hard to speak and so was I and for a while we just held each other. She didn't ask me why I did it and I didn't tell her. We just cried together and handed tissues back and forth and it felt remarkably good, for once, just to feel something with someone else instead of covering it up. I'd never known how good it could feel to be sad.

Eventually Emily and Melissa showed up looking tentative and scared, and while Harrison stood outside talking to Melissa's roommate (who'd given then a ride), we ate the pumpkin pie with a single plastic fork and tried to pretend we weren't in a hospital room.

"So," Em said, eyeing Harrison's back, "what's going on with baby blue eyes?"

Melissa elbowed her, as if asking about my love life while I was wearing a hospital gown was a total faux pas, which maybe it was, but I didn't care. I was just glad to be talking about something other than the elephant in the room.

"It's okay," I said as I chewed on a large mouthful of pie. I handed the fork to Emily to stop her from pushing Melissa off the bed. "I don't really know what's going on. He said...some things."

"Hot things?" Em prompted and Anita rolled her eyes.

"Romantic things?" she guessed instead, swiping Emily's bite before she could get it to her mouth.

"Hey!" Em said. "Are you trying to stop me from eating because you think I'm fat?"

"If she says yes can I have your portion?" Melissa said, snatching the plate out of my hand.

I couldn't help but chuckle as I watched my silly, sharp-tongued, wonderful friends fighting over the half-piece of pie in my lap. I didn't think I'd ever loved three people more in my life.

"Okay," Anita cried, holding up her hands in a T to signal a time-out. Emily had both the pie and the fork hoisted high above her head. "I think we've gotten a little off topic here." She turned to me, suddenly serious, and I was a little worried about what she would ask next. Would she bring up the pills, now, in front of everyone? "Just tell me one thing," she said. "Did you and Harrison have sex in this hospital bed?"

Three pairs of eyes stared at me avidly and I almost

wished I could say yes, just to make them happy.

"No," I said, grabbing the rest of the pie with my bare hands and shoving it in my mouth. Melissa groaned out loud and Emily pouted. As I chewed triumphantly, I added, "But we did get to second base, and we might have made third if a nurse hadn't walked in."

As they all howled with laughter, Harrison poked his head back into the room.

"Everything all right in here?" he asked, his eyebrows raised.

"Yeah," I said, my arms around my friends' shoulders, tears in my eyes again, but tears of laughter this time. Tears of happiness. "Everything's great."

Though I tried my best to convince the doctor that I wasn't going to try to take my life again, that I hadn't even really been trying to do so in the first place—I was pretty sure, anyway—he insisted I stay in the hospital for another night for observation. Harrison stayed with me all day, playing cards with Anita after Em and Melissa left, fetching us snacks as we watched re-runs of old comedies on the ancient TV in my room, even getting me a horrifyingly expensive pair of socks from the gift shop when I said my feet were cold. Eventually I badgered Anita into going home, Harrison assuring her that he would get me home safely the next day while she would be in class. As my friend waved a sad goodbye, we were finally alone again.

"Don't you have to leave too?" I asked him. I'd eaten too much junk food—Anita was a Kettle Chip junkie—and I was slumped on my side on the bed, Harrison lying behind me, my head nestled on his very comfy bicep.

I knew visiting hours were ending in about an hour, but I couldn't bear the thought of being without him. I had the irrational fear that everything he'd said about being in love with me would only stay true if we both remained in this hospital, in this room, in this bed. As soon as he walked back into the world, my little dream would be over.

"You really think I'm going to leave you here by yourself?" Harrison said, placing a soft kiss on my shoulder. I shivered with relief. "Not a chance."

"Well, I don't know if there's enough space for both of us in this tiny little bed," I said provocatively, turning toward him. "We might have to hold each other pretty close, in order to fit."

"Oh, you mean like this?" Harrison said gamely, pulling me tightly into his arms so our chests were pressed together. I was wearing a fleece top and pink sweatpants Anita had brought for me, but it was still pretty hot.

"No, I was thinking more like this," I said, looping my right leg over his hip and hearing him suck in a small breath as certain sensitive places touched each other. "Think you could lie like this all night?"

He reached under the hem of my top and spread his fingers across my back as he feathered little kisses over my cheekbones.

"Oh, I think I could put up with it," he breathed as my lips found his.

We were interrupted a few minutes later by a guy named Ace delivering the cot Harrison had somehow talked him into letting him have, even though sleepover guests were against hospital policy. Ace was young, tattooed, and definitely hot enough to have been around the block a few times, and yet he was exaggeratedly embarrassed at having caught us making out and kept covering his eyes and apologizing as he brought in the cot. He scampered off so quickly that Harrison felt bad for him and jumped out of bed to check on him, not that it was much of a loss. Though it was clear from my contact with his crotch he was definitely interested in kissing me, I'd felt him holding back, his touch tentative, his kisses never deepening, and his hands keeping to the decidedly PG areas of my body.

It made sense. We were in a hospital room, for god sakes! He was probably worried that if he kissed me too hard it would hurt me. And truthfully I didn't really want to have sex with Harrison for the first time in a room that smelled like sour cream and vinegar chips with a door that only locked from the outside.

But it was still hard, when he broke off the kiss, not to assume it was because he didn't want me. It was difficulty not to believe, when he didn't hold me as close as I wanted him to, that it was because his professions of love had been a lie. It was just too easy to give in to those lurking voices in my head, the ones who always believed the worst and told me so, like a mantra.

See? He doesn't want you. See? He doesn't love you. See? He's already running away.

Pulling the pillow out from under my own head, I pressed it to my face and groaned.

By the time Harrison got back from his search for Ace, the prudish orderly, I was already passed out from frustration and junk food bloat. I wasn't sure how much time had passed when I felt myself being shaken awake.

Opening my eyes, I saw that the lights in the room had been turned off and Harrison was sleeping in the cot across from me, one arm flung over his eyes. Then someone crouched down so their face was blocking my line of sight. It was Katie.

"Hey," she said softly, squeezing my hand. "How're you feeling?"

I saw a shadowy figure in the doorway, which I assumed was Lucas.

"I guess I took a nap," I said apologetically, half-sitting up. "What time is it?"

"It's almost seven," she said. "I'm so sorry I didn't stop by earlier. We were in the studio and I didn't check my phone for a while." I sometimes forgot that Katie was an artist. Lucas wasn't half bad either. She was preparing for some big end of semester presentation.

"That's okay," I said sleepily. "Anita and the girls were here earlier. I'm really fine."

But somehow I could tell that Katie, more so than any of my other friends, didn't quite believe me when I said this. She nodded and gave me a half-smile, but she seemed doubtful. She had that same look the counsellor did, that people-who-are-fine-don't-swallow-a-bunch-of-pills look.

"I just wanted to say, I'm sorry you didn't call me," she said softly. "Because, I understand."

"Understand what?" I said.

"I know what it's like to keep secrets," Katie said simply. "Trust me."

Secrets? How could Katie possibly know I was keeping secrets? Had I given myself away? Had I said too much some drunken night? Or did she just recognize something in me, something she'd once seen in herself during all those years of blaming herself for that little boy's death—the boy she'd been babysitting when that psycho Brandon Tomko, her boyfriend, had killed him. Had she picked up the signs of unhealthy coping mechanisms and hidden truths?

"I'm here if you need to talk, Sally," she said, kissing me on the cheek, before retreating to the door.

Although it was insanely early to be going to sleep, I didn't turn on the light or wake up Harrison. Instead, I watched Harrison napping restlessly, tossing around on the cot trying to find that elusive comfortable spot, and I thought about secrets. Because Katie was right, I was keeping secrets, dire secrets, enormous secrets. Secrets that had almost consumed me just the night before. Secrets so big I could hardly face them most days. Secrets about what happened those years ago. And secrets about what had happened just a few days ago. I didn't know how exactly they'd slipped my mind in my hospital bubble of love, but they had, and now that they were back in the forefront of my thoughts I couldn't ignore them, and what they meant for me and Harrison.

As soon as he finds out, you'll lose him, said the voices in my head. *As soon as you tell him he'll walk away.*

Harrison had told me he loved me. Nobody had ever said those words to me before, let alone three times. Maybe that love would be strong enough to withstand all the things I'd been keeping from him. Maybe I could tell him. Maybe.

Maybe…

The real truth was I didn't know. Harrison had said he loved me without all the facts. The girl he'd fallen in love with wasn't exactly me. She was some ideal version of me. A phony. A fake. I had no idea what he'd do if he found out the truth, if he'd stay, or if he'd go.

I had no idea if love could survive in the face of the real me.

With these unsettling thoughts swirling around in my head, I fell back into a troubled sleep. When I woke up again, hours later this time, the dark sky visible through the venetian blinds, Billy was standing over me.

"So, tried to off yourself, did you, little sister?" he said, as I cringed away from him across the mattress.

"What the hell are you doing here, Billy?" I whispered, my eyes darting to Harrison, who thankfully was still sleeping. "How did you even get in here?"

Billy leered at me, digging his talon-like fingers into the sheets as he leaned toward me. "Don't think this gets you off the hook," he threatened. His eyes were little specs of light in a pool of black dark. "You're still mine. You'll always be mine."

"I told you it's over," I said, pulling the blankets more tightly over myself. "I'm never doing what you say, ever again."

It was hard to find the conviction I'd felt two days before given where we were, and everything that had happened. It was hard to feel strong in a hospital bed, but I did my best to be convincing.

Reaching out suddenly, Billy grabbed me by the wrist and pulled me toward him sharply, bending my hand backwards. I gasped as pain spiked up my arm and tried to kick at him with my legs, but they were twisted in the sheets. The pain grew worse as he pulled harder, and I would have cried out but I didn't want to wake Harrison. Biting my bottom lip hard, I glared at my brother.

"You will always do what I say," he said calmly, as if he wasn't at that moment about to break my wrist. As if this was a perfectly normal conversation. "You will always be a whore.

There is no escape for you, Sally. Is that clear?"

Though I didn't think it possible, he bent my hand back even farther, making me whimper.

"It's clear," I said through gritted teeth. A second later, he finally let me go.

"I'm glad we have that settled," he said pleasantly, straightening my blankets as I fell back against the pillow, gripping my throbbing wrist. "I'll be coming for you again soon, Sal. Real soon."

He patted my leg and I had the urge to shoot my heel out just so, and get him right in the groin. It was an impulse I barely resisted.

"Take care, now," he said, and sauntered out of the room, the musky smell of his cologne lingering in the air long after, making me gag.

22

"What do you want?" Harrison said. "I'll get you anything in the world. Well..." he checked his wallet and grimaced, "anything that doesn't cost more than thirteen-fifty." He grinned his half-grin that always left me breathless. "Just name it."

We'd checked out of the hospital with a handful of pamphlets with titles like *It Gets Better* and *Where to Turn* and *Look at the Bright Side*, and an appointment with the stern counsellor for the next week. I'd expected to open the door to the apartment and find myself confronted with the mess I'd left behind—the ripped pill boxes scattered around, the empty whiskey bottle in a puddle on the carpet, the disgusting sickbed I'd left in disarray—but of course it had all been cleaned to pristine perfection, not a trace of my epic meltdown visible on the couch or the carpet. I had to hope Harrison's text got to Anita first, that she hadn't come home to the mess and found out what I'd done that way. But I knew I would never ask her.

"Anything?" I said as the two of us settled on the couch.

I fiddled with the hospital bracelet on my left arm, picking at it absently. My wrist was still hurting from last night, a constant reminder that I hadn't imagined Billy's little visit. He'd really been there. It had really happened.

He was really coming for me.

"Anything," Harrison said, hefting my legs onto his lap so we could sit all that much closer, and running his hands over my calves.

He was doing his best to keep the mood upbeat and cheerful, as if he was worried that being home might trigger whatever feelings had led me down the dark path. It pained me to think he was strategizing how to keep me sane. It made me feel like such a burden.

And here I was, about to ask even more of him.

"Don't leave me alone," I answered, my eyes drifting to the apartment door before returning to his.

A frown creased his forehead and his earlier cheer disappeared, replaced with that pensive seriousness I knew so well.

"You got it," he answered automatically.

He didn't ask me anything further about it, leaving me on the couch so he could go prepare lunch in the kitchen, but I saw the question in his eyes and in the firm line of his mouth.

I knew I wouldn't be able to avoid it for long.

After eating the impressive breakfast-for-lunch meal Harrison cooked for us—bacon, eggs, French toast, and even waffles using the waffle-maker I'd forgotten we owned—Harrison made a long overdue call to his brother. I took the opportunity to slip into the bathroom and take my first shower in three days. As I let the water in the shower warm up I stared at myself in the mirror. My hair was greasy to the point of looking brown instead of blonde. I had terrible bags under my eyes and my lips were cracked. My skin was sickly pale in some places and blotchy in others. I'd never looked less attractive.

Was this the same girl Harrison Leo had been sneaking kisses from at the kitchen table, making her lips sticky with maple syrup?

She didn't look the least bit sexy to me, and yet that didn't seem to bother him at all. And somehow, as much as I was looking forward to my shower, some shampoo in my hair and soap on my skin, it didn't really bother me either. I stepped into the tub, pulled the shower curtain closed and left the girl in the mirror behind. Maybe she was a mess, but I'd clean her up. Maybe she was having trouble smiling, but maybe she didn't need to be happy all the time. Maybe it was okay to be a little sad, a little weak, a little broken once in a while.

Maybe this was the Sally I was meant to be.

I wish I could say that easy-going feeling stayed with me as I let the suds run over me, but a few minutes alone was all it took for other, larger worries than the state of my hair to come rolling in. I hadn't been kidding when I'd asked Harrison not to leave me alone. It was the only solution I could think of to keep Billy at bay. I knew he wouldn't just barge in while Harrison was here to defend me. As long as we were together I was safe from him, safe from the degradation of another night with a man I didn't want. As long as we were together I was out of his reach.

Rubbing conditioner into my split-ends, I considered the thing I'd been avoiding for so long—telling Harrison the truth. If there was ever a time to do it, it was now. If he knew who Billy really was, if he knew what he wanted from me, at the very least he could help me get rid of him for good. Even if he didn't want to be with me anymore once he knew, I didn't think he'd just leave me to my fight. He would help me. He would protect me. That's who Harrison was. He came to the rescue.

But I didn't just want a knight in shining armour who saved me and then rode away the next day without looking back. I wanted to keep my knight. I didn't want to scare him away with tales of my disgusting behaviour. I didn't want to turn him against me just to save myself.

I was starting to believe I was worth saving. I just didn't quite believe Harrison would think so once he knew the truth.

Tell or don't tell. Tell or don't tell.

I weighed my options as I stood under the piping hot

water, all the soap long since washed away. I was so absorbed in my thoughts that I didn't even realize Harrison was standing on the other side of the shower curtain until he spoke.

"We're going to have to talk about this at some point, you know," he said.

I almost jumped under the spray at the sudden sound of his voice in the small echoing room.

"I'm almost done," I said brightly, though he didn't seem the least surprised that I'd been in the shower for half an hour. "Talk about what?"

"Talk about why you ended up in the hospital, Sally," Harrison said gently. "Talk about what really happened the other night."

Here he was, literally coming right out and asking me, and still I couldn't get the words out. Instead, I immediately found myself looking for lies to tell, jokes to hide behind, anything I could say that wasn't the cold hard truth.

"I thought we agreed it was all your fault," I said flippantly as I turned off the water and stood panting in the steam.

Even in my panic I found it pretty shocking that I was managing to stand completely naked in the same room as Harrison, just a flimsy, opaque shower curtain between us, and not throw myself at him like the sex-crazed kitten I was. Well, maybe if he'd been the naked one, and we hadn't been talking about my recent attempted-suicide, the whole moment might have been a lot hotter.

"Sally," Harrison rumbled, a warning tone in his voice.

I was about to ask him to hand me my robe when I saw his hand peeking around the curtain, holding out the blue terry-cloth garment. Like the good guy he was, he wasn't even trying to sneak a peek. He left me alone in the bathroom to towel off, closing the door behind himself respectfully. Which gave me a good ten second window to think over my options at super-speed.

A: Make up some horrific story about my childhood that would explain a sudden desire to die. Not the real story, but some other, dramatic childhood pain, possibly gleaned from a made-for-TV movie.

(Problem: I never watched made-for-TV movies. Gag me.)

B: Completely ignore the subject as if he'd never brought it up and launch into some loud task so he couldn't bring it up again, like vacuuming.

(Problem: I had no idea where the vacuum was, and really, like I was going to vacuum voluntarily?)

C: Tell him I'd tried to kill myself because I'd thought he didn't love me anymore.

(Problem: a little too close to the truth, and super emotionally manipulative and unkind. Did I want to be *that* girl?)

D: Tell. Him. The. Truth.

(Problem: Oh, how about *everything*?)

Still towelling off my hair, I tightened the belt on my robe and pushed the bathroom door open. Harrison was sitting on the couch looking pensive and so goddamn hot he made some deep part of my gut knot itself and knot again. His perfect blue eyes met mine as I perched on the couch next to him, folding one leg under me. I still hadn't decided exactly what I was going to say, but when he reached out and took my damp hand, kissing the tip of each pruney finger, when he smoothed a lock of wet hair off my forehead, when he let the silence linger, giving me time and space to find the words, and did it all without glancing down at the opening to my robe which I was pretty sure wasn't quite staying completely closed—I knew if I was ever going to tell this story, he was the one to tell. And this was the moment to tell it. This moment, right now.

But still…

I found my eyes welling just at the thought of telling the story I'd carried around with me for so long. How could I possibly find the words to tell it? What phrase could I use, what comparison could I make, that would change this story into something that wouldn't make me want to die in the telling?

As afraid as I still was of Billy, of myself, I just didn't have the strength in me to take it on. I simply couldn't get the words out.

Gripping Harrison's hand tightly, I looked into those eyes, so full of sympathy, so brimming with warmth and compassion.

"I really want to tell you," I moaned, the first tears spilling from my lashes. I let him gather me into his lap and shush away my sobs, his strong arms holding me close against him.

"You don't have to tell me now," Harrison said finally. "Not if it hurts you this much." He rubbed my back with his palm and I sank my cheek into the warmth of his chest, wishing I could just melt right into him. "I just don't want you to hold this stuff inside you. Whatever you're not saying, I don't want it to eat you up, Sally. I want you to be free of it. Don't you want that, too?"

"More than you know," I mumbled into his shirt. "More than anything."

"You know, you did mention some things on the night I drove you home from the party," he said tentatively, and I felt my whole body tense in response.

How had I forgotten this? The horrifying sobbing mess I'd been. Harrison carrying me through the apartment. Me accusing him of not wanting me. Our first kiss. And somewhere in between, my humiliating admissions of…what? What exactly had I said?

Stupid girl. You can't even remember which secrets you've told and which ones you haven't. You idiotic, dim-witted, bone-headed, moronic—

"I shouldn't have brought it up," Harrison said hastily, interrupting my mental diatribe of insults by kissing me tenderly on the forehead. "I thought it might make it easier. Give you a place to start."

Except there was no place to start with a story this big, a story that encompassed practically my whole life. Because every first sentence cut to the quick. Every memory burned.

Clinging to his body, my arms wound around his ribs, I said the only thing I could.

"I will tell you," I said, my voice shaking, because even this was a huge step. Even this was far more than I'd ever told before. "I promise I will. I'll tell you everything from start to finish. Just not today, okay? Just give me today."

Harrison leaned down and kissed the tears from my cheeks.

"I'll give you as long as you need," he whispered. "I'll give you forever, if that's what you need. I promised you that, didn't I? And I keep my promises."

Falling back against the couch cushions, I pulled Harrison down beside me and burrowed into his arms, losing myself in his sweet promises and his precious words. One arm under my head, he braced my back with his other hand to stop me from falling off the couch, as if I was ever going to let him go.

"I don't deserve you," I said as I looked up at him, the truest words I could think of.

Harrison shook his head at me. "You don't listen to a word I say, do you?" he teased.

Closing my eyes, I settled against him and waited for sleep to come, as it always did at times like this, to rescue me, but instead of feeling my senses dull and the world begin to get fuzzy, I found the very opposite happening. Little by little, I felt my senses begin to awaken.

First came scent, the delirious smell of oranges that was so specifically Harrison. Then came the sound of his heart, and was I imagining it, or could I feel his pulse quickening, as mine was? I could feel the heat of his body against practically every part of me, the tickle of his breath against my cheek, and all of a sudden I could feel quite keenly the cold air against all the places my robe wasn't quite covering anymore, and there were a lot of them. In fact, if my suddenly heightened senses were in any way accurate, my little robe was barely being held together by the loose knot at my waist.

Apparently realizing this very same thing, Harrison very carefully moved his hand toward the collar of my robe and was about to pull it closed over my chest when I caught it and slipped it inside the material instead, pressing his palm to my breast.

Harrison's eyes met mine, and I could see the desire there—I could feel it too, suddenly jumping to attention against my thigh—but also the hesitation.

Are you too broken for this? his eyes asked me. *Will this hurt you? Will this make it worse?*

In answer, I undid the knot of my robe and pressed my bare body against him, opening my lips to his and letting his tongue find mine. He hesitated for just a second, kissing me without really kissing, his lips mostly still, and then he made a sound in the back of his throat and his body suddenly came alive under my hands.

Burying his face in my neck, nibbling at my skin in a way that made me bite down on my bottom lip, hard, he slid his hand down my body inside my flapping robe, and cupped my ass, pressing me toward him with emphatic firmness. My hands tangled under his shirt, desperate to feel the soft skin of his chest as his lips found my breast and I arched against him, my body humming with pleasure, my senses overloading.

This was the moment, or somewhere around here, where Harrison always tried to slow things down, and I was adamant that he wouldn't be able to convince me this time. I knew what I wanted, and it was this feeling, this kiss, this guy, this this this.

In a quick move that I think shocked the both of us, I pulled him back into a sitting position and climbed on top of him, straddling his lap. His eyes widened and then darkened with the strength of his desire as I reached down between us, unbuttoned the fly of his jeans, and took him in my hand.

"Don't tell me to stop," I whispered into his ear as I began to move my fingers up and down his length.

He replied something inaudible and then his lips were on my breasts again, his hands finding the globes of my ass as his sighs turned to groans. My arms were still stuck in the sleeves of my robe and I longed to shrug it off, to be completely naked in front of him for the first time, this feeling of anticipation so different than the same moment with any other guy. Because it wasn't just about what he wanted. It was about what I wanted, too.

Pulling my hand away for a second, I slipped my robe completely off my shoulders, ready to let it fall, when Harrison's eyes flew open and he said, "Wait." His hands moved around to the outside of my robe and pulled it back up, pressing the material to my back.

Frowning at him in exasperation, sure whatever excuse he was going to give to put off this moment a second longer would never fly, I said, "No more waiting."

I reached again for the fly of his jeans, but he stilled my hand on his thigh, pressing his forehead to my shoulder.

"Just wait," he said and I paused, hardly deterred but willing to hear him out, for a few seconds, anyway.

When he didn't speak right away—he seemed to be trying to catch his breath—I did instead.

"Harrison Leo, if I don't have you inside me in the next five minutes…"

He groaned loudly into my shoulder at the suggestion, and I licked the edge of his ear in response, until he gently pulled me away and, infuriatingly, pulled my robe closed, though his eyes told me he wished he was doing anything but.

"I swear to God, if this was happening at literally any other moment," Harrison said painfully, "I would have you moaning under me in that bed right now."

Running my fingers through his short hair, I said with a sly smile, "Sounds like a plan."

But with some kind of inner strength I did not possess, Harrison shook his head, even as he kissed my smiling lips.

"I can't, Sally," he said. "I took the entire day off yesterday to be with you—which is exactly where I wanted to be. But that means right now I have a Software Development midterm due that I've barely started work on."

He nodded at the coffee table where his laptop sat, indecipherable numbers scrolling over a black screen.

"An exam due the day after Thanksgiving weekend?" I said skeptically, still straddling his lap.

"My professor's a sadist," Harrison answered.

"When's it due?" I challenged him, my fingertips inching under the hem of his shirt.

"At one," he said. We both glanced at the clock on the side table, which read 11:07 A.M.

"And how long would this assignment normally take you?" I asked, the true urgency of the situation beginning to dawn on me.

"About a week," Harrison admitted.

"Shit," I blurted, slipping off his lap at last and tying the belt of my robe.

I knew Harrison didn't consider school to be an irritating impediment in his life the way I did, or at least the way I had. He took his degree seriously. And now my crisis and raging hormones were standing in the way of his success.

"You get to work," I said, popping to my feet. "I'll make you some coffee to keep you going."

"Hey," Harrison said, catching my hand as I scooted past, his eyes settling on mine, "shall we say, to be continued?"

His gaze drifted down my body, now fully covered, just once, and I knew he wasn't seeing the robe at all.

I swatted him on the head and gave him the severe look Anita usually reserved for me.

"Focus!" I said. "What kind of work ethic is this? You've got an assignment to finish, mister!"

But when he raised his eyebrows mournfully, I couldn't help but grin.

"Well, I guess once you finish your work, you'll deserve a reward. I'll have to make sure it's a good one."

I swayed my hips as I walked toward the kitchen and I heard Harrison let out a painful sigh.

"Sally Jarvis, you are killing me," he called after me.

In response I lifted up the back of my robe and mooned him.

23

I was underwater. I wanted to breathe, I needed to breathe, my lungs were screaming with the effort, but I couldn't. All around me there was nothing but blue and I knew I had to kick for the surface, but something was holding me down, a fisherman's hook around my neck. It seemed like such an effort to fight against its pull, such a useless effort. I was Rainbow deep under the water, except without her deep-sea diving helmet. I was drowning.

Just let it happen, I thought. *Just let the end come.*

I felt myself sinking, down, down, down into the deep, dark, swirling blue. Then, from somewhere deep inside me I felt a spark, a determination I hardly recognized, and instead of letting myself sink, I began to fight back.

I kicked hard with my legs and pulled against the hook with my hands, only discovering as I did that it wasn't a hook at all, but a pair of hands, and the blue wasn't water, but my own blankets twisted around me as he held me down, as he told me I was his, as he brought his bloodshot eyes close to mine and I saw his face, my brother's face, and I realized he was strangling me.

Where's Harrison? I thought wildly, even as my vision

narrowed and darkened, even as I clawed at Billy's hands, which loosened one moment—allowing me to take a single breath—only to tighten again the next. *What's he done to Harrison?*

My mind went in two directions at once. A part of me focused only on dislodging my stupid brother who, though he was technically trying to kill me, didn't seem capable of truly pulling it off. Each time I kicked him he tottered—he was clearly drunk and possibly high as well—and he was losing his grip on me, though not his ability to curse and malign me with his every breath.

"You're a whore," he hissed at me. "You're nothing. Nothing but a slut."

Unlucky for him, I'd spent the last day teaching myself not to listen to anybody's put-downs. And I was a fast learner.

The other part of my brain veered toward the recent past, going over the day to try and figure out how I'd gotten here. What time was it anyway? The window was dark, that meant it had to be late afternoon at least. I'd gotten in bed to take a nap when Harrison had gotten the two-hour extension on his assignment. But where was Harrison now? Had Billy hurt him? Had Billy strangled him as he was strangling me?

A vision of Harrison's bloody knuckles after he'd beaten up that guy outside The Limo swam through my mind. Just the thought of Harrison hurt again because of me, just the idea of him injured, made a ferocious energy course through me. I reared up like a bear, shoving my brother away. Billy bounced off the side of the bed and fell to the floor as I gasped for breath, reaching for that lethal weapon, my hair straightener, but finding the drawer of my bedside table empty.

"You bitch," Billy cried from the foot of the bed, and I cringed at the very sound of his voice.

Was my dear brother never going to stop being a constant source of pain in my life? If I could have found the strength in that moment I would have crawled to the end of the bed and stepped on his face.

"What did you do to Harrison?" I said, my voice a

surprising croak. Just getting those words out led to a bout of uncontrollable coughing.

"Worried about Loverboy, are you?" Billy sneered, and my heart lurched at the sound because he seemed to be getting his second wind.

Instead of answering, I tried pushing myself off the bed, but managed only to fall onto the rug, my legs too weak to hold me up. It wasn't just the lack of oxygen—something else wasn't right. The room shifted around me strangely. I still couldn't quite focus my eyes.

Billy's head came suddenly into view as he got back to his feet unsteadily.

That's what I feel like, I thought.

But how could I be drunk?

"Worried about your nerd boy when you should be worrying about yourself," Billy said as he loomed over me. "That's just too pathetic for words."

My head lolling, my thoughts reeling, I realized I couldn't move at all just around the moment I understood why Billy had been strangling me.

Because he'd already drugged me, of course.

Billy always had been the one to take the easy way out.

"What did you give me, Billy?" I said.

"Don't tell me you've never been roofied before, Slutty Sister Sally," Billy taunted, one foot on either side of my hips. "Because I'm not buying it."

Leave me alone, I said in my head, slapping at his leg, but it came out more like, "Lemmelone."

"No, I don't think I will," Billy said with a sickening smirk. "I don't think the customer I've got lined up for you tonight will, either. He's expecting a first-class whore, and I promised to deliver."

The world was closing in again, the water rising over my face. Just before I blacked out, I turned my face to the side, opened my mouth, and sank my teeth into Billy's ankle.

He gave out a pleasing scream—sounding exactly like a little girl—before he swung the hair straightener at my face and everything went black.

I've got to stop waking up like this, I thought to myself as I opened my eyes, once again, to strange surroundings.

I was lying on a pristine white duvet cover, on a bed in a room with dark panelled walls. To my left was a bank of windows which I could see through a sheer curtain, though it was dark out. A tasteful lamp on the side table, which was on, was the room's only adornment. But it was only when I saw the open mirrored closet door, and the perfect line of identical shirts, the impeccable shoes lined up beneath them, that I knew.

This, of course, was Billy's room.

Not that my aching throat and tender forehead wouldn't have given me that answer a few seconds later.

Sitting up shakily, I looked at myself in the mirror opposite the bed, and even from across the room I could make out the bruises on my neck and the ugly red bump on my forehead where he'd hit me with my own weapon of choice— which somehow made it worse than if he'd hit me with anything else.

Goddamn you, Billy.

The outfit I had on was a strange combination of clothes that weren't mine. I recalled that when I'd grappled with my brother I'd still been wearing my robe, which meant he'd taken that robe off and dressed me himself. The nausea which had been brewing in my gut took it up a notch at the very thought, and I shuddered. I had on a pair of Anita's jeans, which were much too short for me, a white tank top I thought belonged to Emily (when had I even borrowed it?), and the red hoodie Harrison had had on earlier in the day. It still smelled like him. Pulling the collar of the sweatshirt up over my nose I inhaled deeply and tried not to explode with worry for him.

Billy might have been stronger than me, but Harrison could overpower him easily. I didn't see how he could possibly have hurt him. Unless he'd gotten him from behind. Unless he'd hit him over the head before he could react. Unless…

Unless…

Lurching to my feet, I shook my head to clear it.

Gotta focus. Gotta get out of here. Gotta get Billy out of my life for good.

I didn't know why my brother had left me alone, but I knew it was an opportunity I couldn't pass up. There had to be something in this room that could help me, something I could use as a weapon. Just something.

As I stumbled around the room, still woozy from the drug he'd slipped me—although, clearly not a full dose, since here I was awake just a few hours later—I kept up a mantra to counteract the one he'd thrown at me earlier.

I am not a whore. I am not nothing. I am not Slutty Sally. I am not a whore. I am not nothing. I am not Slutty Sally.

I checked the door first. Locked. There was no en suite bathroom, and the closet was just row upon row of expensive shirts. The shoes were Italian leather and light as socks. His drawers were similarly boring, full of sweaters and even one cardigan, which I made a face at before shutting the drawer with a click. There were a couple of business books in the drawer of the bedside table with the titles *Be The Job* and *Getting There First*, but I didn't see how they could help me, unless I was going to read him into a coma.

I didn't understand it. Had he thought ahead and emptied the room of belts, letter openers, golf clubs, and for that matter, personality? Was this really how my brother lived?

I almost felt sorry for him.

Actually, no I didn't.

I finally spotted my own pink overnight bag by the window and cracked it open. The last time I'd seen the bag it had been in the trunk of Billy's town car driving away from me, so I was surprised to find it packed with items from my bedroom. (Clearly my brother hadn't actually been trying to kill me, just to strangle me into swift unconsciousness. You didn't pack a bag for a corpse.)

Of course Billy had chosen the most humiliating outfit for me to wear, a black lace negligee I'd been given once as a gift by a horny lover. I'd never worn it because it was so tight it pinched me around the torso, and because my breasts strained against the too-small material in a very unsexy way. It just made me look desperate. That, a stick of deodorant and a hairbrush were the only things in the bag. Apparently my brother wanted me to wear this piece of lingerie as a dress. He hadn't even included a pair of shoes.

Leaning over the bag, I felt something fall out of the pocket of Harrison's hoodie and clatter to the floor. I glanced at the door fearfully, sure Billy must have heard, but the apartment was utterly silent. Reaching blindly into the shadows under the bed, my hand closed around something small and hard. My heart skipped a beat.

It was Harrison's phone.

Breathing heavily with excitement, I squeezed the phone between my fingers and cheered silently. I was saved! I could call Harrison right now! I could find out if he was okay! I could hear his voice!

Except, of course, I couldn't call Harrison right now, because I only knew his cell number, and I was holding his cell in my hand.

My delight wilting just a little, I flipped open the ancient phone and turned it on, trying to think of who else I could call. With some alarm I noticed there was only one power bar left, and of course I didn't have the power cord to charge it. I could have screamed with frustration. Whoever I was going to call I'd have to do it fast. But who was there?

Anita, of course, except I didn't know Anita's cell number either, since I always saw her at home, and since I didn't have a cell I never called her.

Emily, Melissa, or Katie? Except I didn't have their numbers memorized either. I kept them written on a sticky note beside my answering machine.

One of the people in Harrison's address book? Winston or Mo? Sure, why not, except Harrison liked being cute on his phone and had saved everyone's number under funny pseudonyms like Perry Como and White Man Can't Dance.

Did I really want to waste my two minutes of phone time calling some stranger?

9-1-1.

Of course! All I had to do was call the police! My brother drugged me and is holding me captive in his condo, trying to force me into prostitution—what a call. I could practically hear the sirens.

I was just about to dial the number when I heard the door open behind me and I was forced to close the phone and slip it into the side pocked of the bag with what I hoped was casual deftness.

When I turned around, Billy was standing in the middle of the floor, looking unkempt and a little green around the edges.

"Awake, I see?" he said.

His eyes were rimmed with red and his hair was standing on end, as though he'd been pulling at it. He couldn't seem to stop moving, pacing between the dresser and the bed, like a caged animal.

"Let me go, Billy," I said, though really I was looking past him at the open door. If he was as unstable as he looked, maybe I could somehow get past him. "I'm not playing this game anymore."

"Desperate to get back to your fantastic life of whoring, are you?" he said with a strangely high-pitched laugh. "Worried this time will cut into your dirty plans?"

"You're the one who's dirty," I spat back, looking him up and down. "What the hell is wrong with you anyway?"

"Not a thing tonight won't fix," he responded, the skin of his face shining with clamminess. "Time to do your duty. You know what you're good for."

Had these lines really worked on me once upon a time?

You're dirty, Sally. You're a whore, Sally. This is all you're good for, Sally.

Because now, somehow, they sounded exactly like what they were: nonsense Billy spouted in order to control me. Clichéd insults he used to get what he wanted from me. His words were flimsy now, toothless. They had no power over me.

"Maybe you didn't hear me," I said in a low, controlled voice, as I approached him. "I'm not going anywhere with you or doing anything you say, ever again, Billy. I'm not a whore, and I'm not for sale. It's over."

His eyes jumped from my face to the wall to the bed and back to my face again. I didn't know what he was on, but it was obvious he'd taken too much of it.

"Your *boyfriend* tell you that?" Billy said. "Did he teach you to love yourself and now suddenly you think you can talk back to me?"

I didn't bother answering.

"Let me tell you a little something about your beloved Harrison," Billy went on, his face creasing into a smirk. "He walked out on you, did you know that? I didn't even have to wait long. Brought you home from the hospital and then just left. Such chivalry. Just walked out while you were sleeping."

I narrowed my eyes at Billy and tried to stand firm against his lies, but inside I felt the creeping itch of doubt.

Why would Harrison have left the apartment when I'd begged him not to leave me alone? Why would he have done such a thing unless he really didn't care about me?

"He had to hand in his assignment," I countered, but Billy shook his head at me pityingly.

"I know you might not be so familiar with the protocol for exams these days, my dim-witted little sister, but nobody prints out their homework and hand-delivers it to the professor's office anymore. He would have emailed it in."

"He was probably going out for groceries," I said uncertainly. "Or to get me a gift."

Even to my own ears it didn't sound true, and I cringed at Billy's self-satisfied grin.

He's lying, I told myself. *Maybe Harrison didn't leave the apartment at all. Maybe he was in the shower when Billy smuggled you out. Don't listen to him. Don't listen! Harrison loves you.*

But it was so hard to believe love existed when I was with Billy.

When I was around him, sometimes it was hard to remember anything good in the world was real.

"I'm not doing it, Billy," I said, backing away one step and then another as my brother stared me down. "I'm not doing it again. I won't."

Even if Harrison didn't love me, even if he'd left me alone, I could still do this. I could still stand up to Billy. I could make this choice for myself. Couldn't I?

"Oh, I think you will," Billy said with a sudden uncharacteristic calm.

Then, with glazed, almost dead eyes, my brother lifted up his shirt to show me the gun tucked into the waist of his pants and I sat down on the bed, defeated.

For the next hour I was in a daze. It was as though the moment I saw that gun a part of me completely detached from the rest and sat in a chair at the side of the room, watching, as I got ready for whatever Billy had in store for me. She watched as Billy threw my things at me and left the room with the empty bag—unknowingly taking the phone and my only hope of getting out of there with him. She watched as I wiggled into the skimpy outfit and brushed my hair, staring blankly at my own reflection. She watched as I sat on the bed, waiting for Billy to unlock the door. She watched as I waited to cry, but couldn't. She watched as I shook with fear.

She watched as I tried to understand.

Billy with a gun? Billy threatening my life? Billy strangling me, kidnapping me, holding me against my will?

How had we come to this?

Billy had always been self-centred and nasty, even when we were kids, and he'd certainly been horrible to me these past years—it was only beginning to dawn on me how horrible—but I'd never imagined he would go this far. Did he really hate me that much? Or did he just hate being told no? Would tonight's upcoming events really be a part of some shady business deal, or would it just be a punishment for me?

Would he hurt me even if I went through with it? Would

he hurt our mother?

The gun changed things, that was for sure. As much as sleeping with another guy I didn't love turned my stomach, I wasn't about to risk my life over it. I'd slept with tons of guys I didn't care about. What did one more matter? If it meant I could get away from Billy. If it meant he would let me go, I would follow his rules. I would do what he said. Once I was away from him I could think about my next move. Going to the police, or going into hiding, or moving to Japan and changing my name.

I promised myself I would never again be in a room alone with Billy and his gun.

This would be the first and last time.

As Billy opened the door and took my arm, forcing me through the apartment and out into the hall, I tried to think of Harrison. But it was hard to picture his face. It was as though this reality—in which Billy once again showed me the gun in the elevator—existed on a completely different plain than the one I'd been living on with Harrison. I couldn't wonder if he was okay, if he loved me or if he didn't, if he was tied up in some closet or walking across campus, oblivious. I couldn't focus on much more than a single fragment of him, a memory of the kiss we'd shared on the couch as we lay intertwined, our arms around each other.

Though I could barely picture his face, at least I had this memory, this one memory, as Billy marched me down the hall on a floor two storeys above his and knocked on a door.

Harrison's soft lips. Harrison's warm hands. Harrison's beating heart.

I took a breath as we waited for the door to open, and could almost feel his arms around me, like an embrace in a dream.

Then the door opened and the dream came to a screeching halt.

Standing at the door, wearing the same squinting grin I remembered, was Connor Buckley, the boy I hadn't seen since high school. The boy who'd once told me my eyes were bright as stars and just days later sent a video of me that spread like wildfire across the school, a video called *Slutty Sally Pleasures the Team*.

Standing there was the boy who ripped my life apart.

24

"Surprised to see me?" Connor said as I gaped at him.

He was pretty drunk. I could tell by the way he leaned hard on the door. I, on the other hand, felt suddenly amazingly clear-headed. It was as though my head had been dunked in a bucket of water even colder than the one Billy's gun had upended over me. I felt suddenly completely sure about a number of things, and this certainty made me feel strong. I was almost glad Connor had answered the door and not some anonymous nobody.

It had been the three of us at the start of this thing. It was fitting that it would be the three of us at the end.

"Connor Buckley," I said, meeting his gaze and holding it, unwilling to show the slightest weakness. "Molest any cheerleaders lately?"

I was referring to a scandal during his and Billy's senior year of high school when a girl named Ginger Cho accused Connor of fondling her breasts and taking off her underwear while she was passed out drunk. In the end there hadn't been enough evidence to arrest him for sexual assault, mainly because the video a bystander had taken on their phone was found to be inadmissible due to a technicality.

This had all happened a few months after my own mistreatment at Connor's hands. I remembered it so well. I remembered the look on Ginger's face as Connor walked the halls, high-fiving his friends and spreading damaging rumours about her. I remembered her rage and her humiliation. I remembered thinking, *I know how you feel.*

Ignoring my comment, I watched as Connor and Billy greeted each other like chums, even exchanging their old team handshake, which I was surprised I even recognized. I hadn't seen it in years. I hadn't seen anyone from high school in years, and as far as I knew neither had Billy. Yet here was Connor Buckley appearing suddenly from behind a door like a monster out of a nightmare. Connor Buckley and Billy, thick as thieves again, or was it thick as thieves as always?

Had they stayed friends all this time?

The very idea made my blood boil.

At long last, Connor gestured for us to come through the door, which was a relief, given what I was wearing. As I passed between his body and the doorframe, Connor looked me up and down appreciatively.

Billy's gun, I thought to myself as I considered scratching out his eyes. *Remember Billy's gun.*

"You weren't kidding," Conner said to Billy as he closed the door behind us. There was a mirror across from the door and I could see him staring at my ass in it. "It's just like I remember it."

It? Was "it" supposed to be my ass, my body, or just me?

Shaking with anger, I simultaneously felt incredibly exposed in the stupid lingerie I wished I'd had the sense to throw away months ago. I felt my resolve begin to weaken, the chin I'd been holding so high begin to fall. I felt just like a sixteen-year-old girl standing half-naked in a locker room full of guys, trying so hard not to cry.

The calls came from all directions, from all sides.

"Hey, look at me, Sally!" A camera flashed and I blinked, disoriented.

"Take it off, girl!"

"Want to feel how much I like you, Sally?"

A hand reached out and tried to take mine, but I yanked it away.

And then Connor leaned toward me and whispered in my ear. "This is what you get for saying no to me, Sally."

My hands tightening into fists, I spun around to face them both. So what if I was mostly naked and barefoot? All it did was make him want me more. All it did was give me the upper hand.

"I don't know what he told you, Connor," I said, "but I'm not having sex with you tonight."

Billy's eyes hardened. His hand went to the butt of his gun over his shirt as a warning, but I ignored it. He wasn't going to shoot me in front of a witness was he? Even Billy wasn't that stupid.

Connor raised his eyebrows at my statement and ambled over to the bar along the far wall, unperturbed. I noticed with some satisfaction that he still had a slight limp.

"Sure you won't, honey," he said good-humouredly. He looked over at Billy once again. "She's sure become a feisty one, hasn't she?"

His shoulders relaxing, Billy joined Connor at the bar and suddenly it was as though I wasn't in the room at all. I stared at their twin backs for a moment, incredulous at being so ignored—because what the hell was the point in taking a stand if nobody was paying attention?—then realized, now was my chance to get away and stop this nightmare before it even began.

Swivelling on the balls of my feet, I darted back to the door and tried to yank it open, but it was locked. There was a keypad below the knob. Apparently a code needed to be typed in to open the door even from the inside.

Damn paranoid rich people.

Because it was clear that Connor was rich, and possibly disgustingly so. Turning back around, I took in the room as I stepped onto the plush, cream-coloured carpet. The place was much nicer than Billy's, and at least three times bigger. There were floor-to-ceiling, sheer drapes covering the floor-to-ceiling windows. The seating area in the centre of the living room was sunken, a crystal chandelier shimmering over the coffee table. The furniture was expensive and tastefully trendy; rich brown leather armchairs with brass studs, a large chinoiserie lamp, a dining room table of reclaimed wood with reupholstered antique chairs.

I wanted to vomit all over it.

Still hovering by the door, I glanced down at my feet and noticed my bag sitting unobtrusively right next to me. I had no idea why Billy had brought it, or what he planned to fill it with, but it was still the most beautiful thing I'd ever seen. I had to stop myself from leaning down and kissing the canvas as I quickly crouched and slipped my hand into the outer pocket, palming Harrison's phone, my lifeline, my only hope.

I found it difficult to walk forward into the room again, toward Billy and Connor instead of away from them, but I forced my legs to move. A part of me still couldn't believe I was standing in the same room with Connor Buckley, who I'd seen in my nightmares for so many years. Was I dreaming? Was this all a bad dream?

But if this was a dream, would the phone be burning a hole in my hand as though it were on fire?

Naturally my outfit had no pockets to hide what I was holding—Billy, being Billy, had wisely, or maybe just meanly, seen to this by not bothering to lend me so much as a sweater for the walk down the hall. I knew I had mere seconds before the two of them turned around and saw me with the phone, my only chance at escape taken from me.

Holding the cell behind my back with my eyes on my captors, I neglected to look where I was going and tripped down the stairs toward the couches, falling crookedly onto an armchair and bumping into the coffee table.

Connor and Billy turned around at my yelp, but their eyes skated over me quickly, landing instead on the pyramid of brick-shaped packages I noticed tumbling from their pile on the table to the floor. I pressed the phone between the cushions of the armchair as the two of them rushed over, Billy looking stricken, and Connor merely amused.

"Stupid bitch," Billy said, shoving me back into the chair. "Look what you did."

He kneeled on the carpet, carefully recreating the pyramid.

The pyramid of bricks.

Bricks of cocaine.

Cocaine. Actual cocaine.

I blinked and blinked again as Billy continued to mutter to himself, caressing the packages wound with brown duct tape as if they were his babies.

Suddenly, a number of questions I'd been asking myself, and others I'd never wanted to ask myself, had an answer.

Billy wasn't a failed entrepreneur, or a restauranteur, or a sketchy small business owner. Billy was just a plain old drug dealer.

"Calm yourself, bro," Connor said easily as he sunk down onto the sofa across from me. "This carpet's like butter. They're not going to break open."

Still all too aware of the cell phone hiding just behind my ass in the seams of the chair, I looked Connor over a second time. The suit jacket he wore casually unbuttoned looked incredibly expensive. Armani? He had a diamond ring on his middle finger. His jeans were distressed, expertly so. Even his socks dripped with cash. Billy's clothes were pristine, but I knew he had only one perfectly tailored suit. His shoes were expensive but not designer. And most importantly, Billy was the one on his hands and knees frantically handling the bricks of blow, while Connor lounged, unworried, flicking his lighter.

Maybe Billy was a drug dealer, but he definitely wasn't in charge. It looked like Connor was the head honcho, the kingpin, the man. And Billy was just one of his little minions.

"I really appreciate this, man," Billy said once he'd finished stacking his drugs.

Stepping over my legs like I wasn't even there—and really, for a while there I had trouble believing I was. Neither of them were paying me any attention. I might have been an ottoman—he went over to the door, retrieved the bag, and began moving the drugs into it.

"You won't be disappointed."

"No, I won't," Connor replied without looking up from his lighter.

The threat in his voice was subtle, but all too obvious. I noticed Billy's hands still on the last brick, for just a moment. Then he zipped the bag shut.

"Well, I'm sure you'll enjoy the token of my appreciation. I know you've been waiting a long time for this one."

"Oh, I most certainly will," Connor said, his words stinging like curses as I understood what they meant. As they sunk in. "Somehow I'm sure I'm going to get a lot of use out of it."

As their attention turned at last back to me, I didn't have more than a minute to piece together what had just taken place. Connor was letting Billy have these drugs as a favour, or maybe a test. Were they higher quality than what he usually sold? Or higher quantity? Whatever the difference, it was obviously significant enough that Billy felt he needed to give Connor something in return.

And what better gift than the one he'd been giving out for years? What better card than the willing whore he kept in his back pocket, ready to play her whenever the need arose? What better bargaining piece than his own slutty sister?

I am not a whore. I am not nothing. I am not Slutty Sally. I am smart. I can think myself out of this. I can. I can.

I wondered why Billy had needed to sell me all these years. Obviously there had been deals going on, though not the kind I'd imagined. Why would a drug dealer need to sell sex? To convince his customers to pay a premium price? As an added bonus—buy from me and you'll get an extra prize? Just to keep the clients happy when the drugs weren't enough?

Or maybe I had no role in his drug dealing life at all. Maybe he'd just forced me to whore myself for his own amusement. Maybe there was no benefit beyond some extra cash and my humiliation.

I bristled with rage, and felt it making me stronger.

Connor got back to his feet. I took in the whiskey glass in his hand and the unsteadiness of his gait once again as he took my arm.

He's drunk, and Billy is high. You can use that. You can figure this out. You're smart. Just think.

Without a better option, I left the phone where it was and let Connor lead me away. Apparently my brother wasn't about to let me handle the rest of this alone, because he and his gun made no attempt to get up from the couch as Connor and I left the room. I looked back at him over my shoulder and (sickeningly) he winked at me.

The bedroom was down a short hallway. The room was similarly large and impressively decorated, not that I took much of it in. I scanned all surfaces for a phone, or a weapon, or anything, but came up empty.

Unless I wanted to strangle him with the sheets. Or hit him over the head with a chair.

But even if I did—and I didn't really think I was capable of either—there would still be Billy to contend with right outside.

Connor turned so suddenly that I nearly walked into him, my hip brushing against his in a way that made my skin crawl. As he gripped my waist I had the distinct memory of being touched exactly the same way by him once upon a time.

Come on, Sally. Just give me what I want.

Connor, no. Stop. That doesn't feel nice.

I'll tell you what feels nice.

The room was unlit and dim. His face was mostly in shadow as he said, "So, how long has it been, Sal? Five years?"

"Four," I corrected him as he chuckled, his sour breath hitting my face in a gust.

Think. While he's still joking around. While he's distracted. Just think. What would Rainbow do?

"Seems like yesterday," Connor said, reaching around and pulling my lacy underwear down over one ass cheek, grabbing my skin roughly.

But no, Rainbow wasn't who I needed to be now. Rainbow was strong. She could fight. She persevered. But Rainbow wasn't always clever. She was constantly being duped by two-faced companions and making the wrong decisions. I didn't need to be like Rainbow. I needed to be smarter.

What would Anita do?

As Connor continued to grope my body in the most unsexy ways imaginable, I held my hands behind my back to stop myself from strangling him and tried to think clearly. What did Anita always say? Drink less. Go to class. Clean up your dishes. You're better than this. You're smarter than this. Use your head. Use your assets.

Yes. She'd told me that once, when we were moving into our apartment and she'd wanted me to go flirt with the guys on the lawn to convince them to carry the heavy boxes.

"You're good at it," she'd said. "So use what you've got. Just don't give it all away."

Use what you've got. Use your assets. Be smart. Be better than them.

I could do that.

Smiling sweetly at Connor, and dodging his lips as he tried to kiss me, I backed him up against the bed, then pushed him firmly, sending him sprawling on the mattress. He was a tall guy, and broad—he had been a football player, after all—but he was drunk and his defenses were down. And he didn't have a plan.

"Is that how we're playing?" he said as I climbed on to the bed beside him, scooting up toward the pillows.

"No point in wasting time, is there?" I said smoothly as he rolled over and moved toward me, his hand reaching for my breast.

But as soon as his head hit the pillow I pivoted up, straddling his crotch. Luckily he was drunk enough that he hadn't gotten hard yet. I didn't think I would have been able to stop myself from doing something mean and painful to his most tender place if he had been.

When both hands slapped my ass, I gritted my teeth.

"Now, if I remember correctly, it was around this part where you told me to get my hands off you, the last time around," Connor said, moving his hands up my body to my breasts.

"Well, I'm not that little girl anymore," I said, smiling seductively at him as I leaned forward, playing the oldest trick in the book—the boob attack. Shove your breasts in a horny guy's face and he'll be completely distracted.

As he nuzzled the barely concealing lace covering my chest, scraping my skin with his stubble even through the material, I reached into the pockets of his jeans, front and back, searching for something, anything I could use…And finally finding it in the pocket of his jacket.

Bingo.

"Oh, you are most definitely not a little girl," Connor mumbled. Then, without warning, he grabbed a shank of my hair and pulled my head back so hard I nearly saw stars. The muscles in my neck twanged in protest. "But that doesn't mean you don't need to be punished."

I tried to control my breathing, so as not to let my fury show, as he continued to hold me in place by my hair while letting his other hand explore my body. My hands were free and I was pretty sure I could have pulled myself out of his grasp and skipped ahead a few steps in my plan, but there was still a chance he might be stronger than me, even while inebriated. I needed him to believe I was into this, just for a few more minutes. Even if the sixteen-year-old Sally inside me wanted to reach down and show him how it felt to be manhandled. Even if that's what I wanted, too.

When his hand approached the place between my legs, I knew it was time to jump into action.

By this point his hold on my hair had relaxed some, and I was able to ease out of it as I shook my head at him.

"Oh no, you don't," I said playfully as I pressed his arms over his head. "This night isn't about me. It's all about you, Mister Buckley."

I felt the pressure of his resistance at first, that little fire of defiance in his eyes, but when I bit my lip and rolled my hips against his, that pressure let up.

God, men were so easy sometimes.

Pulling the rolled up tie I'd found in his pocket out from under my knee, I quickly and expertly tied his hands to the headboard—tight enough to be believable, but not quite tight enough that he wouldn't be able to pull himself free with a few good tugs—all the while whispering warmly in his ear: "You know, when Billy first asked me, I wasn't sure I wanted to come tonight. But then he told me I'd get to play with Connor Buckley, and I knew I couldn't stay away."

Realizing his hands were bound, Connor leaned forward and tried to bite my lips, but I backed away smoothly, just out of his reach. He grinned and bucked his hips under me and I leaned in again. I had him right where I wanted him.

It was time for the kill.

"When he told me he wanted me to go into the bedroom with Connor and keep him busy for a while, I didn't know what to think," I said, doing my best to appear simple-minded and innocent. I paused for a beat, watching Connor's expression. Nothing yet. "I mean, I didn't hold any ill will toward you. I didn't know what he was talking about when he told me it was time to teach you a lesson, time you got knocked off that pedestal of yours."

"Wha…" Connor said, his face falling slack with confusion. "What pedestal? What are you talking about?"

He strained a little at his bonds, but he wasn't pulling on them yet. Good. Just a few more seconds. Just a little more.

"And then he told me it was all part of some plan to steal from you, and I just didn't know what to think."

Yanking hard on the tie, which held fast, Connor pulled himself into a half-sitting position and looked me up and down, suddenly a lot more sober. Climbing out of his lap, I sat innocently beside him on my knees.

Keep it up. You're almost there. You're almost home.

"Steal from me?" Connor laughed. "Honey, your brother works for me. He unloads the product and gets a cut of the profits. This is how it works, how it's always worked. He's playing you."

I shrugged my shoulders.

"Well, Billy said it would be easy enough to rob you blind while I had you occupied in here. He didn't say anything about stealing drugs. I think he was talking about cash. I know he mentioned a safe."

I was taking a chance on that one, assuming there was a safe somewhere in the apartment, but by the look on Connor's face it seemed it had been a chance worth taking.

"And besides, he said all your things would go for a pretty penny. He said, we could easily empty the place. You know, after we shot you in the head, but before anyone found the body."

Connor pulled hard on the tie now. I could already see the knot coming loose as he growled, his eyes flashing.

"Steal from *me*?" he cried. "He wouldn't dare. Shoot *me*? I'd rip his head off first and he knows it. And my guns are locked up tight. He can't get to them. What's he going to shoot me with?"

I blinked once, and cocked my head to the side. "With the gun in the waistband of his jeans," I replied. "He's probably coming in here any minute to do it. I had to warn you. I couldn't just let him kill you like that. Tied up. In your own bed." He pulled harder. I had seconds only. No, milliseconds. "But shhhh. Don't tell him I told you, okay?"

With a roar that echoed in my ears for days afterwards, Connor wrenched himself free of the knotted tie at his wrists and shoved me sideways off the bed. I sprawled across the floor as Connor leaped off the bed, yelling Billy's name, and stomped out of the room. It was so ridiculously dramatic I was surprised there wasn't a Connor-shaped hole in the door where he'd barrelled right through it.

I desperately wanted to listen at the open doorway and hear the exchange between my brother and Connor, but I knew I had to work fast. I threw myself to my feet as I heard my brother's muffled exclamations of surprise and Connor's yells—the words "betray" and "murder" and "big fucking mistake" the only ones I could hear clearly.

Pulling open the doors to the walk-in closet, I searched for what I knew I would find. Connor hadn't decorated this condo. Somebody lived here with him. Someone who, I was sure, had no idea how her man made his money. Someone who would probably be just about my size.

I couldn't find the light switch, but it didn't take me long to find a pair of jeans and a top and sweater in decidedly female styles. Even the ballet flats fit. I threw off the slip of lingerie I had on and struggled into the clothes as quickly as I could, Billy's girlish screams of protest jolting me to move faster.

Fully clothed, I darted to the door and began to move stealthily toward the living room.

Maybe if their backs were turned. Maybe if they were on the other side of the room. Maybe if the gun hadn't made an appearance yet.

Maybe... Maybe...

Their argument blasted into me as I edged toward the end of the hall.

"She's lying, man!" Billy said, desperation dripping from his every word. "I'm not trying to rip you off! There's no plan. She made it all up. She's just trying to turn you against me!"

Peeking around the corner, I saw that Connor had Billy backed against the front door, barring my escape route. And even worse, he had Billy's own gun in his hand and was pressing it directly to Billy's temple.

Oh God.

It was clear that Connor was past hearing anything, which was something I'd been counting on. I knew what not getting his way did to Connor. I'd paid the price for it myself, four years before. Now it was Billy's turn. I just hadn't factored in what the intervening years, his line of work, and plenty of drugs might have done to his impulse control.

"Double-crossing me? Blinding me with that whore? Taking what's mine? I trusted you, man!"

With every yell Connor pressed the gun harder into my brother's head, and with every yell I saw Billy shrink further back until his head was pressed into the wood of the door.

"I didn't!" Billy whimpered. "I'm not! Just check the bag. I didn't take your cash. I didn't!"

"I don't have to check the fucking bag!" Connor cried, and stepped back a foot, then another, continuing to aim at my brother.

Stepping back to put some room between himself and the mess the bullet would make.

Stepping back to take the shot.

"Don't!" I cried, and without thinking, ran right into the room.

Without looking at where the gun was aiming now, I jumped onto the armchair, and stuck my hand into the seam, my fingers closing over the phone.

If there'd ever been a moment to call 9-1-1, this was it.

Then I looked up and saw the gun aimed at my heart, and my fingers stilled.

"It's her!" Billy cried and Connor swung his arm back toward him. Billy gestured toward me frantically. "Shoot her! She's the one who's fucking with your head. Shoot her now!"

Lovely. Had I really just run into the room to save that goddamn waste of space?

Widening my eyes, I put on my most startled expression. "But you said you'd be the one doing the shooting, Billy. You said you'd gun him down and we'd both make off like bandits. You said you'd buy me a diamond necklace and a matching tennis bracelet. Where's my tennis bracelet, Billy?"

"She's fucking *lying*!"

"Shut the fuck up, both of you!" Connor yelled, the gun aimed at me again, and then my brother. Every time it swung my way my breath caught. I was starting to hyperventilate.

Billy was sweating profusely and I couldn't be sure, but I thought I caught the tell-tale scent of someone wetting their pants. It was hard to really feel it given the circumstances, but there was something very satisfying about the sight of my brother being bullied and threatened by somebody else. It almost made the whole you're-about-to-die part worthwhile.

Suddenly breaking into motion, Connor stalked toward me and yanked me up by my forearm, roughly shoving me toward my brother.

So he can shoot us at the same time? One bullet for two bodies? Is this how I'm going to die, in a kingpin's condo, standing in a puddle of my brother's piss, wearing some other girl's clothes?

My back pressed into the door, I was finally able to picture Harrison's face.

Harrison who loved me.

Harrison who'd never even learned the truth about me.

Harrison who I couldn't leave behind, not now, not like this.

Our story wasn't over yet. I wasn't done yet. I wasn't!

"Wait," I said, but Connor's gun swinging toward me silenced me once again.

Breathing hard, he said, "I don't know what this shit is about, but I'm not about to go down for offing two miserable fucks like you." I felt the muscles in my stomach suddenly unclench at his words. "I want you to get the hell out of here, and never come back. I don't ever want to see either of your faces again."

He didn't have to tell me twice. I turned toward my brother expectantly, waiting for him to move aside so Connor could enter the door code and open the door, but he was staring at Connor, his mouth open.

"But..." he whined and I clenched my hands to stop from strangling him.

"And don't even think of taking that with you!" Connor barked, pointing the gun at the pink canvas bag by the couch.

"I've worked hard for you," Billy continued to protest. "All these years. I made deals, bought people off, did your dirty work. I've done everything you asked!"

"Doesn't mean a thing if I can't trust you," Connor said emotionlessly, his arm still outstretched, the black metal of the gun glinting.

Then, his voice low as a rumble, he said, "Now. Get. The. Fuck. Out."

My brother made a strangled sound in his throat as Connor punched in the door code and turned the knob. We both fell into the hallway, the door slamming shut behind us with a bang that sounded a lot like a gunshot.

Except we were both still alive.

For the moment, at least.

25

I leaned on the wall for a long time, my eyes refusing to focus. For some reason my ears were ringing as though I'd just walked out of a club. Every few seconds I shook my head to clear them, but it didn't work.

I didn't have a single thought in my head.

"You don't know what you just did," Billy croaked.

He was crouched on the ground a little ahead of me, his back against the wallpaper, his head in his hands. My eyes finally cooperating, I focused on his splotchy, pinched, little ferret face and immediately wished I hadn't. I didn't want to look at the person who'd just tried to have me killed. I didn't want to look at his face ever again.

Pulling the phone out of my pocket, I shook my head at him wearily.

What I just did?" I said. "Are you seriously trying to blame all that on me?"

There was nothing to stop me from calling the cops now. If Billy tried to run I was sure I could trap him somewhere, hold him until they came. I had bruises on my neck, a lump on my forehead. But would it be enough? I wished I'd told someone, anyone who could corroborate what he'd done to me for the past four years. I wished I'd saved all the threatening messages he'd left on my machine instead of frantically deleting them. I wished I'd thought ahead to this moment and been smarter.

You are smart. You're smarter than he is. Just think it through. Just think.

"You are to blame, Sally," Billy said. "You screw up everything you touch. You can't even spread your legs without fucking everything up. I should have known."

He doesn't know you. He doesn't know anything. He never has.

"Too dumb to follow simple instructions. Dumber than a bag of rocks, that's you."

Be smart. Don't fall for his lies. Outsmart him. You can do it.

"And now my life is over, and it's all your fault. If Connor comes after me, if he puts me down, that'll be on you. So what do you have to say for yourself, *sister?* How are you going to make this up to me?"

His beady eyes bore into mine, so full of malice, of anger, of contempt, all the things I should have been feeling for him. But there was nothing left in my heart or my soul for Billy, not even hate. There was nothing left inside me but a yearning for the truth.

My thumb hovered over the 9, but I punched in a different number instead. Then I slipped the phone into my pocket without hanging it up and turned toward my brother.

"Make it up to you?" I said, folding my arms. "You want me to make up the fact that you've been pimping me out for years? That you've been blackmailing me into sleeping with strange men so you could make a profit? Stalking me? Threatening me? Kidnapping me and dragging me to Toronto so you could prostitute me at your will? Telling me our mother won't get the medication she needs unless I do what you say? Is that what you want me to make up to you, brother?"

Billy snorted and slithered to his feet, so smoothly, like a python unravelling.

"You enjoyed every second of it," he said. "You were dying for it. Ask any guy at that two-bit school of yours. They all know what a slut you are."

"You're pathetic," I said, watching his face for the flash of anger I knew would come. "For a while in there I thought maybe you were his second-in-command. But you, second to Connor Buckley?" It was my turn to snort. "For all I know you're lowest man on the totem pole. I bet Connor never respected you for a second."

"Little sister, you don't know a thing," Billy said, his voice lowered with barely suppressed rage.

"I know what you are," I said, repeating the words he'd said to me so many times. "I know what you've always been. A pretender. A hack. A little boy riding on Connor Buckley's coattails, hoping he'll take you somewhere grea—"

So quickly I barely even saw the movement, he jammed his forearm into my windpipe and shoved me back into the wall. He didn't have enough strength to cut my air off altogether, but he could still hold me there, his face a mask of rage, which hardly phased me. It was hard to be afraid of a guy who smelled of his own piss.

"Dumb bitch! You don't know anything. You don't know how long I've been working at this. All this time and you never knew," Billy said, and all I could think was, *Tell me more. Tell me everything.* "You never even knew that I was working with your high school tormentor. That's right, three years Connor and I have been running drugs. That's three years of my life you just pissed away!"

I had to stop myself from grinning from ear to ear. It wasn't easy.

"We started small, pot mostly, then expanded into pills, coke, whatever the higher clientele was looking for. Connor made connections, I moved the product. God, the money we made. It was beautiful." His eyes were actually shining. "I've worked hard all these years. Don't you dare say I haven't paid my dues!"

I made a face. "Well, well, Billy Jarvis. The world's first hardworking drug-pusher."

"I was good at this!" Billy cried, punching the wall beside

my head hard enough to make the lights flicker. "And now it's gone!"

Slowly, I felt his hand moving toward my neck, his fingers closing over the same bruises he'd put there earlier.

"Are you going to kill me, Billy?" I said, unblinking, staring him right in the eye. "Are you going to finish what you started? Do what Connor couldn't? Show him you're a man? Is that what you're going to do?"

He'd never be able to do it. I knew he wouldn't. He was too broken, too fragile, after what had happened with Connor. But if he tried, just a little... If he said he wanted to...

"I should," he said, and I felt the pressure on my throat, felt his fingers tighten. "You're nothing. We'd all be better off if you were gone. If I just press a little harder. It would be so easy..."

His fingers didn't close any further around my neck, but I exploded in a fit of coughing and gasping all the same, shoving him away, begging him to stop, to let me go, to leave me alone!

"You're crazy!" Billy cried in surprise as I kicked him backward, hard, and he fell on his ass.

Then I was sprinting for the elevator, jamming my thumb into the down button with a shaking hand, waiting for the doors to slide open.

Come on, come on!

I stepped into the elevator and turned around to find my brother curled on the floor, howling like the child he was.

"Fucking bitch! Fucking whore! You're nothing, do you hear me? You'll never be anything but a slutty piece of shit."

"You've always got everything backward, Billy," I said. Pulling the phone out of my pocket, I held it in the air as Billy's eyes widened, and then snapped it shut. "You're the piece of shit."

Billy reared up on his knees. "You'll never get away!" he yelled.

"Watch me," I said steadily, and the doors slid closed between us.

It had been a while since I'd been mind-blowingly drunk and walking a club, categorizing guys as A, B or C, looking for my next tryst. There was a certain feeling to it, a high that came from knowing what I wanted and going after it. A high of being on a mission. As I crossed the lobby of Billy's building, I felt that same buzz come back to me. I knew what I had to do. I had to get away, get safe, call for help, wait for rescue. These were my steps, clear as day.

It was nice, especially when I was on the verge of a full-on breakdown, to have a plan.

It must have been later than I'd thought when we'd gone to meet Connor, because as I emerged onto Lakeshore boulevard the sun was just rising. I made decisions then, one after the other, like some kind of self-propelling robot. I turned onto a side street and walked through an unfamiliar Toronto neighbourhood until I found a convenience store that happened to have a pay phone out front. I looked up Anita's mother's number, and called her on Harrison's cell—since I didn't have so much as a penny to actually use the pay phone—eyeing the last blinking bar. I managed to compose myself enough to apologize for calling so early and ask for Anita's cell number. I made jokes about my forgetfulness and asked about Anita's father's birthday party. I was patient as she read the number out to me one digit at a time. I made small talk. I laughed. I said I hoped I'd see her again soon. Then I hung up the phone, mumbling the number to myself over and over, and started walking.

I got myself to King, a major street, and began searching for a good place to hide. Somewhere warm—it was October after all, and I wasn't wearing socks or a coat—somewhere that would be open at this hour and where I could stay for a while without being bothered or asked to leave. Finally, after several blocks of searching for a library or a subway station, I found an empty bank vestibule and stepped inside.

Then I dialled the number.

She picked up after the first ring.

"Anita!" I croaked.

A feeling welled inside my chest, a desire so strong to hear my friend's voice that I felt as though I was about to have a heart-attack.

"Sally?" a male voice answered. A voice I knew. A voice which didn't attack my heart so much as rip it right out of my chest.

I crouched down on the floor and held the phone to my ear with both hands, barely able to breathe.

"Harrison?" I whispered.

"Are you okay? Sally? Where are you? I'm coming. Are you there?"

His voice was staticky and sounded very far away, but it was him. It was Harrison. Harrison not dead. Harrison not tied in a closet or unconscious on the disgusting living room rug I never vacuumed. Harrison alive. Harrison coming for me.

I felt suddenly as though I could fly.

"I'm here. Where's Anita? I'm okay. I'm at the bank."

I didn't even know what I was saying. I felt delirious, feverish, like I was dreaming and tripping at once.

Harrison hadn't abandoned me. Harrison was coming to rescue me, like he always did, like I'd hoped he would.

"I couldn't find my phone, so I took Anita's," Harrison said. "I'm in your car. I'm coming to Toronto to get you. Just tell me where you are."

"But how did you know I was here?" I said stupidly.

Was this really important when the phone was about to die? I wasn't thinking straight at all.

Harrison hesitated before answering, and something caught in my chest. I knew before he even answered me.

"I heard the message you left on your machine," he said, and my legs suddenly gave out under me, my ass hitting the tiled floor with a thud.

If a moment ago I'd been flying, now I felt like I was plummeting to earth at super-speed, like Rainbow when she fell from her tree-top world, only faster. And there were no Wittlings to catch me, no soft bed of pine needles and leaves, no branches to slow my decent.

I was just falling.

I'd assumed the apartment would be empty when I'd dialled my own number and recorded my conversation with my brother on my machine. I hadn't for a second imagined Harrison sitting on my bed listening. And since he had Anita's phone, had she been sitting right beside him? And how much exactly had he heard? All of it?

Please Lord tell me he didn't hear all of it.

"But… How did… I can't…" I blubbered incoherently, panting with the exertion of knowing this. Of knowing Harrison knew the truth about me. I could hardly wrap my brain around it. I could hardly bear the excruciating shame.

"Oh *God*," I cried out, covering my face with my hands.

"Babe," Harrison said in that low and patient voice of his, "it doesn't matter to me. None of it matters."

I barely took in this endearment, which he'd never used before, or his words. He was concerned for me, sure. He'd come and get me. And then everything would fall apart. I knew it would. And after the day I'd had, I just couldn't handle it.

"Oh God, oh God, oh God," I said, rocking on the floor.

I could feel the rant of terrible names I usually called myself rising in volume in my ears. I could feel the self I thought I was disintegrating.

I'd been so close, so very close to having at all. That was the worst part.

"Sally," Harrison said, raising his voice to be heard over my moans, "tell me where you are. I'm coming for you. I'll be there in a couple of hours."

His words were starting to fade out. The phone in my hand was beeping its electronic death. I realized I didn't have more than a few seconds, and the part of me that still cared about being found pushed the rest of me to my feet and back outside to look for an address, which I relayed, tonelessly, hopelessly.

"Don't move," Harrison ordered. "I'll be there soon. I love y—"

The phone cut out before he could finish, which I

thought rather fitting.

Folding myself into a corner, I settled in to wait. I settled into my horror. I settled into my shame. I settled into my failure, and let it hold me until the doors opened hours later and he came inside and kneeled beside me.

"I love you," he finished, kissing my cheeks, holding my face, stroking my hair. "I'm here, Sally. I'm here for you."

But by then it was far too late. I was past believing.

26

I was unresponsive, catatonic. I followed Harrison into the car and sat, staring forward but seeing nothing, hearing nothing but a faint buzzing in my ears. Eventually, he stopped trying to get through to me and pulled into a small parking lot at the back of an old building. He led me around the front and into the lobby of what seemed to be a tired and sketchy-looking hotel, the kind that charged by the hour, for obvious reasons.

Because I looked distraught and slightly drugged-out, and because I was severely under-dressed for the weather—although modestly. If only he'd seen what I'd had on a few hours before—the guy at the desk assumed I was a street-walker and insisted I show him some ID to prove I wasn't underage, though of course I had none on me. An argument ensued during which Harrison raised his voice impressively and threatened some kind of legal action I thought sounded far-fetched, but which seemed to intimidate the guy just enough to get us the room we wanted.

As we climbed the stairs to the top, Harrison took my hand and I let him. I was too exhausted to object.

The room was oddly shaped, triangular, as was the whole

building, the window at a diagonal to the street below, looking out over the intersection. There was a creaky double bed covered by a worn, red chenille bedspread and the furniture was dated. The walls were marked and badly needed to be painted. The faucet in the bathroom leaked and the steady plop, plop, plop of the water sounded like the slow beat of my own dying heart.

"Why don't you lie down, have a rest," Harrison said, gesturing to the bed.

Too afraid he would lie down with me out of pity, I shook my head and folded my arms around my middle. I didn't want to rest anyway. I'd been resting for the past two hours on the floor of that dirty vestibule.

I knew what I needed to do. I needed to tell, finally tell.

Harrison already knew some, he knew the end, but he needed to hear the beginning.

So I could stop hiding from the truth. So we could both stop pretending.

All of a sudden he was standing in front of me, his hands on my arms, looking at me with those devastating eyes, and I nearly lost my nerve.

"Sally—" he began in that silky smooth voice of his, but I cut him off swiftly.

"Just sit there!" I said so loudly he took a step back, his hands springing free from my arms.

Watching me carefully, he took a seat at the edge of the bed and watched me pace back and forth from the door to the window as I tried to find the words. What was it Melissa, the English-major, always said about essay writing? Begin with your thesis statement.

"I'm going to tell you everything now," I said, and I could almost hear Mel's voice in my head: *Too broad!*

"You don't have to tell me—" Harrison started, but I shook my head at him so violently, he frowned and stopped mid-sentence.

"I'm going to tell you all the things I haven't been telling you," I said, looking at the walls, the window, the dresser, anywhere except at him. "I'm going to tell you the truth. I need to tell the truth."

"Okay, Sally," Harrison conceded, though he sounded far from okay with it. "Okay."

"Okay," I echoed, pausing at the window, looking for my starting point. I fell still, gazing out at the frozen street. "When I was sixteen a boy named Connor Buckley asked me out on a date. My first date."

It was the story to start it all. It sometimes seemed like the first story of my life. The story of how I lost everything.

I said, "I was a different girl back then. I was studious, shy, very inexperienced. My brother Billy was the popular one, the good-looking jock, while I kept mostly to myself. I didn't know anything about boys, especially a boy like Connor Buckley. I had no idea what he wanted with me, but of course I said yes. It was the most exciting thing that had happened to me in my entire life. Connor Buckley, star of the football team, had asked me out. I couldn't believe my luck."

I shook my head at my younger self.

God, if only I'd said no.

"Billy was trying out for the football team that year, and he had a lot to say about this date. It had to go well, or Connor would hate him and he'd never make the cut. I protested that it was the coach that decided who made the team, but Billy knew Connor had major influence. He told me what to wear, instructed me on how to behave. He practically wrote out cue cards for my every word. It was almost as exciting as the date itself, my big brother suddenly showing all this interest in me. I planned to do exactly as he said.

"Connor took me to a basketball game at the school, a very public first date, which made me pretty nervous. I barely knew what to say to his friends, all these older guys. But he was so sweet, introducing me to everyone, putting his arm around my shoulder, including me all the time. I remember walking out of that gym thinking he was perfect..." My lips curled, the words sour in my mouth. "But teenage boys are never perfect."

"Billy was waiting for me, but Connor wanted a few

minutes alone, so we walked around the back of the school, near the stairs that led down to the locker rooms. I remember wondering when he was going to kiss me, would it be here on the grass, or against the wall, or…I was *so* naive. I was thinking of romance, while Connor's thoughts were far more…inventive."

I heard Harrison breathing hard behind me. In anger? Disgust? I revelled in this feeling of having him on my side.

I knew it wouldn't last.

"Before I really knew what was happening, he leaned me up against the railing at the top of the stairs and stuck his tongue down my throat. I remember being vastly disappointed at how aggressive he was being, but trying to keep myself excited. After all, he was kissing me. He wanted me. That was good, wasn't it?

"He tasted like beer even though we hadn't been drinking, or at least I hadn't. He told me he'd treated me nice, he'd showed me off. He'd showed me a good time, hadn't he? Then he put his hand up my shirt. And I let him, even though he was being too rough about it. I let him unhook my bra and knead my breast and French kiss me. I wanted to please him. Billy had told me I had to keep him happy. But when he reached his hand up my skirt and tried to pull down my underwear, I told him he had to stop. I told him no."

I nodded at my own reflection in the mirror, nodded at my one moment of good sense.

"But Connor Buckley wasn't used to hearing the word no."

"In a flash he went from overly enthusiastic make out partner to hostile predator. He shoved me back against the railing so hard I cried out and ripped my underwear off in one violent yank. I was so shocked I didn't even start to cry. That would come later. Instead I screamed for help as he fiddled with his belt buckle, holding me with his other hand. Just one hand and he was so much stronger than me. I heard yells, someone coming, but I knew they wouldn't come in time. So, I kicked him hard in the balls—a first for me—and we wrestled, him trying to push me back, me trying to shove him off. He kept saying I owed him this, that I should stop being such a tease, that he knew I wanted him too. I barely heard him. I thought maybe he was deranged."

Given the events I'd just lived through, I realized I was probably right.

"I don't know exactly how we got twisted around, but just as I pushed him away with all my strength I realized the stairs were behind him. I watched him lose his footing and fall, dramatically, ridiculously, his legs going over his head, all the way to the bottom of the cement stairwell, ten stairs down.

"A second later, Billy was at my side and Connor was moaning. Billy kept asking me what I'd done, accusing me, blaming me. He saw my torn underwear but he didn't care. He called me stupid and selfish, said it was all my fault. I'd ruined everything. I'd ruined his life, and through my tears, I believed him.

"Connor didn't die, unfortunately, but his leg was broken in such a way that he was off the roster for the rest of the year, his senior year. His hopes for a football scholarship evaporated. The team treated my brother like he was a pariah. Connor wouldn't even look at me in the halls. It was a nightmare. I went from being beneath notice to being the most hated girl at school, at least as far as the jocks were concerned. And their girlfriends too, of course, the mean girls who made sure nobody sat with me at lunch, that every girl in the school gave me dirty looks.

"And then at home, Billy was relentless. He hissed threats at me across the dining room table, broke things, valuable things of my mother's, and insisting I'd done it. He couldn't exactly turn our mother against me—she isn't so easy to manipulate—but she did insist I be extra nice to him, because he was so devastated about not making the team, which was torture. Basically, I couldn't decide which was worse, my life at school, or my life at home. So, it wasn't surprising that when Billy came to me, all earnest, and told me he'd come up with a way for me to make it up to him, to get the team to stop hating us, I jumped at the chance. I still hadn't learned my lesson, I guess. I hadn't learned who to trust."

Gripping the window frame with both hands as if to hold myself up, I let my mind fill up with the night I usually couldn't stand to think about at all, not directly, not in anything more than painful snippets that cut like jagged glass.

And I found that once I'd let it in I couldn't get it to stop. I was falling, falling into the memory, falling into my own nightmare, and there was nothing to do but let go.

"Where are we?" I say for about the hundredth time, and as before Billy doesn't answer me.

I wish I could take off this stupid blindfold he put on me, but I know it will only make him mad. And that's the opposite of what I want. Tonight is about making Billy happy, making him like me again. Tonight is about making things better.

"Okay, now go down these stairs," Billy says, and when I trip on the first step he laughs. He isn't being the best guide—I've fallen twice—but I try not to be angry.

I hear my mother's voice in my head, reminding me that he lost his dream and I should be kind.

I try to be kind.

"All right, stop," Billy says with a hand on my arm. "We're here."

I wonder where here is, because he still hasn't taken off my blindfold. I've been imagining where on earth he could be taking me, what I could possibly do to make things up to him and Connor, but I haven't been able to come up with anything. The room is cold and smells sour. It feels like a big room, something about the echo of our footsteps. A warehouse? The school gym? An arena?

I try not to feel afraid when my brother lets go of me and I'm standing alone in the dark.

"What should I do now?" I ask him, but it isn't Billy who answers me, it's someone else. Someone whose voice fills me with dread. Someone I was hoping, somehow, I wouldn't have to face tonight, or ever again.

It's Connor Buckley's voice.

"Take off your top," he says.

My entire body tenses at the suggestion. So, this is how I'm going to make things better? A strip-tease for Connor? A chance for him to see everything he didn't get to see that night? I wrap my arms around myself, gripping my ribs.

I won't do it. I can't.

Then Billy's voice is in my ear, cajoling, convincing.

"If you do it, he promises he'll back off. He'll make the girls stop being mean to you. I might even get a spot on the team after all. He just wants a peek. He promises he won't touch you. Just pretend you're in a room by yourself. Pretend you're getting into the shower."

I can hear the need in his voice, his desperate desire for me to do as he says. And I can hear his sympathy too. He feels for me, he does, but this is what has to happen to make things right again.

So, even though I don't want to. Even though I've never undressed in front of any boy before, I do as he asks.

I do it for Billy.

With trembling fingers I reach down and pull off my sweater.

"And your jeans, too," Connor says.

I hear a brief snicker, but I can't tell if it was Billy or Connor. It disorients me for a second, and my hands still on the button of my jeans, but I push through it. The faster I get this done, the faster it will be over. I kick off my sneakers and pull off my jeans and my socks.

I try not to shiver with cold. I try not to think: You're standing half-naked in front of Connor Buckley.

"There," Billy says, his voice taking on a different tone now. "Was that really so hard?"

Then I hear a click and it's obvious the light in the room has been turned on. I feel a hand on the back of my head, someone undoing the blindfold. As it falls away and I blink in the sudden glare, a loud cheer rises up, a cheer of many, a cheer that could only be made by a crowd.

I'm in my underwear in the boy's locker room, and the entire football team is standing around me.

I feel all the blood drain out of my face, possibly out of my whole body. Am I going to faint? But I know I can't, because who knows what they'd do to me then.

The guys surround me, laughing, pointing, jeering. I search for Billy in the crowd, but he's somewhere behind me. Connor is impossible to miss, though. He's right at the front on his crutches. He's the only one who isn't smiling. Instead, his face is contorted with hate.

"Take your bra off!" someone yells.

Instead of complying I fold my arms over my breasts. I don't answer him. Maybe if I ignore them all they'll go away. Maybe this is all just a dream.

But it isn't.

The calls come from all directions, from all sides.

"Hey, look at me, Sally!"

A camera flashes and I blink.

"Take it off, girl!"

"Want to feel how much I like you, Sally?"

A hand reaches out and tries to take mine, but I yank it away.

"Leave me alone!" I cry. "Billy, tell them to stop."

I want to cry but I know I can't. Not while they're watching, taking pictures. I can't cry now.

"Don't be silly, Sal," Billy says, his voice in my ear again. "This is what you wanted, isn't it? Didn't you want everyone to like you again? This is what you asked for."

No, I think to myself. I didn't ask for this. I don't want this.

I feel fingers on the clasp of my bra, and I try to reach up, to stop whoever it is, but someone else holds my arms at my sides. I want to believe neither of these people is Billy, but they're behind me and I can't tell.

I realize I've lost Billy. He isn't on my side. There's nobody to help me.

The guys have moved closer, crowding around me. I notice someone in the back is holding up a phone. He's filming.

"Stop filming me," I moan, covering my face. "Please just go away."

"Oh, come on, sweetie. Don't get shy now."

A hand reaches out and brushes my breast, and I flinch so hard I nearly fall over.

"Stop it!"

"We just came for a show. So, go on. Give us what we came for."

Panic truly begins to sink in when I try to push them away from me, and I realize they're all bigger and stronger. My pushes make no impact at all on their hard, massive bodies. I'm trapped here with them. There is no getting away.

I twist around, hoping to find an escape route, but they close in *behind me. Someone pulls me backward by the waistband of my underwear and I stumble onto the bench behind me. I fall hard on my ass, right next to Connor, who laughs appreciatively.*

He leans in and whispers, "This is what you get for saying no to me, Sally."

Then I'm pulled up, forced to stand on the bench so my body rises above the crowd. I go into a kind of shell-shocked trance, my eyes lidded, my mouth hanging slightly open. I'm there, but I'm not there as they pull off my underwear. As they touch where they shouldn't touch. As they photograph and film me. As they put my hands on them.

Billy speaks to me, but I can't be sure it's really him, or just his voice inside my head. A voice of my own creation.

"This is what you deserve," he says. "This is what you're good for. So, enjoy it, Sal. Drink it in. This is what it is to be loved."

A chant starts up, a repetitive beat that I can hear in my ears whenever a guy is rough with me for years and years to come: "Slutty Sally. Slutty Sally. Slutty Sally. Slutty Sally."

When it's over they leave me there on the bench, naked.

I walk myself home.

I opened my eyes as if waking from a terrible dream. My cheek was pressed to Harrison's shoulder, his arms locked around me. A part of me objected, recalling that I didn't want this, I didn't want to have him only to lose him again, but I didn't have it in me to say so. He stroked my hair and whispered in my ear, warm words, sweet nothings. I leaned into him, I didn't think I would have the strength to stand without him.

"Come sit with me," Harrison said softly, and led me over to the bed, seating the both of us without letting me go.

I wasn't crying, but there was a strange sound coming out of me. A kind of whimper-moan that was disturbing to hear, even for me. I covered my mouth with my hand to stop it.

"Don't," Harrison said, gently pulling my hand away. "You'll choke yourself."

He held my face and took the sound into him instead, seeming almost to suck it in through his eyes, which never left mine, until eventually it died away and I slumped into his arms again, spent.

"I can't believe they did that to you," Harrison whispered, his voice thin, as though the pain of my story had wrung him out. "My God, you were so young."

"I didn't stop there," I said tonelessly, and I felt Harrison's hand still on my back. "There's more."

I could feel his disbelief. More? How could there possibly be more? I could feel him having trouble getting the next words out, but forcing himself, for my sake. So I could say my piece. So I could get it out once and for all.

"Tell me," he said.

27

"They didn't rape me. I remember thinking I should be grateful for that, as if having my virginity intact meant something. But the next month at school would prove that it really didn't. It didn't matter what I'd done or hadn't done. It didn't matter what the truth was, or who was to blame. Because I was to blame. They all thought so, everyone at school, everyone I knew practically. They all thought I was a slut, so that made it true."

Harrison shook his head. "But how did they…" Then it dawned on him and he sighed, a defeated sound. "The photos, the videos."

I nodded, remembering when I'd first seen the pictures of my own naked body taped to my locker, when I'd come upon a couple of guys I didn't know, and who I wasn't even sure went to my school, playing the video of my assault at a bus stop. I remembered how I'd run home crying, so ashamed, as if I, and not them, had done something wrong.

"The videos and pictures spread through the school like wildfire," I said. "What made it worse was the expression on my face. I remembered being in a daze, checked out, but on the video it looked like I was aroused, enjoying it even. They had pictures of my hands down their pants, and you couldn't tell they were holding me in place. They had pictures of me with two or three guys at a time. Within days the whole student body was calling me Slutty Sally. I even caught my gym teacher almost saying it once. She caught herself just in time, but I heard it. No girl would so much as look me in the face. They made a Facebook page about it, and all the guys posted pictures. There were literally hundreds."

I exhaled long and loudly, as if I was trying to expel the entire episode from my mind.

But there was no breathing this out. It was a part of me, like my arms, or my feet, or my heart.

Harrison said, "Didn't the faculty step in, force them to take the page down?"

There'd been a number of similar stories in the news lately. We all knew how this type of cyber bullying was dealt with. But that was now.

"You'd have thought so. I know at least some of the teachers knew what was happening. Lots of them had kids who went to the school. You heard things in the halls. But nobody ever approached me. The principal never called my mother—and man, was I glad about that. Nobody tried to protect me. Instead, my teachers just seemed unsurprised. When I started failing tests because I couldn't bring myself to study. When I started feeling so sick in class from everyone's watching eyes that I couldn't answer any question I was asked. They all acted like it was inevitable, like the good grades I'd gotten before were some fluke. They believed I was what they'd heard. I was a stupid, slutty girl to them now. After a while most of them just ignored me. And as their attention faded I started getting a very different kind of attention instead."

"What do you mean?" Harrison said quietly, but I knew he could see it coming. Everyone can always see a train wreck coming except the idiot stalled on the tracks.

I sat up straight and rubbed my face. The cheek that had been resting on Harrison's chest was warm, the other cold as ice.

"I started getting asked out five, sometimes six times a day," I said. "Older guys, younger guys, druggies and nerds and student council types. They were all talking behind my back, calling me names, but that didn't stop them from wanting me, or my body anyway. At home the phone rang off the hook, and both Mom and Billy stopped bothering to answer it at all. Mom thought I'd suddenly gotten popular. Little did she know…"

I smiled humourlessly.

"It was kind of nice for a while. A little break from the never-ending misery. If I tried I could pretend the dates were real, that all these guys were really lining up just for the chance to take me out. It was something, anyway. It was better than nothing. And if I had to give them what they wanted to make them like me, well, what did it really matter? They all thought I'd done much worse already. They were all already talking about me. What harm could it do?"

I dipped my chin as Harrison breathed, "No."

"I lost my virginity against a dumpster behind the movie theatre," I said. "I don't remember the guy's name. I think he was on the debate team. I did it with a bunch of his friends too, one evening after another, like dominoes. In exchange they invited me to a few of their parties, although that didn't last long. Their girlfriends started to object. So I moved on to another group, another team. It was my way of making friends, of getting them to like me.

"Eventually I discovered the joys of alcohol and its wonderful ability to dim my memory and make everything, even awful degrading moments, seem like lots of fun. By the end of the year I'd gone through so many guys I even circled back to the football team. I did it with every one of them, and I didn't even care. I did it with Connor Buckley on his living room couch. I became the girl they thought I was. I made myself into Slutty Sally."

Ever so gently, Harrison raised my chin until I met his eyes. "You promised me you'd never call yourself that again," he said.

"Give a girl a break, huh?" I said, pulling out of his grasp, if only so I could look away.

"What about Billy?" Harrison asked then, his voice low and dangerous.

"My beloved brother Billy?" I said bitterly. "Billy got everything he wanted. He got a spot on the team, the status he craved, the cheerleader girlfriend. And all the while he took every chance he could to remind me that I should just keep doing what I was doing, because it was all I was good for anyway. It was the only way they'd ever like me now. I was damaged goods. I was ruined. I deserved whatever I got."

I saw Harrison's hands tighten on the thighs of his jeans, the tendons in his arms tensing. "That son of a bitch," he muttered.

Sliding off the bed, I walked back over to the window. I couldn't be sitting so close to Harrison when I told this part. I couldn't bear it.

"And so a few months later, just after graduation, when he introduced me to this guy and encouraged me to make him happy, to do what I was good for, I went ahead and did it. At least if I did what he asked Billy would still talk to me. And at that point I didn't really care who I screwed anyway. None of it seemed to matter. Plus Mom was getting sicker, and her insurance was about to lapse. Billy told me he'd take care of it. He'd take care of anything. I just had to help him out once in a while, sleep with this guy or that, help him close a deal. I just had to do whatever he said. He'd even pay for my housing at school, as long as he could pimp me out whenever he wanted."

Taking a deep breath, I turned away from the window. Because sometimes you just had to face the truth head on.

"I'm a prostitute, Harrison," I said as he stared at me. "I sleep with men for money."

There, that did it. The final nail in the coffin.

I sure did love to go out with a bang.

There were a few different reactions I thought he might give me, in the hundreds of times I'd imagined this moment.

A: Complete revulsion, possibly followed by vomiting.

B: Disbelief, which would require me to provide further proof of my sluttiness, followed by A.

C: White hot anger. Because I was a liar. Because I'd tricked him into being with me. Because I wasn't good enough.

As it turned out, Harrison chose D, none of the above. He didn't realize that wasn't one of the possible answers.

My words still hanging in the air between us, Harrison blinked at me once, and then again, his brow slightly furrowed in contemplation before he said, "Why'd you do it?"

"Why?" I said, hands on hips. "What do you mean *why*? I told you why. Because that's all I'm good for."

"We both know that's not true," he said patiently. "That's a lie Billy told you, a lie you swallowed as truth because he fed it to you when you were at your lowest. I don't believe that for a second."

"Well, then you're an idiot," I snapped, scowling at the wall.

I didn't want to keep talking about it. I wanted him to come to the conclusion I knew he would—that I wasn't worth a thing, that I wasn't worth his time or his love—and just go. Couldn't he see that?

"Why'd you do it, Sally?" Harrison persisted, rising from the bed.

I flinched at the movement. I flinched at the idea of him touching me now. I was revolting. I made my own skin crawl.

"I liked it," I burst out, my lips quivering. "That's the truth, okay? After a while I looked forward to Billy's calls. I liked sleeping with those guys, feeling their desire for me. I *lived* for it. Is that what you want to hear?"

Harrison stepped closer. He was within a foot of me now.

"You liked feeling desired. You liked that they wanted you, because you wrongly assumed nobody ever would unless you gave yourself up to them. Because your asshole of a brother told you so. Because you told yourself so."

"Because it's true!" I raised my hands to push him back as he stepped closer still, but he took my hands in his and gripped them, held them, until they lost their tension and he could step between them.

His eyes engulfed me as he brushed a lock of hair out of my face, his touch so very gentle against my skin.

"Why'd you do it, Sally?" he said softly. "Why'd you *really* do it?"

"Because I…because…"

I fumbled with the words, pinned by his eyes. How could I think straight when those eyes were on me, when his hands were smoothing my back, pulling me close?

"Because my mother was sick!" I cried finally. "I had to. I had to help her."

I stared at Harrison, stunned. I'm pretty sure my mouth was even hanging open.

"You had to help your mother," he agreed smoothly, without missing a beat. "She needed help, and you were persuaded by a terrible person, a person who'd spent years breaking you down, that this was the only way you could give it. The only way you could help her. So you did as he said. And now you think I'm going to turn on you for it? For wanting to care for your mom?"

I blinked at him. I wasn't sure why, but every word he said made me incredibly uneasy. It was like being told you had an alligator head, but there were no mirrors to check if it was true. You knew it wasn't. You knew what you really looked like. But he was *so* sure.

In a way, it felt just the same as being told by Billy that I was a slut.

He was manipulating me.

His arms were closing around me, but before my chest touched his I broke away and tripped across the room, putting the bed between us before I turned to face him again.

"No," I said, shaking my head. "This isn't real. It's because you don't know the whole story. You don't know everything. If you knew everything you would hate me."

"I could never hate you, Sally," Harrison said, and in his eyes I could see that I'd hurt him. Somehow, in hating myself I'd hurt him. Did that even make sense?

Of course not, because *nothing* made sense anymore.

I shoved the heels of my hands into my eyes and rubbed hard in frustration. I wanted to be alone, to sink into my self-loathing and drown. Just the fact that Harrison knew as much as he did about my past was like swallowing a burning coal and feeling it work its way through my intestines inch by painful inch. I wasn't sure how much longer I could take it before I cut myself open just to get it out.

"Listen to me, Sally," Harrison said, his voice so close it made me jump.

He was standing in front of me again, his hands gripping my forearms so I couldn't wrench away again, his chest heaving with some restrained emotion.

"Really listen."

"Fine," I said tiredly, because hating yourself and trying to convince the only guy you've ever loved to do it too could really take it out of a girl.

"Do you remember, in the hospital, when I told you I've fallen in love with you three times?"

His voice caught on the world hospital, and I realized, as he gazed at me, that it wasn't because he was ashamed that I'd tried to kill myself, but that it hurt him to see me hurt and lying in a hospital bed. Because he cared about me.

But caring is not the same as love.

"That's what you said," I replied, unwilling to agree completely.

"Do you think I said that blindly, that I fell in love with you without really looking at the person you are?"

The slut I am, you mean.

"I saw you behind the club with that guy you barely knew," he went on. I squeezed my eyes shut at the memory, but he waited until I opened them again to continue. "I knew you had a past, even if you wouldn't tell me your number. I knew you'd been with a lot of guys."

"That's an understatement," I muttered and he shook his head.

"I heard every word you said on that answering machine,

and I came anyway. Doesn't that tell you something?"

His eyes searched mine, looking for some spark of understanding that I refused to give.

"It tells me you're a nice guy," I replied. "It tells me you're the guy who comes to the rescue."

Bizarrely, he smiled at me, a full smile, with a little chuckle thrown in for good measure.

"Sally," he said, "I'm really not that nice of a guy."

Then, gathering me into his arms—which I was too exhausted to resist—he pressed his cheek to mine and said into my ear, "I came because just hearing about what your brother had done to you made me feel like I might explode. I came because I couldn't stand to think of you in danger and alone. I came because I couldn't stop myself from coming."

His lips brushed the edge of my jaw and my body pressed against his, my arms tightening around him, involuntarily.

"I came because I love you," he whispered, "like I told you, like I promised. Only you. Always and forever you."

I felt a strange tearing sensation in my gut, that coal pushing its way through my skin and out of my body. I felt myself collapsing against Harrison and sobbing in my crazy, over-the-top, unrestrained way, and I felt him lift me onto the bed and cradle me against his chest and tell me that he loved me again and again until I had it memorized, until I didn't need to hear it anymore, because I knew I loved him too, without conditions, without reservation.

Because I believed him.

Harrison Leo was in love with me, the real me, the ugly me. I could keep him. This was real.

This, finally *this*, was what it was to be loved.

A long while later, once my tears had finally subsided, I told him all the rest. Waking up to find Billy strangling me. Being drugged. Finding myself locked in Billy's room. Finding his phone, losing his phone. Coming face to face with Connor. And the drugs. And my plan of escape. And the gun. And Billy. And the gun. And Billy.

Harrison was quiet through most of it, though I could feel

his burgeoning anger when I explained how Billy had been so willing to sacrifice me. How Connor had aimed the gun at my face. I could feel the rage coursing through him, and for once I understood that he wasn't angry with me. He was angry for me.

"You see?" he said when I was done. "You didn't need rescuing. You rescued yourself. You've always rescued yourself. You just never realized it."

I smiled a small smile, not quite willing to believe.

"And it's over now," I said. "I have that recording, Billy admitting to every one of his sins. That should keep him away from me for good."

Or at least I hoped so.

"You're amazing," Harrison said, drawing my face up to his.

When his lips met mine, it was the sweetest kiss of my life. A kiss free of guilt, of desperate need, of doubt.

A kiss that was sure.

28

After the interminable couple of days I'd had—the release from the hospital, being kidnapped by my brother, the tussle with Connor, the escape from my brother, waiting for Harrison, telling my secrets, believing I'd lost his love, and finding I hadn't lost it after all—I was surprised to find myself still standing, and starving. I couldn't even remember the last time I'd eaten. Luckily, Harrison had come prepared, and we feasted on chips, snack cakes, and liquorice whips on the hotel rug, chasing it all down with diet Cokes from the vending machine at the end of the hall. I ate with my back snuggly against Harrison's front, his legs curved around mine, his gentle breath against my cheek. He offered to go out and grab some take-out, concerned that all the junk food would only make me sick, but I refused to let him out of my sight, holding tight to a handful of his shirt until he relented.

As soon as we were done eating I dragged him over to the bed and pulled him down beside me. He complied without protest, wrapping me in his arms and moulding his body to mine in the spooning position I'd found so strange all those weeks ago, but which now felt just exactly right.

I fell asleep to the feeling of his warm hand caressing my

stomach, his lips against my shoulder.

I fell asleep knowing when I woke up he would be there.

And he was.

"Morning, babe," Harrison said in a rough, sleepy voice that somehow surpassed his usual deep rumble in sexiness.

I grinned against the pillow at his use of the word "babe" again. I'd had a lot of nicknames in my life, but never before one that was so…personal. Shuffling around in the bed, I turned toward him and found myself struck once again by his good-looks—even in the morning!—his bed-head hair, his second-day scruff, his brilliant blues.

And he was all mine.

The scent of oranges surrounded me as I sank into his arms, the smell so reassuring.

"I love the way you smell," I said to him. "It's so fruity, so you. What is that?"

He shrugged. "I think it's just my fabric softener," he admitted, and I laughed.

"Promise me you'll never start using different fabric softener," I said as I slipped my arms around him.

"You got it," he agreed.

I hadn't brushed my hair, or my teeth, in hours—I hadn't even looked in a mirror since we'd entered the room—but I couldn't have cared less as he dipped his face toward my neck and kissed me there, his hand encircling my hip. As I sighed against him I wondered, was this what it was like to wake up next to a guy you loved? Because I could get used to this.

The top I'd slept in was twisted around me and as I reached down to fix it I remembered that this top wasn't even mine. Neither was the underwear I had on, or the jeans hanging over the back of the chair, or the shoes I'd flung off at the door. Suddenly all the events of yesterday came streaming back and the warmth that had been steadily filling my body frosted right over.

I met Harrison's eyes and he seemed to know how I was feeling without asking, without my saying a word. He placed a small kiss on the tip of my nose and pulled me toward him, my head against his chest. I'd never known how comforting it was to be held before. I'd spent so much time kicking guys out of my bed, or running from theirs before the sheets were even cold.

God, what an idiot I'd been.

"I guess Anita will be wanting her phone back," I said, lazily drawing my fingers up and down Harrison's stomach, making him shiver.

"I don't think she'll mind if we keep it for a while," Harrison said. "But you should call her at home. We really should have called her last night. She's really worried about you. You know, she also heard…what I heard. Your message."

I closed my eyes at the thought, readying myself for the hot burn of shame, but none came. I think I was just too tired to feel it. Besides, now that I'd told Harrison it seemed stupid to continue keeping this secret from the people I cared about most. I probably would have told her as soon as I got home anyway. This way, I didn't have to.

Still, the thought of actually having a conversation with her about it wasn't exactly on the top of my list of fun things to do this weekend.

"She loves you," Harrison said sympathetically, handing me Anita's phone. "It'll be okay."

"Maybe it would just be easier to move to another province, assume new identities," I posited, my eyes following Harrison—wearing only his boxers—as he rounded the bed and went through the pockets of my jeans looking for his own phone.

Was it possible to be both turned off and turned on at the same time? Was that normal?

"Yes, starting a new life is definitely a perfectly sane alternative to having an awkward conversation with your best friend," Harrison said, giving me his half-smile as he pulled on his jeans. "I'm going to go find us some breakfast. Call her!"

"Wait," I said. He'd finished pulling on his shirt—which had some kind of equation on it—and was reaching for his coat. "Don't I get a goodbye kiss?"

Grinning some more, Harrison climbed back onto the bed, planting a hand on either side of my body so he was hovering above me.

"I'm only going to be gone for ten minutes," he said.

"An eternity!" I said dramatically, placing my hands on the back of his neck so I could pull his face toward mine.

"Excruciating," he agreed as his eyes lowered to my lips.

"Agony," I breathed, and then his mouth found mine and neither of us could think of any more words.

The call with Anita wasn't half as bad as I'd imagined. She cried and I cried and she was mostly so relieved I was okay that her protests over all the lies I'd told her never came. I knew there were more questions to come, that they would probably keep coming for a long time—I'd been keeping this secret from her much longer than I'd kept it from Harrison—but for today there were only two.

"So, that guy I met, Billy. That was your brother? That was him?"

I could hear the revulsion in her voice as she realized she'd been in the same room as my kidnapper, that she'd actually spoken to him.

"That was him," I said, staring up at the ceiling.

I didn't like the idea of Billy being in the same room as Anita either. I didn't like the idea of him being in the same country.

"I knew he was a dirtbag," she muttered and I couldn't help but smile. As I recalled, she'd called him cute and asked if he was one of my former boyfriends. But I appreciated the solidarity.

After a pause, Anita sighed, a sound that seemed to come from her very soul.

"But you got away," she said, her voice very small over the line. "You got away before they could hurt you?"

"Yeah," I reassured her. "I got away. And Billy's never going to hurt me again. Nobody will ever hurt me like that again."

I finally felt strong enough to say that and mean it. With Harrison by my side and no more secrets weighing me down, I finally felt that it might be true.

"You've got that right," Anita said loudly, in her sassiest voice. "Or they'll have me to deal with. I mean, you know, me standing behind Harrison, who will be doing most of the dealing."

"Sounds like a plan," I said with a laugh.

When Harrison returned with our fast food breakfast a few minutes later, I was dressed in my borrowed clothes, my face washed, my hair finger-combed, ready to get on the road home.

"There's something we need to do first," he said cryptically between bites of hash brown.

The determined look in his eye told me this "something" wasn't going to be a quick stop at his favourite Toronto burger joint. There was something else going on, but he didn't want to tell me.

"A quick visit to your mistress?" I offered, raising my eyebrows.

"I mean, after that," he said, without missing a beat.

"Harrison…" I said, tilting my head to one side. I didn't want to play any games today.

"I need you to trust me," he said, giving me his serious face.

Whatever this was, it was important to him, which made it important to me.

"All right," I said, wiping the grease from his lower lip with a napkin. "But if you're thinking of pulling a bank job you really should have brought me a pair of better shoes. I can barely run at all in these."

"I'm sure you'll do fine," Harrison said with a creeping grin. "You'll be driving the getaway car."

Twenty minutes later, sitting in traffic on the Don Valley Parkway, I couldn't get over how strange it was to be sitting in the passenger seat of my own car while my boyfriend—I was practicing saying it in my head—was behind the wheel.

"You should probably change lanes now," I said, craning to check the blind spot.

"You're such a back seat driver," Harrison admonished me. "And how do you know we need to change lanes when you don't even know where we're going?"

"Woman's intuition," I retorted, putting my feet on the dashboard and hugging my knees. "You're lucky I'm even letting you drive my car. You may not know this, because I let you drive her after that party, but I normally don't let *anybody* drive her but me."

"Well, I didn't realize what an honour you were bestowing on me," Harrison said with a smirk, which only made me want to make out with him—an unbearable urge that had been coming over me, periodically, ever since we'd left the hotel. Since he was driving, I resisted it, but just barely. Who knew a smirk could have so much power?

"Can I ask you something?" I said suddenly, my eyes on the car in front of us. There was a question I'd been meaning to ask him, but after all the talking I'd done last night I hadn't had the energy until now.

"Anything," Harrison said.

"Why did you leave me alone?" I asked. "I made you promise to stay with me, but when I woke up Billy was there and you were gone."

Harrison sighed and rubbed the back of his head. I could tell the question cut him deeply. I almost wished I hadn't asked. What did it matter anyway? He was here now. He would never leave me again. Case closed.

"I know I shouldn't have gone," he said, his voice thick with regret. "If I'd just stayed with you…if I hadn't left the apartment, then Billy would never have—"

"He would have," I said, my hand on his arm. "He would have found me eventually. You couldn't have stayed with me every second. I'm not blaming you, Harrison. But why?"

He let out another frustrated breath before replying.

"Jason called," he said. "He was on the verge of checking himself into a rehab facility, but he was waffling, about to change his mind. I had to go over there, talk him into it."

"That's great," I said.

I felt a little guilty that I hadn't given a single thought to Harrison's druggie brother's health or whereabouts since we'd found him in that rancid apartment. Though, of course, I'd had a couple of other things on my mind.

"He just decided to go, out of the blue?"

"No, actually, he met a girl," Harrison said, the surprise obvious in his voice. "They've been together for a little while now—she's a recovering addict—and she was the one who convinced him to get some help." He glanced over at me, hunching his shoulders. "All those years of me harping on him to get help, and she talked him into it in just a few days."

I could tell it disappointed him a little, that this new person had been able to help his brother, and not him.

I squeezed his arm in support.

"I guess true love really does conquer all," I said.

"Seems like it," he agreed. "I went over there determined to get him to check himself in, but it was Kelly—that's her name—he ended up listening to. I think he might really get clean this time."

"I'm so glad," I said.

Coming clean and getting clean. Maybe Jason and I would both be saved from ourselves.

Maybe we'd both get our happy endings.

"After that, I would have come back to your place right away, but I had to stop and pick something up for you," Harrison said, gesturing toward the back seat.

"What is it?" I said, craning my neck.

There was a plastic bag on the back seat that I managed to reach after a lot of straining. Inside was the thirteenth issue of *The Forever Place.*

"Johnny knows a guy who gets the next issue before the stores are even stocking them," Harrison said. "I had to promise to help him pass Software Architecture next semester to get him to give it to me. I thought it would cheer you up."

Pressing the comic to my chest, I felt tears prickling

behind my eyes and I didn't even know why. There was just something so *Harrison* about running around town to help his brother and get me the comic I loved. I had no idea why I thought he'd left the apartment that day, but this truth made it okay.

He didn't leave me, I thought to myself. *He was coming back.*

"I'm so sorry, Sally," Harrison said, gripping the wheel so hard his knuckled turned white. "I left you alone and he took you."

"Don't you dare apologize," I said. Leaning as far over as my seatbelt would allow, I put my head on his shoulder. "You found me in the end, that's all that matters. You came for me."

"I always will," he replied softly.

A few minutes later we pulled into the parking lot of a bank and I gave Harrison a look.

"You were kidding about the bank job, right?" I said.

"Mostly," Harrison said cryptically.

He stared through the windshield at the half-empty parking lot for a minute or two and I did the same, puzzled. Then he turned to me suddenly and pulled me into a kiss that was over much too quickly, a peck I wished could just go on and on. It was hard for me to believe whatever we were doing here could be more important than making out. But then, making out with Harrison was ranking at the top of my list of things to do just then. And possibly more than making out. Preferably a whole *lot* more.

"Do me a favour and stay in the car, okay?" Harrison said, looking me directly in the eye like my mother used to when she was trying to catch me in a lie.

"Whatever you say, Sir," I said, holding up my hands in innocence.

"Okay," Harrison said quietly, talking mostly to himself. Then he stepped out into the swirling snowflakes of a flurry that had just begun.

With a sigh I sat back in my seat and turned the key in the ignition so I could listen to the radio. Lord knew how long he was going to be, and I didn't do well without something to occupy my mind. In grade school my teacher had once commented on my report card that I was "likely to get bored if left to her own devices for more than two minutes at a time."

As I fiddled with the radio stations, I glanced up and noticed that Harrison hadn't gone inside the bank as I'd thought but was actually standing on the curb talking to someone in a sleek car.

A sleek black car.

A sleek black town car.

My heart began to pound as I saw Harrison shake his head vehemently and gesture at the bank over his shoulder with his thumb. His face had taken on the hard look I recalled from that moment behind The Limo, his knuckles bloodied, his chest heaving. He looked about ready to kill someone.

Then the car door swung open, a skinny figure all in black stepping out, and I actually felt my blood run cold.

Billy.

Billy talking to Harrison.

Billy, that bastard who had ruined my life, who I'd hoped never to see again, interacting with *my* Harrison, feeding him lies, taking him from me. He would take him from me. I knew he would, as he always had, as he'd taken everything else. But no more. No way.

Not this time.

Before I could even think about what I was doing I was out of the car and charging across the parking lot, screaming my brother's name. Billy swung around, startled, but it was Harrison I ran into, Harrison who held me back as I tried to lunge at my brother's throat, Harrison saying my name.

"What the *hell* are you doing with that piece of *shit*?" I shrieked, pointing at my brother, who sneered predictably.

"I'm the piece of shit?" Billy retorted. "Maybe you should take a look in the mirror, Sal."

Harrison swung toward my brother. "You don't speak," he thundered, and though I couldn't see the look he gave Billy, my brother slunk a few feet back, sulking.

"Harrison, what the f—" I began when he turned back toward me.

"You see, this is why I wanted you to stay in the car," Harrison said calmly, though he didn't loosen his grip on me for a second. He knew I'd wring Billy's neck if I could.

"Did you call him and tell him to meet us here?" I asked incredulously, wiping the melting snowflakes from my face. "How did you even get his number?"

"It's amazing what you can find with a little ingenuity," Harrison replied, subtly steering me back toward the car.

"Harrison stop it," I said, pulling my arms free and turning to halt his advance. "Tell me what the hell is going on. Right now. I don't want you around him. I don't want you to—"

"What, get infected with his evil?" Harrison said, that half-smile appearing again, though it couldn't have come at a worse time.

Anything having to do with Billy was no laughing matter.

"No, but…" I protested. "He's such a…he'll make you think…"

Taking my face in his hands, Harrison stopped my babbling in an instant. "He won't make me think anything. Not about you. Not about us. You don't have to worry, babe. I'm yours, no matter what."

Leaning in, he kissed me again, and this one he let last long enough for a pleasing warmth to spread through my belly and down my legs, into my freezing toes.

"Awww, isn't that precious," Billy called over to us. "I'm about ready to vomit!"

This time I stopped myself from rushing over to drive my thumbs into his eyes, but just barely.

"All right, I trust you," I said before Harrison could ask me again. "I don't get it, but I trust you." I pulled the knitted hat he was wearing down over his forehead. "I'll wait in the car."

"Thank you," Harrison said a little formally, kissing my hand. "I'll explain everything as soon as I get back."

"You'd better," I warned as I got back into the car. He winked at me through the window.

That was the longest twenty minutes of my life. I did everything I could to stop myself from thinking about the fact that my loathsome brother and my boyfriend were in an enclosed space together. I turned up the radio to maximum volume and screamed along with the songs. I used Anita's phone to text Emily and Melissa and reassure them I was okay. I played that stupid cell phone game with the candies that Em loved so much, losing all her lives because I didn't understand the rules. I counted the colours of the cars driving by on the road, and the ones in the lot, and the ones in the lot next door. I did just about everything but run around the block or drive away, though I was strongly considering both, when Harrison got into the car, pulled the door closed behind him, and handed something to me.

"What's this?" I said, turning the white bank envelope over in my hands.

Behind us, Billy was standing in the middle of the lot, ranting inaudibly—or at least it was impossible to hear him over the blasting music. I reached forward to turn it down, but Harrison stopped me.

"Just leave it on," he said as he put the car in gear. "There's nothing he could say we'd want to hear."

So, we backed around my brother who pounded on the hood of the car, still yelling bloody murder, and as we did I reached inside the envelope and pulled out a strip of paper I'd never seen before—though I did recognize my name across the middle—and below it a number. An astonishing number. A number that included a lot of zeroes.

"What's this?" I said, my mouth so dry I could barely get the words out. I flapped the slip of paper at Harrison, feeling dizzy.

As he pulled into traffic, Harrison said, "That is Billy's payment to you for years of pain and suffering."

"He just gave it to you?" I said, staring at the certified cheque so hard it blurred.

"I called Anita and got her to play your message for him. And then I reminded him of how easy it would be for me to drive to the police station across the street and play it for them, too," Harrison answered.

"Did you clean him out?" I said.

I couldn't quite believe my brother had this much money in his bank account. Could this really be true? And now it was all mine?

Harrison shrugged and grinned in my direction. "I left him a couple of thousand. It seemed more than generous."

"You extorted several hundred thousand dollars out of my brother?" I said, astonished.

Suddenly Harrison Leo was taking on a whole new, cunning personality I hardly recognized. And it was pretty hot.

"I also got him to tell me Connor Buckley's exact address, and precisely where in that fancy condo of his he keeps his drugs stashed, and his guns. The cops should be showing up there shortly, if my anonymous tip does its job."

I blinked at him, my mouth opening and closing several times without sound. My eyes kept darting back to the slip of paper cinched in my trembling hands.

As much as I wanted to just shut up and let this news sink in, I couldn't stop the questions from bubbling at my lips.

"But, this money...How—" I began.

"You deserve this, babe," Harrison interrupted me. "Now you can pay for your housing for the rest of your degree. You can pay for grad school if you want, for a vacation, for a new car. No more living under that dirt bag's thumb. Now you're really free."

Turning around in my seat, the cheque still pinched between my fingers, I saw my brother standing in the road, carrying on like an idiot, even running after us, though we were too far away for him to ever reach us.

Harrison was right, this money put me entirely out of his reach.

There was nothing more he could threaten me with. Everyone I cared about knew my secret, or would very soon. I was self-sufficient now. And most importantly of all, his words couldn't hurt me anymore.

He couldn't hurt me anymore.

"Goodbye, brother," I whispered as I watched him give up on running and just stand there, staring after us, his eyes like slits.

Slipping back into my seat, turning away from my brother for the last time, I faced the road ahead with Harrison by my side.

For the first time in a long time the world seemed bright and I felt goddamn cheerful.

29

Instead of driving home we went back to our cheap hotel and checked into the same room. Harrison kept telling me I could afford a fancy hotel suite. I could afford to buy a hotel if I wanted! But there was something charming about this room where I'd bared my soul to my one true love. I'd developed a fondness for its shabbiness.

As soon as I got through the door I threw myself on the bed and pulled the cheque back out of my pocket.

"It's kind of mesmerizing," I said as Harrison chuckled at me. "Like, I can't get myself to look away, even though I know I should. Like an eclipse!"

"Just think of all the things you won't have to do now that you have money," he said, sitting beside me on the bed. "Like waiting until the cupboard is completely bare to do groceries."

"Or only shopping for clothes during the end of season sales," I added.

"Or never going to a garage to check why the engine light is on in your car," Harrison said pointedly.

"I thought that meant the engine was okay," I said with

surprise. "If there was something wrong, I thought it would turn red or something."

Harrison shook his head. "Or eating microwave ramen soups every day."

"Hey," I protested, giving him a playful shove. "I love those ramen soups. You can't take my ramen from me!"

"I'll never take anything from you," Harrison replied, suddenly serious, and all at once I became aware of certain things, like the bed beneath us, and the hypnotic scent of oranges in the air, and the bulky winter coat he still had on.

"Maybe it's time to take this off," I said warmly, enjoying the way he was looking at me. I reached down and undid his coat buttons, my fingers brushing against a strange bulge in the pocket. "What's this?" I said curiously as Harrison's hand joined mine and an odd smile slipped over his face.

"I almost forgot," he said coyly, getting to his feet.

I was admiring the way he filled out his shirt as he took his coat off and didn't notice what was in his hand until he held it out to me.

Sitting in Harrison's palm was a thick stack of bills.

As I gaped at the pile, he said, "I made sure they gave the last few thousand in twenties."

"What for?" I said, unable to take my eyes from the stack.

Sure, I had a certified cheque in my hand for far more money, but I'd never seen so many twenty dollar bills in my life.

"For this," Harrison said.

He undid the elastic holding the bills together and held the stack above my head. Then he let them go gradually, creating a green snowstorm of money around me as I squealed.

I was gathering the bills up by the handful and laughing my ass off by the time he was done.

"You know me so well," I said giddily, throwing the money I'd gathered into his face with a laugh.

"I thought you'd enjoy that," he said, his eyes twinkling.

Sitting up amidst my bed of money, I gave him a long look. "It's just so incredible," I said.

"It is pretty impressive," he said, reaching into his pocket. "We should take a picture."

"No," I corrected him, getting on my knees on the bed and shuffling toward him. "I mean, you here, with me, sharing this with me, caring for me. It's incredible to me. You're incredible to me."

My lips found his without reaching, without searching, as though his mouth and mine were meant to fit together, and always had been. His fingers grazed my cheeks and wove into my hair and I marvelled at the taste of him, at his tongue's ability to make me feel faint. I shifted my weight and the bills crinkled under my knees, giving me an idea. A wonderful idea. A naughty idea.

Reaching up to my earlobe, I broke our kiss suddenly.

"Oh, my earring," I said with dismay, patting the bedspread beside me. "I must have lost it somewhere."

Harrison blinked at me, a little disoriented. Lucky for me he didn't notice I didn't have an earring in my other ear, either.

"Maybe on the floor?" he said, crouching down.

"Can you check the bathroom?" I asked, as I continued to search frantically.

"Sure, babe," Harrison said, and dutifully stepped into the small en suite.

Thirty seconds later, he came out shaking his head.

"I don't think it's…" he began, then trailed off as he found me lying across the bed, on top of the pile of money, without my clothes on. Well, I was still wearing my underwear, but since I hadn't had a bra on to begin with, those undies were about it.

"You were saying?" I said, trying my best to keep a straight face as his eyes, those dazzling eyes, left a white hot trail up and down my body, pausing at my breasts, before landing once again on my face.

"I…" he started. "I…was…I…oh, screw it."

He crossed the room in two long strides and crashed into my arms.

Our bodies melded around each other, his warm hands

pressing me against him as his lips found my neck. My hands gripped his arms, his back, as my leg hooked around his hip. Right away we both felt the wrongness of all the clothes he had on, and off came the shirt over his head (no time for buttons), off came the shoes and socks and pants. For a moment I let my eyes feast on his body—I'd never seen him quite this nude before, or at least not up close—until he lowered his face to kiss my shoulder, his cheeks slightly pink.

Oh my God, he's blushing. He's actually blushing. Lord save me.

Capturing my lips with his, he kissed me so deeply I moaned against his mouth. I squirmed helplessly under his touch as he lapped at my lips and down my neck, each caress of his mouth like a dream. Reaching down, I caught the edge of his boxers and was about to explore what was inside them when Harrison said, "Hold on."

"You've *got* to be kidding me," I exclaimed in frustration as he hovered over me, supporting himself on just his elbows.

He was not putting the brakes on this now. No way. I was not having it. I was getting some tonight, period.

Eyebrows raised, Harrison lifted up his hand, which was plastered with sweaty twenty dollar bills.

"Not that I don't think this is hot," he said. "But are we really going to do this on a pile of money?"

With a shared laugh he both got on our knees and swept the bills onto the floor. I could still hear them hitting the floorboards when Harrison scooped me up in his arms and laid me down beneath him, my legs wrapping around his hips automatically as his mouth swept across my upper chest and ventured down to my breasts. My hips strained against his with the force of my desire as he paused there, and looked up at me.

"May I?" he said, his bottom lip just brushing against the tip of my nipple, making me squirm.

"Yes," I gasped, which was all the permission he needed.

I felt his tongue curve around my sensitive nub, and my body bucked hard under his, my back arching under his touch.

I felt dizzy with heat, literally lightheaded with desire. But it was more than that as well, so much more. I wanted him in a way I'd never wanted anything before, the feeling was stronger than lust, and so deep that the very word "want" seemed inadequate.

As this unnameable, overwhelming feeling pumped through me, I reached for the waist of his boxers a second time, then hesitated.

"May I?" I said shyly.

"Yeah," he breathed, rolling us both onto our sides.

With all the confidence of experience, I stripped off his boxers in one quick motion and then took him in my hand. His mouth caught mine and for a second it was as though I could taste his desire.

I began to move my hand, slowly at first and then in a steady rhythm, as Harrison ran his palms down my bare back and over my ass, my panties slipping lower, though not completely off. I longed to have this final barrier between us removed, to be completely bare as he was, to show him that I was all his.

"Let's take these off, shall we?" I whispered. I would have done so too, Harrison didn't try to stop me, but I could feel his hesitation in the way his eyes met mine. "Don't you want me to?" I said uncertainly, not at all liking the way the air was cooling around us.

If he told me he didn't want me now, when I'd finally stopped doubting myself, when I finally felt certain of him, of us…

"Oh I want you to. I *definitely* want you to," Harrison said, running his thumb over my bottom lip—which only made me want to bite it. "But if you take those off, I can pretty much guarantee I won't be able to stop myself from giving you all the pleasure you deserve. I want to make sure you're not caught up in the moment when you make this decision. I want this decision to be yours, all yours."

He kissed me softly, his lips just a whisper against mine, and I felt it again, that enormous, larger-than-life feeling building inside me, building and building and never bursting. All at once I knew what that feeling was.

Drawing his face toward me, I placed kisses on his chin and his cheeks and his sweet, sweet lips.

"I love you, Harrison," I said, and his hands stilled on my hips, his eyes locking with mine. "I love you so much more than I've ever loved anyone. I don't think I even really knew what love was until I met you, until tonight, until right now. I love the way you make me feel safe. I love the way you see me, because it makes me feel like I might actually be the girl you see. I love being near you. I love touching you. And I love that when you touch me back, I know it's not just my body you want, it's all of me. I love that when I want you I'm not wanting something that's going to destroy me. And I do want you, Harrison Leo. I want to be with you, tonight, right now. I want you so much it's killing me."

Harrison held my gaze for one moment more, before reaching down and sliding my underwear down my legs.

Then he took me in his arms and laid my head on the pillow, his body pressed close to mine, the two of us, finally, naked,

"Well," he said with a wry grin, "what the lady wants the lady gets."

Our limbs tangled around each other, our bodies lining up of their own accord as he kissed me senseless, his tongue doing things to me I couldn't even describe. In that moment where he reached for his pants to search for protection I found myself feeling curiously nervous in a way I hadn't even when it was my first time. But then, this was a lot like my first time. First time without any booze. First time with a guy I cared for. First time without the weight of self-loathing bearing down on me. First time with Harrison.

That was a whole lot of firsts.

My breath caught as he positioned himself over me and I wanted to close my eyes, but as usual when he was near, I couldn't. Not when he was looking at me that way. I couldn't take my eyes off him.

"Don't be afraid," he said tenderly. "I'm here."

I smiled at his words, realizing as my apprehension drifted

away that not every first was bad. Not every first was a mistake.

Some firsts were exactly what you needed.

I wrapped my legs around him, losing myself in those blue, blue eyes, and then he was inside me, and I knew, at last I knew the difference between everything I'd done before and the thing all those songs had been written about.

And the difference was love.

This was making love.

We were making love and it was the best thing I'd ever felt for the first time.

30

"Here?" Harrison said, pulling the car over to the curb.

"Yeah, this one," I said as we came to a stop in front of a small split-level house at the end of an unassuming street.

As Harrison put the car in park I took a deep breath, looking out the window at the bare linden tree by the driveway—was it bigger than I remembered, or was I just imagining it?—the unshovelled walkway up to the front door, the garage door that badly needed a new coat of paint, the patches of snow on the sloping front lawn. All of it looked so painfully familiar, and yet so different, as if I'd known the place in another era, another life.

I supposed, in a way, I had.

"Looks like someone's home," Harrison said.

Through the front windows, which gave a view of the living room and dining room beyond it, we could clearly see someone moving around inside.

"She likes to sleep in on Saturdays," I said. "She's probably just finishing a late breakfast."

When I still didn't make a move, Harrison slipped his hand into mine and squeezed it.

"Sally—" he began.

"I want to go in," I interrupted him, trying as I said it to feel as sure as I sounded.

I wanted to go in. I had to go in. This was what we'd come for.

I could see Harrison wanting to ask more, to say more, but holding back, knowing that I needed to take my time, that this moment was about me and I needed his support.

"Okay," he said simply, kissing me on the cheek, awakening my senses in delightful ways.

I'd thought my desire for him might dissipate now that we'd have sex, that my all-consuming need for him might fade, at least a little.

Nope.

"All right, no more stalling, Mr. Leo. Let's get going," I teased with a weak smile.

I took his arm as we walked up the driveway. There were little ramps over the step onto the walkway and onto the front stoop that hadn't been there before, which made me feel sick to my stomach. Why would she need ramps?

At the front door Harrison reached for the doorbell, but I shook my head, holding out my hand for the car keys instead. As I pushed the house key into the lock I felt a wave of anticipation. Maybe she'd changed the locks. Maybe I was no longer welcome here.

Then the door clicked open and I knew.

I was home.

"Is someone there?" a voice called from the kitchen. A voice that soothed my worried mind. A voice I'd yearned to hear for so long. A voice that was as much a part of me as I was a part of it. "Is that you, Albert?"

I heard the sound of something being wheeled toward the door, and then there she was in front of me, sitting in a wheelchair with one leg extended out in front of her and a shocked look on her face.

"It's me, Mom," I said. "I'm home."

Her face was so blank that for a moment I had the

irrational worry that she didn't recognize me.

But then…

"Sally!" she cried, her voice like an explosion in the small entryway, making both me and Harrison jump.

She held out her arms and I fell into them, breathing in the scent of her rosewater perfume, that scent I'd missed for almost three years. I buried my face in her soft hair as she gripped me tightly.

"My baby," she said. "My girl."

Eventually I sat back on my heels so I could get a good look at her. Her shoulder length dirty-blonde hair was a little more grey than I remembered it. She had a rash across her cheeks, which I knew was a symptom of the Lupus, though it was more severe than I'd ever seen it. But her green eyes were just the same, green eyes which were searching my face just as mine were searching hers.

"Why are you in a wheelchair?" I said at last, with some concern.

"Oh this ridiculous thing," she said dismissively. "I broke my tibia is all. Nothing to worry about. Don't start fussing now!"

I tried to go around back so I could push the chair into the living room for her, but she swatted me away, almost making me laugh. My stoic yet hair-brained mother—she was just the same.

"And who's this young man?" she said with bright eyes, cocking her head at Harrison, who was still standing behind me in the front hall.

Still a little overwhelmed with emotion, I turned back to Harrison, the tears which had been welling in my eyes now rolling down my cheeks. He immediately wiped them away, his face serious, as if caring for me was the most important task in the world.

Out of the corner of my eye I could see my mother watching us with extreme interest and had to resist the urge to roll my eyes, and then right away I felt glad. It was nice to have someone to roll my eyes at.

"Mom," I said, turning back around, Harrison's hand gripped in mine, "this is Harrison."

When my mother only blinked delightedly, and it became clear I couldn't think of anything else to say, Harrison leaned forward and shook her hand.

"I'm the geeky boyfriend," he explained.

"Well, isn't *that* nice," Mom said as we all moved into the living room. Then, in a whisper loud enough that Harrison could hear clearly—he was, after all, only two feet away—she said to me, "Oh my gosh, he's just gorgeous, Sally-Anne! And is he blushing? Oh, he's blushing. You can never go wrong with a man who blushes, my dear. I used to tell you that when you were little."

"Yes, Mom, I remember," I said, sending an irritated smile Harrison's way as he sat down on the couch.

Once we were all seated and settled and my mother had offered tea and we'd politely declined, the conversation hit a bit of a lull. Though we were obviously thrilled to see each other, there were so many questions hanging in the air between us, so many years to explain. As I sat next to Harrison, so grateful for his warm presence next to me, I began to worry that we'd never be able to get past the loss of those years, that this is what our relationship would be like from now on, happy smiles and silence.

When it felt like I couldn't handle the quiet a second longer, I opened my mouth to speak, but my mother beat me to it.

"How was the drive?" she burst out. "It's an awfully long way to come for a surprise visit! You should have called first. Were the roads okay? Did you take turns behind the wheel?"

She looked expectantly at the two of us.

"Well, we were in Toronto for a few days," Harrison began uncertainly. "So, it wasn't too far to come."

"Yes, but before that. To come all the way from Florida."

"Florida?" I said. "Queen's is in Kingston, Mom. It's just a couple of hours away."

"Kingston!" she exclaimed. "You mean you've been living

so close all this time? Billy told me you'd dropped out of school. That you'd moved down to Florida with some no-good boyfriend—oh, not you Harrison, dear. Some other boy who came before you, I'm sure. He said you were earning money …well, he insinuated a lot of things, and of course I didn't believe half of what he told me, but—"

I had to cut her off. I knew my mother and if you didn't interrupt she could go on for a good twenty-minutes straight.

"Billy lied to you," I said flatly. "None of that is true. Actually, you should probably just forget everything he told you about me since I graduated high school."

I shifted uncomfortably in my seat, unsettled both by the awful things Billy had told her about me, and by the fact that we were talking about him at all. If I had my way none of us would ever speak of Billy again until our dying days.

"Oh Billy," my mother exhaled. "It's not really surprising. That boy was always a dishonest little wretch."

Harrison perked up beside me as she said this, sensing in my mom a kindred spirit in his hatred of my brother.

"Mom!" I exclaimed in surprise.

"Well, he's my son, isn't he?" she said, raising her chin. "If anyone can tell the truth about a boy it's his own mother. And Billy was a sly little liar, always blaming others for his mistakes. You remember when he tried to blame you for the stereo he broke? Always spinning tall tales. Lying to me about my own daughter! All to keep us apart. I'm sure he told you vicious things about me as well. Is that why you stayed away? Did he tell you I was angry with you? That I didn't want you to visit?"

This was really the crux of the matter—why I'd never come home. I could feel her hoping she had it right, that there was some easy explanation for why I'd never come home for Thanksgiving or Christmas or summer break. Why I'd never even called.

But of course, nothing was ever that easy.

"It wasn't just Billy," I said, staring down at my feet. "I didn't come back because…I felt…I was sure you wouldn't…I was ashamed."

"Oh, no," Mom said, sadness in her voice. "No, Sally-Anne. What could you possibly have to be ashamed of? You're my little pearl. My beautiful princess. It's your brother who put those thoughts into your head."

She was right, he had. He was the one who'd convinced me I wasn't good enough to come home, but I was the one who'd believed him. For all those years, I'd believed him. That was something I had to own up to.

I couldn't bear to look my poor sick mother in the eye, knowing I'd left her alone.

"She's done really well at school," Harrison said, and I looked over at him, surprised. "She passes exams easily, despite not studying as hard as she could. She has good, loyal friends who'd do anything for her, who love her very much. She's far too humble to admit it, but it took a lot for her to come here today. She struggled with it, but she's strong. She's working hard to live the life she wants."

The left side of his mouth curled up in a half-smile as I stared at him. If my mother hadn't been in the same room, I would have jumped him right then. Even though she was, I still considered it for half a second.

"Of course she's strong. Of course she's smart," Mom said. "I always knew it. You were always a smart little thing, so studious. Until that year in high school when things went wrong."

My head snapped up as she said this.

"Yes, I know about that. Well, not all the details, but it was obvious something was wrong. Billy all smug all the time, and you so miserable. You wouldn't tell me what it was about and now, well it's so long ago, but I'd still like to hear about it if you want to tell me someday."

My breath caught as I said, "Maybe someday, Mom."

Maybe someday when the thought of it didn't hurt me anymore. Maybe someday when I'd really put it all behind me for good.

Maybe someday soon.

You've always had so much going for you," my mother went on. "Your only real flaw was the way you idolized your brother when you were young."

knew she was right, but I cringed at the thought of it now. If only I'd thought just a little less of him, maybe he wouldn't have been able to control me quite as well. Maybe I would have seen through his lies.

"I always worried that it would get you into trouble one day. Billy had such a mean streak, even when he was a little boy. He wasn't anything like my sweet Sally-Anne."

I glanced over at Harrison who smoothed his hand over my thigh reassuringly.

Don't worry, his touch seemed to say. *He can't hurt you anymore. You're safe now.*

"How's your health been, Mom?" I said, grateful to change the subject. "I really want to know. How did you break your leg?"

Though a broken leg didn't necessarily have to be related to her Lupus, I knew it likely was. In terms of my mom's health, very little happened that wasn't connected to the Lupus.

"Oh well," she said, shrugging her shoulders as if her health was of little importance. "I had a flare up a while back that caused me to have some complications. Headaches, seizures, that kind of thing."

She threw in the world "seizures" as if it was as common-place as "stubbed toe."

"Seizures!" I exclaimed. "Oh, Mom."

"It really wasn't such a problem until I had one on the stairs of the library and I broke my darn leg. That break wasn't so bad, I was just on crutches for a few weeks, but the medi-cation to stop the seizures made me dizzy and then I went and broke the same leg all over again! Right there on the driveway. And this break is much worse, so they put me in this chair."

She sighed, frowning. "I hate this stupid chair. Did you see the ramps Albert put in for me? Like I'm a paraplegic."

"Mom, who's Albert? Where's Diane?"

Diane was a part-time nurse who'd cared for my mother at home during some difficult times when I was young. They'd become very close friends over the years.

"Di moved to Vancouver to work at a hospital near her son about, what is it, two years ago now? Albert's a neighbour boy. He's very helpful to me."

"But someone else has been coming in to help you, right?" I said, so fearful of the answer. "You insurance covers that, doesn't it? And Billy…Billy told me he was helping you out monetarily…"

"Well, Billy says one thing, when really the opposite is true," Mom said wryly. I blinked at her in horror. I'd known Billy had not been sending as much home as he'd promised, but to not send anything at all… "And I lost my insurance a while back when I couldn't keep up with the full time hours. That time I was in the hospital for a spell—"

"In the hospital!" I said so loudly it was almost a yell.

"It's okay, babe," Harrison said soothingly.

"No, I should have been there," I protested, the tears beginning to fall again. "I can't believe I stayed away for so long, when you needed me, when you were all alone."

What kind of a person was I to turn my back on my sick mother? What had I been thinking?

"Oh now," Mom scolded. "It was just a bit of trouble with my kidneys, and it's all cleared up now. You know how it is, I have a flare up, they have to isolate the cause and find the right treatment, and it's a little uncomfortable while all that's going on, but afterwards I'm right as rain again.

"Besides, the girls at the library took up a collection for me once, and I've been staying away from the more expensive medications. I have Albert to help with little things, and the neighbours. Linda comes by to check on me weekly. I'm doing all right, Sally. I don't want you worrying about me."

"Well, I don't want you worrying about money at all," I said, wiping at my cheeks. "And luckily, now you won't have to. I came into some cash, a lot of it, Mom. We can pay for everything now, experimental treatments, around-the-clock help, whatever you need."

My mother raised her eyebrows so high they disappeared under her bangs. "What's all this about? Did you win the lottery?"

"Well…"

I hadn't exactly thought through how to explain my sudden influx of cash. The truth was obviously out of the question.

"A rich friend wanted to pay her back for a favour she'd done him," Harrison interjected. "It was a big favour, and he was a very rich friend."

"Yes, very rich," I said, nodding.

"Um-hmm," my mother said, narrowing her eyes at us both suspiciously. "And this rich friend, his name wouldn't happen to start with a B, would it?"

Harrison suddenly became fascinated with the drapes as I stared up at the ceiling.

Then my mother leaned toward me and lowered her voice.

"You didn't steal it from him, did you?" she said, with just a hint of a smile, enough to know that if I'd said yes she wouldn't have exactly objected.

"He wanted you to have it," I said, a lie I wasn't even quite sure why I was telling, except that badmouthing Billy to my mom still seemed wrong, no matter what he'd done to me.

Sitting back in her chair, Mom surveyed me carefully.

"I think we both know that's a lie, Sally-Anne," she said. "But if it's the lie you want me to believe, then I will."

I grinned gratefully. "No more worries, Mom. Just think of it. And I'll come visit way more often now. All the time. Maybe I'll even buy a new car so Harrison can drive me up here in style."

"Oh dear boy, she's letting you drive her car?" she said, concerned. "Be sure to invest in some good earplugs."

"Duly noted," Harrison replied as I gaped at them both.

"Money is nice, dear," my mother said, "but it's you I'm glad to have back. I always knew you'd come back to me. I knew it was just a matter of time."

She reached out and took my hand.

"I didn't," I said in a small voice. "I didn't know."

"You always did have trouble believing," she said. "Believing in yourself, in your future. But I had a dream a while back. I saw you coming through the door looking beautiful and happy, just as you do now. And I knew. I believed."

"I'm glad you did," I said, taking hold of my mother's hand with both of mine.

Maybe that was the next step. After healing. After moving on from the past. Maybe the next step was to learn how to believe in myself.

I knew I'd already taken the first step by believing in me and Harrison. And a first step was all it took.

I was on my way.

EPILOGUE

Six months later…

"Can I ask just one more question?"

I look up from the stack of exam booklets at the handsome-and-he-knows-it student standing in front of me, trying my best not to glance over his head at the clock on the far wall.

Make it quick, kid. I cannot be late tonight.

"Will I be able to stop you?" I reply as I try to cram all the booklets into my backpack in one go. They spill out every-where and the student eagerly jumps forward to help me collect them.

A little too eagerly.

"I was just wondering if you'd like me to take you out tonight," he says, handing me the last of the exams with a suave flourish. "Because, as I've mentioned in the past, I'm very amenable to the idea."

Amenable? He totally got that out of a thesaurus.

I give the student (whose name is Justin) a hard look, but before I can answer him, he goes on.

"And might I point out how beautiful you look today? I

mean, I could hardly concentrate all through class…"

"As Professor Paretti explained at the beginning of term, I'm not a graduate TA, Justin," I say. "I'm just assisting him. I don't do any of the grading. So there's no use in buttering me up."

"Who says I'm buttering you up?" Justin says, rounding the corner of the desk and getting all up close and personal, his hand grazing my hip.

The intensity of his flirtation is almost intoxicating. I look for a moment into his wide brown eyes, crinkling at the corners as he grins, and I consider what it would be like to give in to him. There's no hard and fast rule against undergraduate assistants getting involved with students. And even if such a rule exists, aren't rules meant to be broken?

I take a step, bringing us even closer together, and keep my eyes on his as I reach forward…and swing my backpack onto my shoulder before swiftly turning away, trying not to smile in amusement at the look of shocked disappointment on Justin's face.

Justin doesn't strike me as the type of guy who gets turned down by girls very often. Or ever.

It amazes me that there was a time when I wouldn't have been able to resist him, when his lust would have controlled my every move. When I would have believed giving in to him was exactly what I wanted.

I can barely remember what that feels like now.

"Wow. That's how you're going to play it?" Justin says as I walk away. "I know you like what you're seeing. I know it's killing you to walk away from me."

I consider how I might reply to this.

A: Deny his accusation (which would only draw me into a longer conversation with him. Exactly what he wants).

B: Ignore him entirely (which might be the mature choice, but I've always found maturity to be overrated).

C: Give him the finger. (The popular choice. And by "popular" I mean, popular with me.)

D: Come up with some classy retort that will cut him

down to size and make me sound spectacularly witty.

"Next class, try enticing me with baked goods," I offer as I reach the door, flashing him a smile. "I'm a big fan of cherry Danishes."

All right, maybe not spectacularly witty, but clever enough to shut up Justin, who shakes his head as I pass through the door. Though I don't entirely take the high road. I still swing my ass as I walk out.

A girl's still got to have her fun, right?

Checking my watch as I cross the campus to my car, I realize how late it's gotten and break into a run. As soon as I'm in the driver's seat I pull out the phone Harrison got me for my birthday—an archaic flip phone, just like his—and notice the multiple texts from Anita, and Emily, and even Melissa—who, because she's never sure if this really is my number, begins every text with the words "Sally is it you?" There's also a text from Harrison reminding me of what time he's picking me up tonight, which makes me wince as I throw the car into drive and careen through traffic.

I hate that I haven't called him all day. I hate that I can't tell him why. I hate the way it feels to be dishonest where he's concerned. Because I know he would never, ever lie to me.

And yet I've been lying to him all week.

It feels just a little too familiar.

Abandoning my car crookedly parked in the last remaining spot in our apartment lot, I dash into the building through a side door and take the stairs. Anita opens the door to our apartment before I even put the key in the lock.

"Cutting it kind of close, aren't you?" she says as she pulls me inside.

I barely have time to blink as she hustles me to my bedroom where I see a large white box sitting on my bed.

"It came this morning," she says as I stare at it, motionless. "Sally, are you all right?"

I force a smile and usher her out of the room so I can get dressed. As I stand in front of my bed, looking down at the box, I tell myself I'm being silly. But it's still hard to open the box, expecting to find a note tacked to the front of the material inside—though there isn't one. It's hard sometimes, not to remember the way things used to be. But I struggle through. I banish the old memories and look forward.

I try to put the past behind me, where it belongs.

Emily pokes her head into the room just in time to help me pull up the zipper on the back of my dress.

"You look nervous," she says as she applies dramatic smoky eyeshadow to my lids. "Don't tell me you don't like the way you look, because that dress is all kinds of awesome. I can't even believe I let you have it."

"Let me?" I protest. "I practically had to pay you to wear something else."

"And I'm working it, aren't I?" she says, glancing at herself in my full-length mirror. I chuckle as she wiggles her ass. "This night is going to be uber-fantastic, hon. How could it not be, with me looking like this?"

I wish I could be as sure as she is.

Then Anita is at the door looking harried and Emily scampers back into the living room. Taking my arm, my best friend leads me into the dark living room where I immediately feel cramped and disoriented.

"I hate this," I whisper to Anita as we nearly collide with the couch. I step on someone's toes by accident.

"What do you mean? Everything's going to be fine," she assures me.

"I just hate that I had to keep a secret from Harrison," I reply. "It feels wrong."

"This is a different kind of secret," Anita says knowingly. Because of course she knows why this is upsetting me. She knows everything. At least, between us, there are no longer any secrets. "He'll understand."

"I know, it's just…"

But there's no more time. Someone pushes me toward the door. Someone else shushes the room.

I wish I didn't feel such dread as I hear footsteps

approaching the door and hold my breath for the knock.

"Who is it?" I say tentatively, and so quietly I'm surprised he hears me.

"It's me, babe," Harrison replies through the door. "Were you expecting Bradley Cooper?"

"Always," I reply lightheartedly, unsure how to proceed.

"I can accept that," Harrison says. I can hear the smile in his voice. "So…are you going to let me in, or are you stalling for time because you're still in your robe? Because you know I don't have a problem with that."

Emily titters behind me and I elbow her in the ribs.

"It's open," I say, as I'm supposed to. "You can come right in!"

There's a moment of anticipation as Harrison opens the door that terrifies me. A moment where I feel I'm standing at a different door in a different place, wearing a very different outfit, waiting for a stranger to greet me. When he holds the door open and his handsome profile comes into view, the room explodes with sound, but all I can hear is my own beating heart. All I can see is his so-seldom-seen smile. All I can feel is relief.

"Surprise!"

There's shock written all over Harrison's face as he takes in his friends and mine crowded into the room, all of them dressed as characters from *The Forever Place* to celebrate his birthday. Johnny, dressed in head-to-toe fur as the bloodthirsty bear Koda, jumps forward, his claws bared, and tackles Harrison in a hairy hug.

"Just what you always wanted," he says through his bear mask. "A *Forever* birthday!"

"You know me so well," Harrison says, quickly disentangling himself from his friend and struggling through the other well-wishers to get to me.

I'm still feeling a little unsettled, but as soon as Harrison slips his arm around my waist and I feel the warmth of his cheek against mine, I know I'll be just fine.

"A surprise party, huh?" he says into my ear. "Your idea?"

"I'm sorry I lied to you," I say. "But the guys were so excited, and even Anita agreed to put on a costume." I point at Anita who's standing in the kitchen in her adorable Wittling outfit as Winston adjusts her green felt hat. "I really wanted to tell you, but they insisted it be a surprise."

"An awesome surprise," Harrison says. Then he leans into me, his hand slipping into my hair, and says, "Although, you know, I'm hoping to get an even better birthday present later."

He pins me with his unwavering gaze and I find myself wondering if anyone would notice if the birthday boy disappeared into a bedroom with me for about thirty or forty minutes. My cheeks flush at the thought.

"If you're a good boy," I say, putting on my teacher's assistant face.

"I don't know how good of a boy I can be while you have that on," he says suggestively.

I glance down at my long, royal blue gown, studded with jewels. I'm dressed as Rainbow herself, my hair in its natural curls, a pearl tiara on my head. It's the gown she wears in issue nine to meet the woodland King, and it's pretty revealing as far as *Forever* costumes go, backless and showing patches of skin in a crisscross of holes down the sides. It almost makes me laugh to think that just a few months ago I would have found a dress like this terribly prudish, while now I feel uncomfortably on display.

I dip my chin shyly and Harrison gathers me in his arms again as Emily runs by, tripping on the long train of her Kas costume. She chases after Melissa, who's run off with her swirling black headpiece.

"You know you don't have to dress like this for me," Harrison says to me softly.

"Good thing I didn't do it for you, then," I reply sassily.

I wish we could stay in our little group of two forever, but there are so many friends here wanting to wish Harrison well. Pretty soon I have to let him be whisked away, even as he looks back at me regretfully. For a few minutes I just stand back and marvel at the weird and wonderful group of crazies we've assembled.

I wave at Alana dancing awkwardly with Roger, who can barely move in his cardboard tree costume. I notice Emily has found her friend from the last *Forever* party—Tree Antler Guy—though he isn't wearing his antlers this time, for which she seems to be berating him. A girl prances by wearing swathes of material in different shades of blue, like the underwater world's sole survivor, Fiona. The guys pumping beer out of the keg in the corner are both dressed as Lin-Lin in see-through beach-ball shaped hats.

I hear a gasp from over my shoulder as some more guests come through the door. Not surprisingly, it's Katie and Lucas, who briefly steal the room's attention. Katie is another Rainbow in her iconic leather outfit from the first issue, while Lucas is completely astonishing as the villain Hogol, wearing enormous fake ears, dramatic black eyebrows, and of course, the floor-length chain-mail.

Doesn't make much difference, though. He still looks insanely hot.

"I think Emily's making out with that guy wearing the furry vest, on the balcony," Anita announces as she shows up at my side, thrusting a cup of soda into my hand. "For a bunch of comic book nerds, these guys really seem to get a lot of action."

"Good for them," I say, clinking my cup with hers.

"It's funny, isn't it?" Anita says. "How things change."

She doesn't explain any further, but I know what she means. Once upon a time I would have been the one out on the balcony, or in the closet, or in the bathroom with some guy, and we would have been doing a lot more than making out. Once upon a time I would have been dancing on the kitchen counter by now. Once upon a time my life was so very different than it is now.

"I'm glad," Anita says, squeezing my arm.

"Me too," I agree. Because sometimes you have to let yourself be congratulated for your triumphs.

Then Melissa, dressed as Bedly in a fire-engine red cat

suit, pulls Anita away to deal with some ice crisis in the kitchen.

I start to circle the room, searching for Harrison, and trying to stay as inconspicuous as possible. Lately I've learned that, without the booze, I'm not really such a party-girl after all, which has surprised everyone, me most of all. I might be the TA who's supposed to have all the answers, but these past few months I've really been the one learning. Learning about myself and what I want, and what I don't ever want again. Learning about who I really am, post drinking binges, post Billy, post secrets.

And I've learned some enlightening things.

I've learned that I don't ever want to look to a guy for validation. I don't ever want to need his approval more than I need my own. I don't ever want to find myself listening to someone else's opinion of me and hating myself for it. I don't ever want to be that weak again. Not ever.

These days I have a different motivation. When I walk down the hall, when I look a guy in the eye, when I choose an outfit, when I decide what class to take and how to wear my hair and who to befriend, I'm not doing any of it for any guy.

Sure, there are times when I slip, usually where Harrison is concerned. There are times when I need him a little too much, when I ask him a little too persistently for his advice. But he's always there to kiss me sweetly and remind me that it doesn't matter what he thinks. He's always there for me, no matter what. I'm learning to get used to that too.

I still fall back on my old mantra on those days when I feel like I might be about to fall apart again. Sometimes I still have to remind myself that I am smart, that I am so much better than I was. Silently, I go through my list.

I am not a whore.

I am not nothing.

I am not Slutty Sally.

I never really was.

Now, as I finally catch Harrison's intense gaze from across the room and feel that flutter of excitement in my belly, that wave of desire, when I wind through the people separating us, smiling coyly, anticipating the moment when I'll be in his arms again, I don't have to worry that I'm falling into old patterns, or that I'm doing this for all the wrong reasons.

When he pulls me toward him and my mouth finds his, I know I'm safe.

And not because he's such a good guy.

Not even because I love him, although I do.

I know this is right because when I kiss Harrison, I'm not doing it to satisfy him, or to entice him, or even to please him.

I'm not doing it for him at all.

I'm doing it for me.

ACKNOWLEDGEMENTS

Thank you to my husband for giving me the time and always being my cheerleader. You are my favourite. Thank you Arijana for making another cover that makes my heart swell. Thank you romance novels for inspiring me to dream of a love that heals all. Thank you computer for not breaking down and losing half my manuscript. And thank you to every reader who bought this book and read it all the way to the end. I wish you a handful of nerdy suitors (hopefully the blushing kind), a heap of dirty nights (hopefully sober), and a myriad of incredible novels for those nights when your dirty, nerdy suitor is busy. Though I hope he won't be too often. Unless one of my books just came out.

ABOUT THE AUTHOR

I'm Lola Rooney, romance writer and part-time knitter of hats for cats. For a long time I was a lonely girl who didn't believe in love. Now I like to write about lonely girls and the boys who make them believe in love. I enjoy whiskey, boys who blush, cats wearing hats (obviously), writing in my tree house and flirting with sexy men (who blush). When I'm not skydiving in the Alps I call Montreal home.

Lola Rooney is the pen name of Shayna Krishnasamy.

Also by Lola Rooney:

Put Me Back Together (Scars Run Deep 1)

By Shayna Krishnasamy:

Come When I Call You (The Violent and Dead 1)
We're All Mad Here (The Violent and Dead 2)
Macabre Montreal: Ghostly Tales, Ghostly Events,
and Gruesome True Stories
Home
The Sickroom
Regan

Visit me at:

Facebook: www.facebook.com/shaynakrishnasamyauthor/
Goodreads: www.goodreads.com/lolarooney

If you enjoyed reading this book, I'd be so grateful if you would Like it, review it on the site where you purchased it, or recommend it to a friend.